PRESIDEN

To Mary Craig Sinclair - My Beloved Wife

Into your hands I place the five Lanny Budd books with whatever honors they may have won. Without your wisdom and knowledge of the world they could not have been what they are. Without your cherishing love through times of stress and suffering their author could hardly have been alive.

TIMELINE

World's End	1913 - 1919
Between Two Worlds	1919 - 1929
Dragon's Teeth	1929 - 1934
Wide is the Gate	1934 - 1937
Presidential Agent	1937 - 1938
Dragon Harvest	1938 - 1940
A World to Win	1940 - 1942
Presidential Mission	1942 - 1943
One Clear Call	1943 - 1944
O Shepherd, Speak!	1943 - 1946
The Return of Lanny Budd	1946 - 1949

Each book is published in two parts: I and II.

PRESIDENTIAL AGENT I.

Upton Sinclair

Simon Publications

2001

Copyright © 1944 by Upton Sinclair

First published in June 1944.

Reprint 2001 by Simon Publications

LCCN: 44004916

ISBN: 1-931313-05-9

Distributed by Ingram Book Company

Printed by Lightning Source Inc., LaVergne, TN

Published by Simon Publications, P.O. Box 321 Safety Harbor, FL

An Author's Program

From a 1943 article by Upton Sinclair

When I say "historian," I have a meaning of my own. I portray world events in story form, because that form is the one I have been trained in. I have supported myself by writing fiction since the age of sixteen, which means for forty-nine years.

… Now I realize that this one was the one job for which I had been born: to put the period of world wars and revolutions into a great long novel. …

I cannot say when it will end, because I don't know exactly what the characters will do. They lead a semi-independent life, being more real to me than any of the people I know, with the single exception of my wife. … Some of my characters are people who lived, and whom I had opportunity to know and watch. Others are imaginary—or rather, they are complexes of many people whom I have known and watched. Lanny Budd and his mother and father and their various relatives and friends have come in the course of the past four years to be my daily and nightly companions. I have come to know them so intimately that I need only to ask them what they would do in a given set of circumstances and they start to enact their roles. … I chose what seems to me the most revealing of them and of their world.

How long will this go on? I cannot tell. It depends in great part upon two public figures, Hitler and Mussolini. What are they going to do to mankind and what is mankind will do to them? It seems to me hardly likely that either will die a peaceful death. I am hoping to outlive them; and whatever happens Lanny Budd will be somewhere in the neighborhood, he will be "in at the death," according to the fox-hunting phrase.

These two foxes are my quarry, and I hope to hang their brushes over my mantel.

Author's Notes

In the course of this novel a number of well-known persons make their appearance, some of them living, some dead; they appear under their own names, and what is said about them is factually correct.

There are other characters which are fictitious, and in these cases the author has gone out of his way to avoid seeming to point at real persons. He has given them unlikely names, and hopes that no person bearing such names exist. But it is impossible to make sure; therefore the writer states that, if any such coincidence occurs, it is accidental. This is not the customary "hedge clause" which the author of a *roman à clef* publishes for legal protection; it means what it says and it is intended to be so taken.

Various European concerns engaged in the manufacture of munitions have been named in the story, and what has been said about them is also according to the records. There is one American firm, and that, with all its affairs, is imaginary. The writer has done his best to avoid seeming to indicate any actual American firm or family.

...Of course there will be slips, as I know from experience; but *World's End* is meant to be a history as well as fiction, and I am sure there are no mistakes of importance. I have my own point of view, but I have tried to play fair in this book. There is a varied cast of characters and they say as they think. ...

The Peace Conference of Paris [*for example*], which is the scene of the last third of *World's End*, is of course one of the greatest events of all time. A friend on mine asked an authority on modern fiction a question: "Has anybody ever used the Peace Conference in a novel?" And the reply was: "Could anybody?" Well, I thought somebody could, and now I think somebody has. The reader will ask, and I state explicitly that so far as concerns historic characters and events my picture is correct in all details. This part of the manuscript, 374 pages, was read and checked by eight or ten gentlemen who were on the American staff at the Conference. Several of these hold important positions in the world of troubled international affairs; others are college presidents and professors, and I promised them all that their letters will be confidential. Suffice it to say that the errors they pointed out were corrected, and where they disagreed, both sides have a word in the book.

Contents:

Book Four: In the Midst of Wolves

BOOK ONE

Seats of the Mighty

1

Sweet Aspect of Princes

I

LIKE two ships that rest for a while in some port and then sail away to distant seas; years pass, decades, perhaps, and then by chance they meet in some other port; the two captains look each other over, wondering what time has done to an old-time comrade, what places he has visited, what adventures have befallen him, what losses, what gains he has made. So it was when Lanny Budd caught sight of Professor Alston in the lobby of one of New York's luxury hotels. "Long time no see," he said—for it was the fashion of the hour to be Chinese; you greeted your friends with the words: "Confucius say," followed by the most cynical or most absurd thing you could think of.

"Really, Professor," Lanny continued, seriously, "I'm ashamed of having lost contact with you. You can hardly guess how important a part you played in my life."

"Eighteen years almost to a day since we parted in Paris," calculated the other.

"And almost half my life up to now," added Lanny.

Alston still thought of him as a youth, and saw now that the ensuing years had dealt kindly with him. There were no lines of care on the regular and agreeable features, no hint of gray in the wavy brown hair and neatly trimmed little mustache. Lanny was dressed as if he had just come out of a bandbox, and he had that ease of conversation which comes from having known since earliest childhood that everything about you is exactly as it ought to be. When you are so right, you can even be wrong if you want to, and people will take it as an amiable eccentricity.

What Lanny saw was a rather frail little gentleman with hair entirely gray, wearing horn-rimmed spectacles and a linen suit with some of the wrinkles which these suits acquire so quickly. "Charlie" Alston would never be exactly right; he had been a "barb" at college, so Lanny's father had told him, and he would never be free from the consciousness

2

that the people who had always been right were watching him. He was a kind and also a wise old gentleman, and that helps somewhat but not entirely, as all the smart world knows. Lanny recollected that he had come upon the mention of Charles T. Alston as one of the active New Dealers; so perhaps he was no longer teaching classes in college.

"I have heard from you indirectly," said Alston; but he didn't elaborate the remark. It might have been from the newspapers, for the ex-geographer added: "I hope your divorce didn't hurt you too much."

"My ex-wife has moved up the social ladder, and I was one of the rungs." Lanny said it with a smile; he didn't really mean it, for he was satisfied with the position on the social ladder assigned to a grandson of Budd Gunmakers and son of Budd-Erling Aircraft.

II

"What has life been doing to you?" the older man wanted to know.

This was an overture and called for a cordial response. "Have you anything to do for the next hour or two?" Lanny inquired, and went on to say that he had an appointment to view a collection of modern paintings which might soon come on the market. "That's how I have been earning my living. There are people who are naïve enough to trust my judgment as to what paintings are worth, and that enables me to spend the rest of my time as an idler and parasite." Again he said it smiling.

The ex-geographer replied that he would be happy to inspect works of art under the guidance of such an authority, and they left the hotel and took a taxi. A short drive and they stepped out in front of one of those establishments on Park Avenue where you either own your apartment or pay several thousand dollars a month rent. A personage who might have been one of Frederick the Great's grenadiers opened the taxi door for them; a clerk wearing a boutonnière took Lanny's name; a young woman with shiny red lips spoke it over the telephone; an elevator boy with several rows of buttons shot them toward the skies; and an elderly caretaker admitted them to a tier of rooms which apparently went most of the way around the building, and gave a hawk's-eye view of Manhattan Island and its environs.

The family was away in midsummer; the furniture was shrouded in tan-colored robes and the shades were drawn, but the caretaker raised one, and the visitors stopped to admire a penthouse rose garden. Then they strolled from room to room, examining paintings, each with its separate "reflector" which the caretaker turned on. They would stand for a while in silence, after which Lanny Budd would begin one of those well-modulated discourses with which he had learned to impress the most exclusive sort of people, those doubly élite who possess both wealth and culture.

"You observe the aristocratic aura with which Sargent could surround his model. You note that the head is somewhat small in proportion to the rest of the lady. Mrs. Winstead wasn't really that way, I can assure you, for I knew her; nor was it any blunder of the painter's, for I knew him even better. I watched him work in the hills and valleys around my mother's Riviera home, and can testify that he was able to get his proportions exact when he thought it desirable. It was his aim to select the salient characteristics of his subject and bring them to your attention. If you wanted literal exactness, he would say, a photographer could get it for you in the fraction of a second. It was the business of a painter to portray the soul of his subject."

"Not entirely overlooking what the subject might choose to believe about his soul," remarked Alston, with the trace of a smile.

"Surely not," agreed the other. "As far back as the days of ancient Egypt painters learned to make the masters taller and more impressive than the slaves. It is only in recent times, beginning perhaps with Goya, that painters have ventured to mingle a trace of humor with their subservience."

"Would you say that was the case here?"

"This was a sad lady, as you can perceive. They were enormously wealthy and correspondingly proud. They lived on an immense estate, and their two lovely daughters were brought up with great strictness and chaperoned in all their comings and goings. The result was that one of them eloped with a handsome young groom and the other made a marriage hardly more satisfactory. The haughty old father never consented to see either of them again. He has been one of my clients and I have had chances to observe his sorrow, in spite of his efforts to conceal it. I have no doubt that John Sargent, a kindly man in spite of all his brusqueness, thought that if there was any way of bringing a moment's happiness to Mrs. Winstead, there would be no great harm done to art. In his later years he wearied of such charity and refused to paint the rich at all."

III

"Charlie" Alston realized that this was the same informed and precocious Lanny Budd who had accompanied him to the Paris Peace Conference and shared a six months' ordeal. A youth who had lived most of his life in Europe; who not merely could chatter in French, but knew the subtle nuances, the argots, even the bad words; who knew customs and etiquette, personalities, diplomatic subterfuges; who could stand behind the chair of an "expert" during a formal session and whisper things into his ear, point to a paragraph in a document or write the correct word on a slip of paper—thus equipping a one-time farmboy from the State of Indiana to be something less than helpless in the presence of the age-old and super-elegant treacheries of Europe.

Now Lanny Budd was the same, only more of it. He had lived nearly two more decades between Europe and America, meeting the prominent ones of all lands and learning to take care of himself in all situations. Art to him was not just art; it was history and social science, psychology and human nature, even gossip, if you chose to take it that way. You had to get used to the fact that he really knew the "headliners," and that when he mentioned them he was not indulging in vainglory but just trying to make himself agreeable.

"Here you have an interesting contrast, Professor: a John and a Brockhurst side by side, and both dealing with the same subject. It is as if our host had wished to decide the question who is the better painter—or perhaps to provoke a perpetual debate. This is one of Augustus John's earlier works, and in my opinion they put him in a contemporary class by himself. Poor fellow, he is not taking good care of himself nowadays, and his work is not improving. Gerald Brockhurst is technically a sound painter, but I imagine that he himself would admit the supremacy of John at his best. Brockhurst's success can be attributed to his firm line and to his color. Both these characteristics have increased with the years, and that, I am sure, is why he has just been chosen to paint a portrait of my former wife. She has become Lady Wickthorpe, as you perhaps know, and is engaged in renovating a castle whose former châtelaines were painted by Gainsborough. Irma will be delighted with a portrait which will make her appear like a cinema star."

So once more an ex-geographer perceived that art was also psychology and even gossip!

"You have children?" he felt privileged to inquire.

"One daughter," was the reply. "She is seven, which is old enough to make the discovery that to live in an ancient castle is exciting, and that titles of nobility are impressive. It will be her mother's duty to see that she marries one of the highest."

"And you, Lanny?"

"I am the father, and, for having achieved that great honor, I am allowed to visit the child when I wish, and am shown every courtesy. It is taken for granted that I will not do or say anything to break the fairy-story spell under which the little one is being brought up."

I V

With the hot copper sun sinking low behind the long stone canyons of Manhattan Island, the two friends strolled back to the hotel where they had met. Lanny had a room there and invited the other up; he ordered a meal, and when it was served and the waiter withdrew, they lingered long over iced coffee and conversation. So many memories they had to revive and so many questions to ask! A score of men whom they had worked with at the Peace Conference: where were they now and what had happened to them? Many had died, and others had dropped out of sight. Alston spoke of those he knew. What did they think now about their work? He had been one of the dissidents, and Lanny had gone so far as to resign his humble job in protest against the misbegotten settlement. A melancholy satisfaction to know that you had been right, and that the worst calamities you had predicted now hung over the world in which you had to live!

Better to talk about the clear-sighted ones, those who had been courageous enough to speak out against blind follies and unchecked greeds. Lanny's Red uncle, who still lived in Paris—he was now a *député de la république française*, and once or twice his tirades had been quoted in the news dispatches to America. Lanny recalled how he had taken Alston and Colonel House to call on this uncle in his Paris tenement, this being part of President Wilson's feeble effort to bring the British and the French to some sort of compromise with the Soviets. "How my father hated to have me go near that dangerous Red sheep of my mother's family!" remarked Lanny. "My father still feels the same way."

They talked for a while about Robbie Budd. Alston told with humor of the years in college, when he had looked with awe upon the magnificent plutocratic son of Budd Gunmakers, who wore heavy white turtleneck sweaters, each with a blue Y upon it, and was cheered thunderously on the football field. Alston, on the other hand, had had to earn his living waiting on table in a students' dining room, and so was never "tapped" for a fashionable fraternity. Lanny said: "Robbie isn't quite so crude now; he has learned to respect learning and is even reconciled to having one of his sons play the piano and look at paintings instead of helping in the fabrication of military airplanes."

"And your mother?" inquired the elder man. When informed that she was still blooming, he said: "I really thought she was the most beautiful woman I had ever seen."

"She was certainly in the running," replied the son. "Now she contemplates with grief the fact that she is in her late fifties, and with a seven-year-old grandchild she cannot fib about it."

V

The ex-geographer was persuaded to talk about himself. He had made an impression upon his colleagues in Paris and had been offered a post in Washington. Among the acquaintances he had made there was the then Assistant Secretary of the Navy, a tall, robust young man of ability and ambition who appeared to have a weakness for college professors. "Likes to have them around," said Alston; "has an idea they know a lot, and that their knowledge ought to be used. A novel idea in American public life, as you know."

"It is one that annoys Robbie beyond endurance," replied Robbie's son.

"When F.D.R. became governor of New York State, he invited me to come to Albany and take a minor post—not to have much to do, but so that I could have a salary and be at hand to consult with him about the problems of his office, more complicated than any one man could deal with. A strange destiny for a geographer, but you know how it was in Paris; we all had to be politicians and diplomats, linguists, ethnographers, jurists—or anyhow we had to pretend to be. It is the same in government; you have to study human nature and the social forces that surround you, and apply your common sense to whatever problems arise. F.D. seemed to think that I was reasonably successful at it, so he brought me to Washington, and now I'm one of those 'bureaucrats' whom your father no doubt dislikes."

"Don't get within earshot of him!" exclaimed Lanny, with a grin.

"What I really am is a fixer. I have a subordinate who runs my office reasonably well, and I keep myself at the President's disposal, to find out what he needs to know, if I can, and to straighten out tangles if anybody can. When two self-important personalities fall to quarreling I go quietly to see them and persuade them that the Republicans are the only people who will profit by their ill behavior. All kinds of disagreeable and disillusioning jobs like that—and every now and then I get sick of it and decide that this shall be the last; but more troubles arise, and I am sorry for an overburdened executive who is trying to keep a blind world from plunging over a precipice."

"You think it's as bad as that, Professor Alston?"

"I think it's as bad as possible. What do you think, Lanny?"

"You mean about this country, or about Europe?"

"It's all one world—that is one of the things I learned as a geographer, and that the American people have to learn with blood and tears, I very much fear." It was the summer of 1937.

VI

Lanny, as he listened, had been thinking hard. His thought was: "How much ought I to tell?" He was always restraining the impulse to be frank with somebody; always having to put a checkrein on himself. Now, cautiously, he began:

"You remember, Professor Alston, that I was an ardent young reformer in your service. I didn't give up even after Versailles. I used to travel to one after another of the international conferences—I believe I went to a dozen, and met the statesmen and the newspaper fellows, and served as a go-between; I used to smuggle news—whatever I thought needed to be made known. I really believed it would be possible to instruct the public, and bring some peace and good fellowship to the unhappy old continent where I was born. But of late years I have been forced to give up; I was antagonizing everyone I knew, breaking up my home—it was like spitting against a hurricane. You must understand, I have built up something of a reputation as an art expert; I have played a part in making great collections which I have reason to hope will be bequeathed to public institutions, and thus will help in spreading culture. I persuade myself that this is a real service, and that taste in the arts is not just a fantasy, but an important social influence."

"Yes, Lanny, of course. But can you not also have political opinions and exercise some influence on the side of humanity?"

"It would be difficult, almost impossible. Most of the persons for whom I buy pictures are conservative, not to say reactionary, in their opinions. I have met them because I move in my father's world and my mother's, and in neither of these would I be received unless I kept a discreet attitude on the questions which now inflame everyone's mind. I don't doubt that you know how the people of money and fashion abuse and defame Roosevelt."

"He is trying to save them, and they will not have it."

"Not under any circumstances. Every man of them is a Louis Seize and every woman a Marie Antoinette, hellbent for the chopping block. I made enemies by pointing this out to them, and now I have learned to let them do the talking and reply that I am a nonpolitical person, living in the world of art. They take that as my professional pose, and assume that I am after the money, like everybody else. You see I lead a sort of double life; I talk frankly only to half a dozen trusted friends. I'd like to have you as one of them, if you consent; but you must promise not to talk about me to anyone else."

"I use many devices to keep my own name out of the papers, Lanny —so I can understand your attitude."

"You surely will when I tell you that one of my best-paying clients is Hermann Wilhelm Göring."

"Good grief, Lanny!"

"You may recall hearing me speak of my boyhood chum, Kurt Meissner, who became an artillery officer in the German Army. Now I am free to tell you something I was not free to mention at the time—that while I was serving as your secretary I ran into Kurt on the street in Paris; he was there as a secret agent of the German General Staff, and my mother and I sheltered him and saved him from the French police. Afterwards he lived in our home on the Riviera for a matter of eight years, and became a well-known pianist and composer. Then he went back to Germany and became a Nazi; through him I met many of those high in the Party, including the Führer, whose favorite Kurt still is. You see my position: I could tell my boyhood friend what I really think of his party and his cause, and thus break with him; or I could take the color of the Braune Haus and listen to what they told me, on the chance that what I learned might some day be of use outside. So I have played Beethoven for 'Adi,' as Hitler's intimates call him, and General Göring finds me a gay companion, invites me to his hunting lodge, and pumps me for information about the outside world. I tell him what I am sure he already knows, and I market for him the pictures which he has stolen from the wealthy Jews of his Third Reich. My father goes in and leases his airplane patents to the fat Exzellenz, and they try their best to outwit each other, and laugh amiably when they fail. *Geschäft ist Geschäft.*"

"It is a terrible thing to be giving the Nazis the mastery of the air over Europe, Lanny."

"Don't think that I haven't warned my father, and pleaded with him to change his business policy. But he answers that he went first to the British and the French, and they wouldn't pay him enough to keep his plant running. 'Am I to blame because it is the Nazis who have the brains and the foresight?' he asks, and is too polite to add: 'What business has an art expert trying to determine the destiny of nations?' Robbie insists that he believes in freedom of trade, and quotes Andrew Undershaft on 'The True Faith of an Armorer.' But, alas, when I put this creed to the test, it didn't stand up. My father would not, either directly or indirectly, permit the democratically elected people's government of Spain to purchase a Budd-Erling P9—not for cash on the barrelhead."

"You know Spain, Lanny?"

"Not so well as I know France and Germany and England, but I have visited it three times in the past year. Each time I brought out paintings, but also I met and talked with all sorts of people, and kept my eyes open. I saw the putting down of the Franco uprising in Barcelona and the arrival of the International Brigade for the defense of Madrid."

"What do you think will be the outcome of that fight?"

"The people will certainly be crushed if we continue our refusal to let them buy arms, while at the same time we permit the Italians and the Germans to send Franco everything he asks for. I cannot understand our country's diplomacy, and I wish that you would tell me: Why is it, and what does it mean?"

"The answer is not simple. There are so many forces, some pulling one way and some another."

"But the President himself, Professor Alston! He is the head of the government and is responsible for its policies. Can he not see what he is doing to Europe when he permits the Nazis and the Fascists to combine and murder a democratically chosen people's government?"

"The President is not the ruler of Europe, Lanny."

"No, but he is the head of our State Department, or ought to be, and has the say about our foreign policy. Why has he reversed what has been international law since the beginning; that any legitimate government has the right to purchase arms for its own defense? Why did he go to Congress and demand that the arms embargo be extended to apply to the Spanish Civil War? Why does he go on supporting the farce of Non-Intervention after he has had a whole year to see what it means—that we keep faith with Hitler and Mussolini while they keep faith with nobody in the world?"

VII

The ex-geographer was gazing into a pair of earnest brown eyes and listening to a voice that was always well modulated, even when it was full of concern. They seemed to him young eyes and a young voice;

the same as he had observed them in the conference rooms of the Hotel Crillon, where the grandson of Budd Gunmakers had labored so hard to save the district of Stubendorf, the home of his friend Kurt Meissner, from being turned over to the Poles. Now here was this Lanny in the summer of 1937, nearly twice as old, but still stating a complex problem in simple terms. Or, at least, so it seemed to a "fixer" of high state affairs. Why doesn't President Roosevelt see this? Why doesn't he do that? A fixer hears such questions all day and most of the night; and perhaps he doesn't know the answer, or perhaps he's not free to tell it.

Alston listened until this friend had finished pouring out his demands; then, after a moment's pause, and with a trace of a smile, he said: "Why don't you ask him yourself, Lanny?"

"I have never had that opportunity, Professor."

"You could have it quite easily, if you wished."

The younger man was startled. "You think he'd have time to talk to me?"

"He is a great talker; he loves it. Also, he likes to meet people, all sorts—even those who disagree with him."

"I hadn't thought of the idea," said Lanny; but he was thinking now while he spoke. "It would be a great honor, I know; but I might get into the newspapers—and then what would Robbie say?"

He stopped, and the other laughed. "You might go to sell him a picture. He might really buy one, to make it all right!" Then, more seriously, he explained that the President was at Krum Elbow, his mother's Hyde Park home, which was not so closely watched by the news-hounds. "They make their headquarters in Poughkeepsie, some distance from the estate, and they don't haunt the grounds as they do the White House. The President could easily instruct his secretary that your name was not to be included among the daily list of visitors. That might be of advantage to him, also—for it's possible that he might have something confidential to say to a friend of Hitler and Göring."

VIII

It doesn't take long to arrange an appointment when the telephone service is working—and when you are the right person. Early next afternoon Lanny left his hotel, driving a sport car which was at his disposal whenever he visited his father's home in Connecticut. His route took him through Central Park and up Riverside Drive; across a great tall bridge from which he had a breathtaking view; then up the valley of the Hudson River, known to history and legend. Here Major André had been hanged and General Arnold had fled to avoid hanging; here mysterious Dutch figures had played at bowls in the night, thus causing the thunder, and Rip van Winkle had anticipated Freud with his "flight from reality."

The Dutch settlers had moved up this broad valley and with bright cloth and glass beads and other treasures had purchased large tracts from the Indians. Wars and revolutions had left them undisturbed, and now their tenth generation descendants were gentlemen farmers, living in dignified leisure and voting the Republican ticket. Once in a while comes a black sheep to every fold, and so in this staid Dutchess County was a family of Democratic Roosevelts whom their relatives and neighbors looked upon with horror, referring to the head of it as "That Man." The Nazis had changed his name to Rosenfeld and said he was a Jew; millions of worthy Germans believed it, and Herr Doktor Josef Goebbels, who had started the story, had chuckled over it to Lanny Budd.

A well-paved boulevard winds along the edge of the hills, now losing sight of the river and then coming again upon a sweeping view. Every few miles is a village, with houses surrounded by lawns and shaded by ancient trees. Cars are parked in front of general stores, and loungers sit in front of them, chewing cigar stubs, whittling sticks, discussing their neighbors and the doings of their politicians. In the heat of a midsummer afternoon everything is still that can be; only the bees hum, and the motor of a car speeding along the highway at the customary rate of ten miles faster than the law allows.

When Lanny neared the little village called Hyde Park, he found that he was ahead of time, and stopped for a while in a shady spot and waited, going over in his mind for the tenth time what he was going to say to the man who held the destiny of the Spanish democracy in his hands. Would this busy man give him time to say it all? On chance that he wouldn't, what was the first thing to make sure of? Ever since the spring of 1919 Lanny Budd had been trying to change the history of the world—off and on, of course, and in between playing the piano, looking at paintings, and making himself agreeable to the smart friends of his mother and father.

IX

The old Dutch farms run from the highway to the bluffs which confine the river, a distance which may be half a mile or more. Each has its own gates and perhaps a porter's lodge. Lanny drove slowly until he came to gates having a sentry-box with two State troopers on guard. He stopped and gave his name to one who came forward; the man nodded, and Lanny drove on, up a long treeshaded avenue, like a thousand other approaches to mansions that he had visited in the course of his playboy life. This mansion was modest, according to playboy standards: a two-story structure which had been lived in and added to; part frame and part stucco, with towers; the sort of house which really rich people discard as no longer big or elegant enough.

Lanny parked his car in a shady spot on the circular drive. A colored butler opened the door before he rang, and a woman secretary came to meet him in the entrance hall. When he gave his name she led him without delay along the hall and down half a dozen stairs having a ramp alongside. These gave into the library, a spacious room which appeared comfortable and much used. The books were mostly legislative reports; there was a Winged Victory in marble against one of the walls, a model of a ship under glass, and a lady's sewing-bag hanging over the back of one of the overstuffed chairs. These details Lanny Budd took in with swift and practiced eyes. Then he saw a large flat-topped desk near the fireplace, and seated at it, facing him—That Man!

A large man with a large head, powerful shoulders and arms, wearing a white pongee shirt open at the throat. In his middle years he had been stricken with the dread disease called poliomyelitis, and as a result his legs were shrunken; he had to wear braces, and in public you observed him leaning upon the arm of a strong companion. In his home he used a wheelchair, which was the meaning of the ramp leading into the library. Such a stroke would have crushed most men; but one who had the courage to defy his fate, the power of will to persist and train his shrunken muscles all over again—such a man might come out of the ordeal stronger and more self-possessed. Many persons had doubted whether it could be possible for a man so handicapped to stand the strain which the office of President inflicts upon its victims, but F.D.R. had managed to enjoy the job. He was blessed with a buoyant disposition and could make jokes, look at movies or postage stamps, and not lie awake at night trying to solve problems of state.

He was seated in a large leather chair, and offered a cordial hand and welcoming smile. Lanny was to be exposed to the famous "Roosevelt charm," and had wondered: "What will it do to me?" He had encountered various kinds of charm on the old continent where he had been raised; many kinds false, some dangerous, and he had learned to distinguish among them. He saw at once that here was a man genuinely interested in human beings and in what they had to bring him. On his desk within close reach was a stack of reports and documents a foot high. These would be hard going; but when somebody like the grandson of Budd's came along, having traveled all over the cultured world and met its élite—someone who shared F.D.'s own joy of living and his prejudice in favor of the "forgotten man"—then his face lighted up and his eyes sparkled and it was as if he had had a glass or two of champagne. "You two are made for each other"—so Alston had said to each.

X

They talked about the ex-geographer; the President said that he had found him a highly useful man, and Lanny replied: "I made that discovery when I was still in my teens." He described himself, a youngster who hadn't even finished prep school, plunged suddenly into the caldron of old Europe's hottest hatreds. Everybody connected with the American peace delegation, even a secretary-translator, had been pulled and hauled this way and that by national interests, racial interests, business interests. With his father's help Lanny had come to recognize the real forces behind that conference: the great cartels which controlled steel and coal and shipping and banking and above all munitions throughout Europe; which owned newspapers in the various capitals, subsidized political agents, and moved governments about as their pawns. Stinnes and Thyssen in Germany, Schneider and the de Wendels in France, Deterding in Holland, Zaharoff in all countries from Greece to Britain—these were the men who had had their way, and had broken the heart of Woodrow Wilson.

Zaharoff, munitions king and "mystery man of Europe," had been no mystery to Lanny. He told how this Knight Commander of the Bath and Grand Officer of the Legion of Honor had tried to buy a young American secretary, offering him the most tempting of bribes to betray his trust and reveal the secrets of the peacemakers. Later, not being entirely pleased with the treaties, Zaharoff had subsidized a private war of the Greek nation against the Turks. Lanny told how, with the help of Robbie Budd, he had tried to buy the Bolsheviks at the Genoa Conference; and how, in Lanny's presence, he had burned his diaries and private papers and thus set fire to the chimney of his Paris mansion. When his beloved wife had died, this munitions king of Europe had taken to hiring spiritualist mediums. Lanny had brought him one, but the seance had produced, instead of the hoped-for wife, a horde of soldiers shouting vilifications. Among them had been one who proclaimed himself the Unknown Soldier, buried under the Arc de

Triomphe. He had declared himself a Jew—something which would surely have distressed the anti-Semitic military cliques of France.

A President who had distressed the numerous anti-Semitic cliques of his own country listened with manifest pleasure and remarked: "These are tales out of the Arabian Nights. I command you to come and tell me a thousand and one of them."

"Under penalty of having my head chopped off?" asked the visitor, and they chuckled together.

XI

One who had studied the social arts in France would not make the mistake of doing all the talking. Franklin D. Roosevelt had had his own Arabian Nights' adventures, and Lanny let him tell them. "We have our masters of money on this side of the water, too," he said. "They know just what they want, and are greatly shocked because they cannot get it from me. They were not entirely without influence in the previous administration, as you no doubt know."

"Indeed yes, Mr. President."

"You would be amused to hear of the efforts they made to trap me, after I was elected and before I was inaugurated. The country was in the midst of a panic, and if only I would consent to meet with Mr. Hoover and give him some idea of what I wanted done! The scheme was, of course, that I should be assuming responsibility, taking the panic over as my panic instead of my predecessor's. I let him have it all, up to the very last moment."

"It took nerve, and I admired yours."

"You can't imagine the pressure; it never let up, and hasn't let up yet. They persuaded me into a World Economic Conference in London right after the inauguration, if you remember, the idea being to preserve the gold standard and fix all currencies at the then-existing levels. France and Britain had devalued their currencies and wanted to keep the dollar at the old level, so they could take over the trade of the world. When I realized what it was all about I dumped the chess-board, and I don't expect ever to be forgiven for it. You doubtless know the sort of stories they tell about me."

"I have had them straight from the horse's mouth."

"I am supposed to be drunk all the time, and in spite of my physical deficiencies I maintain a large harem."

"Have you heard the one about the psychiatrist who died and went to heaven and was invited to psychoanalyze God?"

"No. Has that something to do with me?"

"St. Peter explained that God was suffering from delusions of grandeur—He thought He was Franklin D. Roosevelt."

The President threw back his head and laughed heartily; he put his soul into his enjoyment of a joke, and it was a good thing to hear. Lanny remembered that Abraham Lincoln had sought the same kind of relief from too many burdens.

"Just now," said the Chief Executive, "I am in the midst of the hottest fight yet, brought on by my efforts to reform the Supreme Court. Those nine old gentlemen in their solemn black robes have blocked one after another of our New Deal measures, and the whole future of our program depends upon my efforts to break that stranglehold. I have called for an increase in the number of the justices, and this is called 'packing the court,' and is considered the opening wedge for Bolshevism. There is nothing the enemies of this plan will not do or say." The President told some things they had done, and after one tale of senatorial skullduggery he asked: "What do you think of that?"

Lanny said: "I think it shows you are almost as indiscreet as the previous Roosevelt." This brought another burst of laughter, and after it they were friends.

XII

The son of Budd-Erling judged that it was time to bring up the subject which lay nearest to his heart: the peril to the democratic nations involved in the Nazi-Fascist preparations for war, and the demonstration of their program they were now giving on the Iberian peninsula. Lanny told about the trips he had made into Spain, and what he had learned there.

"It is called a 'Civil War,' Mr. President, but it is nothing of the sort; it is an invasion of a free people by the Italian and German dictators. Its purpose is to give them practice in the use of their new tanks and airplanes, and to establish landing-fields and submarine bases to attack the shipping of the free nations when the real war begins."

Lanny described the Spanish ruling classes. "I have played tennis with King Alfonso; I know his set on the Riviera and I have met many of the same sort in Paris and London and in Spain itself. I believe they are the most ignorant, vain, and arrogant aristocracy in Europe. The younger set have learned to drive motorcars, and a few of them to fly, but that is as far as they have got with anything modern; I would have difficulty in naming half a dozen among them who have read a book.

Their interest is in playing polo, shooting tame pigeons, gambling, and chasing women. They are superstitious, and at the same time utterly cynical; about government they know nothing, and if their man Franco wins this war they will turn the country into a paradise for Juan March and speculators like him, and a dungeon for every enlightened man and woman."

"I have no reason for doubting your opinion, Mr. Budd. If I could have my way, governments in many parts of the world would be changed. But I am not the ruler of any part of Europe."

"I believe, sir, that you have the say about the matter which is of greatest importance to the Spanish people's government. I am told that up to this year it has been the invariable rule in international affairs that any established government has the right to buy whatever arms it needs for its own defense. That rule was rescinded last January, and it was you who urged Congress to do it. I couldn't understand it then, and I understand it even less now, when you see that it means the death of one of the most enlightened and progressive of governments."

It was a challenge, deliberately made bold; Lanny all but held his breath while he waited for the reaction of the great man in front of him.

The great man paused to think, and to light a cigarette in a long thin holder. The smile had gone out of the blue eyes, and a grave look had come upon the genial features. "Mr. Budd, you ask me about what has been and still is one of the most painful decisions of my life. I am called a dictator, but you know that such a role is farthest from my wishes or my thoughts. I am the duly elected executive officer of a great democratic people; I am pledged to uphold government by public opinion, and I can do only what the people will let me."

"Of course, Mr. President; but you can sometimes lead the people."

"Up to a certain point, but never beyond it. I can present them with one or two new ideas at a time. If I go too fast or too far, and lose contact with them, then I am powerless to accomplish any of the things I wish. The constant study of my life has to be: 'How fast can I move? How far will the public follow me? Dare I do this? Dare I do that?' Such is the art of government in a democracy, Mr. Budd; often it does not seem heroic, but it is the best way that I know of. It is slow, but also it is sure."

XIII

The President took a couple of pulls at the long thin cigarette holder; at the same time watching his hearer, seeking to read the effect of his words. He resumed: "Call me statesman or politician, the fact remains that I must keep in power or I accomplish nothing. And I am not operating in a vacuum, but in a set of circumstances which I am unable to alter. I am the head of the Democratic Party in the summer of 1937. Have you made any study of this party?"

"I am afraid I don't know my own country as well as I ought to," replied this foreign-born and foreign-raised American.

"In my thoughts I compare myself to a man driving three horses; they had such a hitch-up in old-time Russia—a *troika*. I cannot go anywhere unless I can persuade the three horses to take me; if any one of them balks, the *troika* comes to a halt. One of these horses is young and wild; that is my New Deal group, backed by organized labor and its sympathizers, the intellectuals; they want to gallop all the time, and I have to put a curb-bit in that horse's mouth. The second is much older, and inclined to be mulish; that is my block of Southern states. Those states are run by a land-owning aristocracy, and by new industrialists who are still in the pre-labor-union stage of political thinking. The poor, whether white or black, are largely disfranchised by the poll tax; therefore, the majority of congressmen and senators from the South are always looking for a reason to desert the New Deal. Right now they are finding one in the 'court-packing' program. You have read some of their utterances, I suppose."

"I have."

"And then my third horse, a nervous and skittish steed which I seldom dare to mention by name. You will consider my naming it confidential, please?"

"Of course, Mr. President."

"My Roman Catholic charger. There are twenty million Catholics in this country, and the great bulk of them think and vote as their Church advises. That is especially true of those of foreign descent—Irish, Italians, Germans, Poles. They are strong in our great cities, New York and Boston, Chicago and St. Louis and San Francisco, and their vote determines any close election. They have been told that General Franco is defending their faith against atheistic Reds."

"What they have been told is Franco propaganda, and mostly false."

"That may be so—but will they believe it from a Protestant? I must have their support for my domestic program; so there I am."

That was all the President said; but later on Lanny learned from Professor Alston that the heads of the hierarchy had come to Washington and "talked cold turkey"; in other words, votes. They had said: "Either you keep arms from the Spanish Reds or else we defeat your party."

They could elect Republicans to Congress next year and bring to nought F.D.'s Supreme Court reform plan. They had threatened in so many words to do it.

"Mr. Roosevelt," remarked the visitor, "what you say is almost identical with what Léon Blum has told me. He carried an election on a program of domestic reforms, and is very proud of having pushed them all through. But he had to pay the price which the reactionaries exacted—no aid for Spain. I have warned him in vain—what good will it do him to nationalize the armament industry of France while Hitler is permitted to arm and prepare to overwhelm him? What will be the position of France with a Fascist Spain at her back door and German submarines using harbors on the Atlantic and the Mediterranean?"

"The danger to France is plain enough, because Hitler is just across the border; but you can't use that argument with Americans, three thousand miles away from trouble. Believe me, Mr. Budd, the great mass of our people have just one thought with regard to the European mess: they want to keep out of it. They have no ifs, ans, or buts on the subject; they just say: 'Let Europe go to hell in its own way, but keep us out.' They fly into a fit at the thought of anything that might get us in—such as, for example, the sinking of an American ship carrying munitions to either side in the Spanish war."

"Will they feel that way, Mr. President, when they see the Reichswehr rolling into Paris, and General Göring's bombing planes destroying London?"

"The American people will believe that when they see it; and meantime there's no use in you or me trying to tell it to them. I can say to Congress: 'These are dangerous times, and we must have ships and planes to defend ourselves,' and I can get away with that; but if I should say one word about defending the interests of any other nation or group, I would raise up a storm that would bowl me over. Believe me, I know my master's voice, and when I hear it, I have no choice but to obey. If you want to save Spain, persuade your French friends to stick out their necks; or better yet, persuade Mr. Chamberlain and his Cabinet, the real authors and sustainers of the Non-Intervention policy. If the British cannot see that it is their fight, surely nobody can ask *me* to take it on *my* shoulders."

XIV

So that was that. Lanny was just about to get up and offer to take his leave, but his host had something on his mind and said, abruptly: "Charlie Alston has told me a lot about you, Mr. Budd, all of it good. He thinks I ought to make some use of your abilities."

Lanny wasn't entirely surprised; he had guessed what was in his one-time employer's mind. He said: "I am afraid, sir, I haven't enough training to be of any real use to anybody."

"Very few of us have had training for the work we are doing, Mr. Budd; it is all too new. We have to learn as we go along; we try things and see what happens."

"Mr. Roosevelt," said the grown-up playboy, earnestly, "you are paying me a compliment, and I would hate to seem not to appreciate it. I believe with all my heart in what you are doing, and I would love to be of use to you. But I have ties which compel me to return to Europe and make it impossible for me to settle down to a regular life."

"There might be things you could do for me in Europe, and they wouldn't have to be 'regular.' "

There was a silence, with Lanny thinking hard. He glanced about him to make sure they were alone in the room; then, lowering his voice, he began: "There is something I should have to tell you about my own life, before I could be of any service to you. It is so much of a secret that I didn't mention it to Professor Alston; I haven't told even my father and mother, whom I love. Not merely my own life but many others might depend upon it."

"I am used to receiving confidences, Mr. Budd; and you may be sure that I keep them."

"This must never under any circumstances be told or even hinted to any other person."

"I promise—unless, of course, it is something contrary to the interests of the United States."

"It is nothing of that nature. Many years ago I met in Berlin a young couple, artists, also ardent Social-Democrats, working for freedom and enlightenment in their country. When the Nazis came in, this couple took up what is called underground work; the man was caught, and no doubt has been dead for years. The woman went on with her dangerous tasks in Berlin, and I used to give her money which I earned as commissions on picture deals. When the Gestapo had got all her associates and were hot on her trail, I managed to smuggle her across the border. A year or more later we were secretly married in England. You can see how that dominates my life, and makes it impossible for me to be 'regular.' "

"You mean that she is still going on with her activities?"

"Nothing could induce her to stop. I ramble over Europe, buying pictures for American clients and earning sums of money which I turn over to her. I needn't go into details about what she does; it is a question of getting the truth into a country which has fallen into the hands of the Prince of Lies."

"I quite understand, Mr. Budd; and naturally I sympathize with such efforts."

"I make use of the social position of my mother and father, and of their friends; also, of course, the reputation I have been able to build up as an art expert. That gives me a legitimate reason for going into any country, meeting prominent persons, and hearing what the insiders are saying. I have visited Hitler at the Braune Haus in Munich, and at his Berchtesgaden retreat. I have been on hunting trips with General Göring, and had him try to hire me as his secret agent. As I told Professor Alston, I refuse his money, but promise to tell him things in friendship; what I tell him is news I am sure he already knows, or that won't do any particular harm."

"Fabulous, Mr. Budd! Might it not be worth while for you to visit *me* now and then, and tell me what you learn from General Göring?"

"I have thought of it, sir. What I am afraid of is, it might kill my opportunities in Germany, and put the Gestapo on my trail. You live of necessity in a glare of publicity; and because I was until recently married to a very rich woman, I too have had more than my share of attention. Many reporters know me, and how could I come to the White House without its arousing curiosity? I don't need to tell you that the German embassy has its swarm of spies, and that everything of interest is cabled in code to Berlin."

"All that is true; but it happens that I often have to act secretly, and I have ways of arranging it. There is a so-called 'social door' to the White House, and my friends often slip in unobserved. Also, I have among my personal bodyguards a man whom I have known from his boyhood, and whom I trust. He wouldn't have to know your name; we would agree upon a code word, and any time you got in touch with him and gave that word, he would report it to me and I would set a time for him to bring you. You would be known as a 'P.A.,' that is, 'Presidential Agent,' and would have a number. I believe the next number is 103."

"Very well, Mr. President. If you feel that I can be of use to you in that way, I will do my best."

"Keep an expense account; it will come out of my secret fund."

"No, that is not necessary. I am able to earn plenty of money; I have to, because that is my camouflage."

"But you like to use the money for your cause, do you not?"

"I sometimes earn more than can be safely spent by my wife and her associates; and what I do for you would add nothing to my expenses. Let me be one of your dollar-a-year men."

XV

F.D.R. pressed a button on his desk and the woman secretary appeared. "Missy," he said, "I want to speak to Gus at once." When the woman had gone he said to Lanny: "Choose a code name. Something unusual and easy to remember."

The visitor thought. "How about Zaharoff?"

"Fine!" said the other, with a chuckle. "How long do you plan to be in this country?"

"A couple of weeks. I am here to report to some of my clients."

"Will you be able to see me again before you leave?"

"Certainly, if you wish."

"I may be able to think up a list of questions to ask you, and matters about which you might try to get information for me."

"You will hear from me without fail."

A youngish man built like a college fullback entered the room. "Gus," said the President, "this gentleman is a very special friend whom I shall be seeing now and then. Look him over carefully so that you will know him whenever you meet him. You are not to know his name; we have chosen a code name which he will make use of over the phone, or by mail or wire. The name is Zaharoff. Fix that in your memory."

"Zaharoff. O.K., Chief."

"Whenever he calls or wires you, you will name a time and place where he can get you again in a few hours, and then you will come to me, and I will make an appointment so that you can bring him to me. Nobody else is to know anything about him, and you are not to mention him under any circumstances. Is that clear?"

"O.K., Chief."

"You will give him the phone numbers of your hotels in Washington and in Poughkeepsie, and any other place where he is likely to find you." Then, turning to his visitor: "Could you make it convenient to call in a week or two?"

"You bet," replied Lanny, doing his best to make himself at home in the land of his fathers.

"His name is Gus Gennerich, and he used to be a New York cop.

Talk to him a little, so that he will know your voice over the phone."

Lanny turned to the ex-policeman, who had never taken his eyes off him for a moment. "Mr. Gennerich, I have just been spending a couple of the most interesting hours of my life. I have been meeting a great man and a wise man whom we can trust. He is doing a job for all of us, and we have to be ready to protect him with our lives. You agree with that, I am sure."

"I do, sir."

"The name we have agreed upon is that of a Greek peasant boy who was born in a Turkish village and who came to be at one time the richest man in the world. He was called the munitions king of Europe, and he was the embodiment of everything that we in America dislike and distrust. Z-A-H-A-R-O-F-F, with the accent on the first syllable. You think now you will know me and my voice?"

"I think so."

Lanny took out his notebook and jotted down the phone numbers which the man gave him. The President said: "That is all, Gus," and the man went out.

"Mr. President," declared Lanny, "you have done me a great honor, and I appreciate it."

"A lot of my friends call me 'Governor,'" replied the other. "It is easier to say, and reminds me of the days when I had only one forty-eighth of the burdens I have now. May I follow Charlie Alston's example and call you Lanny?"

"Indeed you may; and be sure that if you give me a commission, I will do my very best to carry it out. Unless I am mistaken we have hard and dangerous times ahead of us, and you will need men whom you can trust."

"I need more of them right now, Lanny, and if you know any, tell me about them. I meant to invite you to stay and have afternoon coffee with us; that is a sort of institution in our family, and you would meet my mother and a couple of my secretaries. But in view of the plans we have in mind, I think you had better just walk out quietly."

"I understand, Governor."

"Don't fail to call Gus a week or two from now, for I shall do a lot of thinking in the meantime. Good-by and good luck to you."

Lanny went out and got into his car and drove away, saying to himself: "By heck! I have fallen for the Roosevelt charm!"

2

Wise as Serpents

I

NORTHWARD up the valley of the Hudson and into that of the Mohawk, Lanny began one of those motor trips in which he combined business with pleasure. He had learned to drive as a boy, and loved the gentle purring of a well-cared-for motor. He enjoyed the variety of landscapes slipping by; his subconscious mind was pervaded by the presence of nature, even while his thoughts were occupied with his personal problems or the destiny of the world. If the mood took him he might turn on the little radio in the car, a combination of inventions by which music could be brought to millions of homes and to travelers on all the world's highways.

Lanny Budd had learned to enjoy those pleasures of the mind and imagination which cost very little and do no harm to any other person. He had learned to take care of himself in a world that was often dangerous. He had learned what he could do, and tried not to grieve because it wasn't everything. The world was tough and stubborn and changed very slowly; just now it evidently meant to grow worse before it grew better. Jesus, who had lived in a time not so different, had said to his disciples: "Behold, I send you forth as sheep in the midst of wolves: be ye therefore wise as serpents, and harmless as doves."

In the trunk of Lanny's car was a cardfile listing hundreds of paintings with their prices, also a couple of bags containing photographs. He was what the English call a "bagman" and the Americans a "drummer," but never in either land had there been one so exclusive. He would travel a couple of thousand miles and call upon only half a dozen clients, all of whom had invited him to visit them whenever he could. In each case he had telephoned to make sure the visit would be convenient. He would arrive at a country estate and the servants would carry in his bags; he would spend the night or a week-end, making himself the most acceptable of guests. He would tell about the great ones overseas and what they were doing and saying. He would inspect his host's art treasures, and would say what he thought with judicious and precise discrimination. He would linger over the last treasure he had purchased for this client, asking how it was "wearing"—meaning whether the client still found pleasure in looking at it. If there was any uncertainty in the tone of the reply, Lanny would say: "You know I could probably get you an offer for it."

When the time came to settle down to business and tell this client what the bagman or drummer had in mind for him, it would be one special item which Lanny had come upon in some old castle of the Rhineland or château of the Loire country; something that had caused him to exclaim: "This belongs in the Taft collection"—or whatever it might be. Sometimes he would come in his father's station-wagon, bringing the painting with him; if he came early, ahead of his host, he would make bold to have the butler take down a painting from the head of the staircase and hang the new treasure, so when the host came in there would be a vision of glory hitting him between the eyes.

It was Lanny's practice to let the work speak for itself; never, never could anyone say that he tried to force a sale or revealed anything but critical impersonality. "Be sure, this work will find a home before I get back to Connecticut." And the host would know this was true, for money was free in America again; the fortunate few had floods of dividends rolling in, and it was a problem to know what to do with them. If you were collecting old masters and wanted an expert to bring you choice items, you behaved in such a way as to earn his respect: that is, you sat down promptly and wrote a check for twenty or forty or possibly a hundred thousand dollars.

All his life Lanny Budd had been learning how to handle the rich and powerful. In earliest childhood he had watched his father and mother doing it. In those days Robbie had been selling the instruments of killing. Generals and cabinet ministers had been the customers, and duchesses and countesses had been flattering and cajoling and "pulling them in," all for a fee, of course. Early in his twenties, Lanny had discovered his own line; the sums were smaller but the techniques the same, and the psychology of the victims. The excessively rich were as shy as wild birds; everybody was hunting them and they took wing at the least hint of danger. They were abnormally sensitive and had to be handled as if they were made of wet tissue paper. They would absorb flattery like sponges—but only that subtle kind which assured them that they were above flattery. Each client was a separate problem, and love of beautiful art and love of wonderful self were tied up together in a knot of many complications.

II

The last stage of this tour was Pittsburgh, where Lanny's friend Harry Murchison made and sold immense quantities of plate glass, and was always interested in the latest news about glass-shattering in Europe. Harry had gained about two pounds avoirdupois every year since the outbreak of the World War, when he had come so near to becoming Lanny Budd's stepfather. Now he was married to his former secretary, and Lanny never tired of observing the speed and certainty with which American women acquire the social arts. Adella Murchison was now a stately matron, perfectly sure of herself and her leadership in the cultural life of her grimy home city. Lanny had provided her with the lingo of the arts, and every time he came visiting she acquired a fresh supply with which to impress her friends. She was willing to pay generously, and when Harry objected: "Where on earth will you put another painting?" she replied: "I have heard you say that no excursion steamer is ever so crowded that there isn't room for one more passenger."

Adella was at their place in the Adirondacks, and Harry said: "I have got me the wings of a dove and I fly to my beloved every week-end." He invited Lanny to come along, and when Lanny explained that he had an urgent engagement in Washington, his friend countered: "I'll deliver you in Washington on Monday morning before I come back here." When Lanny asked about his car, Harry offered to have a man drive it to Washington. When the rich want something, they get it.

Harry's dove proved to be a comfortably equipped private plane with seats for a pilot and three passengers. It rose from the Pittsburgh airfield just after business hours and settled gently down on the Lake Placid airfield before sundown. Harry's secretary had phoned to announce their coming, and Adella was waiting, driving the car herself; they wound through pine forests laden with pungent odors and came to what was called a "camp," a quite sumptuous slab-sided mansion on a remote little lake. They supped on a platter of fried black bass which had been swimming in those blue waters a couple of hours previously. The couple plied their visitor with questions—Harry about the prospects for more glass-shattering in Europe, and Adella about the friends he had met and the paintings he had discovered on that unhappy but interesting old continent.

Presently it came out that the Murchisons had seen a play about Queen Elizabeth and the Earl of Leicester, and Lanny perceived that

Adella's imagination had been captured by the brilliant and willful figure of the queen's lover. "I can tell you where you can get a portrait of his wife," remarked Lanny, "the unfortunate Amy Robsart. She was married when they were both mere children, and she was killed by falling down a flight of stairs. There were whispers that somebody had thrown her down, as a means of freeing her husband to marry the queen."

"Is it a good painting?" asked the plate-glass lady.

"The painters of that time were none of them of the best. This is supposed to be the work of Marc Gheeraerts, whom the English call 'Garrard.' I am not sure if the attribution is justified, but it's an interesting work. The painter was apparently more concerned with the subject's elaborately jeweled clothes than with her character. All those Tudor ladies were so stiff in their corsets that it is hard for us to imagine them as having any life."

"Where is the painting?"

"It is at Sandhaven Castle. The owner's wife is Rosemary, my old flame; they neither of them care much about paintings, and every time Bertie gets into debt she invites me to tea and brings the conversation around to the price of old masters."

So it was that Lanny carried on his business, having a cardfile of paintings and another of customers, and matching a card from one with a card from another. Adella lit up right away; she had met Rosemary Codwilliger, pronounced Culliver, and had driven by the castle, and now she asked questions about both, and then about the unfortunate Amy Robsart. Lanny said: "You can read all about her in Sir Walter Scott's *Kenilworth*." He knew that this would make a hit, because Adella liked to have stories about her pictures, things that she could use to interest and impress people.

"What do you think it could be bought for?" she wanted to know, and he told her he hadn't asked for a price, but his guess would be something less than a thousand pounds.

"I'd better not cable, because that might sound as if you were anxious. I am sailing for England at the end of the week and I'll pay a call on Rosemary and take a stroll along the gallery and lead up to the subject tactfully. The Robsart family was connected with Bertie's—I don't remember just how and he probably doesn't either."

"You have sold us so many men," remarked Adella, referring to her two Goyas and her double Velásquez suspected of being a del Mazo. "It's time you got me a woman. Is she really pretty?"

"Sweet and rather pathetic," replied the subtle expert. "I'll send you a photograph, and you can decide whether you'd like to have the lady in your home."

So it was that Lanny made money for the underground movement against the Nazis in Germany. So also it was that Adella made sure of receiving visits from a charming man who lightened the smoke-laden atmosphere of that city where she had been born and had raised herself from far down in the social heap to the very top.

III

Set down at the Washington airport on Monday morning, Lanny got busy on the telephone and gave the password. "Gus" told him to call again at noon, and when he did so the order was to be at a certain street corner at a quarter to ten that evening. It happened to be raining, and Lanny with overshoes and umbrella stood watching the speeding traffic, standing back far enough from the curb so as not to be too badly spattered. A car drew up, and the President's bodyguard looked out and nodded.

"Not a very good night," Lanny remarked, as he stepped in. The other replied: "I'll say!"—and that was all the conversation. They rolled up Pennsylvania Avenue, and into the "social door" of the hundred-and-forty-year-old building which had housed all the Presidents of the United States but the first. At the gate there was apparently no guard; at the door, which is the main front door under the white pillars, the guard looked at Gus and said: "Hello." Avoiding the elevator, they went up a flight and a half by a rather narrow, red-carpeted staircase. An aged Negro servitor passed them, saying: "Evenin', Mista Gus." They stopped at one of the doors which was ajar; Gus tapped gently, and that warm voice which all the world had learned to know over the radio called: "Come in."

The President was lying in bed, wearing pajamas of blue pongee, covered by a knitted blue sweater, crew-neck style. His head was propped up, with a reading lamp at his left shoulder and a "whodunit" lying on the sheet which covered him. "Good evening," he said to his visitor, not naming him; then, to the other man: "Thank you, Gus." As the man started to retire, the President added: "Close the door, please."

So the two conspirators were alone. Lanny took the chair by the bedside, and the other coughed slightly and reached for his handkerchief. "I am supposed to have a cold," he said. "I am growing suspicious of my subconscious mechanism, for I notice that I develop the sniffles whenever I have a tiresome schedule like today."

"I hope I am no part of the cause," replied Lanny, grinning.

"You are what I wanted to be free for. Have you had time to think about the subject of our talks?"

"I have been motoring most of the time, and I've thought about it constantly."

"Needless to say, Lanny, I haven't had that much time: but I have made notes of several things I want to ask about."

"Shoot!" replied the other; and without further preliminaries they got down to business.

Said F.D.R.: "There has grown up a practice on the part of our leading American industrialists to make secret deals with the big European cartels, whereby they share one another's processes and inventions upon a strict monopoly basis. It appears from the social point of view a highly undesirable practice. I am not sure what I can or should do, but it seems clear that with wars threatening as they are, the government ought to get all possible information on the subject. Do you happen to know about it?"

"I have heard my father discussing it with his friends and associates. I know that such deals have been made with I. G. Farben Industrie and with A.E.G., the great electrical trust of Germany. I have been told that the du Ponts have such arrangements, also a prominent lead company and Standard Oil of New Jersey, I believe having to do with artificial rubber."

"I am not proposing that you should do detective work," explained the President. "That is the business of our Intelligence, and usually they get what they go after. But often we can save a lot of time and wasted effort if we know where the big booty is hidden and where to start digging. A casual remark dropped by one of the insiders may be worth more than tons of documents."

"Quite so," replied the other. "I have heard such remarks, and could easily make note of them. My father talks to me freely and tells me what this or that one has told him. I could be present on such occasions; the only reason I haven't is that I am bored by talks about making money, even in the biggest amounts."

"Do you intend to tell your father about these meetings with me?"

"I plan not to tell anyone, even my wife. It wouldn't do any good, and the wisest and most loyal person might drop some hint by accident. In the case of my father, he is very bitter against your policies: income taxes in the higher brackets, and what he called 'doles,' and your 'court-packing'—a long list. Just now the C.I.O. has got into his plant and is threatening a sit-down strike, and that makes him sore as the devil. If I told him I had met you, it would be the occasion of a long discourse, every word of which I already know by heart. My father is a kind and generous man, and has a sense of humor; you, Governor, would find him very good company, if only it weren't for politics and your threatening his control over what he considers his private affairs."

"It is something I have often observed," remarked the "Governor," with a sad smile; "the conservatives have the best manners and are the easiest to get along with."

"I have speculated about it. They have everything they want, whereas the advocates of social change are apt to be fanatical and narrow, and sometimes motivated by jealousy, one of the meanest of qualities. The conservative has a whole community behind him and he obeys its rules; that makes for serenity and pleasant feelings. The radical, on the other hand, has to make his own rules; he makes many mistakes, and tries his own temper as well as other people's."

IV

It was as Alston had said; these two were "made for each other." Both had grown up in comfort and near-luxury, never knowing deprivation; both were generous by nature and dreamed of a kindlier world; both had met with disappointments and disillusionments, but were stubborn and did not easily give up their dreams; now both were fighting-mad in their hearts, but kept a smile on their lips because that was good form, that was "sporting." Also, they both liked to talk, and were tempted to ramble into the fields of philosophy and literature and what not. But the time was short, and they would jack themselves up and come back to business.

Lanny told about his Paris friends, the de Bruynes, to whom he was related in a peculiar French way. Denis was a leading financier, growing always richer; his cousin had been chosen one of the governing board of the almighty Banque de France—and then Léon Blum had broken the private control of that institution. Lanny could hear all the secrets of France talked in Denis's drawing-room; he could meet Laval, Bonnet, Tardieu—any of the other scamps.

He told about his friend Kurt Meissner, who had become one of the top Nazi agents in Paris. A distinguished German musician and composer, Kurt had access to the highest circles, and everywhere he went he talked persuasively about the problems of the two countries. Why should Frenchmen let themselves be used as pawns by the English in their policy of keeping the Continent divided? Was it not easier to shake hands across the Rhine than across the Channel? France and Germany represented the two highest cultures in the world, and why should they not unite? And why should Frenchmen of breeding and social position permit themselves to be ruled by demagogues and Jews, the dregs heaved up from the bubbling kettle of social hates? Hitler was the man who had solved the problem of labor unionism, and his solution was good for all countries. Hitler was the one enemy of Bolshevism who really meant business; what greater crime against the true interests of French culture than to let the Jew demagogues draw them into alliance with Russia, the arch-enemy of all culture and indeed of all civilization?

So thought Frenchmen, especially rich young Frenchmen, the *jeunesse dorée*, after they had talked with Kurt Meissner in drawing-rooms. Lanny said: "I can never be sure how much Kurt trusts me now. He is secretive, but I watch him through the minds of his victims, and I know that he will be worth an army corps to the Nazis when their invasion starts."

"When will it start, Lanny?"

"The day they are ready. Powder deteriorates, planes get out of date, so why wait an hour after your machinery is set to go?"

"You are certain that Hitler means war?"

"Many of my friends cannot believe it, and I put it to them this way: A man who is poor starves himself and spends all his time and labor to build a bicycle. What are you to assume about his purposes? Do you assume that he is intending to sail on the sea? Or to play music? Or to give his friends a banquet? No, because you cannot sail on a bicycle, nor play tunes on it, nor eat it. A bicycle is good for only one thing, to ride a bicycle; every part of it is made for that, and no part of it is good for anything else whatever."

Lanny told of conversations with his client and host, the head of the Luftwaffe. Hermann Göring was a man of many pleasures but of only one business, which was preparing to make war from the air. Lanny described the huge new office building of the Air Force in Berlin, with three thousand rooms; he told about the airports with hangars hidden underground—Robbie Budd had visited one at Kladow, and had been staggered by the completeness of it. Said the son: "Robbie thinks the fat general is making a grave mistake by building short-range fighter planes when he should have bombers to bring England to her knees. But Hermann only laughs and winks. What he means, of course, is to put troops ashore in England and fly those planes from English fields."

"How can he do it while the English control the seas?"

"He expects to do it by parachutes, and by submarines and dive-bombers sinking the British fleet. He figures that it won't take long to ferry troops across twenty miles of water, and they will be specialists, with weapons the like of which has never been seen in the world before."

"The reports I get differ widely, Lanny. I'd like very much to know the real numbers of the German Air Force; I mean actual first-line planes of the different types."

"I think my father comes pretty near to knowing those figures. But you must bear this in mind, Governor—what counts at this stage is not so much the number of planes as the machine tools, the jigs and dies, the stocks of aluminum and rubber and so on. Hitler isn't ready for war yet, and won't be for two or three years. Meantime he tries one bluff after another, but is ready to back down before any strong move of Britain or France."

"The British tell me they daren't move, because they're not prepared."

"That is the statement of public men who have lost the habit of action. Military expenditure in Germany now is two and a half times that of Britain. What good does it do to delay when you're falling behind at that rate?"

<h2 style="text-align:center">V</h2>

Twice Lanny offered to leave, but the President wouldn't let him. "I'll sleep late," he said; then, grinning like a schoolboy playing hooky: "I have a cold and won't be able to keep appointments." He lighted one cigarette after another in the long thin holder—certainly not a therapeutic procedure—and went on asking questions about the old continent which was managing its affairs so badly and might again be calling upon America for help. F.D. had discovered here another self, a self that had lived abroad and knew all the people who were in the headlines there. It was as if the morning newspaper had come suddenly to life, and the persons in it stepped out and started talking.

"Tell me about Hitler," said the President; so Lanny described that strange portent, half-genius, half-madman, who had managed to infect with his mental sickness a whole generation of German youth.

"Years ago I made a remark in a woman friend's hearing: 'There will be nothing to do but kill them.' The remark horrified her so that I promised never to make it again. But it is literally true; they are a set of blind fanatics, marching, singing, screaming about their desire to conquer other peoples; it is their God-given destiny, and they have no room for any other idea in their heads. They have a song: 'Today Germany belongs to us, tomorrow the whole world.' The German word for belongs is *gehört*, while the word *hört* means hears; so in Germany they sing 'belongs to us' and abroad they sing 'hears us,' which sounds less alarming. That is typical of the Nazi technique. Hitler has written in his book that you can get any lie believed if you repeat it often enough; and especially if it's a big lie—because people will say that nobody would dare to tell one as big as that. It is no exaggeration to say that he has made Germany into a headquarters of the Lie; he has told so many and so often that nobody in his country has any means of distinguishing truth from falsehood."

Lanny described the Führer in the early days of his movement, coming onto the platform of a crowded beer cellar in Munich, the living image of Charlie Chaplin with his tiny dark mustache and ill-fitting pants. In those days he always wore a rusty brown raincoat; he was the proletarian leader, the rabble-rouser, the friend of the common man. "People here make a grave mistake," Lanny said. "They think of Nazism as a reactionary movement, an effort of the capitalist class to put down labor and the Communists; but Nazism was a revolutionary movement—that is the only way any movement can get power nowadays. Hitler promised the redistribution of landed estates without compensation, the abolition of what he called 'interest slavery,' the whole program of populist revolt."

"We had such a man in this country—Huey Long."

"I'm sorry I didn't meet him."

"Believe me, I did! He was all set to be my successor. He once had me waked up at one in the morning to give me hell over the telephone from Baton Rouge for some appointment he didn't like. I refused to cancel it and he was my mortal enemy forever after."

"There will be others like him," replied Lanny, "unless we solve the problem of poverty in the midst of plenty. The German middle classes, the little men like Hitler, were being wiped out, and he offered a millennium, also a scapegoat, the Jews. When he got the votes, he took them to the big industrialists and sold them for more campaign funds."

That aspect of the movement had few secrets for Lanny, because his father, a steel man himself in those days, had heard the German steel men talking about the sums they were turning over to their new political boss. "Thyssen alone put up five million marks."

"And now he's very unhappy, I am told," remarked the President.

"Don't let that fool you. Hitler is a wild horse and has taken the bit in his teeth—but he's galloping in the direction the big industrialists want him to go. They are finding it a wild ride, but they expect to arrive at their destination, which is the integration of the industry of the Continent and its control from Berlin."

"Control by the Hitler gang?"

"But under the rules of the big business game. A big industrialist wants to turn out unlimited quantities of goods, and have an unlimited market for them at what he calls 'fair' prices, that is, prices which allow him a profit. He wants to take these profits and reinvest them in his plants and turn out more goods, and so on, over and over—he calls it the 'turnover,' and as long as he can make it he's happy. That is the situation in Germany for every man who can produce war goods; also for every worker who has any sort of skill. Naturally, they all think it is *herrlich,* and that the Führer who has brought this about is some sort of magician, or an emissary from on high."

"It is really Hitler who is directing it?"

"It is the technical men of German industry, and the officers of the general staff of the Wehrmacht. They are probably the most highly trained military men in the world, and of course it is *herrlich* for them, because for the first time all German industry, both capital and labor, does exactly what they, the members of the Herrenklub, direct. Emil Meissner, Kurt's brother, is a member of that club. He was doubtful of Schicklgruber, the demagogue, but now he worships Hitler, the inspired master of the German destiny. I have seen Emil rise from lieutenant to general in less than twenty-five years, and today he is probably the happiest man I know; he has everything exactly the way he wants it. The Communists, the Socialists, the democrats and pacifists are all dead or in concentration camps; every good German is hard at work, living frugally and investing his savings in government bonds; and all the money the wizard Schacht can create is going into the building of that bicycle I was telling you about a while ago, the machine on which the German Army is going to ride to world mastery."

"It is a terrible picture you paint, Lanny."

"I assure you, Governor, I am no painter. I am only a transporter of paintings. When I come on one that seems to me worth while, I bring it to this country and show it to my friends. The most important one for you to look at is the picture of this German war machine being tried out in Spain. Hitler is sending his tankmen, his artillerymen, and above all his airmen there in relays; nobody stays more than three or four months, just long enough to learn the new techniques of swift and deadly mechanized war; then he goes back to Germany, and tells it to his superior officers, and on the training fields in the Fatherland he teaches it to hundreds of others. The Italians are doing the same, but they're not so good; they don't really like war and nobody can make them. But the Nazis like nothing else, and the result is going to be that they will have a large army of trained and eager professionals, while all the other peoples, except perhaps the Japanese, will be bungling amateurs. The Nazis are training some of their stormtroopers right here in America; I have seen them in New York, and they may be doing it even in Washington. You tell me you can't prevent what is happening in Spain, Governor, but surely you ought to be able to do something in America."

Said the President: "I think I can assure you we're not entirely overlooking that part of our duty."

VI

It was after two in the morning when the great man released his visitor. The last thing he said was: "Make your reports as short as you can. One man sent me a long one, and when he asked if I had read it, I told him I hadn't been able to lift it!"

He pressed a button, and told his colored valet to summon Gus Gennerich. The man came promptly, and escorted Lanny out of the building by the same door they had entered. The rain had stopped, the moon had come out, and Lanny said: "It will be a pleasant day." The reply was: "Looks like it." Evidently this ex-policeman didn't consider it his duty to make conversation with "P.A.'s." He drove Lanny to his hotel.

Much later that same morning the art expert turned secret agent set out on the crowded highway to Baltimore. He reached New York before sundown, having approached the city by the Pulaski Skyway, and crossed the George Washington Bridge. He was heading for Newcastle, Connecticut, for he had already engaged steamer passage and desired as much time as possible with his father.

He had phoned that he was coming, and there was always a warm welcome for him. He had allowed his "Pink" ideas to sink into the background and be forgotten; he had kept his second marriage secret, and to his stepmother and half-brothers and their families he was the art expert and man of the world, lover of music and friend of famous and important people. He didn't mention that Franklin D. Roosevelt had been added to the list. He talked, instead, about his art adventures, and especially about the Murchisons, whom Robbie knew. To fly to the Adirondacks for a week-end was a decidedly swanky thing, and

Lanny's half-nephew, Robert Budd III, piped up: "Why don't you build us some passenger planes, Grandfather?"

Grandfather was sixty-three, an age at which most men think of retiring; but Robbie Budd was just getting ready to conquer the world, by way of the air above it. As a preliminary, he had more than once conquered himself. In his youth he had been "wild," or so his stern Puritan father had judged him. Lanny was the product of that wildness, and as a result was still looked upon askance by the older generation of Budds; they were a long-lived and long-memoried tribe. Again, a decade or so ago, Robbie had been "playing the market" heavily, and drinking much more than was good for him as a result of the strain, also of the bitterness in his heart against his father and his oldest brother.

But now all that was over; Robbie's father was no more, and Robbie was on his own, nourishing colossal hopes. He had broken with Budd Gunmakers, which had been taken over by a Wall Street crowd and was making mostly hardware and "specialties." Robbie's heart was set on the dream that some day the new firm, his creation, would have a bigger turnover and pay higher dividends than the family firm which had been wrested from them.

Robbie Budd lived and breathed and ate and talked airplanes: catwalks and bulkhead segments, stabilizers and de-icers, sub-assemblies and spot-checking—a whole new vocabulary which the members of his household had to learn. Robbie's conscientious wife, who had suffered at the spectacle of his weaknesses and had even had to take Lanny into her confidence, now shared his high ambitions, and did everything to encourage and help him: inviting the plant engineers to dinner, and even studying the highly technical reports which determined the obsoleteness of the B-EP10 and the expected supremacy of the B-EP11.

Robbie Budd was a football and polo player who had taken to golf, and had added fifty pounds and a load of dignity. His gray hair became his florid complexion; his manner was hearty, and he enjoyed talking, provided it was with some person who liked to listen to what Robbie liked to talk about. If left to himself, he might have grown slouchy, but his wife kept him in order by the simple device of causing his used garments to disappear and new and spotless ones to be in their place. She kept his home the same way, causing cigar stubs and ashes and used whisky glasses to disappear. The house was large and elegant, but slightly suggestive of a Puritan meeting-house, with plain papered walls and furniture of the sort which Esther's forefathers had made. On the walls of the drawing-room hung several paintings by Arnold Böcklin which Lanny had found in Germany, knowing that they would please his stepmother because they embodied or were supposed to embody philosophical ideas.

VII

Into this household came Lanny on his secret errand. He must get his father to talking, and carefully guide the conversation to the subjects which had been listed for him by That Man in the White House —who was Robbie's pet peeve and the embodiment of all evil and destructive tendencies of the time. Lanny mustn't make the mistake of showing too much interest in any one subject; he must let his father ramble along. No notes could be made, but Lanny would fix names and figures in his memory, go to his room and jot them down, and then come back for another load.

It seemed a mean sort of job, spying on one's father. But Lanny wasn't going to report anything which could do Robbie any harm; he was only going to harm the cause which Robbie had taken for his own, the cause of bigger profits for businessmen all over the land; also the maintenance of that autocratic control of industry which Robbie considered essential to its progress, and which Lanny considered a menace to the higher sorts of progress, political, social, intellectual. There was no use arguing the point, no use trying to reconcile or explain two opposite points of view. Nobody could tell Robbie Budd that the workers had any capacity or any right to meddle with the control of industry; Robbie considered that the workers belonged exactly where they were and were getting exactly as much pay as they were worth. Robbie didn't really consider them competent to have anything to say about politics either, but he was reconciled to that system, having found that he could make deals with the political bosses in his town and county and state. He hadn't been able to control the Presidency or the Congress, in spite of expensive efforts in combination with other Republican big businessmen; they had tried their best and a few months ago had got a sound licking. Now every time Robbie thought about it he got so hopping-mad that it made his veins swell out dangerously.

Lanny had to say to himself: "I am a traitor to my family's ideas; I am a snake in the grass." He had to say the same thing in the home of his ex-wife and her friends in England, and with most of the fashionable ladies and gentlemen who came to his mother's home on the French Riviera. He had to take with them the pose of art lover and ivory-tower dweller to whom politics was a base trade, far beneath a gentleman's notice. He had to listen to the expression of the most reactionary opinions, and if someone asked him a direct question: "What do you think about it, Mr. Budd?"—or Herr Budd, or Monsieur Budd as the case might be—he had to be ready with some playful answer, something that would pass for a *mot* in the smart world: "Well, all sorts of people manage to make politics pay, and I suppose we shouldn't be too much surprised if labor tries the same thing."

VIII

What Lanny did with his father was to ask how things were going in the plant; his father told him they had just installed the "mating jigs" for the new model. Lanny expressed interest in this odd form of the reproductive process, with the result that Robbie offered to take him and show him the latest devices. Next morning he was escorted through that quite extensive plant which had sprung up in a few months on what had until recently been a mosquito-breeding marsh. He gazed down from a balcony into a great room which appeared to be a jungle of complex machines, each one beating and pounding out its own individual tune. Lanny knew, of course, that every machine had been placed exactly on a spot which engineers had measured to the hundredth part of an inch; he knew that the motions of those machines were determined in some cases to the hundred-thousandth part of an inch, and that the finest watch had never been built with such care as the pieces of steel and aluminum and magnesium and what not which were here being stamped or ground or polished amid such a variety of sounds that it all became one, an infinitude of racket which, so Lanny was assured, the ears of the workers soon ceased to record at all.

Down a long line appeared, in process of growth, a row of swift and deadly fighter planes which would be able to hurl themselves through the air at the rate of a mile every fifteen seconds or less. There weren't nearly as many on that assembly-line as Robbie had hoped to see, and the line wasn't moving fast enough to please him; but he stubbornly clung to the belief that old Europe was soon going to war, and then everybody would be calling for Budd-Erling pursuits. Robbie had seen it magically happen in Paris at the end of July 1914, and Lanny had been there, helping as well as a precocious lad could do. Neither had forgotten any detail of it, and so now they could talk to each other in shorthand. Robbie said: "God knows I'm not asking for it, but it's coming." Lanny wondered: Was it humanly possible to stake one's whole fortune on a gamble, and in one's secret heart not be hoping to win?

Inside that fabricating plant was order, but outside was chaos. Going and coming, Lanny passed through a string of real-estate subdivisions full of jerrybuilt cottages and shacks of varied ugliness, with gas stations and sodapop stands and "eateries" scattered along the main road. It had grown that way, because that was the way Robbie Budd had willed it; Robbie was not afraid of chaos, but saw danger in any sort of order except his own. Lanny's heart ached, because in England he had seen garden cities, and in Vienna beautiful blocks of workers' apartment houses built by the Socialist municipality. Why couldn't something of that sort have been done in Connecticut?

But Robbie Budd had his God called Individualism, and this ugly nightmare was His temple. Robbie wanted no government and no workers' movement of any sort in or near his place; if he could have had his way he would have forbidden all meetings and organizations of any sort whatever. But now the C.I.O., most radical of mass movements, was spreading in his plant, and Robbie was fuming and raging, considering it treason and conspiracy. None the less so because it was backed by the power of the United States government—or as Robbie preferred to put it, by a gang of political shysters who had got hold of the government and were using it to wage a war of vengeance against those who owned property and carried the responsibilities of industry. No doubt whatever of the perfect sincerity of Robbie Budd's opinion of the "New Deal"!

IX

In between tirades Lanny gathered details about the arrangements existing between I. G. Farben, the great German chemical trust, and the Standard Oil Company of New Jersey for the sharing and exchange of patents and technical secrets in the production of artificial rubber from petroleum. He learned about similar deals in other industries, and got the names of various persons who had such secrets locked in their bosoms or their safe-deposit vaults. Lanny would say: "Do you really know that, Robbie?" and his father would reply: "Thyssen told me himself"—or perhaps it would be Krupp von Bohlen, or one of the de Wendels or the du Ponts. Oddly enough Robbie Budd himself had somewhat the same arrangement with Göring; Robbie had his men in Göring's plants and the fat Exzellenz had his in Newcastle—Lanny could be sure of it, for he met them. But he didn't intend to mention that in his reports to F.D.R. The President had agreed with his new secret agent that it was all to the good to have an aircraft fabricating plant hidden up one of the navigable rivers of Connecticut, and a force of American technicians and workers acquiring the "know-how" in that vitally important industry.

Also Lanny collected information as to the present status of the Luftwaffe. Some of it came from Robbie, and some from those Nazi technicians, who knew about the younger Budd's connections in Hitler-land, and thought of him as a friend of their cause. He spoke a fluent German and could tell them about visits to Karinhall and Berchtes-gaden. They were bursting with pride over the achievements of their Third Reich, and what more natural than that some of their bursts should be aimed in Lanny's direction?

After listening, the investigator would retire to the room which had been his since his first visit twenty years ago; he would set up his little portable machine and type out the report, not forgetting to make it short. He would seal it in an envelope marked "No. 103," and put this into another envelope addressed to Gus Gennerich at the ex-policeman's Washington hotel.

X

Duty done, Lanny was free to enjoy himself. Early next morning he bade good-by to his father's family and drove half-way to New York, stopping at the home of the Hansibesses, as he called his half-sister and her violinist husband. Hansi Robin was giving a concert for a workers' group in New York that evening, and Lanny's steamer was sailing at midnight. So everything fitted nicely; Lanny would drive the musicians in, after the concert they would see him off, and Bess would drive the car back to her father's next morning.

The Hansibesses had a baby boy, now a year old; they had called him Freddi, in memory of his uncle whom the Nazis had murdered. He was Lanny's half-Jewish half-nephew, with the lovely dark eyes and hair of his father, whom Lanny had called a shepherd boy out of ancient Judea. He was learning to toddle about and to say new words every day, and kept his parents in a state of constant admiration. His grandmother came over from her home to have lunch and meet her adored Lanny, and point out qualities in the treasure-child which might otherwise not be noticed. Hansi was composing a sonata, and he and Bess played the first movement for their visitor, and Bess indicated features in it which her husband was too diffident to mention.

In the afternoon the grandfather came out from the city. Johannes Robin, formerly Rabinowich, was making money again, though on a far more modest scale than that which he had known in Germany. Upon him rested some of the responsibility for keeping that great

Budd-Erling plant going. He had charge of the sales office in New York, and took flying trips to France or Holland or Turkey, to South or Central America, or Canada—for Budd-Erling was making not merely fighter planes, but also an "all-purpose job" which was carrying supplies to mines in the high Andes and to prospectors in the far northern wilderness. Johannes didn't sell anything to Nazis or Fascists —he left that to his long-time partner, Robbie, who had a stronger stomach. Johannes was tireless in reading newspapers and technical journals, watching out for large-scale business enterprises which perhaps had never realized how they might speed up their work by the use of airplanes.

A greatly changed Johannes Robin from the eager and rather egotistical person whom Lanny Budd had happened to meet on a railroad train in Europe nearly a quarter of a century ago. Now he was subdued and humbled, content to be alive and to have got his loved ones away to this safe corner of a deadly dangerous world. It no longer worried him that his surviving son and the son's wife called themselves out-and-out Reds. Johannes would have turned anarchist if he had thought that was a way to bring justice upon the heads of those Nazi barbarians who had murdered his son and come so near to murdering himself. Lanny didn't have to use any subterfuges in asking a one-time *Schieber* for information as to the secrets of European *haute finance* and its deal with the new masters of Germany. Johannes would pour it out in floods, and would have been greatly pleased if he had known what use was going to be made of it.

XI

Lanny drove them all in to the concert, which was held in a hall on the East side, its purpose being to collect funds for the aiding of Jews who had escaped into the countries bordering on Hitlerland. The place was packed to the doors with Jewish men and women, some of them old but most of them young, a few bearded but most smooth-shaven, a few well-to-do, but most poor. Jews of all sorts and sizes, but mostly undersized; Jews with dark curly hair and some with red; Jews with Jewish noses, but many who might have been taken for Russians or Poles or Hungarians or Italians or Spaniards. They had been mixed up with all the European tribes for a thousand years, but alas, it hadn't done them any good. Once upon a time, long ago, a group of Jewish holy men in a fanatical mood had called for the killing of another Jewish holy man, and by an odd quirk of fate posterity had remembered the executed one, but had forgotten that he was Jewish. He was God, and only those who had called for his death had been Jews; so now in the slums of this crowded Manhattan Island tough little Irish boys and tough little Italian boys would frighten little Jewish boys by yelling: "Christ-killer!"

In Germany this hatred had become a mental disease, and Jew-baiting a substitute for social progress. So there was grief in the faces of this crowd and they had come as to a synagogue. It was a labor crowd, and most of them had broken with their ancient faith, but the spectacle of wholesale torture and humiliation had brought them back to the Ark of their Covenant. Hansi Robin, tall and dark-haired, might have stepped out of any of the books of the Old Testament; he stood before them, grave and priestlike, playing the Jewish music that he loved: *Kol Nidre* and Achron's *Hebrew Prayer*, and Ernest Bloch's *Nigun*, from the *Baal Shem* suite. The audience listened spellbound, and many sobbed, and the tears ran down their cheeks. This was a people who made no secret of their woes; who in the old days had rent their garments and wailed, put on sackcloth and sat in their backyards sprinkling their ashpiles over their heads. "My confusion is continually before me, and the shame of my face hath covered me, . . . Behold, I was shapen in iniquity; and in sin did my mother conceive me. . . . Deliver me from bloodguiltiness, O God, thou God of my salvation: and my tongue shall sing aloud of thy righteousness."

Hansi's accompaniments were played by his wife, who was a grand-daughter of the Puritans, and thus had derived a great part of her moral being from those ancient Jewish scriptures. As for Lanny, he had lived most of his life in the Midi; he loved to laugh and sing and dance, and it came hard to him to lament and torture his soul. But he had committed himself to the Jews by sanctioning his half-sister's marriage, thus helping to bring a half-Jewish baby into the world; he had taken Hansi's brother Freddi Robin as his comrade, and in his efforts to save Freddi had got himself into a Nazi dungeon and seen an elderly Jew beaten close to death. So Lanny was bound in soul to that unhappy race; he had to listen to their music and share their torments, to stand by their Wailing Wall and climb to the summit of their Calvary.

XII

There were still parts of the world where the Jews were not tortured and degraded; where they were citizens and free men and women. One of them was America, and another was the Soviet Union, where Hansi and Bess had visited several times. Whenever they played for the workers, which they did frequently, the couple always closed by playing the *Internationale*. Always the audience would rise and cheer, even those who were not Communists; for, whatever their creed might be, they knew that this hymn meant battle against the oppressors. These New York Jews wanted to fight Hitlerism with any and every weapon they could lay hands upon.

After Hansi had exchanged greetings with one or two hundred workers, the three went out to their car, and Lanny drove them west to the pier where a great steamer lay waiting for its passengers. They had an hour or so for a final chat; then the deep whistle sounded, and the two musicians went out to the pier and watched the steamer towed out into the river. A great harbor, and, half-way out of it, the Statue of Liberty with her blazing torch. Lanny had first seen her in the midst of World War, and she had been welcoming him to the land of his fathers. Later, departing from New York during the Wall Street panic, he had thought that she was drunk. Now she had reformed, but was sad, because so few looked at her or thought about her any more. She might have liked to send back a message to her native land of France, which was facing such a dark and uncertain future. Her torch was wavering in shreds of fog, and it might have been a signal.

But Lanny Budd wasn't on deck to see it. He was down in his cabin, hammering away on his little portable, making notes of statements which Johannes Robin had made and which were to be sealed up and marked "No. 103," and sent by the little boat which took the pilot back to land.

3

Trust in Princes

I

IRMA BARNES, once Mrs. Lanny Budd and now the Countess of Wickthorpe, had at last found a way to spend some real money. She had been handicapped for years because Lanny hadn't cared about spending it, but preferred to live in a little old villa on the shore of the Mediterranean. Now Irma was engaged in modernizing one of the most famous of English castles, part of it dating back to Tudor days. She was taking out pretty nearly everything but the walls and floors, and putting in every gadget she could think of, or that was suggested by a lively young architect whom she had met in a New York night club. Wickthorpe Castle was going to show the English upper classes what they had been missing all these years. She went every day to watch the work, and to imagine the sumptuous entertainments she was going to give when it was completed. Meantime the family was living in Wickthorpe Lodge, adjoining the estate. She had rented it years ago and lived there with Lanny; a convenient arrangement, because it had enabled her to get acquainted with her second husband before breaking with her first.

Irma had crowned her career by being taken into the English nobility; everybody showed her deference, the servants addressed her as "my lady," and it was all delightful. She was going to bear an heir to an earldom; at least, she had a fifty-fifty chance of doing so, and was praying for luck. At the same time she was having her portrait painted by Gerald Brockhurst, a painter who was well recommended and who charged accordingly. One hour every morning she sat for him; not being a chatty person, she sat for the most part in silence, considering whether the armor room of the castle should be left in its present gloomy condition, or should be done over in batik or something else cheerful.

The daughter of J. Paramount Barnes was happy. She had had the responsibility of a great fortune placed upon her shoulders in childhood, and now at last she felt that she was making proper use of it. Her husband had an important post in the Foreign Office—he was a careerman in spite of being an earl, something out of the ordinary. He worked hard and took seriously his duty to protect the future of the British Empire in unusually trying times. His wife would help him by entertaining splendidly but at the same time with dignity; she would spread his influence, and get him promoted. Ceddy couldn't become Prime Minister, but he might become Viceroy of India. Mary Leiter had made it —why not Irma Barnes? In any case she would help to preserve an ancient and honorable tradition, and hold in check the forces of discontent which were undermining property and religion in England as everywhere else. Irma was only twenty-seven, but had lived a great deal, so she considered; she had come close to those satanic forces, and been shocked to the depths of her otherwise placid being; she hated them, and knew that she was going to devote her influence, social and political as well as financial, to combat them.

II

In the midst of these labors and planning came a wireless message from her former husband, on board a ship. "Arriving day after tomorrow will it be convenient for me to see Frances reply Dorchester Hotel regards Lanny." Brief and to the point; polite beyond criticism, but Irma knew that inside the velvet glove was the mailed fist. Lanny had a fifty per cent interest in Irma's child; he could claim fifty per cent of the little one's time, and of the control of her rearing. He could come to see her when he pleased, and everything must be made pleasant for him. If there was any hint of disharmony, he might suggest taking the child away with him, and that filled both Irma and her mother with distress. To be sure, the "twenty-three-million-dollar baby," as the newspapers called her, was no longer anywhere near that rich, for Irma's fortune had been reduced by the depression, and she had settled a chunk of the remainder on her new husband and their future offspring. But kidnapers mightn't know that; and while there was said to be none in England, what was to prevent the child's father from taking her to France, where she had been born, or to New York, where Irma herself had been born? No law that Irma's solicitors could find for her!

Irma really knew her former husband. She knew that he called himself a "Pink," using the word jestingly. Irma herself declined to recognize shadings; she called him in her heart a "Red," and generally with the double adjective "out-and-out." No amount of play-acting on his part, no talk about art for art's sake or ivory-tower residences, could fool Lanny's ex-wife. She could be sure that whatever political facts Lanny might pick up from the lips of her highly placed guests he would carry off and repeat to his friend Rick, the bitter and aggressive left-wing playwright and journalist.

But what could Irma do about it? She had agreed with Lanny in their parting that she would not mention his political opinions as the cause of their break. She had granted this in return for Lanny's promise not to propagandize the child with his ideas. Irma had taken her mother into her confidence—and Fanny Barnes cared very little about the safety of the British Empire but very much about her prerogatives as grandmother. Fanny was urgent on the subject—her daughter must not do the slightest thing to irritate Lanny and cause him to assert the prerogatives of the other grandmother. Lanny was socially acceptable, wasn't he? He knew how to make people like him, and most of Irma's friends did like him. All right then, let him come as a guest and treat him like any other guest.

In America it was supposed to be "sporting" to take divorce lightly and remain friends; and Irma, as an American, would take that right. Nobody, save perhaps the rector of Wickthorpe parish, would be shocked to meet her ladyship's first husband at dinner in her home; and Fanny Barnes would take the rector off, explain matters to him, and require him to show a true Christian spirit. If Lanny pretended to be in sympathy with the ideas of the other guests, that was his concession to harmony, his effort to avoid causing embarrassment. For heaven's sake, let him get away with it, and don't say a word, don't even frown, but make him feel that he is the most appreciated of personalities!

So Lanny would have a cottage on the estate; he would have servants to wait on him and prepare his meals; and if an innocent child wanted him to come to lunch with her and her mother and grandmother, she would have her way. Lanny would entertain them with news about the Budd family, whom Irma knew well, and the Budd-Erling plant, in which Irma owned a million-dollar block of stock. Lanny would play the piano for his daughter, dance with her the farandole which he had taught her in Provence, and take her horseback riding on the estate, of course with a groom to follow them.

Seven-year-old Frances Barnes Budd was a happy child, and healthy like her two parents. She had dark brown eyes and a wealth of dark brown hair like her mother; a vigorous and active body, eager for every sort of play, but not much impulse toward the life of the mind—again like her mother. She adored her father, who came to her like a prince out of a fairy story, always with adventures to tell, and music and dancing and games. She had been guarded from every evil thought, including that of trouble between her parents, or that there was anything unusual about having two fathers.

She was the incarnation of six years of marriage, with their joys and sorrows. Lanny could put all these out of his thoughts when he was out in the busy world, but when he came here he saw them before his eyes. Being of an imaginative temperament, he would fall to thinking: "Could I have saved that marriage? And should I?" Six years of shared experience are not to be wiped out of the soul, which has depths beyond the reach of any eraser. He would wonder: "Could I have been a little more patient, more tolerant? Could I have made more allowances for her youth, and for the environment which made her different from me?" He would wonder: "Is she thinking such thoughts now? Is she remembering our old happiness?" He would never ask such questions, of course, for that would be a breach of good form, a trespassing upon her new life.

He had not come to visit Irma, but Frances. He would play with the child, devote himself to her—but how could he help seeing the mother in the child? He would start thinking his "Pink" thoughts about their offspring. Poor little rich girl! Some day she would awaken to the fact that she was set apart from other children, and that what was supposed to be a great good fortune was in fact an abnormality and a burden. She would discover that friends could be mercenary and designing, and that love was not always what it pretended to be. She would discover the secret war in the hearts of her mother and father, and that this war extended over the whole earth and divided all human society, a chasm deeper than the Grand Canyon of the Colorado, or those which lie at the bottom of the ocean floor. Frances' mother was content to live on her own side of that social chasm, while Frances' father insisted upon crossing from one side to the other and back again—a most unstable and nerve-trying sort of life. But he must never let the child know about it—for that would be unsettling her mind, that would be propagandizing!

III

In the evening Lanny would be invited over to the house which for a year or two had been his home and Irma's. Perhaps it would have been tactful for him not to come, but he had his secret purposes in coming. He had known Ceddy since boyhood, and Ceddy's friend and colleague in the Foreign Office, Gerald Albany, who lived near by. They knew that Lanny had been tinged with Pinkness, and they were used to that in their own ranks; they took it for granted that as men acquire experience, they learn how hard it is to change the nature of men and nations. When Lanny said that he had decided to leave politics to the experts, they took that to mean themselves, and the arrangement was satisfactory.

So they talked freely about the problems facing the British Empire. They had a "line," which Lanny understood perfectly: British governments change, but foreign policy never, and that was why Britannia had ruled the waves over a period of four centuries. If in the course of the conversation the American guest put in the suggestion that it might now be necessary for the old lady to give some thought to the air above the waves, that was taken good-naturedly; it was well known that

Lanny's father had airplanes to sell, and one might reasonably assume that the son had an interest in the business. Commercial men weren't looked down upon as they had been in old England; for, after all, this was an industrial age, and business and politics were pretty thoroughly mixed. The recent Prime Minister, Mr. Stanley Baldwin, had been an ironmaster, and the present Prime Minister, Mr. Neville Chamberlain, was an arms manufacturer from Birmingham.

There existed at this time a peculiar situation in the inner shrine of the British government. Intelligence Service, most secret of all organizations, was turning in one report after another showing that the German Air Force had outstripped the British; also, that the German Navy was disregarding its pledged word to limit construction to one-third of the British. Prime Minister Chamberlain, who believed in business and called it peace, was solving the problem by sticking the reports away and forgetting them. But Anthony Eden, Foreign Minister, was on the warpath against this course, and Sir Robert Vansittart, the highest permanent official of the Foreign Office, was backing him up.

Gerald Albany, the embodiment of propriety, would probably not have mentioned this delicate subject in the presence of an American; but Lanny let it be known that he had heard about it. So then they talked. Ceddy declared that the trouble was due to the inability of some statesmen to face frankly the fact that Hitler had made Germany into a great power, and that she was again entitled to cast her full vote in the councils of Europe. Irma supported him, speaking with that new assurance which had come with her title. It was her idea that her new country should make a gentleman's agreement with Hitler covering all the problems of Europe, and should use this as a lever to force France into breaking off the Russian alliance. Thus, and only thus, could there again be security for property and religion. Lanny, listening to her emphatic phrases, thought: "She is still quarreling with me in her heart!"

I V

The basic principle of British policy for a couple of centuries had been to maintain a balance of power on the Continent, and to fight whatever nation attempted to gain dominance there. Before the World War that power had been Germany. After that war, it had been France, which had accumulated a huge gold reserve and used it to build up a "Little Entente" in Central Europe and to demand a share of the oil of the Near East. Thus it had become necessary for the British to lend money to Germany and build it up as a counterweight. Now there were many in Britain who thought the counterweight was growing dangerously heavy, and that France should again receive the support for which she was clamoring, and for which Léon Blum had come a year ago to beg in vain.

The problem was complicated by the upsurgence of Russia, which most British statesmen had written off as a derelict after 1917. Russia now had an alliance with France, but didn't know whether to trust it or not, and the British didn't know whether the French meant it, and whether they should be encouraged to mean it or to sabotage it. French policy, unlike the British, did change with the government, and that was a bad thing for the French, and for their friends and backers. Many persons in Britain took the position that the question of Russia was not merely a political issue, but a moral one; they refused to "shake hands with murder." Gerald Albany, a clergyman's son, was among these; but Ceddy spoke cautiously, saying that in statecraft it was not always possible to be guided by one's moral and religious ideas. "We should have had a bad time at the outbreak of the last war if we hadn't had the aid of Russia; and surely the hands of the Tsar had bloodstains enough."

The fourteenth Earl of Wickthorpe was about Lanny's age, and everyone agreed that he had a brilliant career before him. He was tall and fair, with delightful pink cheeks and a little blond mustache of which he took care. He was quiet and serious, a good listener and slow speaker. He considered himself modern and democratic, meaning that in his own set he did not exact any tribute to his rank. In his dealings with those below him it had never occurred to him to do anything but to say what he wanted in the fewest words and to be at once obeyed.

He had known Lanny well, and had excused Lanny's free and easy ways on the ground that Americans were like that. When he had met Lanny's wife, at one of the international congresses, he had the thought that she had made a poor match, and it was a pity. He wondered if she had realized it, and before long he decided that she had. He had known about the American practice of easy divorce, but the idea had been repugnant to him, and he had been rigidly correct in his attitude to his friend's wife all through the period when they had rented the Lodge and had the run of the castle.

Only when he heard the news that Irma was in Reno getting a divorce had he allowed himself to think about her seriously. Evidently she liked him, and evidently liked the thought of being a countess. He wasn't pleased by the idea of having a second-hand wife or of being a stepfather; but, on the other hand, he was pleased by the idea of getting out of debt and being able to preserve his great estate in spite of outrageously high taxes. He had contrived to be sent to "the States" on a diplomatic errand, and had invited the blooming grass widow to become his bride with the same grave courtesy as if it had been a proposal to lead the grand march in a ballroom. She had been very generous; the trustees of her estate had sat down with his lordship's solicitor and inquired what settlement was desired, and had agreed to everything with no more than a casual reading of the somewhat elaborate document.

V

There were not many guests at week-ends, because of the lack of room in the Lodge; but friends dropped in in the evening and there was talk about the problems of the world. Just now it was Spain, which resembled a bunch of firecrackers going off in the vicinity of a powder-keg; no one could tell which way the sparks were going to fly and when all Europe might blow up. A publisher of newspapers, a little man who himself resembled a bunch of firecrackers going off, urged Wickthorpe to talk to friends in the Cabinet and bring about the recognition of General Franco as a belligerent without further delay. Lanny, who had been informing President Roosevelt that the British and French governments were conniving at the destruction of the Spanish people's government, now heard this powerful British publisher maintain that the British and French governments were favoring the Spanish Red government so outrageously that it amounted to driving Italy and Germany to war against them. "It will come, and we shall be to blame for it," declared Lord Beaverbrook, who had once been plain Max Aitken, company promoter of Canada. He had made a million pounds there, and now he owned *The Daily Express* and the *Evening Standard*, and from his state of mind you would have thought that the Bolsheviks were in the act of laying siege to these valuable properties.

Nearly a year ago the various governments had formed what was called a "Non-Intervention Committee"; it was meeting in London and had held something like seventy sessions, every one of them an acrimonious wrangle. The Italians and the Germans, who had intervened in Spain from the first hour, meant to go on intervening, while steadily denying that they had ever thought of such a nefarious action. Lanny had heard a story of a Kentucky Colonel who knocked a man down, and when asked: "Did he call you a liar?" replied: "Worse than that; he proved it." That was the situation before this Committee, which refused to receive complaints from individuals, but couldn't prevent representatives of the Soviet government from proving that the Italians and the Germans were systematically sending in troops and matériel to General Franco. Then the Italian and German delegates would fly into a fury and fight their share of the war in London.

A German cruiser off the coast of North Africa had been attacked by what Berlin called "Spanish-Bolshevist submarines." Berlin now demanded that Britain and France take part in a naval demonstration off Valencia. France, patrolling the French frontier with Spain, demanded that Portugal should patrol its frontiers, through which Italy and Germany were pouring in supplies; when Portugal refused, France withdrew her patrol officers and left her highways open into Spain. That was the way it went; one crisis after another, and no way to stop them. It was obvious to insiders of every nation that Franco alone could not conquer his people; if "Non-Intervention" were actually enforced, the Fascists would be licked. Italy and Germany were determined that this should not happen. At any and all costs, their man was going to win.

What did the British want? They had great difficulty in making up their minds; all choices were painful. Obviously they couldn't permit the Reds to build themselves a fortress on the Atlantic seaboard, enclosing all Europe in two prongs of a pincers. The British owned immensely valuable properties in Spain—Rio Tinto copper, for example, indispensable in making munitions—and certainly they didn't want strikes and Red commissars in those mines. On the other hand it might be fatal in wartime to have German submarines based on the Atlantic, and France enclosed in a pair of Nazi pincers. On the whole it seemed best to let the two sides fight it out and exhaust each other, and then a compromise government could be set up, the sort the British could lend money to. The only trouble was, neither side was willing to admit that it was exhausted; this was a war to the death, a kind which is bad for trade and every sort of vested interest.

In Downing Street there had been one crisis after another, and people's tempers were beginning to be frayed. Even in the most exclusive drawing-rooms, among English ladies and gentlemen, there were exhibitions of bad manners. Among the guests at Wickthorpe Lodge was an author of novels very popular in smart London circles; he had airy manners and was a great ladies' man, in spite of the fact that he was growing bald. In his thinking he was for practical purposes a Fascist, and did not resent the label. Lanny had met him here and there at parties, and knew that he was a confidant of Lanny's Fascist brother-in-law, Vittorio di San Girolamo. When Gerald Albany remarked that the trouble was that nobody could depend upon the word of Mussolini, he was "such a gutter-rat," this novelist blew up. "My God, man, what sort of world do you think you're living in? Do you imagine you can handle those Italian Reds like members of your Sunday-school class? They are bomb-throwing, knife-sticking anarchists, and before Mussolini put them down they had seized half the factories in Italy. Do you imagine you know how to deal with people of that kidney? And when you have to find men to do the same job in England, do you imagine they'll be polite church members like yourself?"

"I'm not telling Mussolini how to govern Italy," replied the Foreign Office man mildly. "But when he asks for the right to blockade Spanish ports and keep British ships out of them, I naturally have to consider what he offers in return, and whether I can believe what he tells me."

"All I can say is," retorted the novelist, "when there's a killer in your house and you call for the police, you expect them to shoot first and present their character certificates afterward."

VI

Lanny Budd would listen and say little; only now and then a well-chosen question, to steer the conversation if it could be done. He fixed in his memory details which might be of importance; the character of statesmen and their secret purposes, the attitude of great industrialists, the state of popular movements, the military preparations of this country and that. Alone in his room, he would type out the data and address them to Gus Gennerich, not putting the letter in with other mail that went out from the castle, but saving it to be posted in a public box.

Having done this, he would have moods of satisfaction, followed by others of depression. He had fallen for the Roosevelt charm, but the spell did not last all the time. Professor Alston had warned him that F.D.R. was of an "impressionable" temperament. He had been full of sympathy for Spain while listening to Lanny's story, but could it be that next day he had received a visit from someone high up in the hierarchy of the Holy Church and had heard stories about nuns being sprinkled with oil and burned by Spanish Reds? And would he believe these stories—or at any rate let the prelate depart in the belief that he believed them?

Anyhow, even with the best of intentions, could he absorb all the facts which came to him? What a brain would have to be in that large head to classify and retain them all! The President of the United States must have hundreds of people working for him and bringing him information; thousands must be sending it on their own impulse. Where did it all go? Who read it and heeded it? Lanny saw a vision of his reports being handed in by Gus and added to the pile on the desk. Something else would cover them up in a few minutes, and would they ever be uncovered again? Lanny would have to go back and find out if F.D.R. had ever heard of them, or if they had been lost in the files! And suppose the great man happened to be too busy to see him—what then would become of an art expert's bright dream of changing world history?

"Put not your trust in princes," the psalmist had advised, and Lanny was not heeding the warning. In those old days princes had had to take measures to keep other princes from poisoning them; the surest way was to poison the other princes first. Nowadays princes had to think about raising campaign funds and getting re-elected, keeping control over Congress in the off years, and matters such as that. They wanted to make the world safe for democracy, and at the same time to keep the country out of war. When they discovered that these aims were incompatible, they were in a predicament, and what wonder if their words one day contradicted the words of the previous day, and if their actions were not always in accordance with the campaign platforms of their party?

This much Lanny had already learned: that the favor of princes is a very tempting thing. For princes can act, whereas art experts can do nothing except talk in drawing-rooms. One gets so tired of futility, and of seeing things going the wrong way. If only somebody who *could* do something *would* do it! That had been Lanny's thought for more than half his life, ever since he had seen a world war burst upon a horrified humanity. Now he saw another getting ready to burst; black thunderclouds on the horizon, rolling rapidly upward, shutting out the sunlight; and people going about, heedless, as if in a dream; as if they were blind and couldn't see the darkness, deaf and couldn't hear the rumble of the thunder—those guns and bombs in Spain, to abandon the simile and deal with plain facts. The grandson of Budd's had been close enough to the first World War to have shell splinters fall near, and the son of Budd-Erling had already been close enough to the second to see houses destroyed by shellfire and hear bullets whining past his ears. How could he help being nervous about the prospects?

VII

Lanny couldn't visit England without paying a call at The Reaches, one of his half-dozen homes. A lovely thing to have friends, and to know that you have chosen well and aren't going to have to sever precious ties and mutilate your own life; to know that marriage isn't going to change your friend, nor political disagreements, nor weaknesses of character. To see a family grow, and yet always be the same; to see a tradition surviving and being passed on to new generations; to see knowledge increasing and loyalty never failing—yes, if you have a friend like that, and his adoption tried, you grapple him to your heart with hooks of steel:

Sir Alfred Pomeroy-Nielson, Bart., was in his seventies, but as lively as ever and as interested in what was going wrong in the world about him. He had filled two rooms of his rambling old red-brick house with original documents on the contemporary English drama, and was still dreaming that he might find somebody to help him pay the expenses of this unusual sort of collection. His wife had died not long ago, but he had three children and twice as many grandchildren, all living in England and dutifully visiting him now and then. His oldest, Rick, lived with his family at The Reaches; Nina kept the house, a task not too difficult, since servants were plentiful. In 1937, as in 1914, there were young people dancing and singing all over the place, playing tennis, punting on the Thames, and in the evening sitting out in the moonlight, listening to distant music and experiencing thrills the like of which they were sure had never before been heard of in the world. As always, they considered themselves a unique and original and vitally significant generation; they were respectful to their elders, who held the purse-strings, but slightly sorry for them, as being so backward and out of date, preferring Beethoven to hot jazz, and Tennyson and Browning to Auden and Spender.

Rick was no good for punting, on account of his knee which had got smashed while helping to save England; but his oldest son was at home, vacationing from Oxford, and Alfy's long legs and digestion were sound, in spite of his months in a Franco dungeon. It was the first time Lanny had seen him since their parting on the right bank of the Tagus River several months ago; Lanny hadn't really seen him then, just a dark form stepping out of a boat and scrambling up the bank, dislodging the stones of Portugal. Of course Alfy had written, pouring out his thanks, more ardently than he could do now that he was face to face with his rescuer. But he managed to get out: "I'll never forget it, Lanny; and be sure that if I ever have a chance to return it in kind, I'll be there."

"I hope I'll never be in a fix as bad," replied the family friend. "But if I do, I'll holler."

"And be sure I'm going to earn that money and pay it back," added the youth.

"That was a contribution to the cause, Alfy; and both you and I will make more of them, I don't doubt."

"You will make them all until I have paid you back," declared the baronet's grandson. He said no more, for the subject of money wasn't dwelt upon in his world. Rick had already sent an installment of what it had cost to buy the lad out of a Fascist dungeon, but Lanny had returned it, knowing that the large family was in debt and not likely to get out of it, with Rick deliberately refusing to write "potboilers," as he called the sort of plays his rich friends enjoyed seeing.

Lanny said: "I've come on something interesting in the States; a way to put some of our ideas across. But I'm pledged not to talk about it."

"That's all right," replied Rick; "if it's a secret, the fewer who know it the better."

"There's nothing to prevent my passing information on to you as always," added the visitor. He told some of the news from his Connecticut home, and bits of what he had heard at Wickthorpe Lodge.

"The Beaver is on the warpath, privately as well as publicly," commented the playwright. "They call him flighty, but you notice that he never wavers from loyalty to his fortune."

"And to Empire Free Trade," added Alfy. It was the scheme of having parts of the British Empire trade with one another, to the exclusion of the rest of the world; "the Beaver" had been tireless in its advocacy ever since his Canadian days.

"It's all the same," replied the father. "It means that greed and jealousy continue to rule the world, and people spend their substance building fences to keep the rest of the world out."

Eric Vivian Pomeroy-Nielson was a saddened man. He was only a couple of years older than Lanny, but already there were touches of gray in his wavy dark hair and lines of care in his forehead. He had had his success as a playwright, but that had been a fluke, so he declared, and wasn't likely to happen again. He had his ideas of what was decent, and he followed them, even though he saw the rest of the world traveling another road. He slaved to collect material and organize it into a thoughtful article, and then he sold it to one of the weeklies for five or six pounds. He might have got ten times as much from one of their press lordships, Beaverbrook or Rothermere or Astor, on the single condition that he would write what they told him instead of what he believed.

Alfy was tall like his father, more slender, and had dark wavy hair;

his features were thin and sensitive and his spirit high. He had absorbed his father's ideas, and took them with desperate intensity; he had proved it by going off to Spain to fight in the air for the people's cause. Now he was under a sort of parole and couldn't go to Spain again; he had taken up the idea of the law as a career, and Lanny knew that it was as a means of repaying his debt. Lanny didn't think that this idealistic lad would ever be a moneymaker in any field, but he let the matter rest until Alfy should have finished at Magdalen College, pronounced Maudlin.

VIII

The grandson of Budd's was accustomed to refer to himself play-fully as an amphibious animal; one of those prehistoric lizards whose ancestors had always lived in the water, but which was now climbing out onto the rocks and painfully learning to breathe air in its pure state instead of air that was hidden in the interstices of drops of water. The Lanny lizard could manage it for a while, he said, but every now and then the effort would become too great and he would have to slip back into the element which was his natural home.

By that element he meant the world of fashion and pleasure. It was a world where everybody had, or at any rate was assumed to have, all the money he could possibly want. It was the "leisure-class" world, and the people in it were proud of the fact that they had never done and didn't know how to do anything useful. The farther back they could trace an ancestry which had never done it, the more distinguished they were. To them the world provided every luxury the ingenuity of men had been able to devise: delicious foods and rare wines, with skilled cooks to prepare and trained servants to serve them; soft and delicate fabrics, cut always in a manner having esoteric significance; fast motor-cars, swiftly gliding yachts—and not merely physical satisfactions, but intellectual and moral and aesthetic; great music and literature and art —in short, all the delicate and gracious things that life had to offer. The best examplars of that leisure-class life were truly delightful companions.

The Lanny lizard would crawl out of this agreeably warm ocean onto the hard rocks which were called "reality," into the rare and cold atmosphere known as "social reform." Here people slept in uncomfort-able beds, ate poor food badly served, and wore clothing entirely with-out distinction. They were frequently worried about money and forced to borrow it from someone who had it—which usually meant the Lanny lizard. They worked hard and had few pleasures; they were frequently embittered and hard to please; they were jealous, not merely of the idle rich, but sometimes, alas, of their own comrades whose labors had won too great appreciation. They played little and studied and read a great deal; they were apt to be proud of their knowledge, and had invented a jargon of their own, more adapted to repel than to enlighten.

In short, it was a difficult atmosphere to breathe, and the lizard would find himself getting dizzy and yearning for his old-time home. It was fatally easy to slide back into that pleasure ocean; and moreover, it was from there that he got his food; he had to go back for what were called "business reasons," and his friends the reformers were glad to have what he brought out of it. The result was, Lanny was one of those creatures which have both gills and lungs, and spend their time splashing in the tide-waters, being caught by the waves and bumped against the rocks, and never sure what they are or where they belong.

IX

In this world of fashion and pleasure one of the conspicuous activities was the making of love. To these elegant ladies and gentlemen love had become a game; something to cultivate and experiment with, always in refined and elegant ways, of course. It was something which pervaded their beings, like a perfume always in the air, like soft music heard from far off, while eating, sleeping, or conversing. The ladies of fashionable society prepared themselves elaborately for the practice of this gracious art. Their costumes were carefully devised to stimulate and suggest it, by revealing exactly the proper portion of their "charms." Ideas of what was permissible differed widely in different lands, but in those of the West it had been the custom to reveal the face, the arms and shoulders, and the upper part of the bosom; of late years the entire back down to the waist had been added to this list. When stimulation began to fail, exposure must be increased.

The same sort of changes had been observable in the dance. A little more than a hundred years ago Englishmen had considered it grossly indecent to stand face to face with a lady and put one arm around her and hold her ever so lightly while going through the movements of a dance; Lord Byron, usually no prude, had written a vehement protest against a vile new procedure known as "waltzing." Now this practice had had its day and lost its charms; it wasn't tantalizing enough or mimetic enough to interest anybody. Dancing had become still more obviously a form of love play, a way of titillating the most basic of all instincts, of suggesting the most universal of pleasures.

Reflections upon this subject of love and love-making were passing through the mind of Lanny Budd for the reason that he had promised his friend Adella to get a price on a painting in the fine Georgian home of his old sweetheart, Rosemary. She was a year older than Lanny, which meant that she was at the age called "dangerous" for women, and therefore not entirely safe for men. Lanny had been keeping away from her on purpose, but now business drew him to her. He could come near to guessing her thoughts, for he knew her as well as he ever could know any woman. She had been his first love, and memories of her perfumed nearly all his haunts. She had sat with him by the riverbank at The Reaches, and on the shore at Bienvenu, his mother's estate. She had motored with him through France and Germany, and sailed on the yacht *Bessie Budd* all the way to the Lofoden islands.

She was gentle and kind, and had accommodated herself to his eccentricities. When the time had come for her to marry, she had considered that she owed it to her family to choose a member of her own class; at least, that is what she told Lanny, though he suspected that she had wanted to become a countess, and had enjoyed that eminence. Anyhow, she hadn't wanted to hurt him, and didn't see why he should be hurt. The ladies of her class made such state marriages—*mariage de convenance* was the French phrase; they bore their children and then considered their duty done; after that they could be free if they wished, and as a rule they did. Bertie, the earl, had had his affairs, when and as he pleased; in the course of the years Rosemary had become certain that he would play fair and not object to what she did, provided she observed reasonable discretion. Such was the fashion in the smart world, and if you didn't like it you could stay out of it—which you probably had to do, anyway.

Rosemary and Lanny had been happy for a couple of years, and then, after a ten years' interval, for another year or two; why not for a third period? She knew that he was divorced, and she would be frank and straightforward in "propositioning" him. And what was he going to answer? He couldn't say: "I am married again," for that was a secret which he shared with only three persons, Rick and Nina and F.D.R. He couldn't be mysterious and say: "Sorry, old dear," for Rosemary would ask straightway: "Is there another woman?" and if he was the least bit vague about it she would draw her own conclusion. She knew many of his friends, and it was a part of their modernism to talk with frankness about their own and others' sex lives. The story would go out: "Lanny Budd has another woman, and who is she?" Everybody would be watching him, and the longer he kept the secret the hotter would become their curiosity. Reserve was one thing your smart friends wouldn't forgive; it was a mark of distrust and opened you to the suspicion that you were involved in something disgraceful.

On the other hand if he said: "I am no longer interested in you, Rosemary," that would be wounding her intolerably. He couldn't say: "I have adopted a different moral code," for either she would know it was an evasion, or else her curiosity would be aroused; that was one of her characteristics, and she would want to know all about these new ideas and where had he picked them up. He thought of telling her that he wasn't well, but he knew that his looks belied it. In short, he couldn't make up his mind what to say, and had to leave it to the inspiration of the moment, a dangerous thing for a person of sympathetic nature.

X

Rosemary had taken care of herself, as ladies of her world know so well how to do. She did not look her age; a bit "matronly," but nowhere near to "plump"; Lanny knew that it meant heroic dieting, the foregoing of a lesser pleasure for the sake of a greater. She had always had a wealth of straight flaxen hair; she had scorned to bob it in the bobbing season and now she scorned to wave it in the "permanent" season. She was as Nature made her, trusting that great mother and with good reason. She permitted few cares to disturb her, for she had "inherited that good part."

She received him in her sitting-room, newly done in pale blue silk. Windows were open and a gentle breeze stirred the curtains; a bird sang on a branch almost inside. "He gets paid with breadcrumbs," said Rosemary. "Oh, Lanny," she added, "it's so good to see you! Why don't you come often?"

It was a bid at the very outset, and he chose to evade. "This bird has to travel long distances for his breadcrumbs. I have just come from America." He talked about Robbie Budd, who had always been her friend, and who sent his warm regards. He told news about the Robin family, and his mother, and other mutual friends; that was the sort of conversation she liked; she could take an interest in general ideas if she had to, but she found it rather exhausting and rarely did it if the other person would let them alone. She told him about Bertie, who was fishing in Scotland, and about her children, who were nearly grown, depriving their mother of the last hope of concealing her age.

Presently he asked: "Have you any more paintings you would like to get rid of?"

"Oh, Lanny, you are going to make me talk about horrid business things!" But she resigned herself without difficulty, and they strolled through the gallery. She remarked that Bertie was always spending more than he made; women were always "working him" for presents. When Lanny came to the unhappy Amy Robsart he looked at her for a while and then said: "I know a woman in the States who might be interested in that, if you would put a reasonable price on it. The woman has been reading *Kenilworth*."

Possibly Rosemary had never heard of that novel, but she wouldn't be *gauche* enough to reveal the fact. "What is it worth, Lanny?"

"I'm not the one to tell you, because I'd be getting my commission from the purchaser and I'd have to represent her."

"I know, Lanny, but you're my friend, and I have to ask someone I can trust. Tell me what you'd be willing to pay if you were buying it from a dealer."

"Bless your heart, darling, I'd pay the least I thought the dealer would take, and the dealer would ask the most he thought I'd pay. There really is no fixed value for a painting."

"Tell me the highest price you would recommend as fair to your client."

"Well, if you would quote me eight hundred pounds, I'd feel justified in advising anyone to take it—that is, assuming that the person wanted such a painting."

"It's a very old thing, Lanny."

"I know; but the old houses of England are full of old paintings, and unless they have a well-known name they're just curiosities. I have grave doubts whether this is a Garrard, as it is supposed to be, and I wouldn't offer it as such."

"I'll have to telegraph Bertie; you know it's his property."

"Of course." Lanny knew Rosemary made her husband allow her ten per cent commission for her cleverness in making these deals. That didn't hurt Lanny.

They went back to the sitting-room, and after tea was brought, they were again alone. She looked lovely in a Japanese silk teagown which matched the pale blue of her room, and had golden herons and clumps of bamboo on it; he wasn't sure if he ought to look at her, but of course that was what she was made for. Suddenly she exclaimed: "Lanny, we used to be so happy! Don't you suppose we might be again?"

There it was, "plain and flat," as he had expected and feared. "Darling," he replied, "I'm in the same fix as you were when you were young; I have to think about my parents. My mother is so anxious for

me to settle down, and I've made her so unhappy with my entangle-
ments; my break with Irma was a blow."

It was a "red herring," cleverly dragged out for the emergency. Rosemary asked: "What was the matter between you and Irma, Lanny?"

"Well, you know how it is: Irma wants one kind of life and I want
another. I think you had something to do with it. She saw how high
you had flown, and she wanted to sit on the same perch. Now she's got
there, and I hope she has the fun she expects."

"She'll probably find it isn't so romantic as she imagined. Do you
think you'll ever go back to her, Lanny?"

"I'm quite sure that is finished. My mother is begging me to find the
right sort of wife and stick by her. You know my habits; I've never
stayed very long in one place in my life, and I'm afraid it would be
hard to find a wife who could stand me."

A second red herring, brought into being by inspiration! It worked
even better than the first. "Why don't you let me try to find you a
wife?" inquired his old sweetheart.

"Bless your heart, dear, how could I stay here long enough? I have
some picture business in Paris now, and after that I have to go to
Germany."

It amused her very personal nature to talk about him, and the sort of
woman who could make him happy. So long as it wasn't a married
woman, this was a safe topic while he was drinking his tea. When he
was leaving she said: "I'll let you know about the painting—and also
about the wife!" Then she added: "You'd be conceited if you knew
how much I think about you, Lanny. Come again soon!" It was always
hard for her to face the idea of not getting what she wanted.

XI

Once every week while Lanny was on his travels he wrote a letter to
his wife in Paris. She had had a number of names; just how she was
Jeanne Weill, pronounced as the French pronounce it, Vay. She was
supposed to be from Geneva, and Lanny had got her a book so that she
could read up on that old city of watchmakers and moneychangers, not
to mention the League of Nations, which was clinging feebly to life in
a magnificent palace recently completed for it, which Rick in an article had called its mausoleum. Trudi occupied a small studio on Montmartre, and did sketches which were sold on commission by the proprietor of a tobacco shop near by; she lived on the proceeds, and talked

about her work to the concierge and the tradespeople, thus maintaining an adequate camouflage.

Lanny's letters to her were always on cheap stationery, always addressed by hand, and with nothing distinctive about them; the contents were designed so that any agent of the Nazis in Paris might read them and learn nothing, save that a person named Paul was well, and that he had made so-and-so-many francs, and expected to be in Istanbul on such-and-such a date. The city on the Bosporus was code for Paris, and the francs were supposed to be multiplied by thirty; that is, they meant dollars, and Trudi would know from this what plans her underground friends were to make for the future. Lanny had never sent her a cablegram or even a telegram; he had never stopped his car near her place and never entered the building except after elaborate precautions. Nazi agents had found her once in Paris, and they weren't going to find her again if he could help it. She no longer had any contacts with other refugees, except for the one man whom she met at night and to whom she turned over the money and her occasional writings.

Trudi Schultz was one of those persons who, in the words of a German poem which Lanny had quoted, "belong to death." When he left her, he could never know if he would see her again; when he received a note from her saying she was well, it couldn't satisfy him completely for the reason that it was several days or weeks late, and he could never know what might have happened in the interim.

How does a man love such a woman? The first thing to be said is that, unless he is extremely neglectful of his own interests and peace of mind, he doesn't. Lanny had got into this position because of that weakness which his mother and father and all their friends so greatly deplored: a sentimental streak which made him oversorry for the underdog and overanxious concerning evils which have been in the world a long time and are beyond the power of any man to change. Hitler had seized Germany, and his nasty Nazis were beating and torturing poor Jews and others who opposed them. When you met some victim of that terror you were sorry for the poor devil and helped him to get on his feet again; but when it came to declaring a private war on the Hitlerites and setting out to overthrow them—well, Don Quixote tilting at the windmills was a sensible citizen in comparison with such a person.

But this art expert had got himself in for it; he had gone and got married to an "underground" worker so that he could take her away to America—if only he could persuade her to come, which so far he hadn't had the nerve to try! Did he really love her? Could any man really love a woman who led him such a life; who gave him only little snatches of joy, and no comfort or peace of mind whatever? Lanny hadn't told a single one of his smart friends about it, but he could hear their comments just as well in his mind. "Good God, a man might as well fall in love with a buzzsaw!" A woman whom he couldn't hold in his arms without the thought that a gang of bullies might break in the door and murder them both! Whom he couldn't think of when he was away from her without seeing images of her stretched out naked on a table, being beaten with thin steel rods! It was indecent even to know about such things!

Trudi had foreseen all this; she had warned him about it, over and over, in the plainest words. She hadn't wanted to marry him, she hadn't wanted even to live with him. She had insisted that the things she had seen and experienced made it impossible for her ever again to be a normal woman, ever to give happiness to a man. But he had thought that he could give happiness to her; he had argued that men going off to war clutch eagerly at the joys of love before they depart, and why could it not be the same with a woman soldier? Was it because men are naturally more selfish? Or was it because women are not meant to be soldiers, and are less able to bear the strain of belonging to death? *Wir sind all' des Todes Eigen!*

He had given her a lot of happiness, of that he could be sure. He had picked her up on obscure street corners by appointment and driven her out into the safe countryside; they had stayed in little inns and he had seen that she got substantial food. He had given her love, of mind and soul as well as body; he had kept the faith with her and helped to renew her courage. Yes, she had said sometimes that she couldn't have gone on without him. But even while she said it, a cloud would darken her features and she would fall silent; he would know that she was thinking about her comrades who had fallen into the clutches of the German secret police, and about the horrors which even at this moment were being perpetrated upon them.

XII

Did Lanny Budd really love Trudi Schultz, alias Mueller, alias Kornmahler, alias Corning, alias Weill, *et aliae*, or was he just sorry for her and full of respect for her intelligence and integrity of character? It was a question he asked himself, a problem he wrestled with in his own soul. He could never love her completely, for she was a creature of the hard rocks and the rare cold atmosphere, while he had been playing in the warm soft ocean of pleasure. Trudi could never give him what Rosemary had given, or Marie de Bruyne, or Irma Barnes. All these had been "ladies"; they had known how to dress and how to dance, how to talk and how to behave in the fashionable world; they had known how to "charm" their man. Trudi, while she had come out of the German middle class, had voluntarily joined the workers in order to help them; her very names were commonplace—Schultz, while it meant a village magistrate, had become the name for a butcher or a grocer, while Trudi was a name for a serving maid.

Lanny's Trudi had been an art student of great talent, and had worked hard to develop it; all Germans worked hard, whether it was in the cause of God or the devil, and Trudi had lived a Spartan life from the time that Lanny had first met her in Berlin. She had been severe in her moral judgments, even of the Social-Democratic movement to which she belonged. She had not glorified self-sacrifice as an ideal, but had accepted it as a necessity of her time and circumstances. The workers were not going to get freedom and justice without heavy sacrifices, and those who aspired to guide them must be prepared to think wholly about their cause and not at all about their pleasures.

Somewhere inside Lanny Budd a bell rang whenever he thought these thoughts; a great gong with quivering tones which sent shivers all over him. Yes, that was the way to speak, that was the way to live; that was honest and decent, fair to one's fellow humans; that was the way to pay the debt you owed for being a civilized man, an heir to culture, instead of a savage, dirty and diseased, living in a hut with pigs and chickens. Lanny had felt that high regard for Trudi from the very first hour; she had renewed his distrust of the fashionable world and all its beliefs and practices. Lanny had said: "Yes, I know; I am a parasite; we are all parasites. I ought to get out of it and get something useful to do."

But the trouble was, circumstances wouldn't let Lanny get out. Time after time, something had turned up that he could do for the cause, but only by staying on in the leisure-class world, keeping the role of playboy, art expert, moneymaker. It had taken both money and social intrigue to get Freddi Robin out of a Nazi dungeon, and again to get Alfy out of a Franco dungeon. Even Trudi hadn't wanted Lanny to break with his family and his wealthy friends; no, for the underground had to have money for paper and printing and radio tubes and what not, and had even been willing for Lanny to sell General Göring's paintings in order to keep them in funds.

So while other people were tortured in prisons or starved in concentration camps, it was Lanny Budd's agreeable duty to travel first-class on steamships or airplanes, to stop at de luxe hotels, to put his feet under the dinner tables of the richest and most exalted persons. Boredom was the worst of hardships he had to endure—unless you counted that of having to make the greater part of his life into an elaborate lie, to watch every word and every facial expression for fear of revealing his real sentiments. Whatever you did in that *haut monde* you must always be smiling and *insouciant*, and you must always agree that disturbers of so perfect a social order had to be put down with a firm hand.

XIII

Lanny put all doubts and disharmonies away in a cupboard of his mind and locked them with a secret key. He was on the way to his beloved; he ached for her presence and his thoughts were of the interesting things he would have to tell her. She rarely had much news for him, but he was a messenger of the gods, who came from Mount Olympus and their other haunts, laden with the latest installments of international mythology.

He took a taxi to his customary hotel and deposited his belongings. He got his car out of the garage where it was stored, and drove to a spot three or four blocks from his wife's humble lodgings. The concierge who opened the door for him knew him, and had received her proper tip now and then. "Mr. Harris" was the name he had given, so he was "Monsieur Arreece." Now the woman looked at him with concern and shook her head. "*Hélas, monsieur, mademoiselle est partie.*"

"*Partie!*" exclaimed Lanny. "When?"

"I do not know, monsieur. She must have gone out, and she has not returned. It has been nearly a week now."

"Her door is locked?"

"It was locked, monsieur; but yesterday I became alarmed and notified the police. They brought a locksmith and opened the door, but there is no sign of her. Apparently nothing has been disturbed."

"They have no trace of her?"

"No, monsieur; they nor anyone."

Lanny couldn't say that he was surprised, for he had talked about this contingency many times with Trudi. She had said: "Go away. Do not involve yourself. If I am alive I will get word to you." She had his mother's address at Juan-les-Pins, his father's address in Connecticut, his best friend's address in England. He had no way to find her, but she could always find him.

"What did the police say?" he inquired.

"They asked many questions, monsieur. I told them there was an American gentleman who sometimes came to visit mademoiselle. They told me if you came again, I was to notify them."

"It would do no good to do that. I have not heard from mademoiselle and there is nothing I could tell them."

"*Mais, Monsieur Arreece!* It would be a serious matter for me not to obey the police."

"No one will know that I have been here," replied the visitor. He took out a hundred-franc note, which he judged the right size for the cure of such anxiety. "You say nothing and I'll say nothing and it will be O.K."—the French all knew those two letters.

"*Mais sa propriété, monsieur; ses articles!*"

Lanny knew that Trudi didn't have many *articles;* a few sticks of furniture, a few pieces of clothing suitable to the poorest. She never kept a letter or any scrap of paper; when she wrote something for the underground, she took it away or mailed it at once. The only things she might have were a few sketches, and Lanny would have liked to have these, but he dared not take the risk. He would not trust the French police in any matter having to do with leftwing refugees; also, they had records of his own distant past which he wouldn't care to have dug up.

He took out another note and handed it to the concierge. "Keep her property for a while," he said. "If she comes back she will pay you. *Merci et bonjour.*" He turned away and got out of that neighborhood, never to return.

4

Plus Triste Que les Nuits

I

LANNY'S first step was to get his mother on the telephone. Had there come any letter from his friend? The word in English carries no connotation of sex, but Beauty knew whom he meant; her sharp eyes had not failed to observe the weekly letters, which she dutifully forwarded as directed. She had questioned Lanny and succeeded in getting a few details, but not all that she wanted. Now she told him there was no letter. He tried to keep anxiety out of his voice; no use worrying her. "If a letter comes, please phone me to the hotel at once."

He called Rick, with the same results; nothing there. He hadn't expected it, for he had told Trudi that he was on his way to "Istanbul." To Rick he could say: "She has disappeared. I fear the worst." Nothing more over the phone.

Rick was full of concern; he knew what anguish of mind this meant to his friend. "If there's anything we can do, let us know and we'll come at once." But of course there wasn't. "God bless you, old fellow!" the Englishman exclaimed. He didn't really believe in God, at least not that he knew of; but he had to say something different from the ordinary.

Lanny and Trudi had talked this problem over in advance. She had asked, and he had promised, that in the event of her disappearance he would stay quiet for a while, to give her a chance to communicate with him if she could; also, that he would never do anything that might reveal his connection with her, and thus imperil his ability to serve the cause. He had assented to her stern formula that this was a war in which the cause was everything and the individual nothing. That was the Nazis' own law, and the anti-Nazis would have to match them in firmness of purpose.

The husband went over again and again in his mind the circumstances which governed this case. The Nazis were on the aggressive, all over Europe; they were intriguing and deceiving, seducing and corrupting; undermining the power of their opponents and building up that of their supporters, and no law of God or man meant anything to them, only the question of results. When they approached persons of social standing, they sent a fine musician like Kurt Meissner, able to play Beethoven and even to compose Beethoven, and to speak the exalted language of international cultural solidarity. When it was a question of leading bankers and industrialists, they sent a financial wizard like Hjalmar Schacht to show how Germany had solved the problem of unemployment and crisis; how German big business was thriving as none other had ever thriven, even in America in its boom days; how there were no more unions and no more strikes, no more class war, no more political demagogues levying blackmail. When it was a question of the newspapers of France, always for sale to the highest bidder, they sent Otto Abetz with an unlimited expense account and a briefcase full of plausible editorials in the most highly polished Parisian, setting forth the advantages of permanent friendship between France and Germany, and the treason to European culture involved in the alliance with Bolshevism.

Paris was full of refugees from both Germany and Italy; Jews especially, but also Socialists, Communists, democrats, liberals, pacifists, every sort of idealist; all quarreling among themselves as they had done at home; all insisting that their way was the only way to fight Fascism-Nazism. These refugees smuggled news out of Germany and Italy and smuggled in what they called their "literature": newspapers, pamphlets, leaflets. And of course their enemies were fighting back with fury; the Hitlerites had their little Gestapo in Paris, and Mussolini his little OVRA; Dr. Goebbels had his Personal Department B, and the SS had their Braune Haus. German agents came under every sort of disguise: scientists and journalists, teachers of music and languages, students, traveling salesmen, importers, laborers, even refugees. Agents would be trained to pose as leftists; they would be sent to concentration camps in Germany and beaten there, so that the other prisoners would see them and word would go out to the underground that they were all right; then they could "escape" to Paris, and be welcomed by the anti-Nazi groups, and be in position to collect names and addresses of the "comrades" both at home and abroad. The former would be shot, and the latter would be intimidated and silenced by whatever measures it took.

II

What would be the attitude of the French police toward this foreign civil war going on under their noses? The French police represented property, as police are apt to do all over the world. There were Frenchmen who held the same ideas and behaved in the same manner as the refugees, and the police regarded them as public nuisances and potential criminals; if they got any protection, it was because they had strong influence with labor and commanded numbers of votes. The head of the Paris police, the notorious Chiappe, was to all intents a Fascist, in open sympathy with the Croix de Feu and other native organizations, and perhaps with the Cagoulards, the "Hooded Men," whose murder gangs were patterned on the Blackshirts and the Schutzstaffel. The Nazis were helping to subsidize these groups in France and would not fail to have their friends and secret representatives in the Sûreté Générale and the Deuxième Bureau.

Of course there were limits to what could be done in a supposedly free republic. If refugees of prominence were molested, it made a scandal; the Reds and the Pinks had their newspapers with large circulations and they loved nothing so much as having martyrs. Just a month or two ago Mussolini had arranged the murder of his two leading opponents among the refugees, Carlo and Nello Rosselli, editors of the Italian-language anti-Fascist newspaper in Paris; they had been kidnaped and beaten to death in the woods—the same method which had been used in Rome to get rid of the Socialist editor Matteotti, soon after Il Duce had seized power. Lanny had been there at the time, and his efforts to tell the outside world about it had caused his expulsion from the new Roman Empire. Now the newspapers of Paris had been full of the Rosselli story and it had even reached Connecticut. It was bad publicity for both Fascism and France; it served to alarm the outside world, and the police certainly wouldn't want any more of it.

Lanny was in a position to make another Rosselli case by the simple operation of telephoning any one of the American newspapermen whom he knew in Paris. The story would be flashed to the ends of the earth and would make the front page wherever there was a *grand monde* and a proletariat which loved to read about it. AMERICAN SOCIALITE IN PARIS REVEALS SECRET WIFE DISAPPEARANCE, CHARGES NAZI KIDNAPING. Nothing less than a local murder or the outbreak of a world war would take precedence of that. They would bring in Budd Gunmakers and Budd-Erling, J. Paramount Barnes and Irma and Frances and the fourteenth Earl of Wickthorpe. Under the glare of such a searchlight, the French police might conceivably get busy and find what was left of Trudi Schultz, alias Mueller, alias Kornmahler, alias Corning, alias Weill, pronounced Vay. But what would it do to the picture business, and to Lanny's access to the topflight personalities of two continents? What would it do to his new job as Presidential Agent 103? Obviously, all that would be *fini*, *kaput*, knocked into a cocked hat. For the Nazis it would be a major victory—for of course what they really wanted was not to get Trudi, but to find out where she was getting the money.

If they had her, that was why they had her, and they would be working right now to draw the secret from her. She had said many times that she would die with it in her heart; that was the first duty of every conspirator, the first pledge they all made. But who could tell what any person would do under the most cruel tortures that modern science could contrive? Who could say that in some delirium she might not cry out the name of Lanny? Who could be sure that she might not be hypnotized and told that she was speaking to her lover? Many things might happen, and Lanny Budd had plenty of time to imagine them. If the torturers managed to break the secret, they wouldn't be apt to kidnap the son of Budd-Erling, but they might slug him on some dark night and it would be an ordinary case of robbery; they might force his speeding car off the road and it would be a lesson to other reckless drivers.

III

The unhappy husband went to his hotel and inquired if there had been any call for him. Then he went to his room and sat there; when he got tired of sitting, he got up and paced the floor for a while. He didn't want to go out, because there was the possibility that Trudi might call on the telephone. She had done that once, to this very hotel; the time when strange men had been following her on the street, and Lanny had had to think quickly and tell her how to evade them.

Waiting; just waiting. Like a man deprived of all his senses, and of all powers, but who still retains his consciousness; who knows that something terrible is happening, but cannot find out what it is and cannot do anything about it. He didn't want to eat, he didn't want to read, he didn't want to see anybody; his thoughts were altogether occupied with Trudi. Her image floated before him; those fine, exquisitely chiseled features, expressive of intelligence, of sensitiveness, of moral fervor. She was a saint; he had often told her that, half teasingly, for she didn't like the word with its ecclesiastical connotations. But religion takes different forms; new faiths are born, spurning the outworn faiths of the past. Trudi was a saint of the new religion of humanity, of solidarity, co-operation, and justice. Her image was that of an early Christian martyr, with trembling eyelids and the sweat of anguish upon the forehead; a Nordic blond martyr with fair hair and blue eyes. He had no photograph of her; the only one she had let him have made had been put in a sealed envelope along with their wedding certificate and sent to Robbie Budd, to be put in his safe and opened only in the event of Lanny's death.

But Lanny didn't need any picture; he had an art critic's trained eye and memory. He knew every detail of her features and her form; he knew them as line and color, he knew them as living things, expressions of a mind and character. He had come to Paris with his senses warmed by the thought of her embraces; now he paced the floor of a hotel room like a wild creature caged, tormented by the thought of her torments. He had a vivid imagination, but needed none on this subject. He was back in that dungeon in the basement of the Columbus Haus in

Berlin, its floor slimy and stinking with stale blood; he saw the heavy wooden bench with the elderly Jewish banker—"Jewish-Bolshevik plutocrat" was the Nazi phrase—stretched out naked on his fat stomach and being whipped on his flabby white buttocks with thin steel rods. Lanny heard the rods whistling, four of them, like the wind in a chimney on a stormy night; heard the shrieks, the moans, the gabble of the tortured old man.

Quietly, methodically, mechanically the Nazis did that to people; they did it to long strings of men and women, one after another, until the whippers were dripping with sweat, until they became exhausted and had to be replaced. The victims would fall unconscious and be dragged away and dumped into another room, piled sometimes on top of one another. A wholesale procedure, the mass production of suffering, intended to terrorize all Germany, and then the whole continent of Europe. *Heute gehört uns Deutschland, morgen die ganze Welt!*

They had called in their eminent physiologists and psychologists to tell them how to humiliate and degrade human beings, to break their wills and subject them to the National-Socialist will. They built chambers of concrete of a carefully devised crookedness, so that a human being could not stand up or sit down or lie without having sharp corners sticking into various parts of him; they would throw him in there and leave him for days, for weeks. They would bring him to an inquisition chamber and strap him in a chair with a bright light glaring into his eyes, and there they would question him, with relays of inquisitors, giving him not a moment's rest for days and nights. At intervals they would burn his flesh with cigarettes or stick slivers of wood under his fingernails to liven him up and make him more attentive. They had ascertained scientifically the exact amount of heat and humidity which would reduce the human will to impotence and turn the mind to putty.

Now they had Trudi Schultz somewhere, and were putting her through that sort of ordeal. Doubtless they would rape her—why not? It was one more way to horrify and shock a woman, one more way to subjugate her, one more way to impress her with the might and majesty of the *Neue Ordnung*. They made a sort of ceremony out of it; both Freddi and Trudi had described such scenes: the Stormtroopers in their shiny black boots and shiny leather belts lined up awaiting their turn, dancing with amusement, cracking their jokes and roaring with laughter; the women victims, also awaiting their turn, compelled to witness unspeakable obscenities, sometimes fainting with horror and having buckets of water dumped over them so that they might miss nothing.

If all that didn't cause them to talk, their loved ones would be brought in and tortured before their eyes; a child one day, an old mother or father the next. "*Nun, sag'! Wer ist's, was ist's?*"—whatever the inquisitor wanted to know. With Trudi it would be just two things: "Who gave you the money?" and "Who got it from you?" Perhaps they already knew the latter; perhaps that was how they had got Trudi. Or perhaps they would pretend to know; they would tell her that her comrades had betrayed her, and why should she continue to spare them? They would have an endless string of devices, psychological as well as physical; they would never give up until they found out who had been putting up the money for the hundreds of thousands of anti-Nazi leaflets and pamphlets that had been smuggled into Naziland.

IV

Such was the technique in Nazi Germany. Could it be that the same things were being done to German refugees in Paris? Trudi's comrades had informed her that there was a Prussian nobleman connected with the Embassy, a man of wealth who in the normal course of his life was entitled to reside in a fine château. He had rented in the environs of Paris an historic place with splendid grounds and a high spiked fence around them. No residence of such pretentiousness would be without its wine cellars, and in these places the Nazi agents could carry on their operations under the shelter of diplomatic immunity. Of course they couldn't do it wholesale, but they could handle a special case—and one was enough for Lanny's imagination.

He told himself that he couldn't stand it. But he had to stand it; what else could he do? He would resume the nerve-racking experience of waiting for something to happen. He had begun it when the Nazis had seized the Robin family in Berlin and Lanny and his friends were in Calais, expecting the yacht *Bessie Budd* to arrive. Then again in Berlin, with endless waiting for Freddie Robin to telephone—and he didn't. The same with Trudi, in Berlin several times; and now again. He mustn't see any of his friends, because he couldn't trust them with his secret and he couldn't hide his agitation. He wouldn't attend to business, for what was the sense of making more money if Trudi wasn't there to put it to use?

Remorse seized him, because he had let this woman go to her terrible fate. He ought to have stopped her at all hazards. But what could he have done, except to wreck her peace of mind and her health? He had known what she was doing before he had tied his life to hers. And what could he have said to her, except arguments of selfishness which would have shamed them both? Loyal comrades were in the clutches of the enemy; many of them murdered, others suffering the whole gamut of abuse. Freddi Robin and Lanny had helped to maintain a Socialist school in Berlin; in the carefree old days they had pledged their faith to a cause and its supporters. Trudi and her former husband had been among these, and Lanny's memory was full of names, faces, personalities of scores whom he had met there—students, teachers, guests. Most of them were now paying the price, and Lanny and Trudi owed them what support and assistance it was possible to bring. How could the Nazi monster ever be overthrown, if those who had the weapons were to turn tail and run away from the battlefield?

The very idea of doing so was a humiliation; it was a bourgeois idea, born of primitive selfishness and nurtured in the system of competitive greed. Dog eat dog! Look out for number one! Each for himself and the devil take the hindmost! Such were the maxims of the business world; a shame to humanity, a denial of the fatherhood of God and the brotherhood of man. On what basis could Lanny have said to his wife: "Come off with me and forget our comrades and their needs. I have money, and we can spend it on ourselves and be happy together."

Such ideas belonged in that world which called itself the "great world," the "high world," the "select world,"—all in French, the language of elegance and corruption. Lanny had come to hate that world, and now he hated himself because he had been born in it and was flesh of its flesh. His conscience tormented him because he hadn't been good enough for Trudi; because sometimes—frequently, in fact—he had wondered if he hadn't made an unfortunate marriage; if he wouldn't have preferred having a wife who knew how to dress and could go to dinner parties in the fashionable world and exchange polite conversation with his elegant friends. Yes, sometimes he had actually been bored with the life of heroism and self-sacrifice! Sometimes he had wanted to make love to his wife, while she had wanted to talk about the comrades and their sufferings and needs! Many times he had been all too human and had had to lie persistently in order to keep his superhuman wife from finding it out.

Well, now he had no wife; now he was free to slide back into the warm ocean of pleasure. He could forget Trudi Schultz and let Rosemary and his mother find him the right sort of darling, perfectly "finished" in a high-priced school and equipped for the offices of leisure-class wifehood. He sat with his hands clenched and tears running down his cheeks, vowing that he would never commit that act of treason to his ideals. No, he would stick by Trudi, or at any rate the memory of

Trudi, and by her cause. He would move heaven and earth to help her. But then, as soon as this grandiloquent phrase came to him, he realized that he had no lever and no fulcrum to move even a small portion of the earth. He sat in a hotel room waiting for a telephone call which was never coming, and he tried in vain to think of a person who could give him real help. Those who were willing wouldn't be able, and those who might be able couldn't even be trusted with his secret.

V

Trudi had forced her husband to anticipate this situation, and to agree upon his course of action. "Some day they will get me," she had said. "They get all of us in the end." She had given him the name and address of the middle-aged German teacher of the clarinet who was the medium whereby commissions on picture sales were converted into anti-Nazi literature. Professor Adler was not his real name, but that under which he lived and worked in Paris. He earned meager sums by his teaching, and he lived on those so as to awaken no suspicions. If at any time Trudi were to be missing, Lanny must never go near the garret where this musician lived, but mail him a note enclosing one of Trudi's sketches by way of password, and appointing a place on the street for a meeting at night. This professor had never been told where or how Trudi got her large sums of money, but he had been told that in the event of anything happening to her, he would receive a letter which would enable him to get into contact with the source of the funds. That was the way the underground was built, in separate units, each having contact with no more than one or two others.

Lanny had asked: "What if they should get the professor?" and Trudi's reply had been: "I know another name, but I am not permitted to reveal it. If both Adler and I should be caught at once, it will be up to you to try to make contact through some one of the French comrades whom you can trust; or give your money to them, to be used for the propaganda here." She added: "God knows they need it! They are at the same stage as we Germans were a year or two before Hitler struck."

Lanny spent most of his time in the hotel room, and whenever the phone rang, his heart hit him a blow underneath his throat. Several friends called up, inviting him out, and he made the excuse that business tied him down; when people called on business, he made the excuse of social engagements. Never did he hear the one voice that he wanted; his grief told him that he never would hear it again. For why should she fail to telephone, unless she was in the hands of the enemy? And if she was in their hands, what chance was there of her escaping? He would go out and walk for a while, turning unexpected corners and stopping to look in a shop window to see if anybody was trailing him. But the only persons who paid attention to a well-dressed and young-looking American were the ladies of the *trottoir*.

After four days he could wait no longer, and wrote on his typewriter the fateful note which he and Trudi had agreed upon. He asked Professor Adler to be on a certain obscure street corner in Montmartre at ten o'clock on the following evening and to wear a blue flower in his buttonhole. The letter was signed "Toinette," in the hope that if it fell into the hands of the enemy it might be taken for an assignation. At the hour appointed Lanny walked to the place, taking every precaution to make sure that he was not being followed. He strolled past the spot, looking for a smallish German with prematurely gray hair and a blue flower. There would be, of course, the chance that it might be a Nazi agent taking the musician's place; but this chance had to be taken.

However, there was nobody resembling a professor of clarinet playing. Lanny passed the corner several times, and then, thinking that the musician's knowledge of geography might be defective, he crossed to the other corners—but in vain. He went back to his hotel and wrote another note, making another appointment for the evening after next; he went again, and walked as before, seeing no blue flowers and no one who looked like either a musician or a Gestapo agent—Lanny had met a number of both. His notes doubtless went to the dead-letter office and were burned, along with thousands of other attempts at assignations.

VI

Lanny might have told himself now that he had done all he could; he might have written finis to that chapter of his life and closed the book. But the very fact that he hadn't loved Trudi as wholeheartedly as he ought to have loved her bound him to her memory. Now that it was too late, he really yearned to live the heroic, the saintly life! The fact that he had held a martyr in his arms poisoned his thoughts of the fashionable world which beckoned him from the Riviera, from Biarritz and Salzburg and Davos, and the other places where his mother's friends were to be found in late summer.

Day and night his mind was obsessed by one thought: "How can I save her?" His reason told him that the chance must be slim, and growing more so. What would they do with such a prisoner? Chloroform her and drop her body into the Seine, so that she would pass for one of those unfortunates who every night put an end to themselves in all the great capitals of an unhappy world. Or put her in a closed car and drive her by night to the border—say at Strasbourg, where there was a bridge which Lanny knew well—one half of it France and the other half Germany, the only thing owned in common being a barrier painted with black and white stripes. With the diplomatic immunity which Nazis enjoyed and shamelessly abused, there would be no chance of search; a prisoner well gagged, perhaps unconscious and hidden under a robe, would be safely restored to the land of her origin.

Who would help Lanny Budd? He thought first of his powerful father. Robbie had said that he would be coming to Germany before long. If Lanny had cabled: "I am in serious trouble please come immediately," Robbie would have taken the first steamer. If Lanny had added: "Bring Bub Smith," Robbie would have understood that the trouble was serious indeed, and would have put someone else in charge of his company police force at the Budd-Erling plant and brought with him an ex-cowboy from Texas who was a straightshooter in both the literal and figurative senses of the word. Bub was getting on in years, but he could still toss a silver dollar into the air and hit it with a pistol shot. He had done many kinds of confidential work for Robbie in France, including the bodyguarding of Baby Frances. He had learned to talk the lingo, also to know many kinds of people, including the *flics* both in Paris and on the Riviera.

If Robbie had said: "Bub, I want to know all about the Château de Belcour, which the German Graf Herzenberg maintains in Seine-et-Oise, and where I understand they have a woman prisoner,"—Bub would have said: "O.K., Boss, I'll see what can be done." Robbie would put some new one-thousand-franc notes into Bub's hands, and add: "There's more where these came from, but don't spend them without changing them, for they can be traced." Bub would grin and say: "I'm no sucker, Boss," and that would be enough. Lanny would have been willing to wager that before the week was over Bub Smith would have one of the Graf's servants drunk, and it might be right in the servants' quarters of the château.

Lanny, being of an imaginative temperament, lived through this whole episode. Having included in his cable a request to his father to bring the sealed letter from the safe, Lanny opened the letter and showed the marriage certificate and the photograph of Trudi. Robbie, who had been raised in New England where they grow saints and ascetics wholesale, looked at the portrait—all this in Lanny's imagination, of course—and recognized the sort of woman his susceptible son had "fallen for." He understood without argument the peril in which the wife now stood, for he had been in Germany and knew the Nazis, and had heard the story of Johannes Robin from Johannes himself, and the story of Freddi from Lanny. He was ready with his answer even before his son had finished outlining the situation. "Yes, Son. It looks pretty black but I'll do what I can for you. But you'll have to understand that this is the last straw, and I won't move a finger unless you give me your word that both you and your wife will settle down and drop all sorts of radical activities from now on."

And of course Lanny couldn't say that. Trudi would never make such a promise, and wouldn't admit Lanny's right to make it for her. As for Lanny himself, he had given up one wife because of his unwillingness to make that same promise, and now, apparently, he would have to give up another. He said: "I'm sorry, Robbie; it's no go." The father demanded: "Then what on earth did you bring me across the ocean for?" Lanny replied: "I didn't"—and so ended that abortive piece of imagination!

VII

The bewildered husband's thoughts turned to Léon Blum, who had ceased to be Premier of France a couple of months ago but had become Vice-Premier, and therefore was still chained to the whims of a Cabinet. Lanny had had with Blum much the same sort of session as recently with Roosevelt: that is, he had challenged Blum on the issue of the Spanish war, and heard the defense of a Socialist who held power only on the sufferance of capitalist politicians; of a pacifist and humanitarian who found himself confronted by a many-headed hydra of war; of a Jew who saw anti-Semitism being spread like an artificial plague all around him, and who questioned his right to put that added burden upon his overburdened party.

But Blum was still the leader of that party, and still dreaming of justice in a world of maniacal greeds; still pleading for peace with two psychopathic dictators bent upon war. Privately he could be a friend and wise adviser; if Lanny should go to his apartment and tell him the painful story, Blum would respect his confidence and might be able to give helpful advice. He might name some trustworthy police agent who knew the ropes in Paris and could go to work among the Nazis. It would cost money, of course, but Lanny wouldn't mind that—the money he had brought with him was burning a hole in his pocket, and it seemed to him he would never again have use for it if he couldn't save Trudi. But the more he thought over the plan, the more unlikely it seemed that any police official could permanently keep such a secret as Lanny had to impart. Sooner or later there would be a leak; and anyhow, Lanny would be always in dread of it, and would no longer dare go into Naziland and do his work. He had pledged Trudi that never under any circumstances would he imperil this privilege he enjoyed; and now, since he had become a "presidential agent," he was more than ever committed to preserving it.

So it would have to be some comrade, and preferably someone of the underground. An image arose in Lanny's mind, and he relived a scene of three years ago when he had sat in a tiny second-story bedroom of a workingman's home in the Limehouse district of London, talking in whispers to a German sailor with a round shaven head and a typical Prussian neck that came up in a straight line in back. A tough, hardfisted fellow, this Bernhardt Monck, and Lanny had been suspicious of him; but Trudi had sent him from Berlin, and Lanny had given him money for Trudi's work, and since then nothing had happened to Lanny—which would hardly have been the case if Monck had been a spy of the Nazis. Less than a year ago Lanny had seen him marching at the head of a company of the International Brigade on that forever glorious day when it entered Madrid and stopped the Moors of Franco at the little Manzanares River. Certainly no man was going to walk into any such deadly scrimmage unless he believed in the cause for which it was fought!

There had been many scrimmages since then; and was Monck still alive? If so, perhaps he had earned a furlough, and Lanny could bring him to Paris and put him to work, meeting him secretly and guiding his efforts. Lanny could find out about him through Raoul Palma, his Spanish comrade who for many years had run the workers' school in Cannes, and who was now in Valencia with the Loyalist government. One of the letters which Lanny had found awaiting him in Paris had been from Raoul, telling him the news and pleading with him to move the British government so that the embargo might be lifted and the besieged people of Spain might purchase arms. Just a little thing like that was all a retired school director wanted from his one friend among the ruling classes of the world!

If it hadn't been for war and censorship, Lanny would have got Raoul on the telephone and asked him the whereabouts of Capitán Herzog, the name under which Monck was going in Spain. But with conditions as they were, mail, telegraph and telephone were "out" so far as this matter was concerned. Lanny would have to go to Spain;

and the question which troubled him was, suppose he went, and in the meantime Trudi were to smuggle a letter to him, or try to get him on the phone at this hotel!

VIII

Lanny couldn't sleep. He paced the floor of his room, tormenting himself with thoughts about his wife in the Château de Belcour. He had forgotten to eat; then he decided that he ought to eat, and ordered some food, but found that it had lost its savor. He went out and walked the pavements of Paris in the small hours of the morning; then he came back, and lay down on the bed without undressing; he had managed to exhaust his body but not his mind, and he lay with his eyes closed, thinking every terrible thought possible about Trudi.

Did he doze, and then awaken? He would never be sure. People would tell him in after years that perhaps he had been asleep all the time; but he knew that he was awake and in full possession of his faculties. A strange feeling began to creep over him and he opened his eyes slowly, and there at the foot of his bed was what appeared to be a trace of light, a sort of pillar of cloud, so faint that he couldn't be sure whether it was the first glimmer of dawn coming in at the window. But dawn doesn't come and gather itself into one spot, nor does it make one begin to shiver. The thought flashed over Lanny: "It's happening again!"

It had waited twenty years to happen again. Twenty years ago to this very month Lanny had lain in bed in his father's home and had had this same feeling, and seen a pillar of light turn into the form of Rick, who had been flying in battle over France. One of the most vivid memories of Lanny's whole life, something he could never forget if he lived to be as old as Methuselah. Hundreds of times he had wondered if it would happen again, but it had never happened.

This time it was Trudi; standing there, full size, dim, but otherwise real as life; wearing a plain blue gingham dress with which Lanny was familiar, a dress for which she had paid perhaps twenty-five francs, less than a dollar; with her blond hair drawn back tightly from her forehead and doubtless hanging in two braids—though Lanny couldn't see these, because she was facing him and never moved. She was two or three feet from the foot of the bed, looking at him, slightly downwards; her face pale, her expression gentle, sad, not to say grief-stricken.

When this had happened to Lanny the first time, he had been a youth, entirely uninformed in the strange field of psychic phenomena.

The feeling of grief had overwhelmed him and he had thought: "Rick is dead!" But in the course of twenty years he had read many books on the subject and had tried series of experiments with various mediums, weighing evidence and trying one hypothesis against another. He knew that "apparitions" or "phantasms" have been appearing to men since the beginning of recorded history. What do they mean and how do they arise? From the mind of the beholder or of the person beheld? Are they hallucinations? If so, why do they so often correspond to facts which the beholder cannot normally know? If you say they are "hallucinations telepathically induced," you have to decide what you mean by telepathy and how it works; otherwise you are just fooling yourself with a long word.

Twenty years ago Lanny had said: "Rick is dead!" But Rick hadn't been dead; Rick had been lying on the field of battle, badly hurt and near to death. The apparition had borne a bleeding wound across the forehead—and Rick carried the scar of that wound to this day. Rick had been in France and Lanny in Connecticut; a circumstance which took more explaining than either of them had ever been able to find in any book. Now Lanny looked at this vision of his wife and saw that she had no wound of any sort; just an expression of infinite sorrow. She would have felt that, of course, because she was separated from him, and knew that he would be suffering because of her; that he would forget to eat and wouldn't be able to sleep.

The vision of Rick had filled the youthful Lanny Budd with awe. For twenty years since then he had been thinking: "If I ever see another, how shall I behave?" He had decided that he would not have the least fear or excitement, only scientific curiosity; he would make the most of every instant, like an astronomer during an eclipse of the sun. The astronomer prepares for years and travels half-way around the earth—all for a few seconds. Now Lanny had the seconds and he found that he was awed, even frightened, in spite of himself. Trudi of course would never hurt him; but Trudi came from another world, Trudi represented a break in those veils which hide mankind from its destiny and conceal secrets which may well be unbearable. Lanny felt that his skin was creeping and crawling; he couldn't know that his hair was rising, but it felt like that, a sort of tickling. He was staring hard, and at the same time thinking—the thoughts of twenty years in a few seconds.

He had called out to Rick, and the apparition had faded. So he had decided that he wouldn't speak the next time. But he found that the impulse to speak was hard to resist. To lie there staring at his wife and see her gazing at him—that wasn't normal, it wasn't the part of love. He had become familiar with the idea of thoughts being communicated without words, so he decided to try that. He said: "Trudi!"—moving his lips, perhaps, but not making any sound that he could hear. It seemed to him that the apparition leaned forward slightly and turned its head, as if trying to hear. He said again, soundlessly: "Trudi!"—and could it be that her lips were moving, that she was speaking to him without sound? He had no knowledge of lip-reading, but he imagined that she was saying his name. Afterwards, when he tried the experiment, he discovered that you do not move your lips in saying "Lanny" —you say it with the tongue.

"What shall I do, Trudi?" he thought—and that takes a lot of moving. Did he deceive himself when he imagined that she answered: "Do what I have told you." An obvious enough thing for her to say; any wife, alive or dead, would say it to her husband if she thought that by any chance he would heed. Did he imagine that he heard: "Talk to me in your mind"? That, too, was obvious enough—with a husband who for twenty years had been speculating about psychic phenomena, visiting mediums, persuading his friends to do the same, and making elaborate records of significant communications.

Anyhow, there it was in Lanny's mind, and it stayed while the apparition slowly faded into the light of dawning day. Lanny found himself with a dew of perspiration on his forehead and a chill which was in no way normal in Paris at the end of summer. He found himself with an almost irresistible conviction that Trudi had been there; at least something of Trudi, or from her, and that she had put something into his mind. Nothing that he had read or thought had inclined him toward "spiritualism," but now he was thinking: "Suppose it could be!" And again: "Suppose the Nazis couldn't kill her!" Lanny recalled the *Visit of Emmaus*, so vividly painted by Rembrandt. "And he said unto them, Why are ye troubled? . . . These are the words which I spake unto you, while I was yet with you, that all things must be fulfilled."

IX

Intellectually Lanny didn't know any more about apparitions after this experience than he had known before it. Had this been Trudi—the body, the mind, or the soul of Trudi—or had it been his own subconscious mind, building up a synthesis of ten thousand memories of Trudi? He would never be able to say. But emotionally, Trudi had been there. She had made herself real to him; she had brought his ten thousand memories into active life; and moreover, she had given him a directive.

Lanny had always been, from earliest childhood, a ladies' man. His father he had seen but rarely; it had been his beautiful and warmhearted mother who had shaped his personality, and when she had gone off to take her part in the social whirl, she had left the child with women servants. She had come back trailing clouds of glory—she and her lady friends, dazzling and fascinating creatures, birds of paradise, whose conversation resembled a gramophone wound up and set to run at its highest speed. They had made a pet out of one bright little boy, the only one in a household, and he had watched them primping and powdering, getting armed for their forays into the masculine world—Lanny drinking in words which would never have been spoken if the gay ladies had dreamed that a child could understand them.

Then Rosemary had come into his life; a second mother, but more than a mother, initiating him into the mysteries of love. She had been gentle and kind—they were always that way with Lanny, because he was that way with them. She might have stayed with him for life, only the world wouldn't let her. The world was far more powerful than any individual; it was stern and harsh and made demands upon you which you disobeyed at your peril. *Le grand monde, le haut monde, le monde d'élite*—Lanny had heard these phrases from childhood, and it had taken him many years to understand this *monde*, how it had come to be, and from what its overwhelming authority was derived.

Then had come Marie de Bruyne, one of the creatures and agents of that authority. A lady of high position in Paris, she had been his *amie* in the French fashion, and had handled him with the tact of the woman who accepts intellectually the supremacy of the male creature and does not admit even to herself that she is managing the life of the man she loves. Whenever Lanny did or said anything that was not in accord with the conventions of Marie's class, she had not scolded, she had not even mentioned it; she had just become unhappy, and when Lanny observed it, he decided that it was hardly worth while to do or say or even believe too strenuously that forbidden thing.

And then Irma Barnes, who had come out of the so-called "New" world, and gave no heed to the conventions which bound the women of aristocratic France. Irma had never hesitated to say what she thought; and far from considering herself subject to the male creature, she took it for granted that this creature existed to dance attendance upon her and keep her from being bored. But she had been placid and easygoing; out of her superabundance she had been willing to give Lanny anything he might want, and her only complaint was that he wouldn't make adequate use of his opportunities. What had broken up their marriage was the black crisis which was now gathering over their world. No longer could one just live from day to day and ask no questions; one had to take sides—and Lanny had taken the side opposite to his wife's.

That was how Trudi had come into his life. She represented that other side of his nature, the side which Irma couldn't and wouldn't tolerate; the gullible and softhearted side which made excuses for what called itself "social justice," but which Irma called class jealousy and plain organized robbery. Trudi was—or had been—like Marie de Bruyne in that she had her creed, her set of beliefs and code of conduct from which it was unthinkable to depart. In Trudi's view the workers of the world were struggling to release themselves from age-old servitude and to build a co-operative society, free from exploitation and war. That effort called for the utmost loyalty and consecration, and any weakening in one's efforts was a form of moral decay. Trudi had managed her newly acquired man in much the same way as Marie; she never scolded or found fault, but Lanny would see the distress in her features and would hasten to withdraw the evil words and to suppress the evil tendencies which derived from his leisure-class upbringing and made it so difficult for him to become a singlehearted champion of the oppressed.

X

And now, from the spirit world—if that was it—Trudi was renewing her control of the susceptible Lanny Budd. A new religion had been born and a new martyr was saying: "I am with you alway, even unto the end of the world." A new evangelist was preaching: "Be sober, be vigilant; because your adversary the devil, as a roaring lion, walketh about, seeking whom he may devour: Whom resist stedfast in the faith, knowing that the same afflictions are accomplished in your brethren that are in the world." This world, it appeared, had changed very little in nineteen hundred years; the same human weakness confronted terrifying tasks, and the same moral efforts had to be made, the same injunctions to be laid down, over and over, world without end, Amen.

Without speaking a word, Trudi had said everything she had wanted to say to Lanny—or would have wanted to say if it had really been Trudi instead of Lanny's subconscious mind! Lanny's subconscious mind knew Trudi extremely well and would have no difficulty in making up words for her. So now, for the rest of Lanny's life, Trudi was going to be standing at the foot of his bed, asking: "What have you done for the cause today? Are the workers any nearer to freedom from exploitation and war because of your efforts? Have you really had your mind upon it or have you just been having a good time as in the past?"

Unconsciously, automatically, in Lanny's mind these exhortations would shade into those of the old-time religion which he had read in his boyhood and which his Puritan grandfather in Connecticut had hammered home in a Sunday-morning Bible class. "I beseech you therefore, brethren, by the mercies of God, that ye present your bodies a living sacrifice, holy, acceptable unto God, which is your reasonable service. And be not conformed to this world: but be ye transformed by the renewing of your mind," and so on. "Not slothful in business; fervent in spirit, serving the Lord; Rejoicing in hope; patient in tribulation; continuing instant in prayer; Distributing to the necessity of saints"—this last word would have to be altered, of course, for they were no longer called saints, but comrades and fellowworkers. Their necessity was exactly the same, however, and Lanny had been one of the "distributors," to the endless exasperation of his mother and her friends, of Rosemary and Marie and Irma, each in her turn resenting the coming of ragtag and bobtail to their homes, the flood of begging letters and of leftwing publications with flaring incitements and indecently bitter cartoons.

These begging visitors and letters came no more of late years, for Lanny was pretending to have lost interest in the "cause," and only half a dozen friends shared his real thoughts. What Trudi now exhorted him was: "Get in touch with the underground again, and give them money so that the work may go on. Do not try to save me, because I am beyond help. Do not waste your time in grief or regrets, because what has happened cannot be changed, and your duty is to the future."

Yes, he heard it all and knew it by heart. Trudi had said it, and he had assented, and must now obey her stern directive. He hadn't intended to tell her about President Roosevelt, but in that ghostly meeting he had known that it was all right to tell her, and she had replied: "That is a truly important thing for you to do. If you can persuade That Man and bring him along with us, it will be the greatest service to the cause."

"But can we trust him? Will he really do anything to help us?"—so he had asked, wavering in his soul.

"Nobody can be sure; perhaps he doesn't know himself. But do what you can to open his eyes, and watch him and see what use he makes of your efforts."

This from the Trudi-ghost bore a striking resemblance to what Lanny himself had been thinking. But that wasn't evidential, for Lanny's own thoughts had borne a close resemblance to Trudi's. She had been occupied during a year of marriage and several years preceding marriage to make certain that this should be the case. She would hardly give up the effort now that she was in the spirit world—or was she in that world? Where was she, and what was she? Find out if you can!

BOOK TWO

Wrong Forever on the Throne

5

Forward into Battle

I

LANNY took up his life where he had left off. Zoltan Kertezsi, Hungarian art expert who had taught him his trade, had been to Salzburg for the festival and now arrived in Paris. Lanny dined with him in his apartment, and they talked shop through the meal; what paintings they had bought, or sold, or had orders to buy or sell, and the prices paid or offered. It might happen that Zoltan knew of something that met Lanny's requirements, or vice versa; they helped each other, and would argue over a share in the profits, but reversing the usual procedure, the receiver insisting that he hadn't really earned that much. Lanny had never told his friend what he was doing with his money, but the other must have guessed that he was giving it away for some purpose.

They talked about politics. Zoltan despised that vile world, but just now there was so much murder in the air of Europe that the smell of it reached even to the highest ivory-tower dweller. The urbane and gentle art expert described the plight of Salzburg, famous for its baroque architecture and its music festivals, conducted, as it were, just below the entrance to an ogre's den. Hitler's retreat at Berchtesgaden was a couple of miles up in the mountains, barely across the Austrian border, and now the Führer was summoning the statesmen of various small nations and setting forth his demands—which meant in every case that they should cease their resistance to Nazi agents who came in as tourists and occupied themselves with throwing the affairs of the country into turmoil. Every day Hitler felt himself stronger, and with each concession he wrung from others he was stronger yet.

When the two art lovers could no longer bear these painful thoughts, they played music. Zoltan was a violinist; no great artist like Hansi, but with a fine style of bowing and a lovely tone. He played the sort of music which corresponded to his gentle nature and delicate tastes. Lanny accompanied him, and it was just what he needed to soothe his hidden grief. They played early Italian arias by Tenaglia and Pergolesi, and the haunting cry, *Have Pity, O Lord* (*Pietà, Signor*), which is said to have been written by the tenor Stradella. After that they played the slow movement from the Mendelssohn concerto, and when the tears ran down Lanny's cheeks, he could exclaim: "Oh, how lovely!" without seeming affected or sentimental to his friend.

Before they parted, the American remarked: "By the way, Zoltan, do you happen to know anything about the Château de Belcour? I met someone who told me about interesting old French paintings there."

"I have never heard them mentioned," replied the other.

"The party I was talking to is no judge of art, but the descriptions sounded interesting, and I thought we might go some time and have a look."

"Do you know the owners?"

"I think I have met the Duc de Belcour; but I understand the place has been rented to Graf Herzenberg, who is connected with the German embassy."

"Not so good," said the Hungarian. "But if you like I'll make inquiry among some people who might know, and see what I can find out."

"Good, and I'll do the same. Be as quick as you can, because I have a deal that may take me to Valencia, and I'd better go before Franco gets any nearer."

"That's a pretty dangerous trip just now, Lanny."

"I suppose so, but people get afraid that their art treasures are going to be destroyed by bombs and they offer them at bargain prices. One of my American clients has been tempted by some of the things I described to him, and he's anxious for me to have a try at getting them out."

II

From there the investigator went to call on his Red uncle, tough old warrior of the class struggle, who had been the means of seducing the youthful Lanny away from the faith of his fathers, suggesting to him that *la belle France* was not the altogether admirable lady she had seemed. Jesse Blackless still lived in the tenement on Montmartre, among the humble people whose cause he had espoused; he had moved to an apartment on a lower floor, because the climbing of stairs was too hard on his heart. His faithful wife had given up her work in the Party offices and was helping him as secretary; with the class struggle intensifying, there were more speeches to be made, more documents to be filed, more funds to be raised.

Jesse hadn't seen his sister Beauty Budd in a long while, and Lanny told the news from his home on the Riviera and the one in Connecticut. Jesse, for his part, rarely had any news, except on that filthy subject of politics. He was even more contemptuous of it than Zoltan, for he knew its real insides; but somebody had to clean the Augean stables, and a third-rate portrait painter had made himself into a first-rate muckrake man. He had lost nearly all his hair, and his scalp, which had once been browned in Riviera sunshine, had been bleached in the close atmosphere of the Palais Bourbon, which housed the deputies of the French parliament. Député Zhess Block-léss, as the French called him, was wrinkled and lean, but his tongue was as sharp and active as a whiplash.

He had always talked freely to his nephew, who was not to be converted to the uncle's Communist Party line, but was a good listener and also a mine of information about the class which Jesse desired to "liquidate." Just now the deputy was especially stirred up, for the civil war in Paris appeared to be near the boiling point. The French Fascists were split among themselves by the ambitions of their rival leaders; and, said Uncle Jesse: "When thieves fall out, the Reds come into their own!" A story had come to the deputy's ears, and he was collecting evidence with the intention of blowing it wide in the Chambre. The Cagoulards, the "Hooded Men," who had been beating and murdering their opponents, were preparing their final coup to overthrow the French republic and set up a dictatorship of the Right. They had got arms from both Germany and Italy, and had them hidden in hundreds of places all over the land.

It was the Franco procedure all over again, and among the conspirators were Marshal Pétain, the hero of Verdun, and General Weygand, who had been Foch's chief of staff; also Chiappe, the Corsican head of the Paris police, and Doriot, former Communist leader said to have sold out his party and bought himself an estate in Belgium with money got from the Nazis. CSAR was the name of this group—*Comité pour Secret Action Révolutionnaire*—and their funds were coming not merely from abroad but from anti-labor forces in France, including the tire manufacturer Michelin, and Baron Schneider, the armaments king. Again the parallel with Spain; Franco having got his funds from Juan March, ex-smuggler who had become tobacco king of that country, and his guns and tanks and planes from Hitler and Mussolini.

Uncle Jesse said: "The de Bruynes ought to know a lot about all that. Can't you get them to talk and bring me their story?"

"Sure," said Lanny. "But for heaven's sake, don't mention my having been here. And by the way, Uncle Jesse, here's a story that may be of use to you. I have heard a report that the Nazis have a château not far from Paris, where they take people from the underground and hold them. Do you know anything about it?"

"I have heard such stories more than once, and I don't doubt them. Manifestly, the Nazis aren't going to let the underground operate without hindrance."

"The story I was told is quite specific. It has to do with the Château de Belcour, which has been leased by someone in the German embassy. The person who told me doesn't want it talked about at present, because he believes they have an important prisoner there, and if they are alarmed, they'll take the prisoner into Germany."

"I'll see what I can find out," replied the Red deputy.

"And one thing more," added his nephew; "I want to go to Valencia on a picture deal. Can you get the visa for me?"

"Any time you say," replied the uncle, who had close connections with the Spanish embassy in Paris because his party in Spain was collaborating in the national defense.

"Make it as soon as you can," said the nephew. "Things look bad there and later might be too late."

III

Next on Lanny's list was one of his oldest friends, Emily Chattersworth, châtelaine of the very grand estate known as Les Forêts. A childless woman, Emily had tried to find happiness in a career as *salonnière;* now her health was failing and she was sad, because in the rage of these times she saw the death of urbanity, dignity, even common honesty in that France which was her adopted home. She loved Lanny as a son, and he could never pass through Paris without driving out to see her. Old friends are a part of life's treasure—also old places, such as this château with an artificial lake behind it, and a lawn shaded by plane trees, where Anatole France had sat and discoursed upon the scandals of the long-dead sovereigns of his country. Inside was a drawing-room where Isadora Duncan had danced to Lanny's piano playing; also where Bessie Budd had fallen in love with the violin playing of Hansi Robin.

Emily now had snow-white hair and a slowing step; a stroll in her rose garden was all that she was equal to. She had invited two nieces from the Middle West to live with her, and both of them were fine young women whom Lanny might have invited to go for a drive with him; he was in the embarrassing position of being supposed to be "eligible" when he wasn't. What he did was to tell the three ladies the news he had collected in America and England and Paris, omitting for the most part the distressful subject of politics. He talked for a while about paintings and finally said: "By the way, Emily, do you know the Duc de Belcour?"

"He used to come to my salons, but I haven't seen him for years."

"I understand he has some paintings that he might like to get rid of. He has rented his estate, you know."

"I heard so—to some German."

"No doubt I can get Kurt to introduce me to the German; but first I'd like to make sure the comte approves my inspection."

"I don't know where he is now," said Emily; "but I'll give you a letter to him with pleasure."

"Thanks, darling," replied the art expert. It is convenient to know people who can introduce you to anybody in the great world. It is like having a large library at your disposal; you don't know everything that is in every book, but you know what book to go to.

As a matter of precaution he asked: "Can you tell me anything about his politics?"

"I haven't heard of late. He's *le vrai gratin*, so doubtless he's a Royalist."

"A Royalist these days can be anything from an intellectual bandit like Maurras to a devotee of the Church."

"Belcour was a reserved and proper little man. I cannot imagine him joining the *enragés*."

"Thanks again," said Lanny.

IV

His next duty was to call up Denis de Bruyne. He had promised Marie on her deathbed that he would help to guard and guide her boys —and little could that dear soul have dreamed the use he would make of the intimacy! Denis always invited him out to the château; he would call at Lanny's hotel on Friday afternoon and return him on Monday morning. On the way out they talked about the two families; Denis, a business associate of Robbie Budd and a heavy stockholder in the airplane enterprise, was interested to hear all news about the plant. The head of the family was nearing seventy; his spare frame erect and active, his white hair and little mustache always neatly trimmed, his manner that of a grave *père de famille*. The château was no more than a fair-sized villa, with lovely but unpretentious grounds. A long wall facing the south was covered by carefully trained grapevines and peach and apricot trees. The house was of red stone, and its furnishings had been handed down through half a dozen generations. The place had been one of Lanny's homes, and whenever he came here he lived over his happy years with Marie de Bruyne.

On the drive out, Denis imparted a strange item of news to his guest. He lowered his voice, even though there was a glass shield between him and the chauffeur, and though this chauffeur, the son of an old family servant, had been jokingly described as "the most conservative man in France." "You will find changes on the place," said the master. "I hope you won't be too greatly distressed."

"What are they?" asked the guest, who understood that all changes are distressing to a conservative Frenchman.

"We have felt it necessary to protect ourselves, and have erected a small fortification in the garden."

"Good God!" Lanny wanted to say; but he had learned to guard his tongue, and remarked: "Not for the *boches*, I suppose—but for the *canaille*?"

"Precisely," replied his host. "I have reason to feel sure that the present tension cannot continue much longer."

"But why should you think that troublemakers would pay any special attention to your home?"

"We have something in storage that they will surely be interested in."

"I see," said Lanny. There was nothing in this idea to startle him unduly, for there was a partly underground storage room at Bienvenu, once used as an ice-house, and ever since Lanny could remember Robbie had kept it full of machine guns, rifles, carbines, automatic pistols, and ammunition for all of them. Robbie had never had any idea of using these weapons, except for demonstrations; they were samples of what he had to sell, and he meant for people to use them a long way off, in China, South America, or the Balkans.

When they reached the château, Denis took his guest and showed him a perfect little "pillbox" of reinforced concrete with firing-slits on all sides. It stood on a knoll which commanded the rest of the estate and a valley slightly below it. Only the wall with the vines and fruit trees stood in the way, and Denis remarked, casually: "We shall have to blow that up, of course."

V

Lanny learned what this was all about when he met the sons at the family dinner table. Denis *fils*, now over thirty, had a gentle and well-bred wife who ran the household; they had three children, who had been taught to give Lanny the honorary title of "uncle." Charlot, two years younger, was an engineer, and had been put in charge of the technical side of a plant which his father had recently taken over; his wife and two little ones were also part of the household. Charlot was especially fond of his mother's former *ami*, considering him as his teacher in political and economic affairs. In fulfillment of his duties as a sort of foster father, Lanny had tried to awaken a social conscience in these two boys. As time passed, he had come to realize that he couldn't make them think as he thought, and that if he did so, he would be only breaking up their home life; so he had given up and let them travel their own way. But they had not forgotten his early attempts, and had the idea that they were applying the lessons in their own fashion. Of late years, since Lanny had decided to crawl "underground" and hide, he had assented to everything the de Bruynes had told him; so now he was, in their estimation, one of themselves.

The children had their supper earlier and apart, and the young wives listened while the men of the household discussed the state of public affairs. The franc was declining again, labor was seething with revolt, and *la patrie* was in dire straits. For all of it they held the "Reds" responsible; and by this term they meant anybody who expressed dissatisfaction with the existing economic system or proposed any change which would weaken the control of the country by the present owning class. More than any other person they blamed Léon Blum, the Jew, whose utopian dreams were a subtle camouflage for the scheme of that oriental race to seize the mastery of the world. "Better Hitler than Blum!" was the cry of the conservatives. They didn't really mean that, of course; they were just trying to say the worst possible about a Socialist vice-premier.

Frenchmen were going to keep their country French; they were going to preserve the Catholic religion, the institution of the family, and the private property system; they were going to teach the young to be loyal to *la patrie* and the ideals which made her great and kept her so. Because the democratic system put the ignorant mob in control and put the country at the mercy of venal unprincipled politicians, that system was accursed and must be abolished. The de Bruynes had put their faith in Colonel de la Roque, who had promised action. Because of Charlot's efforts at action as a member of the Croix de Feu, he bore an honorable scar across his face. But now, Lanny learned, they had lost faith in their former leader; he had yielded to the blandishments of the politicians and had pledged his organization to a fraudulent device known as *légalité*.

The de Bruynes were at the point of espousing the program of the Cagoulards, a sort of Ku Klux Klan of France. The noblest, the best names in the land had been enlisted in that cause; arms were being smuggled in from abroad—for since Blum had been able to put through his cunning scheme to nationalize the munitions industry, it was no longer so easy to get them from French factories. Depots were being established at strategic points all over the country; officers of the Army and especially of the Air Force were being won over, and *le jour* was being prepared. The Third Republic would be dumped into the dust-bin of history, the rascal politicians would be jailed, and a committee of responsible persons would restore order, stabilize the franc, and bring back prosperity to *la patrie*. Denis named the persons: Pétain, Weygand, Darlan, Chiappe, Doriot—the very same men whom Jesse Blackless had listed.

A few years ago Lanny would have said that his old friends had gone mad; but he had seen Hitler come, and after Hitler anything was pos-sible, even probable. What he said now was: "What will Hitler be do-ing while you are carrying out this program?"

"It will take only a few days," replied the eager Charlot, who talked more than he should, seeing that he was the youngest of the men. "No longer than it took Hitler to move back into the Rhineland."

The *père de famille* added: "We have very positive assurances that Hitler will find nothing to object to in our program. Why should he? He has said many times that he has no quarrel with France, except for the Russian alliance, which commits us to the anti-Nazi side, as well as to every evil that plagues our domestic life. It is either we or the Com-munists, and the decision cannot be delayed much longer. One more series of strikes, and the situation may get entirely out of hand; the Reds may have our factories and repeat everything they did in Russia."

"How soon will the concrete in your pillbox be set?" inquired Lanny of the young engineer. He meant it playfully, but the answer was given without a smile: "It was poured three weeks ago. That is enough time for safety."

VI

"Baron Schneider dines with us tomorrow," said Denis. "Do you know him?"

"He was in my home when I was a boy," replied Lanny, "but I don't suppose he would remember me. He knows my father, of course."

That was Schneider of Schneider-Creusot, famous throughout the world. Since Zaharoff had retired, he had taken over the title of munitions king of France. But not content with that high rank, he had aspired to be emperor. That was always the way, apparently; when you owned so much, why shouldn't you have the rest? The advantages of large-scale management were so obvious, and likewise the painfulness of letting somebody else get profits which might be yours. Baron Schneider of Schneider-Creusot was getting close to his end, but his hands itched as Zaharoff's had done and he could not keep them from reaching out and clutching at power.

"I think he expects to persuade me to join actively in his CSAR," remarked Denis.

"Doubtless he needs your moral support," responded Lanny, tactfully, and added: "He probably won't want me present."

"I'll tell him you're to be trusted. You of course understand the highly confidential nature of what we are discussing."

"*Cela va sans dire*," replied the American. He had a distaste for lying, and never told a whopper unless it was absolutely unavoidable. By way of a diversion he added, quickly: "I suppose it's all right if I tell Robbie."

"Of course," assented Denis. "Robbie is going to have to do something of the sort himself before long."

It was natural for Lanny to wish to know all about the great man he was to meet, so he asked questions about the Baron Charles Prosper Eugène Schneider, who had a German name but belonged to a family which had been in the business of manufacturing munitions in France for just about a hundred years. "As long as Budd Gunmakers," remarked the American. "Our family has lost its heritage, and I suppose the Baron feels that he has lost his." This was a reference to the recent nationalization procedure.

"He owns more plants outside of France than in, so he's in no danger of starvation."

"How many, do you suppose?"

"It must be over three hundred. He has formed a colossal holding company, the Union Européenne Industrielle et Financière." Denis himself had formed such a company, though on a far smaller scale; he went on to sing the praises of the cartel, as it was called—the "vertical trust," the greatest of all social inventions, according to the Frenchman. It was an institution which would continue from generation to generation, and give society the benefits of mass production without any of the risks incidental to the system of inheritance. "The managers will always be competent technical men, so it doesn't matter whether the owners know anything about the business or not. The owners can go off and get drunk if they want to."

"That seems helpful to everybody but the owners,"—so Lanny would have liked to say, but it was the sort of remark which he had learned to choke back into his throat. "Is Le Creusot the biggest of his plants?"

"I think Skoda, in Czechoslovakia, is bigger. It has been French policy to build up the defenses of the *cordon sanitaire*, to protect not merely France but all Western Europe against Bolshevism. Schneider has built great plants also in Poland."

"I always understood that Skoda belonged to Zaharoff," remarked Lanny.

"Zaharoff wanted to sell, and Schneider was ready to buy. You know how these great enterprises are built; it's purely a matter of having credit."

"Oh, don't I know it!" replied the son of Budd-Erling. "I went around with my father while he was raising the money for his start."

"Your father didn't keep enough for himself," commented one of the father's investors. "He should have started by getting control of some bank. That way, you get thousands of investors without the bother of going to call on them; they don't even know what they're investing in. That is what Schneider did, and you can be sure he kept a sufficient share for himself. He built up this huge cartel in the last thirty or forty years; the family business was comparatively small before that."

"Naturally he wants to hold on to it," remarked Lanny; to which his host replied: "*Vraiment.*"

VII

Baron Schneider of Schneider-Creusot proved to be a dapper and most elegant aristocrat in his late sixties. He wore a neat little white mustache, and had that feature which had struck Lanny about Zaharoff —a prominent nose, like an eagle's. Robbie had said: "It is used for smelling money." Like Zaharoff, the Baron was soft-spoken and mild of manner; no doubt, when he smelled money and was demanding it, he would scream, as the eagle does, and as Robbie had said Zaharoff would do. But Lanny had never heard Zaharoff scream, nor did he ever hear Schneider.

A munitions king was by virtue of his job the man of intrigue, the man who pulled wires behind the scenes of history, putting up the money to protect his properties both at home and abroad. Since this protection had to be intellectual and political as well as financial, Schneider had purchased *Le Temps* and *Le Journal des Débats*, the two newspapers of Paris most influential with those who governed Europe, and whom the Baron must persuade if he was to have his way. Since his business was on an international scale, his intrigues had to be the same. It was not enough for him to control the government of France; he had to make sure of those countries with which France was allied and for which he was providing magnificent new machinery for the manufacture of the machinery of killing. Having bought so many politicians in his day, the Baron could hardly be blamed for taking a cynical attitude to the breed; now, since they were refusing to stay bought, he could hardly be blamed if he had decided to get rid of them.

That was why he had come to have dinner at the Château de Bruyne on a Sunday evening; not because he was interested in the dinner, or impressed by a modest estate, but because Denis, who had begun by owning the taxicabs of Paris, had come into control of other enterprises, including a couple of banks. His sons were active rightists, and the Baron, being old, needed some who were young. He addressed Denis by that name and Denis called him Eugène. He was embarrassed to find a stranger present, and directed his conversation to this stranger, giving him an opportunity to reveal his point of view. Lanny, knowing the ways of the world, took occasion to say: "I believe you know Emily Chattersworth, who has been a sort of godmother to me."

Yes, indeed, the Baron knew this leader of the Franco-American colony, and how during the World War she had taken leadership in aiding the French *blessés*. Denis, who also knew the ways of the world, mentioned that Lanny had had unusual opportunities to know both Adolf Hitler and General Göring personally. The Baron was quick to reveal his interest, so Lanny explained how in boyhood he had been a guest at Schloss Stubendorf, and had come to know a young German who had been one of "Adi's" earliest converts and had visited him in prison after the *Bierkeller Putsch* in Munich. Thus Lanny had been taken several times to meet the Führer of National Socialism; the last time he had seen him was at Berchtesgaden two years ago.

The Baron warmed up quickly. He had sent emissaries to both Hitler and Göring, it turned out, but what they had brought was of necessity formal stuff; they had met the Führer and the Chief of the Luftwaffe on dress parade, as it were. Schneider wanted to know what sort of men they really were, their private lives, their weaknesses, and possible ways to reach and influence them. Evidently the new munitions king of Europe looked upon the son of Budd-Erling as something of a "find"; he occupied most of the time at dinner in drawing him out on the subject of the National Socialist German Workingmen's Party and what it meant to France.

What was Lanny to say? He might have stated flatly: "In my opinion the Führer is definitely psychopathic. His whole being is dominated by irrational phobias. First of all he hates the Jews, and after that come the Russians, then the Poles, then, I think, the French. It may be the Czechs come ahead of you, I'm not sure. He has said in his book that the annihilation of France is essential to the safety of Germany, and there can be no doubt he means it; he didn't mind saying it, because he has a sort of double cynicism: he tells the truth in the certainty that that is the last thing anybody will expect or believe. He is infinitely cunning, and will make you any promise, for the reason that no promise means anything to him. He has only one faith and one idea in the world, and that is the Germans as the master race, destined to conquer the world under himself as the inspired Führer. That is the magnetic pole to which his being turns, and the one thing you can count upon in dealing with him."

That was the truth, but it was surely not what the munitions king wanted to hear. Was Lanny there to convert him? *Could* Lanny have converted him? It seemed most unlikely. If Lanny had said it, the Baron would have made up his mind that the American guest was some kind of Red or near it. He would have dropped the conversation, and after dinner would have requested the opportunity to talk privately with Denis; Lanny wouldn't have heard a word of the things he wanted to hear, and as a presidential agent he would have been the world's worst flop.

So, following his usual practice of telling no falsehood where it could be avoided, he explained that "Adi" was a complex personality, highly emotional, and that his actions were difficult to predict. He had written bitterly about France, but had shown in other cases that he could change his policy when his interests required it. In Berchtesgaden he had assured Lanny that he desired friendship with France, and that the only thing which stood in the way was the treasonable alliance with Russia.

"*Précisément!*" exclaimed the Baron. "We may find Hitler hard to trust—but surely not so hard as Stalin!"

"*Malheureusement*, I have not had opportunity to know Stalin," replied Lanny. He said this with his best smile, and the young de Bruynes helped him out by laughing as if it were an excellent *mot*.

VIII

So now the son of Budd-Erling was not merely a left-handed member of the de Bruyne family, but also of the Cagoulards, the "Hooded Men." When the meal was over they adjourned to the library, where the ladies tactfully refrained from coming, and for two or three hours the five gentlemen discussed the state of Europe and the part which France was playing and about to play therein. First in their thoughts was Spain, which the Reds were trying to get into their clutches.

"I had occasion to be in Seville last spring," remarked Lanny, "and to visit General Aguilar, just returned from the Jarama front. He was quite sure the Reds would not be able to hold out beyond the end of this year."

"They have all been free with their promises," responded the Baron. "The Reds can hold out so long as they are allowed to get arms from Russia; and it is going to bankrupt us all if it is allowed to continue. Ten billion francs is my guess at the amount of the bill."

Lanny wanted to be sympathetic with the so-nearly impoverished armaments maker, but he was afraid of sounding sarcastic. He managed to think of something apposite: "It is too bad that Zaharoff had to die before he saw this victory. He told me he was contributing his quota."

"Basil was inclined to be optimistic when telling about himself," remarked Eugène, dryly. "I can assure you from personal knowledge that he set his own quota, and the rest of us thought it was far from adequate."

Lanny smiled again. "The old gentleman always pleaded poverty; you would have thought he was on the verge of actual hunger. He became one of my father's heaviest investors, but I personally never had any sort of business dealings with him, so we were able to remain friends. He even came to see me after he was dead."

Naturally, the Baron looked startled and Lanny felt it was permissible to laugh. "You may have heard that Sir Basil used to visit spirit mediums, in the hope of receiving communications from his deceased wife. I happened to know one such medium, and in a séance she reported that the spirit of Sir Basil was present, and was crying for his duquesa, but couldn't find her because she was 'twice dead,' whatever that could mean. It was the first news I had had of the old gentleman's passing, which had taken place a few hours previously; so naturally I was startled."

"It is strange how those things happen," commented the old gentleman's successor.

IX

However, Baron Schneider hadn't come there to learn about spiritualism. He had come to plan for a repetition of the Spanish coup, but with more finesse and better management, so that civil war could be avoided, and *la patrie* might become an equal partner of the German Führer, instead of a vassal, as Spain was bound to be. The Baron was emphatic about that; he had received assurances on it and talked freely about the program. It was a most respectable conspiracy; the names involved were literally holy, since they included high dignitaries of the Catholic Church, whose publications, all the way between Warsaw and Brooklyn, were repeating stories about Spanish nuns having been soaked in oil and burned by the Spanish Reds. The name of Marshal Pétain was the most honored in the French army, and that of Admiral Darlan in the navy. There were a score of other high generals and naval officers involved, to say nothing of politicians, including ex-Premier Laval. Schneider called the roll, because he had come to enlist the de Bruynes and to have the *père de famille* promise an adequate "quota" without having to be asked for it.

There was one question which Lanny wanted to have answered; the most delicate of questions, to be approached with infinite tact. "Permit me to venture a suggestion, Baron Schneider. It happens that the piano virtuoso and composer Kurt Meissner is one of my oldest friends; in fact, he lived in my home on the Riviera for many years after the war, and is accustomed to say that he owes his career to the support which my family gave him. He has been in Paris for some time, and I have reason to feel sure that he would be interested in what you are now planning."

Lanny was aware that this statement would appear naïve to the great man, and he wanted it to be just that. Said the Baron: "I thank you, M. Budd; it so happens that I enjoy the honor of Herr Meissner's acquaintance. He has given me valuable help in the organizing of our Comité France-Allemagne."

"What I have in mind," continued the double-dyed intriguer, "is that

Kurt is one of the Führer's intimate friends, plays music for him frequently and enjoys his confidence. He would be the best of persons to put your proposals before Hitler and to explain your point of view."

"Your suggestion is excellent, M. Budd, and I am indebted to you for it."

The other continued: "I hope I am not intruding, Baron,"—knowing, of course, that the Baron would be forced to say that he wasn't. "The subject is delicate, and I am merely making suggestions, to which you need not feel compelled to reply. I realize that Hitler has even more reason to desire a change of government in France than in Spain, for France is his neighbor, and is extending credits to Russia, his one permanent enemy. If Hitler is finding it worth while to put up billions of francs to support General Franco, it seems to me he would be financially interested, as a cold business proposition, in securing a government in France which would promise to seal the Spanish border and stop the present flow of supplies to the Reds. Wouldn't it seem so to you, monsieur le Baron?"

Eugène Schneider's keen dark eyes were fixed intently upon this presumptuous American's, as if he were reading every one of the thoughts written upon the mental scroll behind them. Lanny knew that trick well, and knew that a skillful rascal must meet the gaze with one equally firm. At last the munitions king replied: "M. Budd, the subject is, as you say, one of great delicacy. I can only tell you that that aspect of the matter has received our careful consideration."

"I respect your reticence, Baron. I am told that the decline of Doriot's influence is due to the fact that he has been accused of receiving German funds, and has apparently not felt in position to deny it. All I wish to say is that I have known Kurt Meissner since boyhood, and there is a certain warmth of intimacy one attains then that can never be entirely reproduced in later life. Let me tell you, in the strictest confidence, that Kurt was a secret agent of the *Generalstab*, operating in Paris at the time of the Peace Conference. Prior to that he had been an artillery officer, and was wounded, and lost his wife and baby because of war privations; so you can understand that it is difficult for him to love the French. He came into Paris in civilian clothes on a false passport, and as it was still wartime, he would surely have been shot by your police, who were on his trail. My mother helped me to smuggle him into Spain and thus saved his life, something which Kurt has acknowledged many times. I tell you all this so that you may understand why he would trust me more than he could ever bring himself to trust any Frenchman."

"Your story is most interesting, M. Budd."

"What I have in mind to say is that if the suggestion meets with your approval, I should be happy to talk over with Kurt the plans we have been discussing tonight and to bring you his reactions and advice."

The cautious magnate turned to his host. Having been a member of the *haut monde* of Paris all his life, the Baron was no stranger to the practice of *la vie à trois*, and must have heard rumors as to the situation in the de Bruyne household years ago. *"Eh bien, Denis?"*

Said the *père de famille:* "I could not think of a better method of procedure."

"You understand, M. Budd," said the other, "you are dealing with the most inviolable secret of our movement. The political life of all of us depends upon its being preserved religiously."

"You do not have to tell me anything about that, Baron," replied Lanny—again avoiding an outright lie. "I have lived the greater part of my life in France, and I understand your political relationships fairly well. Also I have enjoyed the confidence of a number of your statesmen, and have never betrayed it."

X

Lanny's first action on returning to his hotel was to call Kurt Meissner's apartment. He hadn't seen Kurt for more than a year, and the composer's pleasure when he heard his friend's voice seemed unfeigned. "Come to lunch," he said, and Lanny replied: "Sure thing."

The presidential agent sat at his little portable and typed out a detailed account of the Cagoulard conspiracy to overthrow the French republic. He didn't say how he had got this information, but he wrote: "This is first-hand and positive." He gave the names of the persons involved and the program, signed it "103," addressed it to Gus Gennerich, and put it into the mail.

To himself he said: "F.D. won't believe it." But of course Lanny couldn't help that; it was his fate to be living in a time when so many things were unbelievable, even after they had happened.

Kurt lived in a fashionable apartment, suitable to his station in the musical world. He had a man-servant to wait on him, a shaven-headed Silesian who had fought under him all through the war and still kept military discipline; the man probably added spying to his other duties, and Lanny got the impression that he disapproved of having foreigners around. Even when Lanny talked about his visit to the Führer, Willi Habicht refused to relent; perhaps he thought the Führer oughtn't to

keep such company. Or perhaps it was just that the servant was naturally glum, the result of having fought victoriously for four long years,
and then discovering at the very last moment that he was unaccount-
ably licked.

Also there was a secretary in the apartment, a Nordic blond young
lady, a devoted Nazi, brisk and efficient. Lanny was left with little
doubt concerning her double role in the household. Kurt had a wife
and several children at home, and now and then went back and begot
another. In the old days he would have considered it his duty to be true
to that wife, but now there was a new *Weltanschauung*. The Nazi
world was a man's world, and the first duty of woman was to submit.
Kurt's superiors would undoubtedly see to it that he had a trustworthy
German companion, so that he might be proof against the wiles of se-
ductive enemy ladies. No Mata Haris this time; at least, not working on
the Germans! Perhaps also—who could say?—it might be one of the
duties of Ilse Vetter to check on Kurt's activities and report now and
then.

If so, she could have nothing but good to say; for Kurt was competent, he had the best connections, and he was laboring with single-
minded devotion to break down the intellectual and moral defenses of
Marianne and bring her into the orbit of the New Order. So true was
this that Lanny had come to find his boyhood chum quite intolerable;
that long lean face which he had once found grave and even priestlike
now seemed to him fanatical, touched with madness. The phrases of
abstract philosophy and ethics with which Kurt had so impressed
Lanny in his boyhood now sounded hollow to his ears; for of course
there could be no general or universal truth in the mind of any devotee
of National Socialism. For him the good, the true, and the beautiful
were limited to Germany and Germans, and for other peoples and individuals the words were a fraud and a snare. Perhaps in the deeps of his
heart Kurt might still have affectionate memories of the little American boy whom he had undertaken to inspire and guide; but if so, he
would regard those feelings as a form of weakness to be repressed.
Lanny, like everybody else both inside and outside Germany, would
be used for the furtherance of Adolf Hitler's dream of glory, and every
word that Kurt spoke and every attitude he assumed to the son of
Budd-Erling would be for some carefully studied purpose.

All right, since that was the game, Lanny would learn to play it. He
would keep his friendship with a respected German musician, and
speak no word to him that did not have some carefully studied purpose. For many years Lanny had never voiced his real ideas on political

and economic subjects in Kurt's presence. He had made a cautious withdrawal from the field, saying that he realized he was out of place there; he had become an art expert, in Kurt's eyes a money-making art dealer; he had become a dilettante in all the arts, and if Kurt chose to assume that he was playing around with ladies such as the Countess of Sandhaven, that was Kurt's privilege and did Lanny no harm.

In recent years the playboy had been dropping hints that he was following along the path of least resistance, and being impressed by the phenomenal success of Adi Schicklgruber—but of course never calling him by that humiliating name. Adi, the former army *Gefreite* and dere-lict painter of picture postcards, had become not merely the master of Germany but the master politician of Europe. He had compelled all the world to talk about him, to heed his words, and to tremble at his frequent rages; he had sent his armies into the Rhineland and now had it securely fortified; he had restored conscription in Germany and was now militarizing the entire Fatherland. He had got away with both these dangerous moves, in spite of all the threats of his enemies and the fears of his own General Staff. Wonderful man! A twentieth-century Napoleon! If Lanny was impressed, that was a part of his role as a weakling, and if Kurt looked down upon him for it, that was what all Nazis did to all the rest of the world.

XI

During the luncheon with Kurt and Fräulein Vetter, Lanny told the news of his mother and father, and of Rosemary and her paintings. He told about his last trip into Spain, saying nothing about Alfy, but mak-ing it a picture-buying expedition, in course of which he had met many of Franco's officers and witnessed the triumphs of Franco's arms. That he should have been thrilled by them was a proper role for an American playboy. General Franco's class was Lanny's class, and Lanny had slipped back into his proper place in society.

Afterwards, alone with Kurt in the study, and with the secretary's typewriter clicking busily in the next room, Lanny opened his mind completely and revealed the changes which had been taking place in it. Kurt had been right all along, and Lanny had been blundering for the greater part of his life. Kurt had been right about the Versailles Treaty, he had been right about reparations and the cruel inflation which had been forced upon Germany; about the *Schieber* and the Jews, and above all about Adolf Hitler, from the first time they had heard him speak in Munich. Lanny had trusted the Reds, and had found that they were unworthy of his trust; he had hoped for some sort of humane social order in France, but had come to realize that the French democracy was hopelessly corrupt, that the Russian alliance was a device of political rascality, and that the only hope for the French people lay in co-operating with the New Order which Adolf Hitler was successfully constructing.

Of course Kurt was pleased. He said that he had been deeply wounded by the separation from Lanny, who had been like a brother to him in past times. He clasped Lanny's hand, and said that this news had restored his youth to him; he said: "My family will be happy; Heinrich Jung will be happy; the Führer will be happiest of all!"

Did Kurt mean all that? And would he continue to feel that way after he had had time to think matters over? Lanny could never be sure on this point. It was obvious that Kurt would have acted this way, whether or not he believed in his old friend's sincerity. He had probably long ago passed the stage where he gave full faith to anybody, or to anything that anybody said. He would watch his old friend and weigh the chances for and against; Lanny would do the same, and they would continue their intimacy so long as it served the purposes of both.

XII

The time had come for Lanny to reveal the business which had brought him here. He had, he said, news which he thought would be of special interest to Kurt. Last evening he had been in conference with Baron Schneider at the home of the de Bruynes. Kurt knew all four of these persons, but now he pretended to have had no idea that they were engaged in a conspiracy to overthrow the government of their country. A most extraordinary thing! A proof of the decadence which prevailed in France! "I always told you that, Lanny. It was the reason I couldn't bear to live any longer on the Riviera, in spite of all your dear mother's kindness."

"Again you were right, Kurt! That world was falling to pieces."

"Do you mind if I make notes?" Kurt asked; and when Lanny consented, he jotted down the names of all the army and navy officers who were in command of the "Hooded Men," and the great manufacturers and landowners and bankers who were putting up the money to pay for the hidden stores of arms. Lanny wasn't naïve enough to believe that all this was really news to the German; Lanny's guess was that Kurt was riding in the very center of this whirlwind, perhaps even directing it. But Kurt would be glad to check his information by so high-up an authority as the munitions king of France, Czechoslovakia, Poland, Belgium, and other countries. Every detail was important; and of course it was good to know that poor blundering Lanny Budd had at last seen a glimmer of the light. No doubt that he could be made use of, though of course not in the ways he naïvely supposed.

Lanny went on to explain his bright idea. "If it has been worth while for the Führer to put up so much money for Spain, he might wish to do the same for France, and make sure of success at the outset. Of course I understand that you may not feel free to discuss such matters with me, and I'm not suggesting that you should. I told the Baron I would take the matter up with you, and report what you said if you wanted me to—though of course there's no reason why you shouldn't get in touch with him direct. If you send anybody else, you'll have to vouch for him, because a man like Schneider doesn't talk unless he's perfectly sure about the person's credentials. I doubt if he'd have talked before me if he hadn't known my father and if the de Bruynes hadn't vouched for me."

Very tactful of the American, but at the same time a trifle self-important; telling Kurt how to handle his most secret negotiations; taking it for granted that Kurt was engaged in such affairs, something which Kurt had never admitted to Lanny, or to anybody but fellow-members of the service. In short, something of what the Americans call "a buttinski," and the Germans *ein zudringlicher Geselle*.

But of course Kurt would take pains not to let Lanny see any trace of such feelings. He would be deeply grateful and assure an American playboy that his revelations were of the utmost importance; however, Kurt could do nothing but pass them on to the authorities in Berlin who handled such matters. He would promise not to mention Lanny in the report, and if Lanny got any further information he could be sure that Kurt would be grateful and would deal with it in the same ultra-confidential way.

From all this Lanny learned that Kurt wasn't going to trust him, but just use him. Kurt wasn't even going to admit in plain words that he was a Nazi agent! All right; Lanny was keeping his secrets also. It would be a duel of wits, and let the best set win.

"By the way, Kurt," said the art expert, "there is a favor you can do me. Do you know Graf Herzenberg?"

"I know him fairly well."

"I'm told he's connected with the embassy. He has leased the Château de Belcour, and I'm told there are some interesting old French paintings in it. Have you been in it?"

"Many times. I noticed some paintings but didn't pay any special attention to them."

"Emily has given me a letter to the Duc de Belcour, and I've no doubt he'll be willing for me to view them; but of course it will have to be subject to the Graf's approval."

"I'll speak to him about it, if you like."

"As soon as possible, please. I have to go into Spain again, to see some paintings there."

Said Kurt, as if the idea had occurred to him for the first time: "You do really know quite a lot about painting, don't you, Lanny?"

"Some people gamble their money upon it," replied his friend. "And that includes the commander of your Air Force!"

6

Blondel Song

I

WHY was Lanny Budd taking so much trouble to get inside the Château de Belcour? He asked himself the question many times without finding an entirely satisfactory answer. His head told him that Trudi probably wasn't there; but on the other hand, his heart told him that she must have been there; they surely wouldn't have two prisons near Paris. Said head: "If she is still alive, she is in Germany by now." Said heart: "I want to see the place where she was." Said head, with a trace of mockery: "Do you want to sing a song outside her dungeon, like Blondel, the minstrel of King Richard the Lionhearted?" Heart replied: "I went and looked at the old palace where they had Alfy, and I found a way to get him out. Perhaps I might do it again." In the most vital of men's concerns, heart usually wins over head, and this is reprobated by a school of philosophers who call themselves realists, materialists, monists; on the other hand it is sanctioned by another school who call themselves idealists, Platonists, mystics.

The mail brought Lanny a note from the secretary of the Duc de Belcour, saying that so far as Monsieur le Duc was concerned it would be entirely agreeable for M. Budd to inspect the paintings, but that the decision necessarily rested with the occupant. A few hours later Kurt called up, to report that he had made an appointment for Lanny to visit the château at three o'clock the following afternoon. Lanny thanked him cordially, and called Zoltan, who with his customary efficiency had got a lot of information about the art contents of the building. He retailed this to his friend, but said that unfortunately he had an appointment for the hour Kurt had set. This suited Lanny, who couldn't foresee what situations might arise and might have a hard time explaining them to Zoltan.

Five minutes before the appointed hour, Lanny's automobile halted before the entrance to these very splendid grounds. He gave his name to the porter who, he observed, was a German. The gates swung back, and he drove between two rows of ancient beech trees. In the back seat of his car lay Trudi Schultz, bound and gagged; at least, so Lanny visioned her. His head said: "Perhaps!" and his heart said: "Oh, God!"

The building was of gray granite, four stories in height and quite extensive; it had been built by a cousin of Louis Seize for his favorite mistress, and had to be big enough so that royal personages could be entertained there. It had towers and crenelations suitable to a castle, but its windows were wide for comfort; at that time artillery had made stone walls hopelessly vulnerable, and noble gentlemen and ladies had learned to rely for their security upon the majesty of the kings of France. Now the driveway was paved with asphalt, and motorcars instead of gilded coaches waited in the wide curving spaces.

II

Promptly on the hour Lanny ascended the steps, and the door was opened before he knocked. A German in livery took his name and led him to a high-ceilinged French drawing-room with elaborate frescos and gilding. In front of Lanny's eyes was a Largillière, and he didn't wait for any invitation to begin his art-experting. One eye surveyed a lady of two hundred years ago, having a tower of hair on her head like a Chinese pagoda, her bosom and arms smooth-shining and white, while voluminous folds of cerise silk encased the rest of her. Lanny's other eye was on the door, through which he expected a more modern costume to appear.

It came; a young Schutzstaffel officer, all in shiny black boots and belt, and with the death's head insignia on his sleeve. The instant he appeared Lanny swung about, clicked his heels, threw up his arm with fingers of the hand extended, and snapped out: "*Heil Hitler!*" The young officer could hardly have expected this, but his response was obligatory and automatic: he halted and returned the salute. Then he said: "Herr Budd?"

Lanny replied: "*Lanning Prescott Budd, Kunstsachverständiger seiner Exzellenz des Herrn Minister-Präsident General Hermann Göring.*"

The Germans love to string titles like beads on a necklace, and they like to put long words together to make what small boys in frivolous America call "jawbreakers." The title which Lanny had conferred upon himself was no more than "art expert"—but how much more honorific and impressive it sounded! It took all the starch out of the young Nazi's collar, and he said, lamely: "*Leutnant Rörich gestattet sich vorzustellen.*"

"*Sehr erfreut, Herr Leutnant,*" replied Lanny. The man appeared to be in his early twenties, and had a round, rather naïve face and closely clipped yellow hair. Lanny's heart cried: "You have been beating Trudi!" His head advised: "No, he wouldn't do menial work; he would direct the rank and file and make sure they did a thorough job."

Employing his very best Berlinese, Lanny explained that he was an old friend of the second-in-command of Germany, and for years had been aiding in the disposition of certain of the General's paintings and the acquisition of others more suited to a great man's increasing honors. At present Lanny had in mind a project to be put before the General for the setting up of a museum of art works illustrating the development of the various European cultures; he was preparing a list of examples suitable for such a grandiose undertaking. Had the Herr Leutnant himself made any study of the subject of historical painting? The Herr Leutnant modestly confessed that he knew very little about it, and Lanny set out to remedy his deficiencies. Each time they stopped before a new work the expert would give his appropriate *Spruch*. Zoltan had given him the names of the painters, and he had refreshed his memory by the reference works in his suite; the same for the château, which was in the guidebooks, with all the dates and information about the Belcour family.

Lanny really looked at the paintings, and formed opinions about them, and expressed competent judgments; but every now and then a part of his brain would be swept by a storm. He would be thinking: "You had her in a dungeon, perhaps under this very spot; and did you violate her yourself. or is that also something you delegate to your *Gemeinen?*" Heart said: "*Nazi Schweinehund!*" Head said: "Perhaps he has taken a fancy to her and is keeping her here indefinitely."

Now and then the lecturer would find some modern simile or allusion and thus lead his discourse away from historic times. Was it a battle scene, with artillery thundering? He would remark: "How startlingly fashions in war have changed! Nowadays you wouldn't stand much chance with a cannon like that." The young officer assented, and Lanny began foretelling that the fighting would be forced into the air; this gave him a chance to mention that his father was Budd-Erling Aircraft, and had leased many of his patents to General Göring, being favored in return with the secrets of the newest Messerschmitts and Focke-Wulfs. Lanny himself had shot stags with the General, and had visited Karinhall, and met the Frau Minister-Präsident General, who was Emmy Sonnemann, the stage star, whom no doubt the Herr Leutnant had seen many times.

"*Ja, gewiss,*" said the Herr Leutnant, and found this conversation most exhilarating.

Or was it a painting by a Spaniard? Lanny had just come from Franco Spain; he had traveled with his brother-in-law, Il Capitano Vittorio di San Girolamo, an officer in the Italian Air Force who had lost an arm in the fighting in Abyssinia. The Italians hadn't shown up so well in Spain, alas; they were having to call on General Göring for more and more help. In the judgment of Lanny's father there was no organization in all the world so efficient as the German Air Force. The founder of Budd-Erling had been taken by Seine Exzellenz to visit Kladow, the new secret air-training base, and had raved about the sights he had seen there. The humble Schutzstaffel officer, who had been prepared to be bored by a culture-seeking American tourist, found himself being lifted up from one Nazi heaven to the next. *Kolossal!*

III

Presently they came to a painting of a wounded soldier with his head in a woman's lap. Said the *Kunstsachverständiger:* "That reminds me of a work by my former stepfather, who was the famous French painter Marcel Detaze. Do you know his work, by any chance?" When the officer had to confess that he didn't, Lanny rattled on: "The Führer is a great admirer of his, and asked me to send him an example. I was giving an exhibition of my stepfather's work in Munich three years ago, and Kurt Meissner, the *Komponist*—you know Kurt, perhaps?"

Ja, the Herr Leutnant was glad to be able to say at last that he had met one of the many distinguished Germans whom this extraordinary American knew intimately.

"Kurt is one of my oldest friends. I visited Schloss Stubendorf the Christmas before the war broke out and ruined Europe. Kurt is the cause of my having met the Führer so early—we went to hear him speak soon after he came out of prison, back in the old days. I didn't become converted at the outset—I used to think I was something of a Socialist at that time."

"We are all Socialists now, Herr Budd," reminded the other; "National Socialists."

"Of course," assented Lanny; "but I had got hold of the wrong kind. Then I visited the Führer in Berlin and he explained matters to me in that marvelous way he has.—But I was telling you about the painting. It is called *Sister of Mercy*, and Kurt and I and Heinrich Jung took it to the Führer at the Braune Haus in Munich. You have been in the Braune Haus?"

"*Nein, Herr Budd, ich bin ein Rheinländer.*"

"*Ach, so?*"—and Lanny talked about that most beautiful country of grapes and old castles, and about Herr Reichsminster Doktor Josef Goebbels, who was from that region, and about the Frau Reichsminster Magda Goebbels and their home and their brilliant conversation. Then he laughed, and reminded himself that he was supposed to be telling about the Braune Haus in Munich; he described the elegant building, which was the Führer's own design; also the Führer's study and its decorations, and how the Führer had admired the *Sister of Mercy*—he had extremely fine taste in art, had been a painter himself and would have liked to be nothing else, so he had assured Lanny; but, alas, the German people had demanded his services and he had been unable to think about his own pleasure.

The Führer had talked with amazing knowledge about French painting techniques—this wasn't true, but Lanny was sure it could do no harm to pile it on extra thick. The Führer had spoken feelingly of his respect for French culture, and his desire that this great people should be reconciled to Germany. All that was needed was the reorienting of French policy, the breaking off of the atrocious alliance with Jewish-Bolshevism.

"That was three years ago," said the art expert, "and you can see the marvelous prescience of the man. Right now the French are beginning to realize the monstrous nature of their blunder. There is a movement under way to change the government of this country suddenly and completely. You can take it from me that it won't be many months before you see the Russian alliance repudiated and a German alliance formed, one that will last for a thousand years—just as the Führer said to me in Berchtesgaden."

For an hour or two the young Schutzstaffel officer had listened to a foreigner ask him if he knew this and that, and most of the time he had had to answer a humiliating No. But here was something about which he was informed, and he said: "I think I know what you mean, Herr Budd. I suppose that you are actively interested in that movement."

"Indeed, yes," replied Lanny; "with everything I have, heart and mind and purse." Then, as if he had committed an indiscretion, he came back to a painting on the wall. "Here we have a David, a later and quite different style from Boucher and Fragonard. He painted charming ladies, as you see; but he became a revolutionist, and did revolutionary scenes, terrible pictures—but no doubt General Göring would wish to have samples, if only as a warning to your German people. All the miseries and corruptions from which France suffers now date from that blind upsurgence of the rabble, which was able to overthrow its rulers by means of pikes and pitchforks, but was not able to keep the control from passing into the hands of Jewish moneylenders and speculators. You agree with that interpretation of French history, Herr Leutnant?"

"*Absolut, Herr Budd.*"

"I am talking too much, I fear——"

"Oh, not at all, I assure you; I have never listened to more instructive conversation."

"I always find myself moved when I come into one of these old buildings. This château, you know, fell into the hands of the revolutionists. Very often they burned the buildings; but somebody had the more sensible idea of turning this one into a revolutionary headquarters. You can imagine the scenes which went on here; the mob of peasants and village people marching in, singing their furious songs, with the bloody heads of their victims on pikes. Probably they broke into the winecellars and got royally drunk—you have winecellars in this château, Herr Leutnant?"

"Yes, of course."

"I suppose you have dungeons, also?"

"There are small rooms in the cellar which may have been used for that purpose."

"With rings set in the masonry, to which prisoners could be chained?"

"I have never looked for them, Herr Budd."

"One sometimes makes gruesome discoveries in these old places. Perhaps it might interest you to go down there with me some day, and see what we could find." The lecturer dropped a hint like that, and then skipped quickly away from what might have been a dangerous subject. He would come back to it later.

IV

They came to the music room, and in one corner was a tiny instrument of French walnut, elaborately carved and inlaid. "Ah, look—*une épinette!*" exclaimed Lanny. "We wouldn't get much music out of it, but doubtless it is priceless as an antique. We have seen in music the same evolution as in war, Herr Leutnant." There was a stool before the instrument, and Lanny said: "Shall I try it?"

He seated himself, raised the cover, and lightly touched the keys. Little tinny tinkling sounds came forth, and Lanny said: "That is what our great-grandfathers' grandfathers considered music. Yet a good many of Mozart's finest works were composed for such—I have seen the little clavichord on which he learned to play, in the humble apartment in Salzburg where he was born."

Lanny played a snatch from a Mozart piano sonata; then he rose and walked across the room to a fine modern French instrument, a grand piano, and seated himself there. He put on the loud pedal and struck the chords, and thunder rolled forth. He played the *Horst Wessel Lied*, the marching song of the Nazis, written by a Berlin Stormtrooper, said to have been a pimp. It has a fine stirring rhythm, and Lanny could be sure that Herr Leutnant Rörich had been brought up on it. Judging by his looks, he had been a youth when his party took power, and his present confidential position indicated that he must have come into the Hitlerjugend as a boy. *Die Strasse frei den braunen Bataillonen*—it was a prophecy which had come true, for when the song was written it was the Reds who had possession of the German streets, and now the last one of them was dead or in a concentration camp. It was a marching tune that would stir anybody's blood, regardless of what he might think of the words.

Lanny stopped and turned to his escort. "*Das klingt besser, nicht wahr, Herr Leutnant?*"—and the other replied: "*Viel besser, gewiss.*"

"Am I taking too much of your time?" inquired the visitor, graciously. "Oh, by no means."

Lanny turned again to the piano, saying: "Let me play you one of the tunes which once rang out in these elegant rooms." Again he pressed the loud pedal and played with vigor another marching tune that would stir anybody's blood, regardless of what he thought of the words. *"Ah, ça ira, ça ira, ça ira!"*—meaning three times over that it is going to go, or to be gone through with, the job is going to be done. In this case the job was to cart the aristocrats "to the lanterns" and hang them from the chains stretched across the streets of French towns. The accent falls on the "a" of *ira,* and when a French revolutionist sang it he hissed and spit it out with hatred to be matched only by the Nazis proclaiming that Jewish blood would spurt from the knife. Alas for the many times the threats of both songs had been made good!

"I don't suppose you ever heard that tune," remarked Lanny, as he rose from the piano. "That is what the mob was singing when it took this château. Have you examined the walls and floors to see if there are traces of aristocratic blood?"

Unspoken in the visitor's mind were far different thoughts. "What are the floors of this château made of? Surely those loud sounds would go through them. Certainly, if Trudi is there, and heard the *Ça irā,* she will know I am here, for she will be sure it would never be played by Nazis. She remembers how I sang it, with comical fierceness. She knows the story of Blondel, too, and will understand that I am sending her a message."

But strange to say, the Trudi-ghost was failing to appreciate this effort on her behalf. What she was saying now was: "Go to Spain and find Monck, and get in touch with the underground again."

V

To his escort Lanny remarked: "It might be the part of wisdom, Herr Leutnant, not to talk too freely about the possible interest of General Göring in these paintings. You know how the French are, a mercenary people, and whenever I ask for a price on any painting, I always have to keep the name of my client a secret."

"I understand, Herr Budd."

"Some day, I doubt not, the commander of the German Air Force may be in a position to compel a reduction in the price of French paintings; but that may be several years yet, I imagine." Glancing at the young officer, Lanny did not do anything so vulgar as to wink; he gave a sly smile, and the other said: *"Jawohl, mein Herr!"*

They had completed the round of the *rez-de-chaussée,* and the escort remarked: "There are paintings in some of the upstairs rooms also, but they are small and I doubt if they are important."

"Probably not," assented the expert. "I am acquainted with an American department-store proprietor in London who has Rembrandts in his bedrooms, but the French are more frugal. However, there is still a favor you may do me, if your patience is not exhausted."

"Surely not, Herr Budd."

"I am interested in this building, as an example of the development in French architecture. We observe in all architecture a gradual process of departure from reality, very interesting to the student of social customs. Some feature originates in a mechanical or historical necessity, and then it becomes accepted and conventionalized, and is continued for centuries after its original purpose has been forgotten. Once upon a time, you know, a château was a fortress, built for defense and compelled to be on the alert day and night. Then, in course of time that strain was relaxed, but a château still had to be a château, because it was the dignified, the aristocratic thing. However, defense features are both expensive and uncomfortable and gradually they came to be replaced by imitations, until now a château is like those Hollywood façades they erect with nothing behind them. If you don't mind strolling with me around the outside of this building, I will show you some of the tricks which the architects of the *ancien régime* in its decadence used to play upon their clients; or perhaps it was the clients playing tricks upon their friends and guests, including members of the royal family who now and then came to visit them."

"Most interesting, Herr Budd. Let us go, by all means."

They strolled to the door while Lanny continued his discourse. "You are perhaps living in a château for the first time, Herr Leutnant, and discovering that it is far from commodious. I venture the guess that the staff of Graf Herzenberg is compelled to send its laundry to be done outside, because the facilities of this magnificent building have been found inadequate."

"You have guessed correctly," laughed the Schutzstaffel officer.

"I recall reading somewhere an old document having to do with the coming of some young princess to marry one of the kings of France. It may have been Marie Antoinette, or possibly Anne of Austria, at an earlier period. Anyhow, the chronicler described the immensity of the princess's escort, a veritable army, with so many hundreds of coaches and so many four-horse wagons, so many servants of this sort and that, forty cooks, perhaps—and the list ended with one laundress. You could see the reason when you came to the items comprising the young person's trousseau: hundreds of elaborate costumes, cloth of gold and of silver, velvet brocade, pure silk from China, and so on—and trailing off at the end to an unimportant item of three chemises."

VI

Discoursing thus entertainingly, Lanny roamed about the grounds of the structure with its many outbuildings, servants' quarters, stables now turned into garages, kennels, aviaries, and what not. Lanny had learned the art of conversation in childhood, and could carry it on while the greater part of his mind was busy elsewhere. How wide were the openings into the basement? Too narrow for a human head to pass through, as in the old castles, or trusting to iron bars, as in later and more orderly days? "Just as I thought, an acetylene torch would cut one of those very quickly! And where does the telephone line run? And the electric light wires? And the servants and workers—all Germans, certainly. No chance of any leak to the outside! And the dogs? Yes, a number of them, and doubtless all turned loose at night!"

Aloud Lanny said: "Beautiful dogs, Herr Leutnant! Are you a lover of these friends of our race? I find it is better to know only one dog at a time—it is just as with a woman, they are jealous, even though they do not show it, even though they perhaps do not know what is the matter with them. Especially these German shepherds. In England they call them Alsatians, and in my homeland police dogs; I do not know why; perhaps people are unwilling to credit the Germans with having created anything so surpassing. May I have the pleasure of being introduced to them? I bought one of these dogs once, from a man who bred and raised him. The man led me to the dog and pointed me to him and said: 'This is your new master; from now on you will have nothing to do with any other man.' And I swear that creature understood the words and took them as his bible. Years later, when I was compelled to be away from my Riviera home for a long period, the dog would not eat and actually perished of starvation. You should have yourself formally introduced to these dogs, Herr Leutnant, so that you can walk out in the grounds at night with safety."

"These are German dogs," replied the Schutzstaffel officer, smiling. "I think they know the German smell."

"Or absence of smell," countered Lanny. "Since you have your laundry done regularly!"

So when they parted they felt themselves to be old friends. Lanny said: "I have no words to tell you how grateful I am for your courtesy. Perhaps you would let me return the hospitality some time. Are you stationed here permanently?"

"So far as I know, Herr Budd."

"*Menschenkind!*—then you might like to join me in Paris some evening and let me show you some of the curious aspects of that city to which the ordinary tourist does not have access."

"*Ich bitte darum.*"

"Just now I have to be away; but a little later, on my return—may I phone you?"

"*Bitte sehr, mein Freund.*" It was a case of *Wahlverwandtschaften*—translated as "elective affinities."

VII

Lanny drove until he was a safe distance from the château, and then drew up in a shady spot by the highway, got out his notebook and pencil, and made maps and elaborate notes of every detail he had observed of the building and grounds, both inside and out. Then he drove on; and the Trudi-ghost said: "You are wasting your time. You cannot help me, and you will risk getting caught. Go to Spain."

Lanny, mannish and stubborn, replied: "I am going to help you. Even if I go and get Monck, it will be to help you."

The Trudi-ghost countered: "Monck will put you in touch with the underground, and you can give them the money."

Lanny, who liked to have his own way but usually gave in when some loved person kept insisting, replied: "Oh, all right, all right; I'll go." It was like still being married.

He telephoned for an appointment and drove to his Uncle Jesse's; parking as always some distance away so as not to attract attention in the neighborhood. All neighborhoods in France are full of curiosity.

The Communist deputy had had his nephew's passport stamped with a visa for Valencia. At the time it wasn't necessary to get an exit permit from the French government, for in one of the shifts incidental to the maneuvers of the Non-Intervention Commission, the border was open into Spain, and the French officials contented themselves with saying: "*C'est très, très dangereux, monsieur, et vous y allez à votre risque.*" The papers of the previous afternoon told of airplane bombs being dropped on the temporary capital of "Red" Spain, and the morning papers told of a cruiser bombardment and the sinking of a merchant vessel in sight of the city. Lanny said: "I won't stay long, Uncle Jesse."

In return for the favor he told his relative a lot about the Cagoulard conspiracy. He didn't mention having met Schneider, and he warned his uncle, as many times before, that he must never let himself be tempted to mention any member of the de Bruyne family, no matter what offenses they might commit. There had been on this point a mutual understanding, never infringed over a period of some fifteen years. The de Bruynes of course knew about the Red sheep in Lanny's family, something he couldn't help and wasn't to be blamed for. Sometimes Lanny would tell them news about the Reds and their doings, treating it playfully for the most part, and confining it to such items as anyone could easily have found out.

There was a curious aspect of this class struggle, even at its fiercest; each side looked upon the other with horror, but this feeling was mixed with a complex of other emotions: fear, awe, curiosity, even amusement. There was something romantic about the idea of actually knowing a real Red; of being able to go to his home and sit down and eat bread and cheese and drink wine with him. What was he really like? What did he talk about when he wasn't making speeches? What did he do? Lanny would answer: "He paints portraits of little street gamins, whom he loves. They are only fairly good as paintings, but people buy them for the benefit of the cause."

Jesse Blackless wasn't doing much painting now; his hands were growing unsteady, he said—he couldn't help thinking about Spain, and that made them tremble. There was a fresh crisis. The Franco invaders who absurdly called themselves "Nationalists" had been trying to get belligerent rights from Britain and France, and failing in this, they had sought to establish a blockade by means of submarines; they were sinking British and French and other neutral vessels seeking to enter Loyalist ports. That of course was "piracy" in the eyes of all neutrals, and it had provoked the first signs of real determination on the part of Britain and France. They had jointly announced that they would sink all submarines in those waters, and they had meant it—with the result that the mysterious pirates suddenly ceased operations about the coasts of Spain.

That was always the way, Jesse said; the moment you took a firm stand with the dictators, they backed down. It was well known that when Hitler had given orders to the Wehrmacht to march into the Rhineland, the General Staff had been afraid of the move, and Hitler had conceded the point that if the French offered resistance, the Germans would at once retire. It would have been the same with Italy in Abyssinia, and it would be the same in Spain, if only England and France would decide to grant real neutrality and let the Loyalist government buy arms like any other.

VIII

Only when Lanny was about to leave, he remarked quite casually: "By the way, Uncle Jesse, did you make any inquiries about the Château de Belcour?"

"I did, and there's no doubt you have a straight tip. The place has been leased by a Nazi named Herzenberg, and they discharged every French employee, even to the laborers, men who had worked there all their lives, and their fathers before them."

"Well," said the nephew, "it strikes me that ought to be a story. I keep hearing reports that this and that member of the underground has disappeared without a trace. Suppose some of them were in the *oubliettes* of that château, surely your Party press would like to know about it! Why don't you find some intelligent and dependable comrade to go to work quietly on this lead? The neighborhood must have reports of what's happening in the place, and there must be ways of finding out more. The Nazis must have gardeners and chauffeurs and what not, and they must come out now and then; they might talk to a woman, or someone might get them drunk."

"You're outlining quite a program," commented the uncle. "It would cost money."

"I know; but I smell what I believe is a sensation, and I'd be willing to put up a good sum."

"How much, for example?"

"First, two conditions: you're never to mention me to anybody concerned; and second you'll keep the story to yourself until I say it can be released. The point is, the tip came to me in confidence, and I haven't the right to jeopardize the life of a person who may be a prisoner in that place right now. It depends on what we find and what chance there might be to do something for the person."

"That seems fair enough."

"All right then. I'll put ten thousand francs into your hands now, and you may draw on me for actual expenditures up to two or three times as much."

"*Sapristi!*" exclaimed the Red painter. "That is a deal!"

"Here's a tip for you," said the nephew. "Make note that the château has its laundry done outside. It might be that some worker in that laundry is a Party comrade."

IX

Lanny was through in Paris for the time being. Early next morning he had his belongings put into the car and took the *route nationale* to the south. He had driven over it perhaps a hundred times, so he knew every landmark. With him rode Rosemary, and Irma, and the Marie-ghost—but not the Trudi-ghost, for she had never seen his Riviera home. Most of the time she had stayed in a small studio; now she stayed in a dungeon beneath the Château de Belcour, where Leutnant Rörich came and tortured her; she clenched her hands and set her teeth and endured it, and now and then heard the singing of the *Ça ira*, and whispered to herself that Lanny was coming—but he shouldn't, for he would surely be caught.

Half-way to his destination, Lanny took the road which parallels the Central Canal, connecting the river Loire with the river Saône; the former flowing to the Bay of Biscay and the latter to the Mediterranean. This is the historic land of Burgundy, rich in coal and iron, as well as in wines and olive oil. The district of the canals is one of Pluto's realms, dingy and smoke-stained; in its valleys grew tall black chimneys instead of trees, and all nature was polluted and defiled. One of its towns is Le Creusot, which means The Hollow or The Crucible—and either might apply. Hither, a century ago, had come two brothers from Alsace and purchased a bankrupt foundry. They had built it up and learned to make arms, and the Crimean War had come at a fortunate time to make them millionaires. The son of one of them had multiplied his riches out of the Franco-Prussian War, and the grandson had done the same out of the World War. Charles Prosper Eugène Schneider had known the right statesmen and the right bankers, also the right words to whisper into their ears; it was rumored that his vast chain of enterprises had drawn sixteen milliards—or what the Americans call billions—of gold francs from the earnings of the French people.

The Schneiders had built themselves a palace called the Château la Verrerie, which means the Glasshouse; the reason not being apparent, since it was made of the most solid stone obtainable. It stood on a hilltop with the village huddled around it for protection, exactly as in medieval days. The hovels in which the workers lived were of materials and style of architecture different from those which surrounded the Budd-Erling plant, but the principles on which they had been erected and the methods by which the community had grown were much the same. The workers of this Hollow or Crucible hated the master of the

Glasshouse, and voted Red on every occasion; so the master feared them, and was financing political conspirators as the only means he could think of to protect himself. The tire manufacturer Michelin and the industrialist Deloncle and the landowner Comte Pastre whom Lanny had on his list were all in the same state of mind and taking the same course.

Lanny had telephoned for an appointment, and the Baron was expecting him for lunch. Afterwards, over the coffee and brandy, he reported on his interview with Kurt Meissner, making it more intimate than it had really been. The *Komponist* had been impressed by the news Lanny had brought him, and had promised to take the matter up with the Nazi authorities. Lanny was on his way south to visit his mother, and on his return in a few days he would see Kurt again and report developments.

After this, Lanny talked about the delicate situation in the British Cabinet with regard to the question of German supremacy in the manufacture of airplanes; he referred to the status of affairs in France at the moment—he had been told that the Deuxième Bureau was getting the same reports on German aerial activities, and that Premier Chautemps was treating the reports in the same way as Chamberlain. Lanny didn't really know this latter fact, but he judged that it was quite certain to be the case, and that Schneider would know it. He took a shot in the dark and it landed in the bull's-eye.

Charles Prosper Eugène, Baron Schneider, confessed that he was greatly worried because modern war appeared to be developing new techniques; leaping into the air and flying over that Maginot Line upon which the French people had based their hopes of security. There came something wistful into the voice of an elderly *entrepreneur* who had invested so many milliards of francs in weapons which might suddenly turn out to be worth so little that it wouldn't pay to move them to the scrap pile. Lanny told how his father had foreseen this development several years ago, and had decided to stake everything he owned on the future of the fighter plane. He told of Robbie's efforts to interest French and British army men—he could give convincing details on this subject, for the dumbness of the "brass hats" had been the theme of his father's lamentations ever since Lanny could remember hearing his voice. French, British, Americans, it was the same with them all; only Germans were on the alert and ready to welcome new ideas.

The Baron sighed and said: "We are compelled to make friends with the Germans, greatly as we fear and dislike them." Then he added: "I think, M. Budd, that it might be well worth your father's while to pay a call upon me the next time he visits Europe."

"I am sure he will be delighted to do so, Monsieur le Baron." Lanny knew that he had achieved a coup for his father, one which might be worth another block of stock for himself if the frightened supermagnate should take up the notion to have a branch of Budd-Erling set up in France. In any case, the son of Budd-Erling had made himself solid with one of the most powerful men in the world. Schneider of Schneider-Creusot would take it as a matter of course that Lanny was trying to promote his father's business, and would respect him for having made an approach in exactly the right manner. That is how the biggest business is carried on, with tact and dignity, and without hurry or worry. Whatever came of Lanny's effort, he would be counted among those who had a right to get the Baron on the telephone, and the Baron would know that Lanny's interest in the Hooded Men was the legitimate and proper interest of one who had property at stake.

"Stop by and see me whenever you are passing this way," said the master of the Crucible and the Glasshouse.

X

Bienvenu was always the same. First came the dogs, clamoring loudly; Lanny had been romancing when he talked about only one, for they kept reproducing themselves and it was hard to find people to adopt them. His mother heard the racket and knew what it meant, for he had telephoned before leaving Paris. But she wouldn't come out into the bright light of late afternoon—she had begun to note the crow's feet in the corners of her eyes, and couldn't endure for even her son to see them. Beauty Budd had never been much of an outdoors person, and now, without making any fuss, she stayed at home in the daytime, and made her social appearances under the protection of the kindly shadows of evening. Everybody said how marvelously she was managing to keep her charms; at any rate that is what they said in her hearing.

Beauty's one serious trouble was, as ever, that known as *embonpoint*. The happier, the hungrier, seemed to be the rule with this one-time "professional beauty." She weighed herself on the scales in her bathroom every morning, and what she saw destroyed her appetite for breakfast; feeling faint in the middle of the morning, she would nibble several chocolates, and at lunch she would gaze longingly at the cream pitcher, which someone always left provokingly within her reach.

She was an intensely personal being; she was curious about every human she had ever known, and always Lanny had to answer a score of questions about how Robbie was, and Robbie's wife, and all their family. Beauty might have had that family herself, but fate in the form of a cruel old Puritan plutocrat had intervened; so Beauty had only her one Budd, whom she adored and watched over and spied upon lovingly. What was the state of his heart now, and was there still no chance óf his settling down? He would soon be thirty-eight and it was surely time.

His adoring mother wanted to know, had he seen Rosemary on this trip? He knew what that question meant: "Oh, Lanny, are you going to get tied up with that woman again?" The alternative was even worse, the *affaire* which she knew he was having in Paris, but she wasn't allowed to know even the woman's name; obviously, she was some variety of social outlaw, and a fond mother imagined the worst. She simply couldn't be kept from scheming to get some suitable wealthy debutante to be brought to the house, or to meet Lanny by accident at the home of the former Baroness de la Tourette on the Cap d'Antibes near by.

XI

Throughout most of Lanny's life Cannes had been a winter resort, and Juan-les-Pins, on the edge of which the Budd estate was situated, had been a tiny fishing village. But advertising and real estate promotion, plus the cult of sun-bathing, had turned the whole Côte d'Azur into a summer resort as well. New casinos had been built, for gambling and dancing and dining; colored bands had been imported from America, and all night long the thumping of drums and the moaning of saxophones resounded over the Golfe Juan. People did their sleeping in the morning on the sands of the beach or on apricot-colored mattresses laid upon the rocks of the Cap; the men wearing little more than a G-string and a pair of horn-rimmed dark glasses; the women adding a light brassière. Nature hadn't always constructed them with a view to such exposure, and when you saw them you desired to avert your eyes, but there was no vacant place. Especially was this so when one of the new German excursion steamers arrived and discharged a cargo of a thousand stout Nordic male and female blonds, and they all made a rush for the beaches to eat sausages and drink beer. Lanny fled before such invaders and shut himself up behind the gates of Bienvenu, where he had a little studio with a piano on which he could pound out his discontents.

The older residents of the Riviera, at least those whom the Budds knew, had their estates with private swimming pools, and so did not have to come into contact with what they politely referred to as "the public." Here you saw more tasteful costumes, on bodies which had been bred for good looks and carefully tended since infancy; you listened to polite conversation about other people and what they were doing, and about dancing and dining and travel; you played a lot of bridge and gin-rummy, and ate modest but excellent meals served with decorum. It was all extremely proper, but dull after you had come to know it. Now and then you heard talk about a new book or a forthcoming election, and if you were in your secret heart a Pink like Lanny, you observed that the point of view was always that of the protection of this decorous mode of life and the property ownership upon which it was based. Nothing was to be changed, and the idea had better not even be mentioned; for times had become serious, and with Spain only a couple of hundred miles away, it was a case of "Under which king, Bezonian? speak, or die."

Now Lanny was going into Spain for the fourth time, and it was undeniably dangerous, and gave great distress to his mother. Paintings, yes—but weren't there plenty of paintings in France and other parts of Europe? Couldn't he busy himself with selling Detazes? Beauty could always use her share of the money, and Marceline, his half-sister, was begging for more all the time. By the way, how was Marceline? Beauty reported that the child's husband was still with the Italian troops in Seville, and the child herself was unhappy in that wretched hot climate, with mosquitoes biting her ankles, and fleas, too; everything topsy-turvy in wartime, the price of everything prohibitive, and Marceline cursing the day she had let her one-armed hero come to this place. Couldn't Beauty force Lanny to send at least some pocket money?

Beauty knew that she mustn't scold her wayward son, or try to force him; otherwise his visits to her home might become even fewer. He was obstinate; he had his duties, as he conceived them, and Beauty had to keep his dark secrets locked in her heart. When he came, she was proud of him; all his old friends wanted to see him, he was invited everywhere, and could have been "in the swim" and towed his mother along in his wake; but he had something serious on his mind, she could see at once, and she didn't believe for a moment that it was picture business taking him into Spain. No, he was going on another of his mad errands, and his mother had to hide her anxiety and let him go.

XII

Beauty Budd was married to what she called the kindest man in the world, and one who was firmly convinced that he was married to the most wonderful of women. Parsifal Dingle showed fewer signs of age than anyone of his generation whom Lanny knew; he permitted nothing to trouble him, he loved everybody, no matter how hateful they might be, and when they got into trouble he talked to them about Divine Love, never referring to their past actions, but assuring them that they could have happiness and healing whenever they were willing to open their hearts to receive it. He said his prayers and read his books and papers dealing with the subject of New Thought; also, as part of each day's routine, he carried on psychic experiments with the Polish medium who had made her home with the Budd family ever since Parsifal had discovered her in New York, eight years ago.

Madame Zyszynski, elderly, rather dumpy ex-servant, was slow-minded and left it for others to be interested in her rare gift; she would sink back into a chair and go into a trance, and straightway would begin to speak with strange voices and tell things about which Madame herself knew nothing, either waking or asleep. Parsifal was still accumulating notes concerning a Buddhist monastery called Dodanduwa, on an island off the coast of Ceylon, and the monks who had lived there a long time ago; he had written and learned that there actually was such a place, and now he was sending copies of his records to be checked.

For most of the time, Madame's "control" had been the spirit of an Indian chieftain named Tecumseh. But recently he had got "tired of talking so much," he declared, and his place had been taken by a voice named "Claribel," who said that she had been a lady-in-waiting to the queen of Henry the Sixth of England. She was a poetical lady, and, if you gave her any subject, no matter how remote or esoteric, she would burst into a sort of sleepy rhapsody in poetical prose. It might be a vision called up by the words; as a rule it was indefinite, but always it was extraordinary as coming from the mind of this dull Polish woman, whose reading was confined mostly to the pictures in the cheapest sort of papers. Parsifal would go to the encyclopedia and look up the most unlikely subjects, such as "the choragic monument of Lysicrates," or "the Old Slavic Josephus," or a fossil called "glyptocrinus decadactylus." Said Claribel of this last: "With my ten fingers I did shake the world,"—and that was true, since it is true of everything that moves on the earth; but the question was: How did any voice coming out of Madame know the meaning of a long Greek word?

Trudi Schultz had had sittings with Madame, and in the last of them Zaharoff had appeared, announcing his own death, just after it had occurred and before the papers carrying the news had appeared on the streets of Paris. So naturally Lanny had the thought: "Trudi might come to me!" One of his first procedures upon reaching home was to take Madame into his studio and get her comfortably seated in an armchair, and then wait with pencil poised over a notebook.

But alas, it wasn't Trudi, only Zaharoff, an unwelcome intruder at this moment. But Lanny mustn't show it; no indeed, for it was Tecumseh speaking, and the two-hundred-year-old Iroquois was extremely touchy in his dealing with the grandson of Budd's; taking exception to his supposed-to-be-scientific attitude, ridiculing him, often teasing him by refusing to tell him the things he most wanted to know. Lanny had learned to be scrupulously polite, talk like a devotee of spiritualism, and omit none of the ceremonies due to a person of royal rank.

"It is that old man who has guns going off all the time around him," declared the chieftain. "Such a racket, it makes my head ache! And people shouting that they hate him. Poor tormented old man, he's always talking about money. What is the matter with him—didn't he have a chance to fix up his business affairs before he left?"

"He left rather suddenly," replied Lanny; "but I know that he made a will. Perhaps he is not satisfied with it."

"He keeps crying: 'Gold! Gold!' Did he have anything to do with gold? He says 'gold at the bottom of the sea.' What is that?"

"I am sure I have no idea, Tecumseh."

"He says it is being covered with sand and mud. It will be lost forever. This old man—Basil, he cries—is that his name?"

"That is his first name."

"He says a human arm floated out in the water and it was from the kitchen—no, he says the Kitchener."

"Was that Lord Kitchener? He was lost at sea."

"He says yes; the ship was full of treasure; he, Basil, tried to bring it up. Was he ever a diver?"

"I doubt it very much."

"He says they got some gold, but most of it is still there. He says it is very important; there were war records."

"Doesn't he know the war is over?"

"It is another war coming. The gold was in the treasure room. It is a fortune for you. The man who can unlock it—his name—I forget the name."

This last was supposed to be Zaharoff speaking to Lanny. The voice was still that of Tecumseh, but the words were supposed to come from the "spirit," and you were supposed to play that game. Lanny said: "You never told me that you had done any treasure-hunting, Sir Basil."

"Many things I never told you. I kept my affairs to myself. The name of the man—he is the key-master."

"Key-master?" repeated the inquirer. "Do you mean the master-key?"—for Lanny had read a few crime and mystery stories.

"Key-master," insisted the one-time Knight Commander and Grand Officer. "He opens all locks. The American. You can find him."

"I ought to have some clue to his name, Sir Basil."

"Huff—is it Huffy—or Huffner? Tell him there is gold—the greatest treasure—it was for Russia—to stop the revolution——"

The voice trailed away, and there was silence. Lanny was afraid the old man would fade out, and he asked quickly: "Sir Basil, have you been meeting any friends of mine?"

"Some of yours, but none of mine," quavered the spirit.

"See if you can find one of my friends named Trudi. Remember the name for me, please." Lanny took that as a tactful way of giving the request to Tecumseh, who might otherwise spurn it.

"Trudi—Trudi—Trudi—!" It died out in a sort of sigh, and quiet followed. The medium began to stir, then moaned and opened her eyes, and the séance was over.

"Did you get good results?" she asked, and Lanny told her: "Very good." That pleased her; she rarely asked more, and he never told her, for that might invalidate later communications. He went away thinking: "A damned strange thing! Kitchener's arm floating in water, and gold at the bottom of the sea." He recalled the name of the cruiser, *H. M. S. Hampshire*, which was reported to have struck a mine in the North Sea during the World War. That was all he had ever heard, so far as he could now recall. He thought: "I wonder if Zaharoff ever did engage in a treasure hunt."

He tried several times more with Madame Zyszynski, but all he got was Claribel and her prose poems. When he said "Trudi," the lady of old England knew that the name was German, but apparently thought it was a milkmaid, and went into a rhapsody about cows, country lanes, and kisses. To be sure, Lanny had walked in country lanes with Trudi, having motored her out into the remote parts of *la douce France*, and having assuredly not failed to kiss her. Some people might have called that "evidential," but it wasn't what the researcher wanted now.

XIII

Lanny phoned and made an appointment with the wife of Raoul Palma, who had been running the workers' school while her husband was in Spain. Lanny gave her some money for the school and learned that Raoul was still in Valencia, in a state of terrible tension over the developments in the war. Lanny said: "I am going in there on picture business." Julie Palma answered: "Take him a lot of chocolate. They are living on horse and burro meat in Valencia now."

He had a couple of Detazes to get out of the storeroom and pack and ship to Zoltan. Then, his last errand, he went to call on the Señora Villareal, one of his clients, who lived near Nice. He had tea with this Spanish lady of the old school, who was in his debt because he had brought some of her paintings out from Seville and she couldn't imagine how she could have got along without the money. He told her now· that he had an opportunity to go into Red Spain. "With money one can do almost anything with that crowd," he said. "You know how the unfortunate city is being bombed, and it is a ghastly thing that its art treasures should be exposed to destruction. I feel that I should be doing a public service in rescuing some of them."

"Surely, Señor Budd; but is it not frightfully risky?"

"I don't intend to stay long. What occurred to me is that you might know someone in Valencia who has some especially valuable work he might like to have brought out. It couldn't be a large one, for I plan to travel by train. I learned the lesson that a car is too dangerous a luxury in a war-torn land."

"Oh, Señor Budd, it is such a horrible thing! How much longer can it go on?"

"I wish I could make a guess," he replied. "If anybody had asked me at the beginning, I would never have said it could last fourteen months."

"There will be nothing left of my poor country!" sighed the lady. "My estates bring me almost nothing, because the army has to have the produce, and they pay in paper money which is without value in the outside world."

"Keep it carefully; it will surely be redeemed." Thus soothingly Lanny addressed a mother who still had one daughter at the age for marriage but who lacked the necessary *dot*. He led the talk to the subject of refugees from Valencia, and the Señora listed several who owned paintings; they all surely needed money, and presently she telephoned to one and made an appointment for the American expert to call. She spoke of Lanny in the highest terms, explaining that he was no speculator but a gentleman with the best connections; his father was the great manufacturer of airplanes, he was an intimate friend of Mrs. Chattersworth, and so on. That is the way the world is run, and the way Lanny Budd was able to travel to any part of Europe and to earn not merely his expenses but the means of indulging his whims.

XIV

He called upon a Spanish grandee—they don't use the term any more but they have the manners and the ideas. This one was living in obviously straitened circumstances in an unfashionable part of Nice. Señor Jimenes owned lands in the suburbs of Valencia on which oranges were grown, and buildings in the slums for which thousands of laborers had been accustomed to pay high rents. But now everything was in the hands of the Reds, and how could an unhappy grandee hope to maintain his grandeur? He spent an hour or more probing Lanny's mind and soul, and when finally he had satisfied himself that this was a man of good will, he confessed that he owned a Murillo, representing some ragged little boys playing outdoors; a superlatively lovely and absolutely priceless work. Before his mansion had been seized, he had had a trusted servant carry this treasure away and hide it in a hut near the city. If Lanny could get it and bring it out, the señor would agree to let him sell it and pay him a commission.

On account of Trudi, Lanny was in a greedy mood. He said: "Señor Jimenes, those are the terms on which I normally work; but now it is a question of risking my life on an extremely dangerous enterprise. If I, a foreigner, go to visit a former servant of a landlord, I am certain to be observed and very likely to be reported; if they caught me, they would quite possibly find out my record and shoot me as a spy. In any case I might have to pay large sums to officials to get the painting out; I might have to take it directly on a steamer to London or even to New York. The only terms on which I could undertake such risks would be that I had an option to buy the painting outright."

"And what would you be willing to offer, Señor Budd?"

"First, I should have to view the work and satisfy myself as to its authenticity. I do not doubt that you, Señor, believe your little boys to be Murillo's; but that popular painter had many imitators, and I have many times seen owners of art works deceived as to what they had acquired. My proposal would be that you trust me with an order for the delivery of the painting; if I am satisfied that it is genuine, I will assume all the risks from the moment it is in my hands. I will put the sum of one hundred thousand francs into escrow here, and as soon as the painting is delivered to me I will order the bank to release the money to you."

"Oh, but, Señor Budd, the painting is worth many times that much money! Perhaps a million francs!"

"Quite possibly, and I am making no attempt to deceive you. What you have to figure on is what the painting is worth in Valencia today; for that is where I would get it, with all the risks of bombs and Reds and crooked officials and firing squads and ship torpedoings—a whole gantlet to be run, and if you expect the full price for the painting, it is surely up to you to do the running."

Lanny was used to the spectacle of persons of wealth and rank arguing, pleading, haggling, fighting for their money; the sums were larger than if it was the purchase of suspenders or cabbages, but the technique was the same. Courtesy required that you should listen patiently and never cut any statement short; never take offense, and when everything had been said several times to no purpose, you must rise to leave with great reluctance. It was expected that you would make some small concession, in order that the other party might feel that he had gained something by his labors. In this case, the seller was badly off, perhaps not able to pay his rent; Señor Jimenes actually wept when he contemplated parting with his sole transportable treasure—so he described it— and in the end Lanny weakened and raised his offer to a hundred and ten thousand francs. This was, he opined, a real fortune in France; a man might live on it in modest comfort the rest of his days.

It was only when Lanny had given up hope, left the house, and was getting into his car that the Spanish grandee called: "Come back, Señor; it is a deal."

There was nothing new about that, and nothing humiliating. Lanny came, and with entire amiability prepared the necessary papers. He went away knowing that he had a satisfactory story to tell to Kurt or the de Bruynes or Baron Schneider or General Göring, in case any of them should chance to hear about his going into Red Spain. He would get the money needed for his effort to help Trudi, without having to sell any of the securities which he had stored in his father's keeping, and which he couldn't order sold without causing worry to both his parents, and causing them to ask inconvenient questions. His main purpose was, of course. to see Monc¹⁻ but to make a profit incidentally could do no harm.

7

Spain's Chivalry Away

I

LANNY BUDD was traveling on a train, something which he did rarely. It was the express which ran along the Mediterranean; a rocky and irregular coast, with now a beach, now a wooded stretch, now bare red sandstone cliffs, and now a spur of mountain with a black tunnel through which the train darted with a loud racket. There were fishing villages, and pink and white villas built into the rocks, and vistas of bright blue sea with many small boats, some with white sails and some with red. When it grew dark there were lighthouses flashing white and red signals.

They came to the southernmost point of France, and the few passengers who were going on had to get out and walk through a tunnel; there it was Spain, and they had to stand in line while officials inspected their papers and luggage. Lanny was traveling light, with only one suitcase, his portable typewriter, and a large package of *chocolat Menier*, one piece of which would suffice to win the favor of most any official. Presently he was in an extremely dingy train, having scars to prove that it had been through battles. Except for the early fighting, Red Catalonia hadn't seen much of the war, and in the judgment of the rest of the country wasn't carrying its share of the burden. Catalonia was anarchist and individualist, and didn't take kindly to the stern discipline which war imposes. The peasants of Catalonia were glad to be free of their landlords, but didn't want to part with their products except at war prices, which was why the people of the towns were having a hard time keeping nourished.

All this was explained to an American traveler by a young workingman who had been into France on some purchasing errand for his collective. He was ardent, full of determination and hope; a new life had begun for him and his kind, and they had no thought of giving it up. It was the final conflict and each stood in his place; the international party would be the human race. What had been done in Catalonia was going to be done throughout the Iberian peninsula, and when the workers of France saw its success, they too would throw the parasites off their backs. In the next stage, the people of the Fascist lands would discover how they had been misled; they would revolt, and Europe would become one commonwealth of workers and peasants, free, fraternal, and dedicated to the life of reason.

Poor old Europe! Lanny in childhood had thought it was a beautiful and wonderful continent; only little by little he had come to realize that it was a land of hereditary evils too numerous to be counted. Then he had become possessed by the same bright dream of social change as this young workingman; he still cherished the dream, because there was nothing else to live for, but he clung to it now with a sort of desperation, like one who knows that a dream is over and that he has come wide awake. Just recently he had been reading a statement by some historian, that during the past few centuries Spain had spent an average of seventy years of each hundred at war, and France an average of fifty. Idealists preached and promised freedom, but what they got was "man arrayed for mutual slaughter."

Of course Lanny mustn't say anything like that to a workingman of Red Catalonia. He had to explain, as well as he could in his imperfect Spanish, the strange indifference to freedom now being displayed by the great American republic, which all Europe thought of as the land of freedom. Dropping that embarrassing subject as soon as possible, he asked questions about the workers' co-operatives. To what extent were they solving the problems of production? Were they actually getting it, in spite of all the controversy, the politics, the sabotage? That was the test, and the only test, in war as it would be in peace. More production than capitalism could give; more than that thing which Robbie Budd glorified under the name of "individual initiative," and which was really the true anarchy. As Lanny had said to his father: perfect order inside the plant and perfect chaos outside!

Yes, said this workingman, the wheels of the factories were turning and the goods were coming forth. The workers had had more than a year in which to organize and solve their problems; in spite of war and blockade and internal conflicts, they were getting materials and turning out goods. "How do you solve this?" and "How do you manage that?" Lanny would ask; and all the time he was thinking: "I must explain this to F.D.R." The smiling and genial President of the United

States had become little by little the center of Lanny's thinking, his refuge from despair. A man who really had power and who really understood! If Lanny should tell him how the Catalan workers were running their own plants, F.D.'s face would light up, and he would chuckle and remark: "How the National Association of Manufacturers and the United States Chamber of Commerce would like that!" But would he really do anything about it? Would he even say anything about it publicly? And if he did, wouldn't the Associated Robbie Budds of America be able to throw him out on his ear at the next election?

II

From Barcelona on, the young workingman's place was taken by a grim-faced elderly peasant woman who had been to town to nurse a son wounded in the fighting on the Aragon front. She had brought in a load of produce to pay her expenses, and now was carrying home such necessities as salt and kerosene. Lanny had picked up many words of the Catalan language, which is allied to the Provençal of the fisher-boys with whom he had played in childhood; and anyhow, he had no shyness about trying to jabber in all the tongues of polyglot Europe. He made out that the peasant woman was dissatisfied because the high prices for farm products were more than balanced by high prices for store products. Lanny knew that this complaint was universal in wartime. He found that this woman didn't like war, and couldn't see that the coming of Franco would make any difference to her—provided only that they wouldn't fight over her hereditary acres! Lanny was interested to understand the peasant mind, which is strictly "isolationist," and as firmly fixed as the boundary-stones of its small plots of land.

The farther south the train went the hotter it was, and the nearer to war. Trains were sometimes bombed; ships and small craft had been torpedoed and beached where you could see the wrecks from the train. Few people went to Valencia who didn't have to, for it was bombed frequently and its defenses were inadequate. It had been the seat of the government ever since the siege of Madrid had begun, ten months previously; now the government was planning to move to Barcelona, so people on the train reported; some departments had already moved. The Italians were pressing in the south, while Franco, with his Moors and Requetes and another large Italian army, was fighting a great battle up on that River Ebro where Lanny had once hidden his car while the Fascists were searching for him. Franco was getting a thumping defeat, so reports indicated, and everybody was exulting in this success.

Raoul's wife had written him that "a friend" was coming with news from home. Raoul had no trouble in guessing who it was, and he was waiting at the badly bombed station. He was several years younger than Lanny, but already his dark hair was streaked with gray and his face deeply lined; he looked years older than when Lanny had last seen him, during the first attack upon Madrid. He had a high forehead and delicate features; a thin nose, with nostrils which seemed to quiver when he was deeply moved, which was often, for he was high-strung and impressionable. People call it the "spiritual" type of face, but to Lanny it meant undernourishment; he was sure his Spanish friend hadn't had a square meal in many a month, and as he handed over a heavy package he said: "This contains chocolate."

"Oh, good!" exclaimed Raoul. "How the staff will welcome that!" Lanny thought, how characteristic! He was going to share it with the whole Foreign Press Bureau! Having foreseen this, Lanny had purchased a goodly stock.

III

The new arrival explained, quickly: "I don't want any publicity about my coming. I have a couple of important errands and then I have to skip out. I don't want to go to a hotel. Can you take me somewhere we can talk quietly?"

"I'll put you up in my room, if you don't mind discomfort."

"Not in the least. Let us go."

The people of Valencia had no *gasolina*, and were eating their horses and burros; but there were a few antiquated cabs at the station, and the two friends and their luggage were driven to one of the smaller hotels set apart for government employees. Raoul had a small room with a single cot, and it was his idea that Lanny was to occupy this while his host slept on the floor. Lanny said: "I won't stay on those terms," and they started an argument, which might have lasted quite a while.

Lanny changed the subject abruptly, saying: "I want to see you eat at least one piece of chocolate." He opened the package, and on account of the heat the contents were soft. It was necessary to unwrap a piece and lick it off the paper. Not a dignified procedure, but a semi-starved man does not stand upon ceremony, and all the time that Lanny talked Raoul licked, and it wasn't long before his mouth and everything around it were smeared a rich shiny brown.

Lanny began: "Do you happen to remember that Capitán Herzog whom we saw marching with the International Brigade in Madrid?"

"Indeed, yes. He has made a good record in the Thaelmann *columna*."

"He is still alive, then?"

"Well, you know how it is in war. I wouldn't necessarily have heard if anything had happened to him."

"Can you find out?"

"I can find out where he was stationed and if there's any recent news about him. His company is fighting on the Belchite front, I'm fairly sure."

"What I have to do is to have a talk with him. I have a message from the underground in Germany; I'm pledged not to talk about it, but you will understand, it's a party matter, and important."

"Of course, Lanny. It wouldn't be easy to get to the front without publicity. We are taking foreign journalists continually; but if you went along, they would know you, and they wouldn't see any reason for not mentioning you." Raoul called the roll—it was a roll of honor —of American writers who had made the cause of the Spanish people their own, and who were now or had recently been in Valencia: Ernest Hemingway, Vincent Sheean, Dorothy Parker, Eliot Paul, Louis Fischer, Anna Louise Strong, Albert Rhys Williams. They had taken a long and perilous journey in the cause of conscience. They turned their hearts' blood into burning words in the effort to overcome the dull inertia of the masses, to awaken the people of America to the meaning of this rape of democracy.

Lanny said: "I have met many of them, and they would know me. That wouldn't do."

"You must understand," explained his friend, "I'm not the boss. I have to take the matter to my chief. and I have to be able to say something that will convince him."

"Couldn't you say it is somebody with a message for Herzog; say, a family matter."

"The answer would be: 'Let the man write to Herzog, and if Herzog wants to see him, it's up to him to make the application.' All that might take some time."

"Couldn't you get somebody to smuggle me up there?"

"But that's not done in wartime, Lanny. You'd be a spy, and might get into serious trouble. It would certainly mean publicity."

"To be suspected as a Fascist spy wouldn't be so bad from the point of view of what I'm doing. Much better than being a friend of the Reds."

"Yes, but you might have to clear yourself before you could get out.

And it would get me into a mess—it might make it impossible for me to be of any use here. You must understand, I am half a foreigner, because I have lived so long in France. We are bedeviled by spies and saboteurs, and by suspicion and fears of them. Once you are suspected, you are guilty."

"Then perhaps it isn't wise for you to be hiding a stranger in your room here."

"It won't be good if it lasts very long, and unless I can introduce you as a comrade."

They talked the problem over from every angle. Whatever story Raoul told he had to stick by; he couldn't try a second. Also, he was bound by the name Lanny Budd, which was in the passport and could not be changed. He asked: "Will Herzog know your name?" and Lanny answered that there could be no doubt of that.

Finally Raoul said: "The best thing is to be open about it. I will go to my chief and ask permission to get El Capitán Herzog on the telephone. Unless he is at the fighting front, that should be possible. I will say to him: 'Lanny Budd is in Valencia and wishes to see you.' If he will say to my chief: 'Please send this man to me,' it can be done, I am sure. Perhaps I can get permission to go as your escort."

"*Bueno!*" said Lanny Budd.

IV

While Raoul went to carry out this commission, the visitor went for a stroll about the city of the Cid. It is more than a thousand years old, and many of its buildings have been made out of the stones of a previous city a thousand years older; ancient Roman ruins, such as Lanny had been used to seeing in the neighborhood of his childhood home. The less ancient Valencia was built in part by the Moors, and has blue and white and golden domes like Istanbul and other places of the Levant. Like all Spanish cities it had dreadfully crowded slums, and its modern industries were carried on in buildings ill-suited to the purpose. Now these industries were in the hands of the workers, who were learning to run them under penalty of being conquered by Franco's Moors, which meant death for the men and worse than death for their wives and daughters.

Italian and German bombers came over at frequent intervals. The interference was pitifully inadequate, and they could come down and pick their targets. They chose places where there might be crowds, for their purpose was to terrify and break the spirit of the population.

What they achieved was to fix in the minds of all a black and bitter hatred of their class enemies, whether native or foreign. The outside world called this the "Spanish civil war," but no worker in Spain ever thought of it as anything but an invasion by foreign Fascists who were pledged to put down and enslave the workers of all Europe and keep them as slaves for the rest of time. Spanish landlords and great capitalists and high prelates of a degenerate Church had hired this crime and paid for it by pledging the national wealth of Spain, the iron ore and copper and all the products of the soil. Foreign troops were doing the fighting, and the weapons were without exception of foreign manufacture—including all the planes which swarmed in Spanish skies and blasted Spanish homes and tore the bodies of Spanish women and children. Some day there would be justice! Some day there would be vengeance!

Lanny didn't see any of the torn bodies, for they had been carted away and put underground; but he saw the blasted homes by hundreds. The bombs were not big enough to destroy whole blocks, but enough to send one five-story tenement sliding down into the street, or perhaps to blow out the front walls and leave it like a set in a modernistic play, with several rooms exposed: a dining room with a table for the family to sit at, a bedroom with a bed for lovers to lie in, a crib for the resulting baby to sleep in. Sometimes the damage was recent, and gangs of men were clearing away the rubbish, taking down loose cornices and tottering walls; sometimes the ruins were still smoking—for the bombers dropped incendiaries, and many stone buildings had been gutted and left mere shells.

Amid all this ruin the people went grimly about their daily tasks. They were drably clad, the men mostly in well-worn black *blusas*. Lanny never saw anybody smile, even the children, unless he caused them to do so by being a wonderful *señor Americano*, asking questions and distributing centavos. He looked like a "class enemy," but did not behave so, and everybody on the Loyalist side knew that there were a few *simpáticos*, especially from that wonderful land across the sea where every worker owned a motorcar and sent back money to his impoverished relatives. *"La tierra de tíos ricos,"* a peasant had once said to Lanny; the land of rich uncles!

V

Back at Raoul's room, Lanny read about the battle of Belchite in a crudely printed newspaper. At last his friend came in, greatly excited.

"I talked with El Capitán," he announced. "We are to start tonight, and I am to take you. *Congratulaciónes!*" But really it seemed that Raoul was the one to receive these; it was a holiday he had earned by fourteen months of incessant labor with few thoughts of himself. Now he gave no heed to possible dangers at the front; when you have been under siege for so many months, first in Barcelona, then in Madrid, then in Valencia, you learn to forget about danger; it is like a thunderstorm—maybe you will be hit and maybe not, but there's nothing you can do about it and no use crawling under the bed.

What Raoul thought of was the chance to be with the wonderful Lanny Budd, who had picked him out of a starvation job in a shoestore in Cannes and given him a chance, first to study, and then to teach others. During fifteen years Lanny Budd had come and gone, and every time he had come it had been with a pocketful of money for the workers' school, and a story of adventures in that *grand monde* which Raoul's Marxist convictions obligated him to despise, but which his human weakness led him to hear about with curiosity.

First they went to a café to get some dinner. Lanny was worried, because he hadn't ever tried the meat of either *burros* or *caballos;* but he learned that, for a much higher price, some fisherman had been willing to risk being machine-gunned. Also there was rice fried with olive oil, and there was the juice of the well-known Valencia orange, and dates which grew in groves of tall palms in the suburbs. Few are the times when one cannot get food in a city if one has a purse full of its currency.

A much-battered Ford runabout had been provided for the trip. The chauffeur, who ordinarily was inseparable from his vehicle (for fear of being drafted into the army), was providentially sick, and so Lanny would be permitted to do his own driving, at his own risk. Raoul had the necessary passes, including a government order for the proper amount of *gasolina*. If you bought it on the black market, you would pay pretty nearly its weight in silver.

Belchite lies in Southern Aragon, something over a hundred miles north from Valencia. It is rather barren hill country, and the front there represented a noose drawn by the invading armies from the west of Madrid to the north and around to the east and southeast. If they had been able to come southwest from Belchite, they would have cut off Madrid from connection with the outside world; if they could have come southeast to the coast, they would have cut both Madrid and Valencia from Catalonia, dividing the Loyalist territory in half. They had marched boldly in full sweep, with one or the other of these plans in mind; but the free men of the Spanish democracy had stopped them cold, and now Raoul brought the latest news from headquarters and was all but dancing with delight. The battle of Belchite, the greatest victory of the war!

VI

Lanny didn't want to sleep; he didn't mind driving on Spanish roads at night, even with a strange car whose motor sputtered ominously now and then. They sped rapidly northward over a wide plain, green with well-tended orchards, the setting sun casting long shadows of tall date-palms across the road. Their destination was Lérida, and Lanny said: "Do you remember—we spent a night there, trying to make up our minds whether to strike north through the Pyrenees, or east to Barcelona. What a difference it made in your life!"

"I'll tell the world!" exclaimed Raoul, who had been perfecting his American in the company of visiting journalists. He talked about the cataclysm of humanity which had turned upside-down the life of an amiable idealistic school director, and made him into a sort of publicity agent in the service of Mars. Incidentally he had met so many famous correspondents and writers that he fancied himself as military expert and authority upon international diplomacy. He was quite sure that Franco had shot his bolt up here in this hard and harsh land; also that Britain and France were at last awakening to the perils of Fascism, and that their stand against submarine piracy would soon be broadened into a policy of true neutrality. Lanny had grave doubts on both points, but refrained from voicing them, for the poor Spaniard had to live and do his work. Let him have hope as long as he could.

Raoul described the manifold duties of a publicity agent of Mars. The head of the Foreign Press Bureau, to whom Raoul tried to be loyal in spite of many obstacles, was a gnomelike little man, pallid-skinned and nearly bald. He was embarrassed because he was assumed to understand the American language but really didn't; therefore he shut himself up in a small room with carefully drawn curtains, wore dark glasses even in that gloom, and left the meeting of foreign journalists entirely to his subordinates. One of these was a charming lady whom Lanny had met in Madrid on his first visit. "Constancia de la Mora. You remember, you bought some art goods in her little shop." Raoul was loud in his praises of this aristocratic Spanish woman, granddaughter of a former premier, who had broken with her old associations and cast in her lot with the people. Her husband had done the same, and was now commander of the Loyalist Air Force.

VII

They climbed into the hills, from which most of the forests had been stripped many centuries ago, leaving the land barren and the population sparse. Darkness stole upon them, except for the feeble rays from their little car, turning this way and that on the winding road and lighting hillsides of red clay and now and then a peasant hut. They reached Lérida soon after midnight, and arousing a sleepy clerk of the Palace Hotel, found that they could have only one room and one bed. In the morning they had orange juice and coffee and *huevos revueltos con tomates*. They bought bread and fruit—for the nearer they got to the front the scarcer food would be.

On the familiar road toward Saragossa they passed those sights of war which Lanny had learned to know so well. The road was worn and rutted, and the dust of vehicles made a reddish-gray fog around them and ahead. Out of this fog emerged trucks carrying wounded men back to the bases, and slow-plodding peasant carts taking families and their belongings away from destruction. Very young children and old people rode, while the rest walked alongside; the men wearing short black trousers and hempen sandals, the women much-worn dresses, invariably black. Sorrow enveloped them, old and young, but they had that patient dignity which characterizes the Spanish people, inured through centuries to every known kind of suffering.

Raoul's papers were in order, and an American visitor was welcomed with old-fashioned courtesy by guard-posts on the way. Always the travelers asked how the fortnight-old battle was going, and made the discovery that the closer you get to war, the less you know about what is happening. Better to stay at home, sitting by a radio! The rumble of the guns grew louder, but there was no way to tell enemy shots from friendly, or which were finding their targets.

La gasolina, otherwise unobtainable, was purchased from government stores, and before noon they were coming down into the valley of the Ebro. The bridge across the river had been blown up, and they went along the bank by a road which had been torn to pieces by shellfire. There were burned-out wrecks of cars and trucks scattered here and there, and a sickening sweet-rich smell that made one reluctant to breathe. The publicity agent of Mars was put on the defensive, and explained: "They can bury all the human bodies, but not the horses and mules."

As they neared their destination, Lanny apologized: "I have a mes-

sage for the Capitán which I am pledged not to reveal to anyone else."
His friend replied promptly: "I much prefer not to know anything
that doesn't concern me. If ever there is a leak, the fewer persons one
has to suspect, the better." He went on to state that he would find some
of the soldiers to talk to; they would tell him not merely about the
fighting, but about the progress of adult education in the trenches. That
was Raoul's hobby, about which he was willing to ask questions without end. The government program called for teaching every soldier to
read and write, and nothing else could have reconciled a pacifist and
idealist to the manifold horrors of civil war. "Even if the Fascists should
win," he said, "that is one thing they will never be able to undo."

VIII

The appointment with Capitán Herzog was at an inn called *El Toro
Rojo*. Raoul didn't know just where it was, and they stopped to get
directions; apparently these were not correct, for they got lost, and
finally approached the place by a sandy path in which the car would
have stuck if the Spanish official had not leaped out and pushed from
the rear. A swinging sign with a fierce red bull told them, as it had told
thousands through the centuries, that they had found the right place.
It was a building so old that it was sagging in the middle, but it had an
inside court with a second-story gallery all around, and carvings which
Lanny would have been glad to study if there hadn't been a battle so
near.

El Capitán was waiting for them: a solidly built, shaven-headed Prussian, the sort whom Lanny was used to seeing in a brown shirt with
shiny black belt and a swastika on the sleeves; but this one was a rebel,
a laborer and sailor who had educated himself and become an active
Social-Democratic Party worker. He had learned war the hard way,
in action, and because of his force of personality had been chosen as
leader by the Germans of all creeds and parties who made up the
Thaelmann *columna*. The Capitán was clad in a much-worn khaki shirt
and trousers tucked into boots, with insignia of his rank sewn onto the
sleeves. His face was drawn, and Lanny guessed that he hadn't been
back from the front more than a few hours.

Raoul stayed by the car, so there were no introductions. Comrade
Monck, as Lanny had learned to call the German, was a man of direct
approach. His first words were the same that he had spoken at their
first meeting: "*Wir sprechen besser Deutsch.*" When Lanny assented,
he said: "*Bitte, kommen Sie mit,*" and led him out of the courtyard and

up a hillside path. Under a cork-oak tree, clear of underbrush and giving a view in all directions, they seated themselves. "Bushes may have ears," declared Monck.

Lanny was in the same businesslike mood. He didn't comment on the crash and rattle of gunfire. He didn't even ask: "How is the battle going?" It was enough that the enemy had retired from this field, if not from the atmosphere. "Trudi has disappeared in Paris," he announced.

"*Ach Gott, die Arme!* How long ago?"

"About three weeks. She had made me promise that if ever she disappeared, I would wait a while before I took any action. Then I tried to get in touch with the man whose name she had given me, a clarinetist, Professor Adler."

"I know him; a true comrade."

"I wrote twice, making an appointment, but he failed to show up."

"It must be that the Nazi devils have got him also."

"That is what I feared. Trudi has given me no other name, and you are the only person I could think of who might put me in touch with the underground."

"I guessed as much as soon as I heard you had come," replied the German.

"There is something I must explain at once," continued Lanny; "something rather embarrassing to me. Trudi has always insisted that I have a special value to the movement, in that I am able to get large sums of money. There are others who can write, print leaflets, and distribute them; so she said, again and again."

"The world being what it is, Herr Budd, she is right beyond question."

"She made me promise that never under any circumstances would I take any step that might reveal my connection with the underground, and make it impossible for me to go on with what I have been doing for her and a couple of other trusted friends. It puts a man in an awkward position, to have to see other people risking their lives while he lives in comfort and safety."

"You can put your conscience at rest," declared the Capitán. "From what Trudi told me I would name you as one of the persons indispensable to our movement. You should under no circumstances let yourself be tempted to break your promise."

Said Lanny: "You will understand better how difficult the decision has been when I tell you that for nearly a year Trudi has been my wife."

"*Oh, wie schrecklich!*" exclaimed the Capitán. Then, gazing into the visitor's face: "Herr Budd, you have my deep sympathy. This is a terrible thing in any case, and beyond words when it is someone we love. It is the time we live in that permits assured happiness to none of us."

"I have known what must be her fate, Comrade Monck; but somehow, it was impossible to be prepared."

"She was a magnificent girl; one of those who should be at the head of the German government, instead of the monsters and madmen who have seized the power."

"You think there is no chance that she may be alive?"

"Alive? Yes, quite possibly; but better dead."

"I wrestle with myself day and night. I ought to be doing something to save her. But what can I do?"

"What can anybody do, except to make war on the Nazis? Here, right now, we are having the satisfaction of putting a number of them where they can do no further harm. We are fighting what is called a holding action; the longer we can keep them busy in Spain, the more time we give the rest of Europe to awaken to its peril. The Nazi-Fascists did not expect this, I assure you, and it has deranged their plans not a little. It may be they will learn what is in the souls of free men and women, and be more hesitant in attacking the next democratic government. At least, that must be our hope."

IX

Lanny realized that he had come to the place of consolation, if any such there was in the world. The noise which filled this air was of a giant sausage machine, grinding up Nazis; here the self-called master-race were being met by the only measures that counted with them, the only argument they understood. If you really wanted to get rid of Hitlerism, these were the weapons and the techniques. The thing to do was concentrate your attention upon them, forgetting everything else.

"You must understand, Herr Budd," went on the Capitán, "I have been seeing men die in Spain for more than a year; men of conscience, of fine minds, many who were or might have become artists, writers, scientists, teachers—intellectuals of all sorts. They didn't have to come here and die; they might have lived quite safely elsewhere. I get to know them, I share their lives—and then in a fraction of a second I see their faces shot off, their guts blown out by a shell burst. I have to go on and leave them; the enemy is out there, and my business is with him. So you must understand, I have got used to death, and I spare my own feelings. There is a limit to the attention I can give to any one person, no matter how worthy."

"I understand perfectly," answered Lanny. "It was exactly the way Trudi felt, and tried to make me feel. It is I who am the weakling."

"That is not the way to put it. Trudi told me a good deal about you, Genosse Budd—may I call you that?"

"Assuredly."

"I have had a rough life, but I managed to hear a little music and read enough poetry to know that there are finer things in this world, and to appreciate people who have been able to live in them and for them. I know the torment you must be enduring, and I sympathize with all my heart. All I can tell you is that the fate of the world—not merely of Spain, but of all the future—is being decided up here in these hot and dusty hills, and we need the sort of help that you can give, we need it worse than any other kind. We cannot fight unless we have the weapons and we cannot get the weapons unless we can get world opinion behind us, unless we can somehow manage to explain why we are fighting—not for ourselves, but for those who are so blind and indifferent to their own danger."

"There is almost nothing I can do, Genosse Monck; I am filled with despair because of my impotence."

"Don't be too hard on yourself. I know about the documents you smuggled out of Germany for Trudi, and I know that they somehow got published and produced their effect. Also, the money you gave us was turned into hundreds of thousands of pieces of paper, and, as a result, millions of Germans know things of which they would otherwise be ignorant. All that will count some day—I don't know when or how, exactly, but we have to keep our faith in the human spirit, in the social mind. I beg you not to let this tragic sorrow weaken your determination and dry up the source of funds for our underground work."

"What it makes me want to do is to stay here and learn to fight like you. It makes me feel myself a coward——"

"To be a coward of that sort takes courage, Genosse Budd, and I beg you to have that special kind. You are one in a million, and you must keep the promise you made to your clearsighted wife."

"I am going to do my best," said the unhappy man. "I have to have your help in getting new contacts with the movement."

"You will certainly have that help. It may take a little time, because I have my duties here, and one cannot write about such matters from a war zone. I do not know how much longer this battle will last, but when it is over, I will apply for a furlough; I have earned it, because

I have been on duty constantly for more than a year. I will come to Paris and meet you and make the necessary contacts."

"That is all right, so far as it goes; but you are taking the chance that you may be killed in the meantime, and I would be left with a pocket full of money and no place to spend it. I do not know anyone else whom I could approach without risk of uncovering my secret."

"Let me think." There was a pause while Lanny listened to the sounds of the guns and endeavored with professional ears to sort one kind from another. Finally the Capitán inquired: "You remember how I identified myself to you, with a little sketch drawn by Trudi?"

"Be sure I shall never forget it."

"You have other such sketches in your possession?"

"Quite a collection."

"Are they signed, by any chance?"

"No; Trudi never put her name on anything."

"Very good; they will serve. I will write a letter to a man I know in Paris; let us call him 'X' for the present. I will say that I have a friend who is an artist; I want X to see his work, which I am sure X will appreciate. That is an innocent-appearing note which should not trouble any censor. I will say that the American art expert, Mr. Lanny Budd, has a collection of these drawings and will be glad to send him samples on request by mail. I will give your address, which Trudi taught me and which I have graven in my memory: Juan-les-Pins, Alpes Maritimes, France. X will guess that this is a party matter, and will write to you and ask to see the drawings you have for him. He knew Trudi in the old days and will recognize her work. In the event that I fail to show up in Paris, you can propose a meeting, and tell him everything and follow his guidance."

"That sounds all right," said Lanny. "But suppose the Gestapo has got this man also? They would undoubtedly make a response to me, and I would hate to be earning money for them to spend."

"The man I am sending you to is a German, about my age, which is thirty-five. He was in the Oranienburg concentration camp for two years. As a result he has a sort of nervous spasm, a tic I believe it is called; his left eyelid cannot be still. The Nazis in their efforts to make him talk used to tie his hands behind his back and then hang him up by the thumbs; that mangled his thumbs and pulled them out of joint; also it broke his shoulders and they healed improperly. You have a right to ask him to show you these various scars."

"I will do so," replied the other. "The Nazis might have difficulty in reproducing such marks at short notice!"

X

They discussed the methods by which they might communicate with each other, without Lanny's having to visit battlefronts. The Capitán said: "You understand that in a war like this, everybody watches everybody else, and often has reason for doing so. Letters may be stolen, or they may be secretly opened and read by others than the censors. We have traitors in our army—and you may be sure that Franco has some in his."

"By all means, Genosse Monck. Let me point out to you how my profession of art expert serves me in this situation. Would it be possible that you have some family heirlooms, old paintings which I might be trying to sell for you?"

"That would not sound likely with a man of workingclass origin."

"You might have a rich aunt—that can happen to the poorest. Let us say that you have a Tante Lize, and I have been to inspect her paintings, and I tell you that I am definitely certain I can sell the one showing the French prisoner of war. You would understand that I have got results from some investigations I am having made as to Trudi's whereabouts."

"Very good, Genosse Budd. I wish I might have a letter from you saying that you have got a good price for the painting showing the prisoner coming out from a dungeon."

"There is no limit to the price I would be able to get for such a painting," declared Lanny, earnestly. "You may assure your friends of the underground that that is the case."

"*Leider, Genosse,* such a work of art is beyond our skill to produce."

"This is one of the subjects I came to consult you about," continued the visitor. "Can you spare me a few minutes longer?"

"Our regiment has been brought back to rest and recuperate; therefore I am entitled to spend a couple of hours sitting under a shady tree talking with a friend from America."

"Even though it is a bourgeois person, and mysterious?"

The Capitán smiled. "This war has received a great deal of publicity, and you would be surprised how many tourists have thought of it as a spectacle for a summer's holiday. By one or another ingenious scheme they wangle a permit to come; they are writers, lecturers, painters, motion-picture directors or actors; sometimes they are businessmen who have goods to sell which we urgently need. Their wives wish to be able to go back to—what are the names of those strange towns in America?"

"Podunk, for example?"

"To Podunk, and say that they have heard the rumble of the cannon and smelled the smoke of powder. They show up here, and have to be fed even though the troops go hungry. They find it highly educational —until they get too close, and the wind brings the stench of human bodies rotting in this blazing Spanish sun. Then they have an attack of nausea and decide that battlefields and picnic grounds are not the same."

XI

Lanny got down to business. "Genosse Monck, there is a member of the German embassy in Paris, Graf Herzenberg, who has rented the Château de Belcour near Paris. Trudi was quite sure that members of the German underground who have disappeared have been hidden there. Have you heard anything about it?"

"No, but I would expect something of the sort to be done."

"It may be an obsession, but I am haunted by the idea that Trudi is in that place. It seems likely they wouldn't kill her so long as there was the slightest chance of getting out of her the information they so badly want."

"That is reasonable, I agree."

"Of course they might take her to Germany; but it might be more convenient to have her in Paris where her statements might be checked against those of others. They wouldn't have much reason to feel worried, for so long as Chautemps is premier of France, the government will be busy with political intrigues, and no one will take any sort of action displeasing to the German ambassador."

"That sounds convincing, also."

"I won't go into details—suffice it that I have social connections whereby I was enabled to make a thorough inspection of the ground floor of the château and of the grounds outside. I have drawn a reasonably accurate plan of the building and its environs. I am now having investigations made to see if I can find out about prisoners inside the place. If I get anything definite, I shall want a dependable man to undertake the job of rescuing Trudi. You understand how I am bound by my promise; I cannot do the job myself, and can only serve as secret paymaster."

"You will have difficulty in finding a man equal to that job, I fear."

"One of the reasons I came up here was the hope of persuading you to get a long enough furlough and make a try at it."

"*Aber!*" exclaimed the Capitán. "How could I work in France when

I do not know the language? I have only my German, and a few words of bad English, and enough Spanish to understand my orders, and to bargain with the peasants for food."

"You are a man of action and judgment. I have contacts with both the Socialists and the Communists in Paris, and could put you in the way to find dependable French assistance. Also, your contacts with the underground might help. Tell me, have you a family?"

"I have a wife and two children in Germany. The wife is working to support the little ones, against the time when I shall have saved up enough to bring them out."

"*Also!* If you will do your best for me, I will, regardless of success or failure, make it possible to bring your family out and to make them secure, at least until you are through with this war."

The Capitán sat in silence for quite a while. "What you are proposing is, in brief, that we shall burglarize a French château?"

"Possibly that, and possibly more, depending upon circumstances. First, we shall find out if Trudi is there, and second, if she is there, we shall get her out by whatever means it takes."

"Have you thought of any plans?"

"I have thought of many, some of them rather wild, I must admit. I succeeded in making friends with a member of the embassy staff, and I have thought that we might kidnap him and exchange him for their prisoner."

"*Aber nein, Genosse Budd!* The Nazis care nothing for individuals, and would sacrifice many lives to find where our underground has been getting its funds. Cross that one off."

"I have thought we might force the embassy man to talk, and perhaps to help us."

"The Nazis have you hopelessly licked at that game, for the reason that they have no scruples, while you have. Do you think you could torture a man?"

"Well, I have the feeling that if I was quite sure the man had Trudi, I would be willing to tear him to shreds to make him talk."

"You think you would, but you would probably find that the effort would wreck your nervous system. Also, you overlook the fact that the embassy would notify the French police as soon as their man was missing; and you do not enjoy diplomatic immunity."

"I have thought that we might have a small vessel and take the fellow out to sea."

"In that case, you would be a pirate, and any nation that caught you might hang you."

"Theoretically, yes; but practically, if you have money, you are sent to prison for a few weeks or months, until the scandal has blown over."

"You are speaking as a member of the leisure classes, Genosse Budd. You are accustomed to having your own way, and are annoyed by the idea of having to submit to law. But you must remember that I am a Socialist and a so-called Red fighter, and we are not privileged to break the laws of France or any other country; if we do, the police are prompt to proceed against us, and what is still more important, the capitalist press leaps to put all the details on the front page. You must bear in mind that our comrades of the underground in France are in that country as guests, and have to proceed with the utmost circumspection. The reactionaries are ceaseless in their watch to get something on us, to support the demand that we be expelled from the country. We face the fact that if crimes are committed against us, the police manifest very little interest, but if we dare to reply with a counter-crime, every form of power in the land rises up in wrath against us."

Said Lanny: "All that you tell me is right, and it means just one thing—that in whatever we plan to do, we must not fail."

"In other words, the perfect crime!" replied the officer, smiling for the first time in this colloquy.

XII

They discussed back and forth for quite a while, and at the end Monck said: "I cannot tell how long this battle will last. We have forced the enemy to retire all along the line, but we have not been able to rout him or surround him, and I doubt very much if we have the resources to do either. What happens in such clashes is that we extend our communications as far as we dare, and use up our supplies, both food and ammunition; then we have to halt, and there follows a long wait, perhaps a couple of months, while both sides bring up fresh troops and supplies. During that interval I can with honor apply for leave for a month, and I will meet you in Paris and see what you have been able to discover and what plans you have been able to work out. If you could present me with a really perfect crime, I might be willing to commit it; but I warn you in advance that I will take no chance of compromising our movement, and would strongly urge you not to do it either. That is what the Nazis would most desire, and what Trudi would forbid, if she had a say in the matter."

Sorrowfully Lanny had to admit that this was correct. He asked: "At your best guess, when should I expect you in Paris?"

"I would say three weeks, possibly four."

"That is a long wait for a woman under torture, **Genosse Monck**."

"You must not put that sort of pressure on me. There will be a long wait for men who are dying up in these hills while we talk, and for the hundreds of thousands of our comrades in all the concentration camps and prisons of the dictators—Spanish, German, and Italian."

"I say no more," replied Lanny. "I will go back to Paris, see what has been learned, and perhaps start further investigations. It may be then that I will take a fast steamer to New York, where I have a chance to get a large sum of money, and also to speak some important words to an influential person. One never knows, in dealing with our governing classes, when one is having any effect. It is like shooting arrows into the dark."

"We in this place do a lot of shooting into the dark. We prefer to use bullets and shells, when we can get them. Do what you can to move the hard hearts of the profit seekers and their politicians, and get us whatever help you can—that is, of course, without endangering your social position."

Again there was a smile upon the face of the speaker; but it faded quickly as there came a burst of machine-gun fire that sounded nearer, up in the hills to the left. "That may be a flanking attack," he said. "I am afraid I cannot talk any longer. *Adios, Compañero!*"

8

This Yellow Slave

I

THE return to Valencia was uneventful. Raoul talked about adult education in the army, and also about the great victory in the making. He was sure the Fascists were finally on the run—all the fighting men agreed on it. Lanny didn't tell him what the Capitán had said; in fact he didn't mention the officer, saying merely that his own purpose had been accomplished and that he was deeply grateful. Raoul said: "Come as often as you can."

They discussed the problem of getting a painting out of Spain. It was against the law, but laws were not being strictly enforced amid the confusions of war, and Raoul knew that the money was meant for the cause. "Our art treasures won't be of any use to us if Franco gets here," he conceded, and went on to say that Lanny might have trouble getting by the border carrying a rolled-up old master under his arm; some official might insist on adhering to the regulations and referring the matter back to Valencia, with endless red tape and delay. "Also it might cause publicity," Raoul opined.

Obviously, the thing to do would be to walk on board a foreign steamer, preferably one leaving for Marseille. No one would pay any attention to the baggage which a passenger took on board; the submarine pirates had been driven away, and the trip would be quick. Raoul undertook to visit steamship offices and make arrangement for the passage; Lanny would drive in the car to get the painting, and then proceed to Raoul's lodgings, pick him up and drive to the harbor of Gráo, where the steamers docked.

The address which Señor Jimenes had given was to the south of the city, beyond the cemetery. *La gasolina* was just about equal to the trip, and Lanny found the peasant home without too great difficulty. The gray-haired old servant was working in a vegetable patch, wearing a black sleeveless waistcoat attached to his cotton trousers with a broad *faja* of dark red. His eyes lighted up with delight when this foreign gentleman offered him a cigarette, something he had not seen for a long time. Lanny said: "I have a letter from the Señor, and he told me to show it only to you."

They found a seat under a heavily laden grape arbor, and the *huertano*, whose name was Tomás, took the letter in his hands and looked at it solemnly; he didn't know how to read handwriting, but was ashamed to confess it. His former master, having foreseen this, had told Lanny how to proceed; he was not to allow the man to take the letter to the village official who served as scribe, but talk to him patiently and convince him that the visitor was a friend of the family. To that end the master had provided various details, and Lanny now told the news about how they were living, the children in school, and so on. Lanny explained that he had agreed to buy the painting if he decided that it was genuine, and described the work as the Señor had described it, including the fact that one of the six little ragamuffins was eating a bunch of grapes. "That will convince Tomás," the owner had said. "He has seen it hanging on the wall most of his life, and his idea of art is the perfect texture of the grape skins."

"*Bueno, Señor*," said the man at last. Putting the letter into his pocket, together with the carefully extinguished cigarette butt, he led the way into the *barraca*, a cabin with a thatched roof, blue-washed sides, and a cross on top. The three women and as many children were not introduced, but Lanny greeted them kindly; the women bowed politely, while the little ones stared with open mouths. Tomás fetched a stool, and from up among the rafters, carefully concealed by old boards and rags, chains of garlic, of onions, and of dried figs, he drew forth a canvas cylinder about four feet long and perhaps a foot in diameter. The dust of a year was wiped from it and it was spread out and held open before the visitor's eyes.

Ars longa! Nearly three hundred years had passed since oils and pigments had been mixed and spread upon this well-woven cloth; kings and queens had reigned and perished, conquering heroes had been acclaimed and turned to dust—but here were half a dozen street urchins who had survived the ravages of time and were still laughing and full of energy. Their costumes were not so different from those of the little ones in this cabin, but their faces had that softness, that angelic quality of love, which must have been the basic ingredient of the soul of Bartolomé Esteban Murillo, for it manifested itself in everything he painted, whether it was cherubs out of heaven or disorderly little urchins on the narrow and crooked streets of old Seville.

If Lanny carried this painting out of the peasant's cabin he was obligated to release to Señor Jimenes the sum of a hundred and ten thousand French francs, which was something over four thousand dollars. If the painting proved not to be genuine, it might possibly be sold for as much as four hundred dollars. So Lanny was not satisfied with the thrill of beauty; he spread the canvas on the heavy wooden table which stood in the center of the all-purpose room and studied the signature and brushwork under his glass. When he was satisfied that it was an early Murillo, he said: "*Està bien, Tomás,*" rolled up the treasure, and tied it with the ragged hempen cord. He said his "*Buenas dias*" to the women, and saw the man carry the roll out and stow it in the car. He knew that Tomás was in a state of suppressed anguish at the idea of parting with this precious object on the basis of no more than some marks on a scrap of paper; he wasn't used to living by paper, like the *gente de la capital*. Having known the peasants of Mediterranean lands since childhood, Lanny spoke reassuring words, patted the old man on the back, and made him feel better with a whole packet of cigarettes and a ten-peseta note.

II

Raoul was waiting in front of his lodgings. He ran upstairs and got the typewriter and the suitcase, and while Lanny drove he explained that he had found a French freighter due to sail for Marseille that evening. He had engaged passage for the American traveler for the sum of four hundred and fifty francs. "Not very elegant," he apologized; but Lanny said: "It's all right if you got a guarantee against torpedoes." Raoul, having learned the American habit of "kidding" about the most serious subjects, replied: "A life-preserver goes with every ticket."

As a matter of fact, it was perfectly safe, for there was a gray-clad French destroyer patrolling off the port and a British light cruiser visible to the north. Chanticleer had crowed and the lion had roared; the Spaniards might kill one another and sink one another's ships all they pleased, but right at the moment nobody was going to sink French or British ships. Lanny walked on board with his precious roll under his arm and his Spanish friend carrying the rest of his luggage. Nobody asked any questions, and before long the engines of the rusty old tramp began to rumble and pound and she stole out past the long môle with her French flag proudly floating over a load of cork, hides, and other raw materials for the factories of Marseille or Lyons.

Lanny, who liked all sorts of people, made the acquaintance of two officers of the French merchant marine, and of sailors from two or three thousand miles of Mediterranean shore. He told the officers that he had a painting in his cabin; but didn't offer to exhibit it, and no one manifested curiosity. In his tiny cabin, reasonably clean, he wrote some notes for his Big Boss, telling what an officer of Loyalist forces on the Belchite front thought of the prospects of that battle and of the supplies which the opposing forces were getting from Germany and Italy.

The trip took two nights and a day. On his arrival, Lanny's first act was to phone to his mother, to ask if by any chance there had come a letter from his *amie* in Paris. No such luck; so he told her that he was alive and on his way to her. He had to come because his car was there, but of course he wouldn't say anything so tactless to an adoring mother. He asked her to phone to Señor Jimenes and tell him that the painting was safe, and that the money would be released as soon as Lanny could get to the bank. He sent a cablegram to a dear old lady in Chicago who purchased babies in paint, telling her that he was making a special trip to her home in order to show her the half dozen most charming urchins who had ever romped on the streets of old Seville. After which he engaged a taxi as the quickest way of getting himself and the aforesaid urchins to Juan-les-Pins.

III

At Bienvenu there was a letter from Rick in Geneva, where he had been sent by the editor of a leading weekly to report the opening ceremonies of the League of Nations Assembly. Rick enclosed a carbon copy of his first article, in which with quiet irony he contrasted the external splendors of the proceedings with their intellectual and moral bankruptcy. The British Indian ruler, Aga Khan, reputed to be the richest man in the world, was to be chosen President of this Eighteenth Assembly. He was a Moslem god, but the most modern of divinities, owning a famous racing stable and contributing twenty-five hundred quarts of champagne for the Geneva festivities. He spent most of his time on the Riviera, where Lanny had met him many times; he had admirable manners, and gave priceless jewels to the ladies who won his favor.

The new Palace of the League of Nations had been ten years a-building and had cost fifteen millions of dollars. It was magnificent beyond telling, and its murals, paid for by the Spanish republic, had as their subject the freeing of mankind from intolerance and tyranny; alas, the painter had gone over to the Franco side, and the Spanish republic was not sending delegates to the Assembly, on account of the failure of the League to act against Franco's intolerance and tyranny. Rick predicted that this Assembly would demand the withdrawal of foreign troops from Spain, and also the ending of Japanese attacks upon China, but that it would be powerless to enforce its decrees and not one of its members would move to make them good. All this took a couple of months to happen, and meantime the delegates from China went home, and Rick went home also, telling his readers that it was no longer worth his while to write, or theirs to read, about the doings of the League of Nations.

Lanny stayed at his mother's home long enough to have another session with Madame. Alas, he got nothing but the wearisome Claribel, and fragments of he knew not what; confused voices, names which he had never heard, references to happenings of no consequence; the contents of a mental junkshop, with goods molded and cracked and covered with dust. Lanny jotted it down in his notebook, and after a month or two would read it over to see if there were evidences of precognition, such as he had read about in the books of J. W. Dunne. But he didn't stay for more of it now, and wondered if Madame's gift was petering out. Poor soul, she was always afraid that would happen, and Lanny would console her, saying: "You have given us our money's worth already."

IV

Early in the morning Lanny stepped into his self-moving magic chariot, and this time he didn't stop at Le Creusot, but went straight through, reaching Paris in the late afternoon. His hands trembled as he glanced through his mail at his hotel. Nothing from Trudi; nothing from Professor Adler; only the silence of the tomb. So he phoned to his uncle. Having decided that it was no longer wise to visit that center of sedition, he had appointed a certain street corner as a rendezvous. Now he drove to the spot and took the elderly painter into his car.

They rolled peacefully about the drives of the Bois while Jesse made his report. He had an investigator—"Let's call him Jean," he said—"a dependable fellow who is a good mixer and knows how to get acquainted with all sorts of people. I didn't tell him what I expected to find; I just said I wanted to know what those Nazis are doing in that château and why there have to be so many of them. Jean found an old unused water-mill near the village, and he read up on the subject and took up the project of leasing it and putting it back into service. So he has an excuse to visit the peasants and ask if they would bring their grain to him; he sits in the *bistro* in the evening and chats with everybody, and the first crack out of the box they were telling him that it was no use expecting the patronage of the château, because those Germans have nothing to do with anybody. The village is bitter against them because men and women who had been employed there, and their fathers and grandfathers before them, were turned off without ceremony. That is an advantage to us, as you can see."

"Possibly a disadvantage," remarked Lanny. "They will be predisposed to believe whatever they hear, provided it is bad."

"Yes; but with hundreds of pairs of eyes watching, they can't fail to pick up some valid details. The Germans don't trade in the neighborhood, but bring all their supplies from Paris. One of their *camions* had a breakdown and halted by the roadside at night, and a peasant driving his cart stopped to see if he could help. Of course he was full of curiosity—and you know how sly they can be. The Germans said they didn't want any help, but he stood there offering comments, discussing the prospects of a storm, and so on; obsequious, but stubborn, and of course they couldn't order him off a highway in France. Tell me, is the party you are interested in a woman?"

"Why?"

"The peasant declares he heard a groan from inside the *camion*, and it seemed a high-pitched voice. It was a covered vehicle, and he couldn't see anything but what the Nazis illuminated with their flashlights."

"Do the people of the neighborhood believe there are prisoners in the château?"

"They are quite convinced of it. But of course it's a natural assumption; it's what the Nazis do wherever they go. A district like this, close to Paris, is tinged with Red, and naturally the Reds believe the worst."

"Has Jean met any party comrades?"

"Several, he tells me. He has let them have the idea that his sympathies lie their way."

"Did he follow up my tip about the laundry?"

"He has made contacts there. The Nazis bring the laundry and call for it, so there's no chance of getting inside by that method."

"Is he being careful not to excite suspicions by too many questions?"

"He's a clever chap, and used to the role of idle gossiper. Once you have established yourself as a Frenchman of the left, able to remember the last war and what *les sales boches* did, you are permitted to hate them. *Que le diable font-ils dans la patrie?* You can be sure it's nothing good, and that they are paying the pigs of politicians a lot of money to let them stay. That is the way Frenchmen talk in the *bistros* nowadays; they don't trust any of their *cochons*, and all they value politically is the privilege of calling them names."

V

Lanny said: "What you tell me fits in with the story I have heard, so let us get more. I have to run over to Chicago to sell a picture. I expect to be back in a couple of weeks and perhaps one or two days over. Meantime, have your man keep on working. We should have detail maps of the district, and a plan of the château. What could that mill be rented for?"

"I don't know, but it shouldn't be much. It is so run down as to be almost useless."

"We can lease it with an option to buy, and we can take our time and do a lot of discussing about fixing it up. Meantime, we have a rendezvous—and the Nazis would find it as hard to get into our place as we into theirs."

Lanny went to the bank next morning and drew out thirty thousand francs in the form of thirty crisp new notes. They looked immensely impressive, and even Americans had a tendency to be fooled and to forget that a franc was only three or four cents. (It had been doing a lot of fluctuating.) Lanny preferred to handle the sum in cash, because he was sure the banks were co-operating with the police authorities, and the last thing he wanted was to have anyone get the idea that he was putting up money for the Red cause. His uncle promised to stick the money away in an empty ginger-jar, and to change every single one of the notes before he paid them in any sort of transaction.

Lanny called Kurt on the telephone. Speaking English, he said: "On my way to Bienvenu I had lunch with Baron Tailor." Kurt knew both the English language and French geography, and would understand the reason for not saying Schneider. "I told him of my talk with you and he was interested and wants to hear more on the subject. You can follow that up if you wish." Lanny was sure that Kurt was never going to admit to him, directly or indirectly, that the Nazis were paying money to the Hooded Men; the proper role for Lanny was to be free from curiosity on all delicate subjects.

He went on to say that he had visited the château near Paris and had found some paintings of great interest. Also he had met a delightful young German, Leutnant Rörich. "What wonderful young men you have managed to train, Kurt! A quite new sort of men. *Unglaublich!*" He knew how Kurt would beam at that. "He reminded me all the time of Heinrich Jung. You remember when Heinrich was at that age, so full of his early enthusiasm for the Führer?"

They talked about old times for a bit, and at last Lanny informed his friend: "I am running over to Chicago to dispose of a painting. I am taking the *Bremen*, because it will be like a visit to Germany. I have been missing it." He inquired if there was anything he could do for his friend in either New York or Chicago, but Kurt said there wasn't. *Glückliche Überfahrt!*

VI

Lanny took a boat-train for Cherbourg. The great German liner was stopping there that night; she was as fast as any, and Lanny wanted to get the smell of Naziland after two years. Also he might pick up some items of information. He had three purposes in the trip: to sell his precious old master, which he now had carefully wrapped in oilcloth; to tell his father about the interview with Schneider and get due credit for this coup; and finally to visit Washington and make sure that his secret communications were being received and read. He hadn't dared make carbon copies of any of them, but he had them all in his head.

The steamer was magnificent and shiny, like everything the Nazis were displaying, and every German on board was as proud of it as of all the other triumphs of the *Neue Ordnung*. The vessel was crowded, for the most part with Americans on their way home from a summer of culture seeking and finding; they were loaded with it and couldn't resist unloading upon Lanny, even when they learned that he had lived in Europe most of his life. He had been able to get on board at the last moment by sharing the bridal suite, the most expensive apartment, with a manufacturer of machine tools from a city of Indiana. He chanced to meet this large expansive gentleman in the steamship office; they both had money, but shrank from paying twenty-one hundred dollars for a five-day journey, and decided to stand each other's company. The gentleman was a devout Catholic and hung a crucifix over his bedpost as soon as he opened his bags; it had been blessed by a bishop, and would keep him from being seasick in spite of equinoctial storms. He had recently kissed the Pope's toe, and received a rather gaudy medal for his contributions to the building of a cathedral.

Opposite to Lanny at the table sat a plump widow who owned most of the stock of a manufacturing plant in Camden, New Jersey. She had with her a lovely daughter, a bold striking brunette just out of Vassar. How Beauty Budd's heart would have thumped if she had been there, and how quickly she would have convinced the mother of the supereligibility of her brilliant son. Mother and daughter had been doing the grand tour, and it had included at the end a ten-day excursion into Russia, entering by way of Leningrad and coming out by Moscow. The only things they had enjoyed had been the paintings, and the palace of the Tsar and Tsarina with the bedrooms and all the knickknacks and bric-a-brac untouched. All the rest of Russia was dirt and bad smells, dingy clothing and water-spigots out of order. Women actually working on the railroads, shoveling dirt! Women paddling along barefooted in the dusty roads, following their men! Most horrible!

A relief to come out into Poland, and find the stations with counters loaded with every sort of delicious foods. And the army officers, with such gorgeous sky-blue uniforms! The ladies had spent a whole day in Warsaw and hadn't seen a sign of any slums; they hadn't heard there was a ghetto, and were quite sure that stories of pogroms were just made up by the hateful Bolsheviks. Lanny had learned to listen to such opinions and smile amiably. In his mind was the thought: "You should have stayed a while longer, Miss Gwendolyn, and married one of those uniforms!"

VII

Studying the passenger list of the steamer, Lanny noted the name of Forrest Quadratt, the poet whom he had met at Irma's Long Island home; American-born of German descent, and said to be a left-handed relative of the Kaiser. He had been a lifelong devotee of *Machtpolitik* and Lanny was sure that he was now a well-paid agent of the Nazis. Their last meeting had been in the days of Lanny's suppressed quarrel with Irma, and he couldn't be sure that she hadn't given the man some hint of her husband's distressing political attitude. Whenever Lanny suspected anything like that, he had a deft way of covering it up; he would say: "I used to have a Pinkish tinge to my thinking, but what I have learned about the wholesale purges in Russia has cured me. I realize now that Europe has to be protected from the Asiatic hordes, and nobody but the Germans can do it."

The one-time decadent poet—he said that he had "given up the genius business"—was in his fifties; rather small and stoop-shouldered, nearsighted and wearing thick glasses through which he peered out at you; leaning forward and speaking with rapidity—English, French, or German, *wie Sie wollen, comme vous voulez*, as you like it. His hand was soft, warm, and moist, and so was his voice. He had sinned heavily and written about it boldly; also he had read the literature of sin, and was cynical about what was in the hearts of men, and what women were doing when they shut and locked the doors of steamship cabins.

Like all the Nazis, Quadratt was convinced that the mass of mankind was made up of dolts and imbeciles who had to be given orders and made to obey. He considered that the Germans were the proper people to take charge of Europe and bring it out of the Middle Ages. The British had their huge empire, and should be content with that and not make Germany the victim of their jealousy and greed. As for the United States, they were the people who most resembled Germans, and should be their spiritual brothers, as they already were their blood brothers—owing to the vast immigration of Germans, who had brought most of the new country's culture. Let America be content with the Western Hemisphere, upon which the Germans had no designs whatever. If you asked Quadratt why the German propagandists were so active in all South American countries, he would answer that their attitude was purely defensive, a result of America's having deprived Germany of her hard-won victory in the last war.

But Lanny Budd asked no questions of that sort. Lanny Budd was the spiritual brother of the Nazis, an art expert who had sold pictures for General Göring and shot stags with him; an amateur pianist who had played the *Moonlight Sonata* for the Führer; a gentleman of leisure and fashion who had been the friend and patron of Germany's greatest living *Komponist*. In Lanny's pocketbook was a clipping from the *Münchner Neueste Nachrichten*, telling how the American *Kunstsachverständiger* was directing a one-man show of his former stepfather's paintings in Munich, and how he had taken the *chef-d'œuvre* to the Führer at the Braune Haus and the Führer had certified to the validity of the art work. This clipping included a photograph of the distinguished American, and thus served as a *Legitimationspapier* to any Nazi anywhere.

Lanny wished to make himself rock-solid with this *Nummer-Eins* propagandist in the land of Lanny's fathers; he swore him to secrecy as to the source of his information and then revealed the new revolutionary movement to abolish the Third Republic of France and put an end to the alliance with Russia. Quadratt pretended to know all about it, but obviously he knew very little, and Lanny let himself be deftly led to make revelations; the Nazi agent enjoyed getting the better of anyone, and the presidential agent enjoyed watching a smooth psychological trickster doing his stuff. Lanny was sure it couldn't do any harm for Quadratt to possess this information, and it was a way of getting a Nazi to unveil his innermost soul.

The talk took place in the ex-poet's stateroom, where they could be sure of privacy—at least the ex-poet could be sure. Lanny wondered if there might be a dictaphone, but decided that it wouldn't matter, for he wasn't naming the de Bruynes or Schneider; only those French politicians whom the Nazis had on their payroll. After this steamship intimacy had progressed to the proper point, Lanny ventured: "We're going to have to do something of the same sort in America, I very much fear."

The Kaiser's left-handed relative didn't consider it necessary to play shy like Kurt Meissner; what he played was sad, for he was a tenderhearted man, a lover of culture and peace, and he hated to see violence and cruelty anywhere. Said he: "I am afraid that you are right, Mr. Budd. There are elements in every country today which are deliberately or otherwise playing the Moscow game, and they have no intention of letting themselves be put down without a struggle."

Lanny knew that Quadratt had sounded out Robbie Budd on the question of the Hooded Men of America and the possibility of their being used to overthrow the New Deal. Now Robbie's son threw out a piece of bait, and was amused to see the speed with which the peace-loving Nazi grabbed it. Lanny said he had heard the subject discussed in American drawing-rooms and that some of the most prominent victims of the New Deal were now in a mood to put up money and save themselves from further victimization. Quadratt made plain that he wanted nothing in the world so much as to know the location of those drawing-rooms; and Lanny promised to invite these wealthy friends to meet Quadratt and hear what he had to suggest.

The son of Budd-Erling went on to discuss some of the more prominent public enemies of the New Deal: Mr. Henry Ford, who had spent a fortune to awaken Americans to the menace of Jewish Imperialism; Colonel McCormick of Chicago, lavish in subsidizing those groups which were struggling to keep America out of European affairs; Mr. Hearst, who had interviewed the Führer just recently, and whose newspapers were the Rock of Ages for all friends and sympathizers of National Socialism; Mrs. Elizabeth Dilling, who ran a sort of volunteer intelligence service and had a dossier on every man or woman who had ever given aid or comfort to Moscow. Lanny said he hadn't met any of these persons, but would like very much to meet Hearst and the wife of Ford for business reasons, since both were noted for their interest in painting. Did Quadratt know of any way to bring him together with either of these highly inaccessible persons?

The reason for this proposal was that Lanny knew the world in which he lived, and was sure that Forrest Quadratt would have more respect for him if he believed him to be engaged in making plenty of money like Quadratt himself, and not just traveling about the world indulging a yen to meet celebrities and put his feet under the dinner tables of the rich. When they parted on board that steamer, they were friends who understood each other thoroughly and were prepared to exchange favors. You scratch my back and I'll scratch yours!

VIII

Arriving in New York, Lanny signed an affidavit to the effect that his painting dated from approximately 1645, which meant that he did not have to pay any duty upon it. Then he stepped into a taxicab and was driven to the airport from which a plane left for Chicago almost every hour. He sent a telegram to Mrs. Sophronia Fotheringay, saying that he was coming. Instead of going directly to her home, he went to a picture dealer and had the painting put into an elaborately hand-carved old Spanish frame. When he reached the mansion on Lake Shore Drive he dined with the hostess, and told her the story of his trip into the land of the Reds—the deepest-dyed and bloodiest of all Reds now operating. Manifestly, a painting must be extremely valuable to justify the taking of so many risks as the expert described.

The old master was hung in the drawing-room, with a proper reflector above it. Before they went in to see it Lanny delivered his spiel about a painter who had been the favorite of Spain all his lifetime, and after three centuries was the favorite of all persons everywhere who loved sweetness and light. They entered the room, and the elderly widow was seated in a padded armchair, after which Lanny ceremoniously unveiled the treasure. Of course she was enraptured; she saw in one of those dark-eyed urchins the perfect image of her only son, who had been killed in the Meuse-Argonne and was now waiting for her in heaven. His photograph stood on the piano, and Lanny had to get it and compare them, and admit that the likeness was extraordinary. The coincidence cost the old lady an extra five thousand dollars.

When the visitor mentioned that he was asking thirty thousand for the painting, old Mrs. Fotheringay never turned a hair. When he told her that he would prefer to have her call in some other expert, say from the Art Institute, to pass judgment on the work's authenticity and the fairness of the price, she waved the idea aside, saying that he had risked his life to get it, and she liked it. She didn't mention, but Lanny knew, that she had so much money she literally didn't know what to do with it. Her husband had left her the royalties upon certain basic patents having to do with machine-tools of which she did not even know the names; all she knew was that several million dollars was paid every year into her bank account, and she wrote checks for any amount that came into her head, often without taking the trouble to enter the item in the stub—which made it rather hard for her business manager. Now she wrote a check payable to Lanning Prescott Budd, and he wrote her a bill of sale.

Afterwards he strolled with her about the many rooms of this old-style overdecorated home, and looked at all the painted babies and children, many of which he had bought for her. She told him that she loved them all, and would not part with a single one at any price. She invited him to spend the night, but he said that he was taking a plane back to New York at midnight, so she told her butler to have a car ready for him at the proper hour. He devoted the rest of the evening to telling her about art in Europe and preparing her mind for the next picture he might bring. He had never been mercenary in the past, but now he had become so, on account of Trudi. Gold, "this yellow slave," was going to perform for him the magic service of getting his wife out of a dungeon cell.

So Lanny told himself. It is an ancient doctrine, and highly dangef-out—that the end justifies the means. Looking upon the matter through Marxist eyes, he could see it as the automatic operation of economic force. How could any man on earth see that amiable stout old lady with her pen poised to write checks, and not say: "I might as well have it as the next fellow"? If you had any sort of "cause," including a Marxist one, you naturally believed it the best of causes—otherwise you would have had some other!

IX

Back in New York, Lanny called Gus Gennerich at his hotel in Washington, and was told to call back in four hours. He telephoned Hansi and Bess to say "Hello," and then Johannes to invite him to have lunch and a gossip. He called Robbie, and said that he was going to Washington on picture business, and would come to Newcastle on his return. He added that he had "big news," but didn't say what, for when he told about Schneider's "bid," he wanted to see the expression on Robbie's face, and if possible lead the conversation into channels of interest to Robbie's son.

When he called Gus the second time, the man asked if he could take a plane to Washington at once. Lanny said: "You bet!" and Gus replied: "Call me at nine-thirty tonight."

This so wonderfully comfortable modern world was getting smaller and smaller, and those who had the price of its services were getting them more and more prompt and efficient. The porter in Lanny's hotel would phone to the airport for his reservation, and meantime a taxi would be speeding the passenger to a newly opened field which was a marvel of administration. Safe traveling "on the beam" would deliver him in his country's capital in an hour, a journey which had taken the founder of the country at least two weeks.

So it came about that Lanny Budd was again picked up on a street corner and delivered through the "social door" of the White House. The "Governor" was in bed, as before, but this time he had no sniffles; his family and guests were looking at a movie upstairs, while he had begged off on the plea of pressing work. "Hello, Marco Polo!" he exclaimed, when his visitor entered the room; he always had comical names for his intimates, and had been struck by the fact that no two of Lanny's communications bore the same dateline.

They had been numbered serially, and he had read every word, so he declared. "It is better than a Cook's tour; you should have them made into a movie some day." Then, his expression and tone changing as suddenly as any movie actor's, he demanded: "What is going to be the outcome in Spain?"

"The Belchite drive has come to an end," replied the visitor; "just as I wrote you it would. Franco has taken most of the north, with its iron ore that Hitler wants so badly. The rest depends upon the British and French Cabinets. If they continue the farce of 'Non-Intervention' while Hitler and Mussolini send in all the supplies needed, the end is certain. It may take another year, but no people, no matter how brave and determined, can fight airplanes and artillery with sticks and stones. Neither side has the manufacturing resources to fight a modern war, and it's purely a question of how much each can get from outside."

Lanny had been told, definitely and flatly, that the "Governor" wouldn't do anything about that. But he couldn't give up; nobody could give up who had been to the battlefront and seen the bloodshed and agony. He was too tactful to say "Please," or "You must," or anything of that sort; he just told what he had seen with his eyes and heard with his ears, and it was better than any movie which F.D. could have enjoyed upstairs. First Trudi and the visit to the Château de Belcour; then the trip to Spain, and what El Capitán had reported under the sound of the guns. Said Lanny: "This raid is the beginning of a war on civilization, and it won't stop until the last bastion has been knocked out. The best military brains in Europe are planning it and this time they aren't overlooking anything."

This Cassandra in trousers was in a strong position, because only a few weeks previously he had warned his hearer that France was to be the next victim, and now he was able to bring the blueprints of this future operation. He told what he had heard from the lips of the de Bruynes and Baron Schneider in two long talks. When Lanny was speaking to the Nazis he lied carefully, but to the President of his country he would bring the precise truth, and wouldn't hide any name, unless perhaps that of his own father. F.D. was the one who had the right to know, and Lanny must count everything else as second to that service. There were things he couldn't put on paper, but in the privacy of this bedroom he got them on the record.

"There are reasons, Governor, why you should understand my relationship to the de Bruyne family; no Frenchman would need an explanation, but an American does. Marie de Bruyne made me a sort of godfather to those two boys, and they still think of me in that relationship; they keep no political secrets from either my father or myself, and so it has come about that I am in the center of the coming storm in France. I mention this so that when I tell you I know something, you will be sure that I really do know it. In future, when I write, let the de Bruynes be St. Denis, and Baron Schneider be Mr. Tailor."

"Have you made a note of these?"

"I have prepared a list of such names. Kurt Meissner is Kaiser; that is where his loyalties began, and may end again. You understand that Kurt was an officer of the old army; it was that army which sent him to Paris at the time of the Peace Conference. His brother Emil is a general, and Kurt is an agent of that same army today. You must know that the Germans have half a dozen organizations doing their secret work in the Ausland; Goebbels has one, and I'm pretty sure that Göring has his own; Rosenberg, the supplier of the official Nazi religion, has his, and so have the SS, and the Gestapo, or Secret State Police. The old army, the Reichswehr, has perhaps the biggest of all. Those officers are exclusive, and they look upon the Nazis as upstarts and intruders; it's all for the Fatherland, of course, but the old army has its own way of doing things, and keeps its own secrets. I am not sure, but I got hints that Kurt and the Graf Herzenberg are not on the most cordial terms. The fact that it was an SS officer who showed me about the grounds of the Château de Belcour indicates that the Nazis are running the Embassy, while Kurt's organization is serving the army."

"Did Kurt admit to you that the Cagoulards are taking his money?"

"No, and I'm sure he never will. Even if friendship prompted him to, he is under a solemn oath. But you know how it is; you can smell things in the atmosphere. Both Schneider and the de Bruynes made it plain that they want all the money they can get and they don't care who puts it up; also, it goes without saying that Hitler would rather take France by a revolution than by a costly war. You have only to ask yourself—what else would Kurt be doing in Paris? When he left my home on the Riviera and went back to Germany to live, he was a musician devoted to his art and living a most austere life; I doubt if he had five hundred dollars a year to keep himself and his family. But now he lives in a fashionable apartment with a blond secretary and an ex-soldier to wait on him and drive him in a limousine. What is all that for? Manifestly, to find out what high-placed Frenchmen are for sale, and to buy them."

"The Frenchmen know what they are selling?"

"Some do and some don't; Hitler is as cunning as the devil when he wants to be. He is holding out an olive branch with one hand, and keeping his dagger behind his back in the other. Perhaps—who knows?—if the Frenchmen take the olive branch he will not use the dagger. Many of them choose to believe so, and not all have been bought for cash; they want to break the alliance with the Reds, and put down the labor unions and the sit-downs, and Hitler is the one who knows how. It is one ideology and one technique all over the world, and it is spreading fast. The dictators are all blood brothers under their skins."

"Under their shirts," put in F.D., with a smile.

"It makes the Communists wild for anyone to say so, but the fact is that Mussolini took over his technique from the Bolsheviks; the Agit-prop, the Gaypayoo, the youth movement, the whole show. When I first met Mussolini he told me: 'Fascismo is not for export'—but that was only until he had got firmly set in the saddle. Then he passed on his bag of tricks to Hitler, and now the two of them have loaned it to Franco, and to the little Balkan dictators. I have been watching the Croix de Feu, the Jeunesse Patriote and all the others in France, and it is a standardized product—if you follow the formula you can produce it in any part of the world where you can raise money for shirts and armbands and banners and drums and the salaries of rabble-rousers. In this country, I am told, the shirts are silver, or gold, or white—more appropriate to a country which can afford laundry bills."

X

That led to Forrest Quadratt and Lanny's negotiations on board the *Bremen*. Like Kurt, the ex-poet had never admitted that he was a Nazi agent, but he had shown wide acquaintance with the art of getting the money of the rich, and also with the names and addresses of persons who might like to see a coup d'état against the New Deal. Lanny said: "He knows exactly what he wants, and again it is the standard product. Quadratt talks to Americans and Kurt talks to Frenchmen, so they have different sets of phrases, but the thing they talk about is identical."

"They really imagine they can make headway in a free country like America?"

"I assure you they are making headway very fast, and are full of confidence. They figure that the New Deal cannot go on piling up public debt indefinitely; and when you have to stop, there will be a smash-up, and that will be their chance. The very freedom we are so proud of is their assurance of success; we are made impotent by it, and cannot imagine taking action against those who use their freedom to destroy ours."

"It is hard to see just what I can do, until they take some overt action." F.D. seemed to be thinking out loud, and Lanny put in quickly: "Are you open to a suggestion, Governor?"

"Always, of course."

"We grant that American citizens who have millions of dollars have a right to use them to poison the public mind; but surely we don't have to grant the right of foreigners to come in and intrigue against us. Why doesn't some congressman propose a law requiring all agents of foreign governments to register, say with the State Department, declaring what government they represent, what payment they receive, and the nature of their duties? If American citizens serve on the payroll of foreign governments, why not make them do the same? That would turn the spotlight of publicity upon them; it would frighten some, and might be the means of jailing a few who would try to keep their doings secret."

"By Jove, Lanny, that's an idea! I'll give some thought to it."

The younger man flushed with pleasure. "You know my position. I can't make any suggestions to congressmen; but you, no doubt, make them now and then."

"Indeed, rather often!" replied the President, with one of his broad grins. "They aren't always accepted, but I keep on trying."

XI

They came back to the subject of Quadratt, and Lanny said: "I believe I have him on the hook, and could get a lot of information about his doings." But the President replied that he had abundant sources of information as to the United States. He wanted the son of Budd-Erling to return to Europe where he had so many carefully cultivated entrées. Roosevelt was really frightened by the prospect of waking up some morning and reading that France was in the hands of the Fascists. He complained that the State Department could hardly be ignorant of these intrigues, and wondered what those well-bred young gentlemen did with such information when they got it.

F.D.R. was a free and easy talker, which was one reason he had so many enemies. He described to his visitor that venerable and somewhat musty building, whose inmates had a tendency to take on the color of their environment. Secretary Hull was the most honorable and high-minded lawyer who had ever come out of the mountains of Tennessee, but he was somewhat old-fashioned in his thinking, and devoted to his idea that freedom of trade would solve all the problems of the nations. He was a former senator, and possessed the confidence of those elder statesmen to a greater degree than F.D. himself; so F.D. had been forced to adopt the method of putting in younger men upon one pretext or another. "But the trouble is, they all take to wearing top-hats and spats, and presently I discover that the new state of the State Department is more stately than the old."

Lanny chuckled. "Perhaps you might like me to investigate them for you."

"No," was the reply; "I know them too well already." Then the laughter went out of the great man's voice and he continued: "I really deplore the spread of these reactionary doctrines all over Europe. I want to know what I can do about it, and when, and how."

This was the opening for which Lanny had been praying, and he stepped into it without hesitation. "May I make another suggestion, Governor?"

"Always, Lanny. Believe me, I am glad to make use of other men's minds. You have lived among these new movements and seen them grow, while to me they are almost incomprehensible; I hear the stories of what the Nazis are doing, and it seems like somebody's nightmare."

"It is primitive barbarism employing all the techniques of modern science. That makes it the most dangerous movement in human history; the last upsurgence of the beast in man against the restraints of civilization. The first step in fighting it is to understand it, and that is where you can help more than any other man. For in addition to being the most powerful executive in the world, you are the greatest educator in the world. And don't think that is just taffy—you can talk to twenty or thirty million Americans any time you wish, and sooner or later what you say reaches every literate person in the world."

"You want me to warn them about the Cagoulard conspiracy?"

"No. The French people would resent your claim to know more about their affairs than they do. I don't mean even that you should name the Nazis, or the Fascists, or the Falangistas, or any other group. But surely, as the spokesman of the world's leading democracy, you can warn our people that the dictatorships which are spreading over the world are an evil force, the enemy of every freedom-loving man, and woman. Surely it is your duty, as the leader of the free world, to speak out against aggression, and say that some way must be found to quarantine the aggressors and make it impossible for them to disturb the peace and order of the world."

Lanny had had his say, and he knew when to stop. The President sat staring before him with a frown on his face, and Lanny watched him. A large and decidedly noble head—or so it seemed to an admirer; graying hair, beginning to thin at the front and on top; broad heavy shoulders and vigorous arms lying relaxed on the bedsheet; blue and white-striped pajama coat open over a powerful chest. In that large head was a brain, and inside it, by some process beyond the comprehension of all the scientists on earth, a chain of thoughts was being generated which might change the destiny of the world. Lanny was afraid to breathe or to blink an eyelid for fear of interrupting those thoughts.

At last the President spoke, his voice low and grave. "You are right, Lanny. I believe I will do it. It will raise merry hell, but the time has come for speaking out. I am scheduled to leave for a trip to the west and I shall be making several speeches. Would you like to write one of them?"

All the *savoir faire* that Lanny Budd had acquired in a leisure-class lifetime failed him at that juncture, and he blurted out: "*Me,* Governor?"

"I have a lot to do, and the mark of a good executive is never to do anything that he can get done. You have your mind full of this subject, and why not get it off? I don't say that I won't change it a lot; but you make the first draft."

"O.K., if you say so."

"Let us get the key phrases on paper without delay. Do you use a typewriter?"

"Yes."

"All right, there's one over in the corner. Turn on the light and imagine yourself the greatest educator in the world. You are going to write a few sentences which all literate people on earth will read and give thought to."

"My God!" exclaimed the son of Budd-Erling. "If I am able to hit the keys straight!"

This amiable great man was not above being pleased by his visitor's naïveté, and he had learned to take his multiple duties with a flavoring of gaiety. "Don't use too violent language," he cautioned. "Remember your responsibilities!"

XII

Lanny went to the typewriter and seated himself, took off the cover, turned on the light, and put in a sheet of paper. His head was in a whirl, but the whirl was full of words and phrases, because he had been a talker all his life, and now for many years his talk had been of the perils of Nazi-Fascist dictatorship. Sentences took form, and he found that his fingers were equal to the task of hammering them out. When he had finished, he read: "The present reign of international lawlessness began a few years ago. It began through unjustified interference in the internal affairs of other nations or the invasion of alien territory in violation of treaties; and has reached a stage where the very foundations of civilization are seriously threatened."

"O.K.," said the President, and Lanny's head was more in a whirl than ever. But still, it didn't keep another sentence from coming. He typed it and then read: "Innocent peoples, innocent nations, are being cruelly sacrificed to a greed for power and supremacy which is devoid of all sense of justice and humane considerations."

Again the listener said: "O.K."

Then a third sentence, one which seemed crucial to its author: "When an epidemic of physical disease starts to spread, the community approves and joins in a quarantine of the patients in order to protect the health of the community against the spread of the disease."

"Excellent!" exclaimed the President. "Take that for your keynote. Everybody in the world understands the nature of a quarantine." Then he ordered: "Read it all over to me." After listening he asked: "If I say something like that, will you be satisfied?"

"Oh, Governor! It will make me as proud as a dog with two tails."

F.D. chuckled. "Where did you get that phrase?"

"Somewhere in England they have such dogs." Lanny liked his fun, too.

The President sat in thought, and it was not about dogs' tails. "Consider this for a moment," he said. "The German people have had some real grievances, have they not? There were clauses in the Versailles treaty which couldn't be enforced and shouldn't have been there."

"Indeed yes, Governor. I got myself into hot water by speaking out against them."

"Then suppose we make it harder for the Nazis by admitting that fact. Let us put in a paragraph that will cut the ground from under them. Take this—" and he dictated, phrase by phrase, while Lanny typed: "It is true that the moral consciousness of the world must recognize the importance of removing injustices and well-founded grievances; but at the same time it must be aroused to the cardinal necessity of honoring the sanctity of treaties, of respecting the rights and liberties of others, and of putting an end to acts of international aggression."

Lanny typed those words, and read them back. "Will that do any harm?" the other asked.

"It shows me what it means to be a statesman."

So both were pleased, with themselves and with each other. "I want a speech of say twenty minutes," explained the President, "about ten typewritten pages. How soon could you have that ready?"

"I'll do it tonight. Believe me, I won't do any sleeping till it's finished."

"Get it to Gus's hotel as soon as it's ready. I'll tell him to expect it. I think I'll use it in Chicago, where I'm scheduled to speak at the opening of the Outer Drive Bridge. How Bertie McCormick will foam at the mouth!"

"Don't lose your nerve and back out on me, Governor."

"I'll probably change your text so that you won't know it, but the substance will be there. I've had something of the sort in my noodle for a long time. I tell you in advance, nothing I have said in my entire career has aroused such a fury of opposition as those half-dozen sentences will—and it won't be only among the Republicans!"

XIII

Lanny went to his hotel room, set up his own typewriter, and went to work. He didn't need to order any coffee, for he was in a state of exaltation. Now, at last, he was going to change the world! Everything he had ever done in his life was preparation for this job. His head was so full of ideas that it was hard to sort them out. An exposé of all Fascist aggression, a call to solidarity of all democratic forces— and all in three thousand words!

He paced the floor and ordered his thoughts. The Nazi-Fascist piling up of armaments; the efforts of the peace-loving nations for an understanding; the Covenant of the League, the Briand-Kellogg Pact, the Nine Power Treaty. When he had got it clear in his head he sat and typed—all through the small hours of the morning. He revised and marked out and tore up and retyped, and worked in a fever, until the sunlight was streaming into the room. The final task—the making of a clean copy—he might have entrusted to the hotel stenographer; but he thought: "Suppose F.D. delivers it as I wrote it, and then she remembers it!" No, he had to do it all.

He allowed himself the luxury of one carbon copy, which he would seal up and put away in his safe-deposit box in the First National Bank of Newcastle, of which Esther Budd's father was president. All the earlier drafts were torn into small pieces and sent down into the capacious sewers of the city of Washington. The first copy was sealed in an envelope and addressed to Gus Gennerich's suite in the Hotel Mayflower. Lanny called a messenger and entrusted him with the precious missive, cautioning him that it was important and giving him a half-dollar to stimulate his sense of duty. Lanny waited until Gus had telephoned: "O.K., Zaharoff." Then he pulled down the shades, shut off his phone, hung out his Do Not Disturb sign, and slept the sleep of one who has succeeded in reversing the foreign policy of his country.

BOOK THREE

Most Disastrous Chances

9

His Honor Rooted in Dishonor

I

IN NEWCASTLE, Lanny found his father in a high state of discontent. Budd-Erling Common had lost seven points on the market in the past week. Other stocks had done even worse; business was receding, and another panic was in the air. After all that New Deal spending, nobody had money enough to buy anything, and goods were piling up in the warehouses. Of course Robbie blamed That Man; Lanny, hiding his guilty secret, felt himself more than ever the snake in the grass. He listened politely and didn't say a word while Robbie denounced the madness of trying to bring back prosperity by spending; here we had piled up a huge public debt—and where were we? No place that Robbie Budd wanted to be!

Troubles never came singly. Those C.I.O. organizers who had slipped into the Budd-Erling plant and poisoned the minds of the workers had now got to the stage where they were presuming to demand a conference with Robbie's executives. There was supposed to be something called a Wagner act which compelled Robbie to negotiate with them, but he had set his jaw; he wasn't going to recognize the act, he would close up his business before he would let any gangleaders come in and tell him how to run it. Lanny wanted to say: "You are the original anarchist, Robbie," but instead he told how he had just sold for thirty thousand dollars a painting which he had bought for a little more than four thousand.

Robbie couldn't but be tickled by news such as that. Better than he had ever managed to do in all his business career! There must be a catch in it somewhere, and he asked: "Won't that old woman find out that you've overcharged her?"

Lanny replied: "Mrs. Fotheringay is a perfect lady, and never mentions what she has paid for her art treasures. I doubt if she remembers for more than a few days. She got something that will bring her happiness every time she looks at it; and nobody found it but me."

The cautious father wanted to know what his son was going to do with all that money. He would have been pleased if the son had answered: "Put it into Budd-Erling." But Lanny was noncommittal; he had something in mind that he would tell about later. The father said: "I hope to God you're not giving it away to those radicals of yours." Robbie cherished the notion that the "radical movement" was in great part the creation of his son's perverted generosity.

Lanny had thought it over and decided to feed his father some of that soothing syrup which he was administering to the rest of the fashionable world. "No," he replied, gravely. "I've about made up my mind that the world isn't going to change as fast as I hoped. I'm definitely done with politics. I'm going to retire and cultivate my own garden." It was pathetic to see how eagerly the father gulped this down. It made him so happy that he forgot the stock market and the C.I.O. for the rest of the evening.

They were settled in his den, and while he smoked a long dark cigar that came out of a gold-foil wrapper, Lanny told about his visit to the de Bruynes and the later one to Le Creusot. He didn't say that he had undertaken to act as go-between for the Hooded Men and the Nazis; he said that he had talked airplanes—which was true—and that the Baron had admitted being uneasy because the Germans were forging so far ahead of his country. Lanny had told him what the new Budd-Erling pursuits were able to do, and now the Baron wanted to have Robbie Budd call upon him. Robbie didn't need to have it pointed out to him that that might mean something really big. "I've been planning to see Göring," he said. "I'll see the Baron first, and that will help me with the General." It is the essence of the munitions man's technique to play two rival countries each against the other.

Lanny told about the Cagoulard conspiracy and the fortification in the de Bruyne garden; also the talk with Quadratt, and the Nazi effort to unite all the different sorts of "shirts" in America. It was Lanny's hope that his father might "open up" on this subject, but all Robbie said was: "The New Deal is doing its best to force something like that on us, and if they keep asking for it, they may get it." Lanny was pretty sure his father had information along this line, but the only way Lanny could have got it was by doing with Robbie what he had already done with Kurt: pretending to change his viewpoint and approve the conspiracy. But Lanny couldn't bring himself to take that step. Robbie would go far enough without any encouragement. With it, he might get himself seriously involved, and Lanny wouldn't take that upon his conscience. Back to the ivory tower!

II

There was another bee buzzing under a psychical researcher's hat. This bee made the noise: "Huff"—and then "Huffy"—and then "Huffner." This bee said: "Key-master," and then "American." Upon Lanny's arrival in New York, it occurred to him to consult the classified part of the telephone book under "Locksmith." He didn't find a Huff, or Huffy, or Huffner; so he looked for a locksmith not too far from his hotel, and strolled there and said to the man: "I have a safe in my home in Connecticut and have lost the combination. What do I have to do?"

"You have to go to a man who knows how to open safes," was the not very illuminating reply.

"Do you know how?"

"No, sorry; I'm just an ordinary locksmith."

"Can you recommend somebody to do it?"

"The best man in New York is Horace Hofman."

Lanny repressed a start. Huff—Huffy—Huffner—Hofman! "Is he an ethical person?"

"He was one of the founders of our American Association of Master Locksmiths. You won't find any better man in the business."

"Where can I find him?"

"He has a place up in Harlem, with more keys in it than any other place in the world, so he claims." The man produced his telephone book and gave Lanny the address. "Hofman with one 'f'" he said, and Lanny thanked him and went to a near-by telephone booth and called the number.

"May I speak to Mr. Hofman?" The voice answered: "Speaking," and Lanny explained: "I am looking for a locksmith who used to know a party named Zaharoff."

The reply set a whole swarm of bees to buzzing in or around Lanny's head. "I used to know a Mr. Zaharoff. I did a good deal of work for him."

"May I ask, did you ever do any deep-sea diving?"

"I did that for Mr. Zaharoff, and very nearly lost my life at it."

Lanny wanted to say: "My God!" But his training in the social arts protected him. "Mr. Hofman, my name is Budd. I used to be a friend of Sir Basil Zaharoff, the armaments manufacturer. Is that the man you mean?"

"That is the one."

"May I come and have a talk with you?"

"Certainly. I am at the shop, unless I am called out on some job." It was a friendly voice, and apparently that of an educated man. Lanny said he would be there in half an hour.

It was a small but well-appointed shop, with large rooms in back. The proprietor was a man with rugged and much-lined features; his hair was white, though he appeared to be under fifty. Lanny introduced himself and was invited into a back room, furnished as a combination of den and museum; its walls were hung with more kinds of keys than Lanny had ever imagined to have existed in the world. "This has been my lifelong hobby," explained the host. "Some of these are the newest and some the oldest keys ever made."

"You are no ordinary locksmith, I take it," replied the visitor. "You might be described as a key-master."

"Now I know that you were really a friend of Mr. Zaharoff's, for that is what he used to call me: *der Meister-Schlosser.*"

"I have a strange story to tell you, Mr. Hofman; but first let me ask one or two questions. Did you ever hear of the cruiser *Hampshire?*"

"Indeed yes. That was where I came near to losing my life."

"You were diving for the gold on board?"

"Exactly."

"Was there anything in your experience to correspond to this: Kitchener's arm came floating out?"

"I couldn't know that it was Kitchener's; but a human hand came floating out of a room we opened, and then two corpses. They nearly drove us divers mad, because we thought they were chasing us. The heavy door was swung by the current and we were trapped. One man was killed, another had his back broken. I thought my end had come, and when I came to in a hospital I found my hair had turned white. Did Mr. Zaharoff tell you that story?"

"He never mentioned it during his lifetime; he told me after he was dead."

That statement never failed to make people listen. Lanny narrated how his father had been the European representative of Budd Gunmakers, and how he had met the munitions king at the age of thirteen and become one of his friends. When Zaharoff's duquesa had died, Zaharoff had taken to visiting spiritualist mediums, and Lanny had brought one to him, and many strange and unexplainable incidents had occurred. In one of the latest Zaharoff had revealed his own death, a few hours after it had occurred and before Lanny had read about it in the papers. Recently, at another séance, a voice claiming to be Sir Basil's had told Lanny about the *Hampshire* on which Lord Kitchener had died, and about the gold at the bottom of the sea, being covered with sand, and about a human arm floating out. Lanny had his notebook with him, and read the phrases he had jotted down.

III

The "key-master" told his story in return. He had become known in the capitals of Europe for his skill in opening safes and locks which no one else could master, and some five years ago his exploits had attracted the attention of "Mr. Zaharoff." (Lanny had never heard Sir Basil referred to in that way, but he recognized it as an Americanism, and adopted it politely.) Mr. Zaharoff had invited the key-master to a remodeled old château at Biarritz, and provided for him a very elaborate dinner-party, at which paunchy and gray-bearded financiers from all over Europe drank champagne and danced with young girls until they could no longer stand up but fell asleep piled on top of one another. Mr. Zaharoff himself didn't dance, and very soon realized that he had got up the wrong sort of party for the American; so the two of them sat at the abandoned dinner-table chatting, with a blond beauty wearing a diamond butterfly in her hair sound asleep across the munitions king's knees. "When you invite such young ladies to parties and then don't pay any attention to them, you are considered discourteous," the locksmith explained; and Lanny answered: "I have been there."

What Mr. Zaharoff wanted was for Hofman to take part in an expedition to bring up the ten million dollars' worth of gold which was known to have been in the *Hampshire* strong room. Hofman had sworn off from diving long ago, but now he let himself be tempted by a "fabulous reward." The sunken cruiser had been located and marked by a buoy, and a German salvage ship was fitted out with every sort of modern appliance. The *Hampshire* lay in some four hundred feet of water, and was found to be covered with deep sand; but this was dredged away and entrance was obtained with electric torches. No explosives could be used, because of the huge quantity of munitions inside the cruiser. The strong room was found to be full of great chests containing gold coins, but they were too heavy to be carried by divers and it was necessary to tear them open and scoop the coins into canvas bags, a tedious process. Storms are frequent in the North Sea, and the salvage ship would have to seek port; when it returned, the wreck would be found buried under sand again. It was heart-breaking labor and there were many mishaps, culminating in the steel door of the strong room slamming to on half a dozen divers and bringing them near to death. In all they had got about half a million dollars' worth of the gold. There could be no doubt that the rest was there, just as Lanny had been told in the séance. "But somebody else will have to go for it," remarked the key-master. "My fingers are insured for a hundred thousand dollars—but even so, I don't want to lose them."

"I have no interest in treasure-hunting," replied the son of Budd-Erling, "except to hear about it. The reason I sought you out is not that I wanted to know where the *Hampshire's* gold is lying, but how it came about that an old woman, a Polish ex-servant who lives in my mother's home, came to know that there was gold in the cruiser, and that Sir Basil Zaharoff had sent a diver named Huff, or Huffy, or Huffner, to bring it up."

"You can search me, Mr. Budd," said the Meister-Schlosser.

I V

Lanny found himself attracted to this unusual personality, a man of French parentage who had made his way in the world by the American method of mechanical ingenuity. From childhood he had been fascinated by every sort of lock and had been tempted to take them apart and put them together again. He had made the subject his life study, and now it was his claim that he could open any safe that men could build. This ability had brought him many adventures, taking him to strange parts of the world and bringing him into touch with princes and millionaires. He had not been awed by any of these, but had told them in American fashion that he was pleased to meet them; he had done his job quietly, and at the same time had studied the personalities of his employers and formed shrewd judgments of them.

Lanny invited him to lunch, and listened to stories, some of them humorous, many terrible: children who had locked themselves in chests and were suffocating, butchers and furriers who had got themselves locked in refrigerators and were freezing; bankers who had lost the combinations to their own vaults; misers who had died leaving their fortunes locked up, and heirs who fell to fighting when green-backs or gold were brought to view. Of course there were unethical opportunities, and it took a strong character and sound judgment to make use of such a talent as Horace Hofman had acquired. He had been called to Moscow to open safes which contained some of the crown jewels, and there had met Stalin, and been allowed to purchase for a nominal sum a wonderful collection of Indian, Chinese, and Russian "animal locks." Taking the gold of the *Hampshire* to Berlin, he had met Hjalmar Schacht, who had invited him to the May Day celebration at which Hitler spoke, soon after his becoming Chancellor. "I was close enough so that I could have stuck a knife into him," said the Meister-Schlosser.

"What did you think of him?" inquired Lanny.

"I wasn't impressed. He was bareheaded, and wore a shabby brown raincoat; he shouted in a high rasping voice—very bad German, I imagine."

"He comes from Austria, the Inn Valley, country of the Steer-washers." Lanny told the story of the peasants who had wished to compete for a prize offered for the best white steer; they had only a black steer, but every day they washed it, and at the competition they had insisted so loudly that it was white that they had carried off the prize.

Lanny himself expressed no opinions about Hitler, but kept the conversation on Germany for a while, so as to discover his guest's point of view. He found that Hofman's mind was not burdened with social theories, but he had the instinctive reaction of a man who has lived in a free country and resents militarism and its trappings. That was enough for Lanny's purposes, and after they had spent part of the afternoon chatting he remarked: "Mr. Hofman, I don't know whether you are able to accept my statement that Zaharoff never mentioned the cruiser *Hampshire* to me during his life. I wouldn't blame you in the least if you couldn't."

"No, I am quite willing to accept it, Mr. Budd. I have heard stories of psychic experiences—though never anything quite so startling, I must admit."

"I have been forced to give thought to the subject, because such things have happened to me many times. It seems to me this case ought to be followed up, and I am wondering if you would be interested to try."

"What do you have in mind?"

"I would like you to try a series of sessions with this Polish medium, and see if you would get any sort of communication from Zaharoff or anybody connected with the treasure hunt."

"Where is the medium?"

"At my mother's home on the Cap d'Antibes. She is getting on in years and I couldn't undertake to bring her to New York, but I would have my mother bring her to Paris, and I am wondering if you, who have done so much traveling, would care to come there as my guest. I would be happy to pay your expenses both ways in return for the satisfaction of my curiosity. Also, you might do a little locksmith work for me; at my mother's estate we have a storeroom in which we keep the paintings of my former stepfather, Marcel Detaze, whose work seems to be acquiring value as the years pass. The keys have been lost, and you may help us to get in. Bring all your tools along, for there might be more work to do on that old place and others."

"That is certainly a generous offer, Mr. Budd. When would you propose for me to come?"

"I am sailing for Southampton at midnight. That is rather short notice, I know, but you tell me you are used to being called at all hours to save people's lives. Is your business in such shape that you could leave it, say for a month?"

"I have a wife and daughter who attend to my affairs when I am away, and we have a competent assistant. It is indeed sudden, as you say——"

"I will be pleased to put a check into your hands, and I will give you bank references."

"That part of it is all right, Mr. Budd; I know your family and also its products. From the point of view of mechanics, there is a certain kinship between a lock and a machine gun. If you are quite certain that you want me to come, and wouldn't be bored before you got through with the experiment——"

"Let me assure you, Mr. Hofman, I have been pursuing this subject patiently since I first got acquainted with this medium, eight years ago. I must have had several hundred sittings with her, and my present stepfather has had one nearly every day. I will show you many notebooks that I have filled, and some of the stories are as strange as any of the real ones you have to tell."

"All right," said the Meister-Schlosser. "You tell me yours and I'll tell you mine!"

V

They traveled on a comfortable English steamer, and all the way Lanny laid himself out to win the confidence of this new friend. He talked psychic research and sometimes art, and in turn listened to locks and keys. He carefully avoided politics, but took the precaution to prepare Hofman's mind for what might be coming, mentioning among

Madame Zyszynski's revelations a young artist couple whom Lanny had met in Berlin many years ago in the course of his business. Ludi and Trudi Schultz were their names, and it must be that they had been opposing the Nazis, for Ludi in a séance had declared that he had been killed by them. Lanny didn't know what had become of the wife, but she had been mentioned and apparently was trying to find her husband, or he to find her. Hofman remarked that the Nazis had evidently found ways to solve the problem of unemployment, but it was hard to excuse their cruelty to their opponents. Lanny answered with words he had heard his father use many times: "The Europeans have not yet learned to change their governments without violence."

They went up to London for a couple of days, because Lanny wanted to see Rick. Nina drove her husband to town, and Lanny told them his story, and a dozen or more of the wild schemes which sprang up overnight like mushrooms in his head. He didn't really know what he was going to do; it depended upon whether the Capitán came, and what that ally would approve. "But I'm never going to rest till somebody gets into the cellars of that château," he vowed.

Rick said: "If there's any way Alfy can help, he will drop his college work and come."

"Alfy is a marked man," was Lanny's answer. "This is no job for him."

He didn't introduce his new friend to the old ones, because Rick, too, was a marked man, and Lanny wished to be rigidly nonpolitical. "Of course I may have to take Hofman into my confidence," he said; "but first I'm going to try to get him to do the work as part of an experiment in psychic research."

"When you get through, give me the story for an anti-Nazi play," said the Englishman.

"You're forgetting the Lord Chamberlain," put in his wife. Nina was a quiet little woman, but now and then she made a remark that showed how well she understood the world she lived in. "Poor Rick! He's always dreaming that if he can get a brilliant enough plot, he can persuade the propertied classes to pay him for threatening their property."

"Beaumarchais did it before the French Revolution," insisted the playwright.

"And then got into trouble, didn't he?"

"He was in jail for a few days, I believe, but he lived to a ripe old age. I hope to do the same, so as to attend the funerals of Mussolini and Hitler!"

VI

Lanny had cabled his mother telling her to bring Madame to Paris for two or three weeks. There was nothing Beauty Budd loved so much in all the world as a trip; she made herself agreeable to her many rich friends so that they would invite her to come along, and one reason she had been heartbroken over Lanny's divorce was that Irma also was a tireless tripper and did it *à la princesse*. This time Beauty was invited to bring her husband, and of course she never traveled without her maid. She guessed that Lanny had had some kind of successful business stroke, and it was like old times to have him spend the money on his mother instead of on some other man's wife or widow.

Arriving at his Paris hotel, Lanny's first thought was of the mail. Nothing from Trudi or Adler, but a note from Monck; he had got a month's furlough, and would be in Paris in a few days. Then Lanny phoned Uncle Jesse and made an appointment to pick him up on the street. Lanny's car had been stored in Paris and now he drove his uncle and listened to the news. Jean had rented the old mill for five hundred francs a month. Also he had found an architectural volume giving the ground plans of famous châteaux, and one of them was Belcour. The Michelin touring maps gave all details about the roads. Jean had become well acquainted with men who had worked in the place all their lives, and he knew several who could be trusted to take bribes.

Another item of information which Lanny had asked for: the Germans who were employed in the château never spent their time off in the neighborhood, but always in Paris, and Jean had found the café which they frequented—a German place, of course. There were several islands of Germans in this great metropolis; Red and Pink and Brown Germans, as Red and Pink and White Russians, and Red and Pink and Black Italians—and so on for most of the nations on the globe. Each of them spoke their home language, ate their home food, read their home newspapers, and argued and fought their home battles; each was a small village, full of intrigue and spying, jealousies and thwarted hopes; each had its heroes and saints, its traitors and informers, and those who lived by pretending to be whatever paid best at the moment.

Uncle Jesse asked no questions; but he was nobody's fool and had his own thoughts. He had known for a score of years that his nephew trailed with the Pinks, at present denounced by the Reds as "Social-Fascists." Jesse knew there was a Socialist underground, just as there was a Communist, and he had no difficulty in surmising that it was some worker of this movement whom the Nazis had seized. Jesse had no idea that his nephew was living a celibate life in Paris, and when the nephew suddenly took to spending a fortune to get somebody out of a dungeon, it was a natural assumption that it was some *Freundin* he was helping.

The deputy knew also that his nephew kept up his old intimacy with Kurt Meissner and the de Bruynes. Manifestly, he couldn't do that without pretending to change his political color, and that was why he had to keep himself in the background. Jesse was willing to play this game for a proper price. He looked upon Lanny in much the same light that Lanny looked upon old Mrs. Fotheringay: a softshell crab that every creature in the sea would take a bite of—and why shouldn't the biggest bite stay in the family? Lanny would bring his uncle large bundles of francs and never ask for an accounting; Jesse would spend part of the money to get Lanny what he wanted, and put the rest away against the time of another election, when a *député de la république française* would have to meet opponents well fortified by capitalist backers. Lanny wouldn't wish to make contributions to Red campaign funds, but he was glad to pay anybody, of whatever political hue, to help him get his Socialist *amie* out of a Nazi dungeon.

VII

In the interest of psychic research, Lanny had agreed not to tell the members of his family anything about Hofman, but merely that he was obliging enough to come all the way from New York to make experiments. Nor would Lanny tell his mother that he was paying the visitor's expenses, because that would excite her curiosity and possibly her discontent. Lanny gave his new friend a check and left it for him to pay his own bills. To Madame he was merely Monsieur Offmah, with a French nasal sound at the end; whenever he requested, she would come to his apartment and take a seat in an overstuffed chair, lean back her head, shut her eyes, sigh and groan a few times, and be in her trance. Lanny said: "I'd better stay out, at least the first few times. It will be interesting to see if Tecumseh connects you with me."

They tried their first séance that evening, and the key-master came out of it quite staggered. The Indian chieftain hadn't appeared, but from the first moment had come a voice which purported to be that of Hofman's mother, who had died when he was a child. She had talked about the farm in the Blue Ridge mountains of Virginia, the house with a red clay floor, the half dozen brothers and sisters, and her own blond hair which had hung in two braids to her knees. She had mentioned various family details, some of which little Horace remembered only dimly. "Really, Mr. Budd, it is most astonishing!" The locksmith had purposely avoided revealing anything about his own origins, and had waited in the full expectation that "Madame" would produce only those episodes of his career about which he had given hints.

"I am glad," Lanny said. "So often the results are disappointing, and I'd hate to have you come all this way for nothing."

Here was a lock that would take the Meister-Schlosser quite a while to open. Was it his mother, or was it only the childhood memories buried in his subconscious mind? The old question of spiritualism versus telepathy; and what was telepathy and how did it work?

Hofman wanted to go right after this problem. He would have liked to have several séances every day, and being a systematic man, he started keeping notebooks like Lanny. He struck up a quick friendship with Parsifal Dingle, who never tired of talking about psychic matters, and had notebooks which would take anyone a long time to study. Parsifal took to attending Hofman's séances, and that brought in the Bhikkhu Sinanayeke, a hundred years dead in a monastery of Ceylon. "Claribel," most fortunately, did not put in her appearance; Parsifal, who had dabbled in hypnotism in earlier years, had tried the experiment of hypnotizing Madame and seeing what he could do with her in that way; all that he got had been Madame's own childhood life, something which had never before come into her séances. He had had the bright idea of giving Madame the hypnotic suggestion that Claribel wouldn't appear any more, and that apparently had ended her.

Lanny in turn had an idea that Madame should be hypnotized and told that Zaharoff would appear. This was done, and the results were startling. "That old man with people shouting at him"—such was Tecumseh's phrase—began speaking with direct voice, and was much pleased to hear the voice of his old friend of the cruiser *Hampshire*. Apparently he had only pleasant memories of this friend, and for the first time since he entered the "spirit world" he manifested that quiet irony which the Knight Commander and Grand Officer had possessed in his life on earth. He mentioned the list of sunken treasure ships which he had shown to Hofman, inviting him to choose the one he would go after; also, he told of the anxiety he had suffered when the salvage-ship came in with one dead and several injured divers, and the time he had had collecting insurance policies and otherwise carrying out his financial obligations to these men. Apparently he was now beyond reach of creditors, and no longer under the necessity of being the "mystery man of Europe."

Horace Hofman got along fine with the "spirits," or whatever they were. He handled them with the same delicate touch he would give to a complicated lock; he spoke in a soft persuasive voice and they responded as if it were magic. He found this fascinating as any game, and remarked to Lanny: "It appears there are stranger things in the deeps of the mind than in the sea."

VIII

Lanny phoned to his friend Leutnant Rörich at the Château de Belcour. "You promised to spend an evening with me"; and the other replied: "You promised to invite me." Lanny explained that he had been to Chicago since their meeting. They made a date for the next evening, and Lanny said: "Bring a friend with you, and we'll make his eyes pop open."

So here came two junior SS officers, prepared to make a night of it. Bruno Fiedler was the name of the other, and he had a tendency to put on fat; his face was round and red, with yellowish bristles which he should have shaved twice a day, but evidently didn't. His eyes were narrow and sly, and Lanny thought at the first glance: "I won't fool you so easily as Rörich."

They were as excited as two schoolboys. They were going to see the real wickedness of Paris, famed throughout the world. Members of the master-race were taught to despise French decadence, but of course they could despise it better if they knew what it was, and they were full of curiosity to find out. Lanny had never gone in for that sort of thing, but he had listened to the conversation of his playboy friends both native and foreign, of artists, journalists, diplomats, munitions buyers, tourists, and the riffraff that came to what they called "gay Paree" in search of thrills which they missed at home.

Lanny took his Nazis to one of the de luxe places of pleasure, where you could have anything for a price. He had ordered a *cabinet particulier* with dinner for six. They noted the extra places and asked who was coming. Lanny replied: "What sort of ladies do you prefer? German?" They said No, they had plenty of German ladies at home. He went on: "Algerian? Senegalese? Or perhaps from Dahomey?" He was being funny; they were starting off on a note of hilarity. They said they wanted French ladies; they had heard reports that French ladies were extraordinarily passionate, but so far they had been disappointed.

Lanny called the waiter and ordered three canapés, three quarts of champagne, and three passionate French ladies. The waiter bowed three times and said "Oui" three times and everybody was merry. Presently there came prancing into the room three ladies, undoubtedly French and reasonably young, all painted and powdered, with bosoms just a trifle more bare than one would find in good society; skirts above the knees, showing embroidered garters slightly soiled, openwork stockings and slippers with abnormally high heels. They came all smiles and dimples, and with practiced eyes each chose her man and made a rush for the seat at his right hand. They gave their first names, and the gentlemen did the same; champagne corks popped and bright conversation in French began quickly. Lanny saw that he had got the youngest and prettiest of the trio, and Leutnant Fiedler didn't like that; in his role of perfect host Lanny said to his lady: "Devote yourself to the other gentleman, Fifi; he is new in Paris and wants more than his share." This was considered delightfully clever, and the fun grew faster.

Lanny left his wine glass almost untouched, and concentrated upon thinking up bright remarks and making his friends have a good time. Presently Hans Rörich noticed that their host was getting less than his share of the delightful sparkling drink, and he said: "You are reneging on us, Herr Budd. Empty your glass!"

"I have to make an embarrassing confession," replied the American. "I cannot drink champagne."

"Why not?"

"It goes straight to my head."

The young Nazis thought that was delightful. An American millionaire, such a man of the world and so self-assured, having to admit that he couldn't carry his liquor! "For shame on you!" cried Fiedler. "Drink it down!"

"You bring us out for an evening and then spoil all the fun!" put in the other Nazi. Of course that was part of the fun.

"I go clean off my head," Lanny pleaded. "I behave like a fool."

"*Kolossal!*" exclaimed Fiedler; and Fifi clapped her hands: "*Ça sera fameuse!*"

The host flushed with embarrassment. "Really," he said, "you won't like it. I say things that are shocking."

"*Merveilleuse!*" exclaimed Toinette, and Belle and Fifi pounded on the table with their knives and forks: "*Buvez! Dites les choses horribles!*"

In short, they were absolutely determined to see Lanny drunk, and he would have been the poorest of sports if he had refused to oblige them. "All right," he said. "It's your funeral," and quaffed his glass of "fizz-water." The waiter, sharing the fun, filled it up promptly, and they wanted their host to drink that, but he said: "No, no, please. Wait a while." So they waited, watching him covertly while pretending to talk about other things.

IX

In the course of two decades of fashionable life, Lanny Budd had had opportunity to observe the effects of liquor upon a number of fortune's darlings; one of them Dick Oxnard, painter of genius and favorite of New York society, who had drunk himself into an early grave. Lanny knew every symptom; so, in a minute or two, he put a silly grin on his face and then tried hard to get it off but couldn't. The Nazi officers looked at one another and winked; Rörich looked at his one lady and Fiedler at his two, and all were delighted. Lanny would blink and roll his eyes, and then all five would giggle and hardly be able to stop.

"Drink some more!" exclaimed Rörich, and Fifi offered Lanny's glass to him. He took it and held it unsteadily, spilling some. He rose, lifted it high, waved it unsteadily in the air, and proclaimed: *"Heil Hitler!"* Of course the two Nazis rose, and held up their glasses; the French ladies, having been hired to do what they were told, followed suit. They drank the toast and resumed their seats. Lanny blinked, gulped two or three times, and rose again, exclaiming: *"Der grösste Mann der Welt!"* All rose and drank again, and he said: *"Mein Freund Adi! Prosit, Adi!"* and drank a bit more. He took it in small sips, talking wildly in between, which enabled him to seem to be taking a great deal.

Drunkenness affects different men in different ways, and now with Lanny Budd it took the form of singing the praises of *lieb' Vaterland* and all its achievements. Hiccuping now and then, and stumbling over his own tongue, he said that German was the language he liked to speak and Germans were the people he liked to be with; he was one of them in soul, and begged them to let him see them often. He hoped they would excuse him for weeping with happiness when he spoke of his visits to Schloss Stubendorf as a boy, and of Kurt Meissner, who had been getting ready to become the greatest musician in the world; of Heinrich Jung, son of the *Oberförster*, who, without knowing it, had been getting ready to become one of the leaders of the Hitlerjugend. He told how, after the war, Heinrich had visited the great Adi in prison, and had told Lanny about this new Führer, destined to redeem first Germany and then the world.

"The world is rotten," declared the playboy. "France is rotten—look at this and you can see how rotten it is." He waved his hand, indicating the room, the table, the food, the *Damen*. He was speaking German, so the *Damen* didn't know they were *Damen* and wouldn't hear that they were *verfault*. Lanny hiccuped and said *Verzeihung*, and explained that it did him grief when he thought about the corruption of *Frankreich*, and he became *absolut schwärmerisch* when he thought about the virtues of *Deutschland*. He didn't mind piling it on, because he was supposed to be drunk, and by that time his friends were somewhat drunk also.

It was a moving speech, received with many a *Hurra* and a *Heil*. It culminated in the announcement that rotten *Frankreich* was going to be cleaned up and so was rotten *Europa*. Lanny knew all about it, and guessed that his National-Socialist friends knew also; but perhaps they didn't realize how near *Der Tag* had come. "We are ready to act, we Hooded Men,"—and Lanny proceeded to take off his hood and reveal himself as a leader of the coming leisure-class coup d'état, one of its paymasters, and an intimate of the men of action who were going to carry it through. Lanny took another sip of champagne and named these leaders and their important social positions; he told where the arms were stored and named the key places which were to be seized— he didn't have to worry about accuracy, because the young Nazis were in a state of exaltation, seeing their Fifth Column taking possession of France without having to fire a shot, and they weren't in any condition to make notes or remember details. Lanny watched the women, to make sure they gave no signs of understanding German, but were proceeding in the normal way to get as much champagne into them as an American millionaire was willing to pay for.

X

This wasn't the sort of conversation the two Schutzstaffel officers had come prepared for; and presently the befuddled host realized it, and hiccuped: "I'm doing all the talking. I am drunk, by God—just as I told you!" He started to grow unhappy because of his bad manners; but his friends consoled him—it was most intellectual conversation. They wished to prove that they too could take part in such conversation, and assured him that Americans were great people and worthy of sharing Germany's high destiny. Lanny Budd and his guests would be friends for life. Yes, they knew what the Hooded Men were doing, and were ready to help whenever called upon.

"*Nein, nein, wartet nur*—you wait—let the French do it—hic!" Lanny had a different role for his Nazi comrades. "What you do is take care of the Germans—German traitors. You know you got German traitors in Paris?"

The host was started on another confused discourse. There were Reds and all sorts of betrayers of the Fatherland in Paris, slandering the great Führer and noble Nazis, and sending their lies back into Germany. "We Cagoulards have spies among them and we know who they are; maybe you—hic—like me to tell you?"

The Schutzstaffel officers said they didn't need any Auslanders telling them about German traitors; they had their own means of watching the vermin—but all the same they were grateful to their American friend for this warning. The three had another explosion of *Schwärmerei;* they clasped hands across the table—this was easy because the corrupted French ladies were by now sunk back in their chairs, about ready to fall asleep. The three uncorrupted gentlemen sang a song telling the dear Fatherland that it could sleep in peace because its hero-sons were keeping watch. They sang about the streets being free to the brown battalions, and then about Germany belonging to us today and tomorrow the rest of the world. In between songs the nazified American would sip a few more drops of champagne and renew his offer to find out for his German friends what the traitors and snakes and vermin were doing here in Paris.

"*Nein, nein,*" Rörich insisted. "We have our ways to take care of them—*nicht wahr, Bruno?*" And Bruno, whose face was now the shape and color of a harvest moon rising over dusty fields, replied: "*Du musst es ja wissen!*"

"What do you do with them?" demanded the American. "Take them back to Germany?"

"We take care of them! They don't spill any more poison in the Ausland."

Lanny became excited. "*Pass auf, Menschenkind!* They are fooling you. They are sending stuff into Germany all the time. I have seen it with my own eyes. Heinrich Jung showed me some of it in his office in Berlin."

Maybe that wasn't exactly drunken conversation; but the young Nazis were drunk enough by now so that they couldn't tell the difference. They were being challenged, and had their honor to defend. Rörich mumbled: "Maybe a few"; and Fiedler proclaimed angrily: "Nobody pays any attention to such *Pöbel.*"

"You are mistaken," insisted Lanny. "The Führer told me himself it is a great menace. Do you mean to oppose the Führer's word?"

No, of course; neither of them dreamed of opposing the Führer's word. Neither of them could say that they had ever been spoken to by the Führer; but here this American made the claim, and proceeded to prove it before their eyes. He pulled out the clipping from the Munich newspaper. "Here is an article telling of my visit to the Führer at the Braune Haus, and here is my picture to prove that it was nobody else. I had called on him once before in his apartment in Berlin, and afterwards I visited him for an evening in Haus Wachenfels, at Berchtesgaden. I played Beethoven for him and he had Kannenberg sing songs for me. Do you know Kannenberg?"

They were staring at him, awestricken. They had heard of the fat and jolly *Bierkellner* who was the Führer's steward, but had never laid eyes upon him. How could they stand up before such authority?

"The Führer said to me: 'It is a grave peril to my *Regierung*, the activity of these *Schweinehunde* in the Ausland. They must be rooted out. They lie about us; they poison the outside world against us. *Sie müssen ausgerottet werden'*—hic! That is what the Führer said; and what are you in Paris doing about it?"

XI

This was, for all practical purposes, as if the Führer himself were here, demanding an accounting. The two underlings were greatly distressed. "We are doing our best," pleaded Rörich. "We know these people and we watch them."

"Watching is not enough. They have to be put out of business. They have to be liquidated—purged!"

"There is a limit to what we can do in France, *mein Lieber*."

"There should be no limit. If I, an American, am willing to overthrow the government of France for you—hic—why should you be afraid of a few sneaking traitors hiding in the slums of this city? You should seize them and break them to pieces."

"We have done it a few times, Herr Budd." It was still Rörich speaking. "That is Bruno's job."

"What do you do, Bruno?"

"I give them something they don't forget in a hurry."

Lanny was working himself into a really fierce mood. He stuck out one forefinger and swung it down toward the table. "Woosh! Woosh!" —the whistling of the whip. "You give them *die Peitsche?*"

"*Ja, gewiss.*"

"*Also!* You may believe me, I know about it! Reichminister General Göring sent his staff officer, Hauptmann Furtwaengler, and took me down into the Columbus Haus, and I watched what they did to a fat Jewish *Schweinehund*. Solomon Hellstein was his name, the banker— you know the Hellstein Bank in Berlin?"

"*Natürlich, Herr Budd.*"

"They stretched him out on a bench with his fat fanny bare and they laid it on good and plenty. How that old Jew did yell! You should have a place like that here in Paris."

"*Zerbrechen wir uns nicht den Kopf, Herr Budd. Wir haben so etwas.*"

We have it! Those were the words Lanny wanted to hear, and there was exultation in his voice. "Give it to them good and plenty!" he cried. "Make them talk!"

"Bruno makes them. It is his job."

"You do it yourself, Bruno?"

"I flay them alive."

"You have good muscles?" The son of Budd-Erling got up, staggering slightly, and felt his Nazi friend's arm. "*Ja*, those are tough! Let's try them!" Laughing wildly, he picked up Fifi, who had fallen asleep in her chair, bored by a long conversation which had nothing to do with ladies. She woke suddenly when Lanny turned her upside down over the chair and pulled up her very scanty skirt. "Show me what you do!"

The woman started struggling and kicking and the two Germans started roaring with laughter. It was truly a hilarious scene. Fifi squealed, but Lanny held her down, and kept calling to Bruno: "Go on! Show me!"

"I have no whip," protested the SS man.

"Take a napkin and tie some knots in it." Then to Fifi: "Shut up! He only wants to whip you."

"But I don't want to be whipped!" wailed the girl. She was starting to fight, and seemed capable; but Lanny said: "Keep still. I'll pay you a thousand francs." A girl in her business learns about the whims of rich gentlemen. She became suddenly still, and Lanny turned to Bruno with mounting excitement. "Now! Go to it!"

"*Aber, Herr Budd!*" protested the Nazi.

"What is the matter? Are you afraid?"

"*Nein, Herr Budd——*"

"Don't you know there are women among those Red vermin? Don't you ever have women prisoners to whip?"

"*Ja, natürlich—aber——*"

"And you spare them? You don't break them down—hic—make them tell what they are up to?"

"*Nein, nein——*"

"Have you got softhearted? Afraid to defend your National Socialism?"

"*Natürlich nicht—nimmer, Herr Budd——*"

"*Also, was ist los?* Don't you know that your Führer whips his women? Have you never heard that?"

"*Ja, ja—aber, hier ist nicht Berlin, Herr Budd; hier ist Paris.*"

XII

Lanny, working himself into a passion, was threatening to become ugly, as many drunks do. Hans Rörich, who had known him longer, felt it necessary to intervene. He laid his hands on his host's shoulders pleadingly. "*Bitte, bitte, Herr Budd*—you must make allowances. We are connected with the Embassy, and we cannot have any sort of disturbance in a foreign country. It is not gentlemanly of you—*nicht korrekt!*"

Lanny's mood changed suddenly—this also being a characteristic of drunks. He had been rebuked, and his feelings were wounded. A look of despair came upon his face, and he turned away and hid it in his hands. "*Ach!* I have offended you! You will never respect me again!"

The two Nazis doubtless had handled drunks before, and understood all this. They grinned to each other as they replied: "*Nein, nein, Herr Budd,* don't take it so seriously."

"You made me get drunk! I told you—hic—I would play the fool." Lanny shook with sobs.

"It is nothing, Herr Budd, *wirklich*—it is all good fun. Bruno will forgive you—won't you, Bruno?"

"Of course, I forgive you, Herr Budd—*macht gar nichts.*"

Lanny was hard to console. He sank into a chair and would not show his face, in spite of the efforts of his friends. They would never love him, they would never respect him again. He kept up this little comedy because he wanted them to have something else to occupy their minds; something to laugh over, and thus forget the grave admissions they had made. A crazy American millionaire who wanted to see a woman whipped and who then wept like a spoiled kid because nobody loved him! Were they all as *verrückt* as that? *Ein verrücktes Land,* full of gangsters and bootleggers and cowboys and wild Indians—you could see it in the cinema, and be sure that such a land would be ripe for taking over when the time came.

At last the wild man let himself be comforted. Then he wanted to drink another toast. "*Der Tag in Frankreich!*" he announced, and of course they drank it; the women, too, neither knowing nor caring what the words meant, so long as it was champagne in the glasses. Poor Fifi, who saw her thousand francs vanish like so many champagne bubbles! The host observed her state of melancholy and gave her a hundred-franc note, which she quickly folded up and stuck into her stocking.

To his friends the son of Budd-Erling pleaded: "*Bitte, nicht mehr trinken*—hic—don't let me have any more." They laughed heartily and said they had learned their lesson—they were scared to death of him. To take his mind off the bottles they started petting the girls, who had been so cruelly neglected. Lanny remarked: "There are rooms upstairs. What do you say?"

They said "Yes," with evident satisfaction. As they started to leave the room, Fifi attached herself to the wild American; but he said: "*Non, non—ce monsieur*," pointing to Bruno, "he wants two." He put her on Bruno's vacant arm, saying to the partly befuddled Nazi: "It's all right; I'll get another." He escorted the five of them to the elevator and saw them inside. Then he stepped back, and the door was closed.

He returned to the *cabinet*. The waiter was there, and Lanny said: "*Addition, s'il vous plaît*,"—and not a single "hic." He examined the account, making sure that it included the rooms and everything. He paid it, together with a generous tip. "*Ces boches sont gentils, n'est-ce pas?*" he remarked. "Those Germans are nice, aren't they!" He took his hat and walked out—strangely enough, perfectly straight, and when an attendant brought his car and started, he didn't weave in the traffic or bump into anything, in spite of the fact that the greater part of his mind was in the cellars of the Château de Belcour. He had got what he had come for—the admission that the Nazis had prisoners there, that they tortured them, and that a woman was among them.

10

Falsely True

I

WAITING for Monck to arrive, Lanny sat in at séances with
Hofman and Madame. He sat as still as a mouse, hoping that Tecumseh
would ignore him, and for a while this succeeded. Lanny concentrated
his mind upon the image of Trudi; he "rooted" as hard as he could for
Trudi to come, and this was a worthwhile experiment, whether one
chose to believe that there were spirits in the neighborhood or that the
subconscious mind of Madame was weaving fantasies. If telepathy was
a reality, a medium's mind might receive suggestions just as if it were
under hypnosis.

No Trudi; but after Lanny's strenuous mental labor had gone on
intermittently for a couple of days, the Indian chieftain said: "There
is a man here named Loodveek. That is a German name, is it not? He
is young and has blond hair. He has been here before."

Hofman had been posted as to what he should do if such a personality appeared; so now he said: "We are trying to get in touch with
Trudi."

"He says that Trudi is not here. He is worried about her."

"Does he know where she is?"

"He says she is in trouble; he feels that, but does not know where.
There is an old man trying to help her, and the old man is suffering,
too. The old man is stout and kind; he is some sort of servant who does
not like what he has to do; he is in a dangerous position. Loodveek tries
to give me his name, but he doesn't know it very well himself. It is
something like Powell."

"The German name Paul is pronounced Powl. Could it be that?" It
was still Hofman asking questions, and Lanny sat there, ready to burst
with a dozen others he wanted asked.

"It might be," said the control. "I don't understand these foreign
ways of saying things and I don't see any sense in them."

"Can you find out if Trudi is in the spirit world?"

197

"This man doesn't say. He says Trudi was his wife; I ask him why he says 'was,' and he doesn't answer. He looks like an educated man but very unhappy. Maybe he can't speak but a few words, I don't know why. He says the old man groans all the time."

There was a silence. When that happened, Tecumseh was apt to fade away; it was necessary to keep talking to him. But Hofman had asked everything that Lanny had told him to. So now Lanny ventured a timid question: "Pardon me, Tecumseh, could one of the old man's names be Adler?"

"Oh, so it's you!" exclaimed the Amerindian, dead a couple of hundred years. "I haven't been having the pleasure of hearing from you. Have you been biting holes in your tongue?"

"I have been trying to oblige you, Tecumseh."

"You are trying to fool me. You sit there thinking that telepathy stuff at me all the time."

"Does that bother you?"

"Of course it does; it is the wrong suggestion; it works backwards. You are one of these smart intellectuals and think you have to understand everything with your mind; but there are things older than the mind, millions of years older. When a bee builds a hexagonal cell, does it have to go to an engineer to find out how?"

"How does the bee find out, Tecumseh?"

"He has it already inside him; his intuition. You have it, too, if you would let it work."

"How can I learn to do that?"

"Have you ever heard the saying: 'Except ye become as little children, ye shall not enter into the kingdom of heaven'? What does that mean to you? Put yourself in an attitude of faith and you experience the reality of faith; put yourself in the attitude of skepticism and you become as a hollow nut, all shell and no meat inside. Take that off and pray over it, Mister Worldly Wiseman."

"Really and truly, I am trying to do that very thing, Tecumseh. I am in trouble and I need help. Can't you give me another chance?"

"Just what do you want?"

"I want that man Ludi to talk to me directly. Can't you persuade him?"

"The man is gone. There is something the matter with him that I don't understand. I think he is the same kind of smart-aleck that you are—he cannot believe that he is a spirit, or that he is still alive and can talk if he believes that he can talk."

"Do a man's doubts follow him into the spirit world?"

"The sin of intellectual pride is self-punishing; God doesn't have to do anything to you—you do it to yourself, and this German fellow is doing it, and maybe also that Trudi who was his wife."

Lanny said: "You seem to know the Bible, Tecumseh. Do you remember the story of the man who said: 'Lord, I believe; help thou mine unbelief'? I say that prayer to you. We have known each other a long time, and you must know there is some reason why I come back again and again, in spite of the bad times you give me."

"Well, if you want to get results, stop shooting that telepathy business at me."

"Just what shall I shoot?"

"Tell yourself: 'There are spirits and I know there are spirits, just as live and real as I am, and I want such and such a spirit to come and talk to me.' Ask, and it shall be given you; seek, and ye shall find; knock, and it shall be opened unto you."

"Thanks, Tecumseh. I'll do my honest best."

"That's enough now. You tire me out with all these arguments. Remember, I was nothing but a stone-age man born too late, and I never heard any of these long words that you highbrows have made up. Where do you suppose I got them from?"

"God knows, old friend."

"God knows—but He won't tell!" With that, Madame gave a violent start, and when she came out of her trance, she said: "Did somebody have a quarrel?"

When the two men had left the séance room, the incorrigible intellectual remarked to his locksmith friend: "It seems to me the stone-age man is taking over the whole mental apparatus of my stepfather."

II

The President of the United States kept his promise and delivered that "quarantine" speech in Chicago. The American *Herald Tribune* in Paris reported the event and gave several paragraphs, some of which Lanny recognized. The rest was of the same tenor, and the effect of the speech was what F.D. had foretold. In fashionable society everybody argued pro or con, and a week later came the New York papers, full of the same debate. The policy of the State Department, carefully built up for the past decade and a half, had been dumped overboard in half an hour. "Stop Foreign Meddling!" clamored the *Wall Street Journal*.

Robbie Budd made it a rule to write his son every month, but this was a special occasion, and the fabricator of airplanes poured out his displeasure in a long screed. Here was definite proof that our national and international affairs were in the hands of a madman. We were going to take all the troubles of the world on our shoulders, and be played for a sucker by every tricky diplomat and his mistress. It was Woodrow Wilson all over again, only worse, because we told the world that we could learn nothing from experience. We would carry this burden all alone; for where in the world was any other nation looking out for any interest but its own? Where was there a foreign statesman who would even pretend to be thinking about any other nation? Even the English, the world's masters of hypocrisy, had given that up as *vieux jeu.*

To Lanny this was playing over an old phonograph record; Robbie had been dinning it into his ears all through the Peace Conference of Paris. Robbie wanted his country to be the best-armed in the world, as its wealth and resources entitled it to be, and then to attend strictly to the affairs of the Western Hemisphere. Let Europe stew in its own juice; let Britain and Germany fight it out—from Robbie's point of view it mattered little which of them came out on top. Just make it plain to them that they had to keep out of South and Central America! In the days when Lanny had felt like teasing his father he had asked: "Suppose that some day there should come a nice, carefully contrived revolution in Brazil—not a Nazi revolution, but one of pure native Brazilian Fascism—what would you do about it? And suppose the thing spread all over South America, and you woke up some morning and discovered that the Germans had the continent in the bag?"

But just now Lanny wasn't teasing anybody. Instead, he wrote: "I had lunch with Baron Tailor again and he asked about you. When do you plan to come?"

III

Bernhardt Monck arrived in Paris. He called Lanny's hotel and spoke one word: "Belchite." Lanny said: "Where are you?" The answer was: "I'll be walking on the Rue du Rivoli, where the jewelry shops are."

Lanny hardly knew the Capitán at first glance. He had got himself a suit of old clothes and had gone back to his role of sailor enjoying shore leave. Lanny drove him out into the country, so that no one might see the grandson of Budd's in unfashionable company. They spent the day, having plenty to talk about. This was the man to whom Lanny meant to tell everything, and he found the telling a great relief.

He set forth the different items of evidence he had collected, tending to show that Trudi was in the château. He told about his Red uncle, and about Jean, and the mill; about the drunken party, and the admissions his Nazi friends had made; about Kurt, and the use Lanny hoped to make of this friendship; about the Führer, and the clipping from the Munich newspaper; about the fat General and his paintings—Monck must have all the details in his mind, for there might come some crisis when there would be no time for explanations.

Lanny saved Madame and Tecumseh and the spirits until the last, they being a hard pill for a Marxist to swallow. The founder of this Social-Democratic religion had lived at a time when mechanistic theories of the universe had prevailed in Germany, and he had included them among his ten commandments; therefore "dialectical materialism" and "scientific Socialism" were supposed to be inextricably bound together—whereas, so far as Lanny could see, they had no connection whatever. He knew the materialist mind, as dogmatic as any Pope's, and he became apologetic when he brought up this subject. "You may think it's all superstition and fraud, but it's a part of the story, and before I get through you will see how it may help us in our job. So I beg you to listen patiently."

"O.K.," said the sailor. " '*Raus damit!*"

Lanny went back to the beginning and told how his stepfather had picked up this old Polish woman in the cheapest sort of medium parlor in a cheap neighborhood in New York, and of the things she had told them which she had no normal way of knowing; how Lanny had brought Zaharoff to her without saying one word about him, and she had revealed among other things the fact that this Greek agent had once pleaded guilty in the Bow Street police court in London to having borrowed money on four hundred and sixty-nine sacks of gall belonging to another man. "As God is my witness," said Lanny, "I didn't even know what gall was; but my friend Rick found the record in the *Times*, of a date more than sixty years ago."

He told about Zaharoff's reporting his own death, and then of his revelation concerning the *Hampshire*, and the "key-master" whose name was Huff or Huffy or Huffner, and who could tell Lanny about the gold. Lanny said: "I had never had anything to do with locksmiths, and I supposed the only men who knew how to open safes were burglars. But I found this man Hofman, and here he is in Paris, absorbed in trying experiments with Madame. He has already heard communications about Trudi—and of course you can see how useful he could be to us in the château, if we could persuade him to take the risk."

"Do you think he would be willing?"

"I don't know; I have waited to get your advice before broaching the subject."

"Tell me just what you have in mind."

"Roughly, this. I shall be a guest at the château. Sooner or later those Nazis will have to invite me, and I'll find a pretext to stay overnight. Also, I'll have some way of getting word to you. I will make friends with the dogs—I've already begun at that, and I'll keep them out of the way while you and Hofman either climb the wall, or he picks the lock of one of the gates. I will leave one of the ground-floor windows open, and you and Hofman will go down into the cellars and open the doors of whatever dungeons you find."

"Do they have a nightwatchman?"

"That's one of the things I have to find out. I may have to stay more than one night."

"And suppose we get caught—what happens to us?"

"There mustn't be any fighting; if you can't get away you must give up. My father employs one of the best *avocats* in Paris, and I will go to him as my father's son and put the case in his hands; he will of course keep me out of it—my function will be to guarantee him a thumping fee. He will go to the French police, and so you will quickly be turned over to them. The *avocat* will take up the matter with the German embassy, and I haven't a doubt that he can bluff them into backing down. You see the situation; you are not burglars but political crusaders, trying to save a refugee who is held in durance in defiance of French law. If you are prosecuted, members of the Embassy staff must appear in open court and face cross-examination as to what was going on in the château. The scandal would be terrific, and I feel certain they would never face it. They would just tell the police that it was all a mistake, and request them kindly to drop the matter."

IV

Such was the program; crazy enough, but not so crazy as the ideas Lanny had suggested in Spain. Monck admitted that if Lanny could really manage to spend a night in the château, and if Hofman could be persuaded to do his fancy work, there might be a chance to get Trudi out. The most serious flaw he could find in the plan was that it involved Lanny's taking the locksmith, a comparative stranger, into the most precious secret of his life. "You will be breaking your promise to Trudi."

Lanny said: "I have been worrying over that. It may be that I can get by without telling Hofman anything of the sort. He is not interested in politics, and I don't have to be either. Suppose you come to me, as a former friend of Trudi's, and tell me the horrible story of her being tortured by the Nazis, and I introduce you to Hofman and let you tell it to him. My heart is touched and I offer to put up the money to save her, but I can't be known in connection with the matter, because of my father's business relations with General Göring, to say nothing of my own. That won't make me seem very heroic, but there's no reason why I should, and I surely don't seem it to myself, with all this lying that I hate so utterly. But it seems to be what the situation calls for; Trudi wanted it, and you want it, and—" Lanny stopped himself; he nearly said: "and the President."

"That part of it's all right," said Monck. "When you set out to kill people, as I'm doing, you surely don't mind lying to them, or about them."

"I'm talking about lying to Hofman, who is a fine fellow, I am certain."

"My guess is, he'd prefer not to know that you're a Socialist or have any political connections. If he doesn't know it, then what he does is a purely humanitarian thing. Those Nazis, holding a woman in prison, are criminals, and nobody has to be squeamish in trying to get the better of them."

"All right," Lanny said. "Then let us say, you learned about Trudi's plight, and came to me because you knew that I had been helping to promote her art work. I'll show her sketches to Hofman and convince him that she is a real personality. I think you had better be something a bit higher in the social scale than a sailor. What else have you been?"

"I was secretary of a labor union for a while—a Socialist union, to be sure."

"We can leave off the Pink label. You were the secretary of a union, and you employed Ludi Schultz as a commercial artist, and in his studio you met his wife. Now you've learned from refugees in Paris where she is and came to me to ask financial support. I explained to you my father's position and my own; I will put up the money, but only on condition that my name is never to be mentioned by anyone. I introduce you to Hofman and you persuade him to help you. You don't tell him that I am going to be in the château. You are a German, and you have a confederate who has a job there. All that I'm doing is putting up a bunch of money. You can tell Hofman I'll pay him anything within reason for the job."

"You will confirm that?"

"Of course. But I think the proposal ought to come from you, because you are the one who has dug up the case and has got all steamed up about it. You present it emotionally, as a friend of Trudi's, while I'm interested only because I consider her a great artist. You know how it is with us rich people—we let others do the dirty work."

The ex-sailor and soldier didn't smile often, but this humor was in accord with Marxist ideology, and he answered, in American: "You said it!"

V

The Capitán went over the story a second time, looking for flaws, and finally he said that he was willing to work over it and see how it developed—even to the extent of attending a spiritualist séance for Trudi's sake! Lanny gave him a sum of money and said: "Get yourself a better suit and a room in a hotel. I'll let Hofman bring Madame to you, because he has learned how to conduct these affairs, and Tecumseh is inclined to waste time in discussions with me." Lanny could read the mind of a hard-boiled "monist," hearing a phrase like that; he added: "Take it as a game, and play it according to the rules."

"All right," said the other. "Tell them."

Lanny set forth the proper way to treat Madame and her "control." Nothing of any importance might happen, and in that case it would be tedious, and seem very silly. "Whatever happens, do me the honor to believe that I haven't said one word to the old woman about you, and I shall not. What name will you take?"

"Any you say."

"All right, you are Monsieur Branting. I'll tell Hofman you are a man I met in Berlin many years ago; you want to make a test, and for that reason I am telling him no more about you. You will take my word for that?"

"Yes, surely, Genosse Budd."

"Don't let that slip past your tongue again. Better call me Lanny. When the séance is over, call a taxi and send Madame to a picture show —that is her greatest joy in life—and you get acquainted with Hofman and tell him whatever you feel the circumstances warrant. Take him out to dinner and get him feeling good. From now on you are the boss!"

So they had a séance, and Tecumseh said there was that old man with the guns going off all around him. The old man said he was lonely and still couldn't find his wife. He said he was trying not to worry about all that gold being lost, for after all, when had gold ever made anybody happy? That didn't sound like Zaharoff, but maybe he was becoming spiritualized. Tecumseh remarked: "His gold is sour grapes"—which gave the impression that the stone-age man was becoming sophisticated. Tecumseh had never liked Sir Basil, and when he took his departure the chieftain said: "Boom, boom, boom—twenty-one guns!"

Next there was reported a little girl with blond hair in pigtails, speaking to someone she called "Pay-tah." That gave Monck a jolt, for it had been his childhood nickname; he had been christened Peter. He had had a little sister who had died young and whom he barely remembered. Now she said that she was happy in the spirit world, and kept her love for him. This wasn't exactly evidential, but the name was unusual, and Monck couldn't figure out how anybody in this company could have heard it.

He was hoping for more news from home; but, alas, here came the insufferable Claribel, bouncing and eager to display her poetical talents. She asked for a name, and Monck took a chance and said "Ludi." Evidently she thought he was speaking Latin, for she started on one of her visions, having to do with gladiators marching into an arena and ending with the lament that "Men can still find no pleasure so great as killing their fellowmen." She asked for more, and Monck tried her first with a German word and then a Spanish. She was equal to both, and perhaps would have understood Tagalog or Marathi if his travels had taken him that far. When the tiresome séance was over, Hofman remarked: "Madame will have to be hypnotized again."

VI

Having the locksmith alone in his hotel room, Monck poured out the sad story of a young woman artist of talent which had attracted the attention of experts even in France, and whose only offense had been refusing to accept the dictates of the Nazi tyrants and continuing to circulate exposures of their cruelty. The Nazis had caught her husband, and for four or five years nothing had been heard of him; no doubt he had been murdered and buried in quicklime. The widow had gone on with her activities, first in Berlin and then in Paris. Monck had got some of her literature from friends of the underground, and he gave it to Hofman to read; the highest and purest idealism, he said; a defense of the basic rights of freedom of speech and of religion which everyone in America took for granted.

The Nazi gangsters had kidnaped this woman, and were holding her somewhere under the Château de Belcour. They would torture her to make her reveal the names of her associates, and if she refused, they would never let up till they had killed her. Several refugees in Paris had disappeared, and everyone was satisfied that this was what had become of them; one of the Nazi spies among the refugees had confessed it.

Horace Hofman simply couldn't believe such a tale. He thought he was living in a civilized world, and such things happened only in movies. Why didn't the refugees appeal to the Paris police? Monck proceeded to set forth a still more melodramatic situation: the chief of the Paris police was a Fascist, at present engaged in a conspiracy to overthrow his own government, and permitting the enemies of his country to accumulate stores of arms for that purpose. The government, the army and navy and air force of France were riddled with such disloyalty, and anyone who went to the police on such an errand as Hofman suggested ran a risk of being himself locked up. Certainly someone in authority would give the Nazis a tip, and their victim would be whisked into Germany overnight.

Persuading an ordinary American to believe things like that was a long job of education. Monck had to tell how Göring and his followers had set fire to the Reichstag building in order to blame it on the Communists and justify their campaign of terrorism. He had to tell about the "Blood Purge" and what that meant—that Hitler, who had got power as a radical agitator and then had sold out to the big steel and munitions interests of his country, had murdered in cold blood some twelve hundred of his own followers who had tried to stick to their old program. He had to tell how the Nazis had killed the premiers of Austria and Rumania who had opposed them; likewise the king of Yugoslavia and the foreign minister of France. Hofman had read about these events, but had hardly realized their significance and had already forgotten them. America was such a well-behaved land, and so far off!

When the locksmith asked what they wanted of him, Monck pledged him to secrecy, and told him that he and other members of the underground were attempting to get Trudi out of the château. They had got an agent inside the place who would keep the dogs out of the way and leave one of the windows unfastened. What they wanted of Hofman was to come along and open the doors of whatever dungeons or lock-ups might be found in the cellars of the building.

"Just as simple as that!" said the Meister-Schlosser, with a smile. "It sometimes takes a lot of time to open a lock that one is not familiar with; it takes tools, some of which it is a near-crime to possess."

"You have them," replied Monck, "and we will carry them in for you and carry them out again."

"And suppose we are caught and these amiable Nazis give us a dose of their torture?"

"Me, yes—but you, no. You are an American, and the last thing they want at this stage is any unfavorable publicity in your country. Our friends will be on watch outside, and if we fail to come out by a certain hour they will go to the American embassy, and more important yet, to the American newspapermen. We have the money to pay a first-class French *avocat*, and of course to pay you."

"I would never think of taking money for anything of this sort. If I did it, it would be because I believe in fair play and decency. I have been asked to commit crimes more than once in my life, and if I did this it would be the first."

"Strictly speaking, it is burglary; but we will go unarmed, and will be acting against kidnapers, who can hardly come into court with clean hands."

"Suppose we opened the doors and found nobody inside, and then we were caught—what then?"

"We would have to produce the evidence we have of various persons who have disappeared in Paris, and what the Nazis have been doing at the château. They would find out what we had on them, and would have to back down; they aren't ready for war, and they don't want to be exposed until that time. I point out that you would be with us in those cellars and could make quite sure that we didn't take anything but Trudi, or some other person we might find being held by force."

VII

The locksmith said he'd have to have time to think this over; and what he did was to come straight to Lanny. "Mr. Budd, I have never in my life let myself be played for a sucker, and if you wish me to have anything to do with this enterprise you will have to deal with me openly. It is one thing if it is supported by a man of property and standing like yourself, and quite another if it is the proposal of a mysterious German who calls himself a 'labor union secretary' and who I suspect is going under a false name. Just what do you know about him?"

"I know him to be a man of good faith, whom I have tested and trust to the limit."

"You believe this Trudi story?"

"I used to know Trudi well, and I did what I could to make her known as an artist of rare talent. You may recall that I mentioned her to you on the steamer. I haven't the slightest doubt that Branting's statements are true."

"This is a serious matter for a man of my calling, Mr. Budd. Such a blunder could ruin me forever. You will have to trust me as I trust you. Are you backing this enterprise?"

"I am backing it to the limit. I cannot come forward myself, because of my father's position and my own business in Germany; but I feel it my duty to help a woman of noble character, of sensitiveness and refinement, who has been made the victim of an outrage. Let me show you her work, which speaks for itself and for her."

Lanny brought out a portfolio of photographs. "I have the originals of these in my storeroom at Juan. Most of them are sketches which Trudi would throw off in a few minutes. She loved to draw children and poor old men and women she saw in the street; she would watch them and then draw them from memory. She has extraordinary fineness and clarity of line, and you see that whether it is pencil or crayon, every stroke counts."

Lanny was launched upon one of his persuasive discourses on art. He dealt with technical matters, but in simple language which an uninstructed hearer could follow. "There is a soul in these drawings," he said. "Hardly one of them is commonplace; each gives you a feeling—weariness or gaiety, sorrow, hunger, despair. When you have looked at them for a while, you begin to know the person who has created or interpreted them; for no artist can make you feel such things unless he himself has felt them. These minute variations of a line do not happen by accident, but because someone has learned exactly what are the indications of a certain emotional state, and how to reproduce them on a small flat surface."

Horace Hofman's life had been lived in other fields than those of art; but he had had to do with fine distinctions and possessed a pair of keen eyes. After he had spent an hour studying these drawings, Trudi Schultz had become a real person, a living presence in the room. He said: "Mr. Budd, this is a dangerous undertaking, and I may be acting foolishly, but I am willing to help you if you can show me any chance of success. Of course I count upon you, in case we should get into trouble, to pay whatever it might cost to defend us."

Said Lanny: "Every dollar I have in the world would be committed to your defense, and if necessary I would borrow from my father. You say that you will not let me pay you, but I assure you that if you do us this service, I will find some way to reward you, and on a liberal scale."

VIII

While these things were going on, Beauty Budd was living at the hotel, having the time of her life, as she always did. She had spent some forty years making friends in Paris, and now they invited her, and she went tirelessly day and night. She had married a "spiritual" man and was quite sure that he had ennobled and reformed her, but somehow that didn't keep her from believing that the *grand monde* was just as great and the *haut monde* just as high as it considered itself. She wanted Lanny to take her about, for he was a charming escort, and when she saw his success with important people she was ready to burst with pride—her corsage being already dangerously tight. Lanny went with her now and then, for that was the way to pick up information as to what was going on; you met the right people, said the right things to them, and guided the conversation into the channels you desired.

At an extremely classy *soirée* he ran into the American ambassador, that same "Bill" Bullitt who had been on the American staff at the Peace Conference, and whom Lanny had joined in protest against what they considered unsatisfactory provisions of the settlement. What a lot of water had flowed under the bridge in eighteen years! "Bill" had been ambassador to Russia, where he had acquired an intense dislike for the regime. Now he had got himself transferred to Paris, where he spoke boldly in opposition to the alliance of France with Russia, at the same time being troubled to discover in what company this brought him. William Christian Bullitt, amiable rich playboy like Lanny himself, had written in his youth a novel poking fun at the solemn snobbery of his native city of Philadelphia. Now he was round-faced and tending to baldness, serious and exactly proper in his evening clothes. He had been one of the original New Dealers, and rumor had it that he sometimes wrote speeches for the President. Lanny might have caused a sensation if he had said: "I wrote the Chicago quarantine speech"; but of course he wouldn't.

He thought quickly, and remarked: "You know, Bill, you are likely to have a new French government to deal with before long."

"You mean Blum again?" inquired the ambassador, ready to talk politics, and thinking that Lanny might have inside information.

"Nothing like that," replied the art expert. "I mean the Cagoulards."

"Oh, my God! You don't mean you take those people seriously!"

"I wish I were at liberty to tell you what I know about their military preparations."

The rest of the fashionable company was forgotten, and Bullitt drew the younger man out onto the terrace. It happened to be a warm evening, though late in the autumn, and they found two chairs. "Listen, old man," said the ambassador. "I am the one person who has a right to know about such matters."

"You must have heard about the plot already."

"People talk to you much more freely than they do to one in my position. Tell me what you have heard."

"It happens that my sources are confidential. You know my father's position, and perhaps you know who my friends are."

"You may count absolutely upon my discretion. I won't breathe your name to a living soul."

"Not even in your dispatches?"

"Of course not. Washington doesn't ask how I know. They are satisfied if I tell them that I do."

Lanny explained: "I can't afford to take sides in these civil wars, because I have business connections in the different countries, and so has my father. But we are Americans, and you really ought to know what is in the wind right now."

So the son of Budd-Erling whispered the news about the arms caches, and the financiers who were backing the enterprise, and the Nazi agents who were pouring in funds. It wouldn't be more than a month before the coup would come off and, in the Hitler phrase, "heads would begin to roll." Bullitt asked many questions, and Lanny chuckled within himself, feeling certain that before the ambassador went to bed that night he would get off a coded dispatch to the State Department, or perhaps to the President direct. F.D. would read it, and know that Lanny Budd had got there first, and so Lanny would be the fair-haired boy!

He had more serious purposes in this bit of play. One good turn deserves another, and in the event that Horace Hofman got into trouble Lanny would be in position to ask favors; also, he wanted to find out what Bullitt knew concerning the Château de Belcour. He said: "I don't know whether it's Kurt Meissner or Graf Herzenberg who is distributing most of the money. I understand one is working for the Wehrmacht and the other for the Schutzstaffel."

"All their agents are stuffed with funds," declared the ambassador. "I wish we had one-tenth the amount for our work."

Lanny asked what he knew about Herzenberg, and the other talked freely. The Graf was one of the early Nazis, and had a strong position in the party, since not many of the aristocracy had come into the movement in those days. Their fellow-aristocrats had rather looked down upon them, considering that there must be something cracked or crooked about persons who really took the Hitler ideas seriously. Now the Junkers had made terms with the Nazis, and were using them, or trying to, but they still looked down their long noses at them and counted the days before they could get rid of this bunch of upstarts and interlopers. Lanny knew all that, but didn't say so; he listened and learned that Herzenberg was a sort of overseer of the German ambassador, like the commissars whom the Russians set to watch their army officers. At the same time he could do the dirty work that it was too dangerous for Embassy officials to do. He had as his mistress a red-headed Austrian actress who was reputed to have some Jewish blood and who very certainly was a spy working in French government circles for Nazi pay.

IX

All that was directly to the point; and driving his mother back to the hotel, Lanny inquired: "Have you ever met Lili Moldau?"

"I met her casually in Berlin, and I believe in Vienna some years ago."

"She is in Paris now, I'm told, as the *amie* of Graf Herzenberg. Would you like to do a little job for me?"

"What is it?"

"You know Herzenberg has leased the château of the Duc de Bel-cour, who is an old friend of Emily's. I went there and looked at some paintings, and I believe I could find a market for several of them, if Herzenberg were willing to release them. Naturally, nothing of the furnishings could be taken out during the period of his lease without his consent. It happens they are historical paintings and I don't think he can especially enjoy looking at representations of French troops winning victories over Germans. What I thought was that if I met him socially, I might lead him to talk about them, and offer tactfully to get them out of his way. All you'd have to do is to get Lili Moldau to invite you to tea, and I'd bring you. I think I could do the rest."

Beauty Budd had lived a long time in the world—longer than she could be persuaded to admit—and for almost thirty-eight years of that time she had been watching her one precious son. "What is this, Lanny? Are you up to some of your radical tricks again?"

"Bless your heart, old dear! This is a deal on which I would stand to make a few thousand dollars, and I could pay you one of them—or keep you a while longer in this center of the world's elegance."

"Is that the reason you invited me?" she asked, ready to have her feelings hurt.

"Goose!" he said. "You know I have to earn my living." He didn't mind hurting her feelings if he could divert her mind from his "radical tricks."

But he saw that he hadn't succeeded. "When are you going to introduce me to that new *amie* of yours?" she demanded.

"She isn't in Paris now, or I would, honestly."

What was that strange intuition which made Beauty almost impossible to fool? "You don't take your mother into your confidence any more," she lamented. "When did I ever fail to help you when you asked me? I know perfectly well that you're absorbed in something more important than selling pictures. I know you didn't bring Hofman to Paris just to try experiments with Madame."

"I'm busy with a dozen things, dear. Robbie asked me to get some information from Baron Schneider for him, and Rick wants to know whether the French government is going to stand by the Nyon agreement. Hofman wanted to come, and I thought he'd be good company for Parsifal while I took you to parties. Haven't I been behaving?"

Why didn't he take her into his confidence? She would have gone to bat for him, and would have kept his dreadful secret; but she would have worried herself full of wrinkles, and she would have tried to exact from him the same payment as Robbie—a pledge that never, never, never again so long as he lived would he engage in the madness of making war on constituted authority or established property rights. Beauty hadn't much more social conscience than a tigress; only a tigress's love of her own progeny. Moreover, she had what no tigress has, the ability to shed tears and to be unhappy for an indefinitely extended period. Every man knows that is hard on the man's nerves as well as the woman's—so what was the use?

X

Jesse Blackless had taken a sheet of note paper and torn it in halves irregularly, giving one piece to Jean and the other to Lanny. The latter had passed it on to Monck, alias Branting, together with Jean's address. The French investigator had been told that some day a man would come to him with the other half of the paper, and by that token he would know the man he was to trust and obey.

Following Lanny's instructions, Monck rented a small and inconspicuous French car, and drove out to the mill where Jean had installed

himself. Ever since the German had taken on this job he had been dili-
gently making use of a pocket dictionary of the French language and
by now was able to make himself understood. He knocked on the door
of a moss-covered old building which stood perhaps thirty feet from
the road, with an open space and a platform against which carts or
small trucks could be backed up. The creaky door was opened by a
smallish, narrow-chested fellow with a straggly brown mustache and
a cigarette dangling perilously under it. That was Jean as he had been
described; and Monck, having rehearsed the sentence, said: "*J'ai un
papier pour vous.*"

He handed out the half sheet, and the other man looked him over,
then took out the paper from his pocket and carefully matched them
against the frame of the door. When he was satisfied, he said: "*Entrez,*"
and Monck stepped into the main room of the mill. It hadn't been used
for a long time, and the white dust had turned gray and moldy. The
water passing over the dam sounded as if it were right in the room;
everything was deadly damp and chilly, but there was a round-bellied
iron stove with a long pipe hung from the ceiling, so presumably the
place could be kept habitable. There was a lean-to at one side which
had been used as bedroom and kitchen, but the roof leaked, and Jean
had fixed himself a pallet on the floor in a dry corner. He had a table
with a little oil stove and some food, and was having a good time camp-
ing out, he declared.

He had been told that the purpose of this campaign was to pry into
the secrets of the château, so as to provide the party press with a red-
hot exposé and the député Zhess Block-léss with material for speeches
in the Chambre. Jean was to be allowed to go on thinking this until
the raid was over, and indeed for the rest of his life. The only persons
who were to know the real truth were Lanny, Hofman, and Monck,
alias Branting. At any rate, such was the hope; of course if Lanny
couldn't carry out his wonderful idea of becoming an overnight guest
of Graf Herzenberg, then it might be necessary to bribe one or more
of the former workers of the estate, or possibly even one of the Germans now employed there.

Patiently, and with much consulting of the dictionary, Monck gathered the facts which Jean had accumulated. The Frenchman was a
Communist and the German a Social-Democrat, which normally would
have led to arguments; but Monck, forewarned, had nothing to say
about politics and parties, or where he had come from or what he was.
His only difficulty was to keep Jean from talking fast. "*Lentement,
plus lentement, beaucoup plus,*" the visitor would say, out of his dic-

tionary. French is hard to learn from print, because the look of the words is so different from the sounds; now and then Jean would have to find the word himself and point to it. Monck would say: "*Ah, oui!*" and repeat the word, learning language along with architecture, landscape, geography, milling, and what not.

He took the man in his car and made a circle of the estate, and then through the near-by village and around it. They did this several times, observing the landmarks, and being careful not to make themselves conspicuous. Monck had already familiarized himself with the ground plans of the château and Lanny's crude map of the grounds. Jean had got one of the former workers in the place to draw him a more detailed map by the device of claiming to have been inside and making assertions as to the position of things which irritated the other by their inaccuracy. When Monck cautioned: "You are sure you haven't asked too many questions?" Jean replied, with pride: "I set up the drinks and get them to arguing. They are stupid, or why would they stay in a place like this?"

XI

Meantime, Lanny was working at the difficult assignment of getting himself into the Château de Belcour. He had called Rörich on the telephone the day after the party and said he was afraid he hadn't behaved very well. The SS lieutenant answered that they had had a grand time and were everlastingly grateful. Lanny exclaimed: "I am immensely relieved. I don't remember what I did or said, but it must have been terrible."

He suggested that they must get together again soon, and the other replied: "The sooner the better." So now Lanny phoned to his friends the de Bruynes. The head of the family was away on one of those mysterious affairs about which no one asked questions. To Denis *fils* Lanny explained that he had met two officers of the staff of Graf Herzenberg, and found them well informed as to National-Socialist techniques both political and educational. He thought the family might like to make their acquaintance. He didn't have to say: "In view of the fact that you are seeking reconcilement with Germany."

An engagement was made for the following afternoon, which happened to be Sunday. Lanny called at Belcour for his two friends, which meant that he had another chance to give his name at the gatekeeper's lodge and then to drive through the double line of beeches to the front entrance of the château. He drove slowly, observing everything he could, for every little might help. He didn't get a chance to enter the front door, for his friends came tripping down the steps, dressed in their elegant uniforms, with tall boots and belts newly shined; all, as the Germans say, poured out of the egg. They were young and full of excitement; they were winning a war—by the most agreeable method ever devised. Who could fail in loyalty and gratitude to Führer Hitler and Foreign Minister von Ribbentrop and the other great minds who had discovered how to conquer a nation by drinking tea with ladies and gentlemen of the highest social position?

Lanny had the pair crowded into the front seat beside him, and while he drove he explained that from the French point of view a great honor was being done them, since Frenchmen of this class rarely opened their homes to foreigners. He explained the basis on which he himself stood with this family; the mother had been his *amie* for many years—which, of course, established Lanny as the very devil of a fellow. He said they would have to be on their best behavior. "I don't think they'll serve champagne, but if they do, please don't ask me to drink any." The amused passengers promised that they wouldn't. Lanny added: "I don't know if you know the reputation of the de Bruynes; they are very old, *le vrai St. Germain*, and the father has become a considerable financial power. All three of them are active politically, and have important plans in hand. I am not free to give you any hint of these, but it is possible they may do so themselves if you win their confidence."

The two officers stole a swift glance at each other. *Herrgott!* The man actually didn't remember anything of what he had blurted out the other night! *Jawohl, um so besser!*

XII

Both châteaux being in Seine-et-Oise, the drive was short. The Nazis met two Frenchmen just in their thirties; cultivated, with gracious manners, high technical education, and military training as well. Some day it might be the fate of one pair to meet the other pair on the battlefield—but why should they? Both pairs found it pleasanter to sit on the terrace of this old red-stone building and sip coffee out of delicate porcelain cups and converse about their countries' ideas and aims. Western Europe had a common philosophic and scientific heritage, a common literary and artistic heritage—and it had enemies still close to a state of barbarism, rapidly preparing for one of those raids which had come every century or so throughout recorded history. So, at any rate, these four believed and said.

They talked about the new kind of training which the Nazis were giving to their youth. Lanny knew about it, for Heinrich Jung was one of those in charge, and had raved about it to Lanny for hours on end. Here were two products of that training and they spoke for themselves. Lanny mentioned the "Party day," a celebration held in Nuremberg the first week in September. Fiedler had obtained a furlough to attend these ceremonies, and described them as the most beautiful and moving in the world. A million German youths assembled in one giant airfield; and such decorations, whole forests of banners and standards; such music and singing, such marching, such eloquence of orators and fervor of consecration on the part of auditors—no one who attended could doubt that a nation had had its soul restored.

The French brothers had been through all that themselves. They too were products of a "youth movement," and had marched and sung, worn insignia and sworn oaths under the banners of the Croix de Feu. But on a scale so pitifully small in comparison! They did not conceal their envy of the Führer and his magnificent triumph; they looked upon themselves as a vanguard of such developments at home, dreaming of some magic whereby they might overcome the cruel skepticism and wicked cynicism of the French masses. Denis *fils* and Charlot had no ambitions for themselves, but were ready to be followers of some Jeanne d'Arc who would lead *la patrie* on a new crusade, a Catholic and conservative revolution against the materialistic and individualistic forces of the modern world. Lanny would have liked to tell them that the National Socialist German Workingmen's Party had succeeded because of the second and fourth words in its title, and that the masters of French industry and finance would have to find themselves a rabble-rouser before ever they would see a million youths assembled to swear allegiance to their cause.

The conservative French revolution was to have reconciliation with Germany as one of its goals, and therefore the two Nazis were cordial to it, and glad to reveal the secrets of their colossal success. Privately, they didn't share the hopes of the de Bruynes, because the French were not Germans, and were incapable of such discipline, or of producing a Führer of such genius. But they explained their methods of organization and training—no secrets, since they were available in books, and both Frenchmen read and spoke German. More important, the Nazis told how it felt to be the objects of such efforts, the material of this discipline; how their doubts and uncertainties had been overcome, what had moved them and ultimately persuaded them, and what now, as finished products, they thought and felt and intended to do. All that was deeply interesting from the psychological as well as the political point of view.

XIII

Driving his SS friends home, Lanny found that they had been impressed by the sincerity and intelligence of the two brothers. Rörich said: "It is something that must not be allowed to happen, that Germany and France go to war again. Why should we destroy each other for the benefit of others?"

"It would not be the same next time," said the more practical-minded Fiedler. "The French army will not be such an obstacle."

"It is supposed to be a pretty good army," ventured Lanny, mildly. "*Lächerlich*," said the Nazi. "We would blow it to pieces in a few weeks."

"It must not be allowed to happen," put in Rörich, quickly. "If we could bring it about that France was governed by such men as the de Bruynes, there would be no excuse for it."

They expressed their gratitude to Lanny for having brought about this meeting. They would be glad to know more such Frenchmen. It was an overture, and he responded at once: "Let us see more of one another."

"By all means," said Rörich, the more genial of the two. Lanny waited to see if he would add: "Will you come to see us at the château?"

But alas, no such luck! The SS lieutenant asked: "Will you be our guest some evening in Paris?" Lanny could only answer that it would give him pleasure.

When they came to Belcour and he stopped in front of the steps, they didn't say: "Won't you come in for a while?" Nothing of the sort; just "*Danke schön*" and "*Auf wiedersehen.*" Lanny drove away, completely balked, and reflecting: "That place is a concentration camp, and I might as well expect them to invite me for a social call at Dachau or Oranienburg!"

11

Time by the Forelock

I

IT IS in the nature of social affairs that they cannot be hurried, and so Lanny Budd had to spend a lot of time waiting. He couldn't use it all in living through imaginary scenes in the Château de Belcour, nor yet in listening to Hofman's speculations as to what kind of locks he was likely to find on the doors of that place. There was Madame, always in the hotel, and Lanny kept thinking up schemes to get information by way of the psychic underground.

There were some of his acquaintances who looked upon him patronizingly because he had let himself be drawn into this sort of activity. An aroma of fraud hung about it, and only a weakminded person would waste time on it. Lanny had heard this said by gentlemen who played the stock market and wore out their nerves trying to win great sums of money for which they had no need; by others who got drunk at night, or amused themselves seducing other men's wives. He had heard it also from ladies whose occupation in life was decorating their persons with expensive clothing and jewels, and from others who found diversion in staking their fortunes upon the turn of a card or a roulette wheel. Such occupations were fashionable; but to try to find out something about the mysterious universe you lived in was a waste of your own time and a deprivation to your friends.

Lanny had read enough to know that it was truly a mysterious universe, and the clues to its secrets had been found in odd and unexpected places. An old-time Italian had occupied himself with touching a copper wire to frog's legs and watching them jump; a retired merchant of Philadelphia had taken to flying a kite in thunderstorms—which must surely have seemed eccentric to the neighbors. So it must have been with the grinding of curved glass, which had opened up a universe of the infinitely large and another of the infinitely small. One could list hundreds of men who had watched some puzzling phenomenon—the falling of an apple, the bubbling of a tea kettle, the fer-

218

menting of liquids—and had persisted in asking why and how it happened, and so had expanded man's powers over nature.

And what about the mind, most familiar of our possessions, yet the least investigated? Lanny was coming to the conclusion that his mind was one with all the other minds existing—and this, not because his mystical stepfather had dreamed it, but because of facts which he was observing and for which he could find no other explanation. He saw himself as a bright and lovely bubble, floating on the surface of a vast dark ocean; he was keenly aware of his own existence, and somewhat less keenly aware of other bubbles, dancing in the sunshine all around him; but of the infinite ocean from which he had come and to which he was destined to return, he knew next to nothing, and was considered an oddity because he kept trying to find out.

An ocean of mind-stuff, a cosmic consciousness, or unconsciousness —whatever that could be and however it could function. Some called it evolution and others called it God. Whatever its name, it brought you into existence and kept you going. Very certainly you hadn't made yourself, either body or mind; very certainly you didn't know how to make your own blood or to repair your tissues; your thoughts came, but you didn't know how, and the wisest scientist had no explanation of the process whereby a thought, desire, or act of will could cause your muscles to flex and your hand to move. You had some control over both mind and body; you lived your life, as you said, and did what you pleased; but why you pleased this and not something else was a question you left to the learned psychologists—very few in number, and mostly not agreeing with one another.

Dipping into the subconscious mind of a dull old Polish woman, Lanny had discovered fragments of the minds of other people, mostly dead, but now and then a living one. Were these disembodied minds, spirits, or ghosts, or did they exist as fragments of mind-stuff—just as long-buried fragments of bones exist in the grave? No scientist had to apologize for studying a piece of the skull of a Piltdown man and learning what he could about that ancestral being. Why shouldn't some of them get busy to study the mental fragments of a long-dead Amerindian chieftain, or a Greek munitions king, or a victim of the Nazis murdered in a concentration camp? Nobody could give any reason that satisfied the son of Budd-Erling, so he went ahead holding séances and jotting down notes.

II

He had watched his stepfather hypnotize Madame; he had read books on this subject, and now he wanted to try it once. He asked her permission, and she said Yes without hesitation. She would do anything for this family who had been so kind, solving all her problems for her and granting her every request. In her secret heart she held Lanny as a son, and at the same time as a lover; when she went to the cinema, he was the hero upon the screen, and a lonely old woman dreamed dreams which she would not put into words or perhaps even admit to herself.

With Horace Hofman watching, Lanny seated himself in front of her and fixed his eyes upon hers; he made the gentle passes he had seen Parsifal make before her face, and murmured slow words of command. He was himself surprised by the quickness with which she passed into a trance; quite evidently a different kind from those which she herself induced, tapping a different level of consciousness, or at any rate bringing a different set of phenomena. No "control" and no "spirits"; only passivity and silence. If he had told her that she was a bird flying, she would have got up and waved her arms; but he wasn't interested in parlor tricks. He wanted to find out what sort of mind he now had to deal with. He asked questions, and she answered; she was satisfied and would do what he told her. Yes, she knew about Tecumseh, but he wasn't there now; there were no "spirits" anywhere about, and she didn't know how to get any.

Lanny said, in a quiet, firm voice: "Listen carefully, Madame, and remember what I say. You will have nothing more to do with Claribel. You will take control of Tecumseh"—how Lanny would have liked to find a way to get Tecumseh under hypnosis!—"and ask him to bring me a man named Ludi Schultz whom I very much want to talk to. You will remember the name?"

"I will remember."

"Also his wife, Trudi, if you can find her. They are good people who will do you no harm, but will tell you about themselves if you can find them. You will remember all that?"

"I will."

"And above all no more Claribel. No more Claribel. You will wake up now." Lanny snapped his fingers, and the old woman came to herself. "You feel all right?" he asked—having been worried by the thought that he might put her into a trance and then not be able to get her out. She said she was all right, and he asked her to go into her own kind of trance. She sank back in her chair and closed her eyes, and it worked like magic—there was no Claribel and no Tecumseh, but a voice, speaking German, and saying that he was Ludi, and that he was well and happy in the spirit world.

A most unsatisfactory Ludi, far different from the aggressive Social-Democratic Party worker whom Lanny had known in Berlin. He didn't have very much to tell that he hadn't told in previous séances; he took some time to speak, and his answers were vague and sometimes faint. He said Yes, he knew Lanny Budd, and remembered having met him in Berlin. He, Ludi, had been a prisoner of the Nazis, and had "passed over" a long time ago. The spirits apparently didn't like the word death, and in general were as mealy-mouthed as if they were in church. Ludi said he had had different ideas when he was on earth, but now he had changed. He said Yes, he knew what was happening to his friends on earth—sometimes, at any rate; but he didn't prove it by giving details. He said that he knew some of those he had known on earth, and what had happened to them since they had passed over. Lanny named several persons whom Trudi had mentioned as having fallen into the hands of the Nazis, and Ludi said they were here and they were well and happy. It was a formula.

III

Lanny had found that these fleeting and unsatisfactory beings didn't like to be pinned down and forced to answer questions, and he was taking no chances of having the voice of Tecumseh suddenly break in and scold him. However, there was one subject nearest to his heart and he came to it quickly: "You remember Trudi, and your life with her?"

"I remember her, of course."

"Have you seen her lately?"

"I thought I saw her, but I wasn't sure. I think it must have been her ghost."

"How interesting! Do you mean they have ghosts in the spirit world?"

"Sometimes; at least, some believe in them, but I never did."

"But you saw something that you thought was Trudi?"

"Yes."

"And did she speak to you?"

"A few words. She called my name, and said she was coming."

"Did you answer her?"

"I tried to, but I am not sure if I could."

This cross-questioning went on for quite a while. Lanny was interested to know if Trudi had been near to death and had appeared to her former husband in the "spirit" world in the same way that she had appeared to her second husband in the world which called itself "real." He wanted to know if people appeared on the threshold of the spirit world and then receded into the real world again. He wanted to know how Trudi had looked, and what Ludi had thought about her near-appearance, and why he was so vague in telling about it. "Is it because when you were on earth you were so much opposed to the idea of spirits? Maybe in your heart you are still opposed, and that is why you don't see Trudi and others of your old friends. Could that be possible?"

The voice admitted that it might be, and Lanny proceeded to give him the same advice which Tecumseh had given to Lanny. "Try to change your attitude, and be more receptive to the fact that you yourself are a spirit, and that there are other spirits you might learn to know and love." A strange kind of auto-suggestion, given to beings who perhaps weren't beings at all, but merely imaginings taking form in some mind-stuff, fragments out of the minds of Madame and Lanny or perhaps the former minds of Ludi and Trudi.

Lanny asked about that old man who was said to be helping Trudi; and again it was all vague and unsatisfactory. Ludi said the old man might have been a ghost, too; he had spoken Trudi's name. He was rather stout and had a kind face. Yes, he was called Paul, pronounced German fashion, and Teich, or something like that—it was the German word for "pond." Perhaps it was Teicher. No, Ludi had never met him before, and didn't know where to find him. He would try to find out more about Trudi, and would come to another séance. Lanny, trying to give suggestions, pleaded in the name of friendship, and said he would be glad to have Ludi's company at any time; but Ludi said it wasn't easy to arrange. The man in the real world explained that he was trying to help Trudi without being sure what world she was in. Ludi ought to help them both; but instead of reacting to this with ardor, as Ludi on earth would have done, the spirit voice said that he was *müde, erschöpft*—very tired, and his voice trailed away, and it turned into the moanings of Madame, coming out of her trance, something which Lanny had learned to recognize and never to oppose.

So there was one more not very successful experiment. Lanny said to Hofman: "Do you suppose we are shaping all this ourselves? Imagining the way things ought to be, and so getting them that way?"

The locksmith answered: "I admit that Ludi's bewilderment is about what is in my own mind when I try to imagine the spirit world!"

IV

It didn't take Beauty Budd very long to think of somebody who would know Lili Moldau, and she called up this friend and invited her to tea, along with a couple of other ladies so that they could play bridge. Lanny had been to a newspaper office and inspected what they had in their files concerning the actress. Thus it was brought to his mind that he had once seen her in a play in Vienna; he had forgotten the event, but didn't have to tell her that. Posted on the details, Beauty had no trouble in leading the conversation, first to the stage and then to her favorite performer. "She is living in Paris at present," remarked the friend. "Oh, do you know her?" exclaimed Beauty. "I would love to meet her, and Lanny would enjoy it, too."

The friend promised to invite Beauty and her son to tea. That is the way things go in smart society; people are always being "used" for some purpose or another, and they try not to know it, because they have a natural human desire to believe that they are loved for themselves alone. They don't like to become suspicious and distrust other people's motives; but they learn by sad experience, and the older they grow, the less faith in human nature they retain.

A date was made, and Lanny and his mother dressed themselves in their glad rags and he drove her to a mansion on the Boulevard des Malsherbes, and there was the lovely Lili in all her Titian-haired splendor, clad in a sheath dress of green silk with a sort of patina of gold, tight-fitting as if to say: "See how I have kept my figure!" She had been in her time the most charming of ingénues, and now, at an age where that was no longer plausible, she was too proud to take older roles, and preferred to serve as a sort of scout for her lover and patron, exploring the wilds of French public life to find out who was in the market and at what price.

Mother and son laid themselves out to be charming, and they knew all about it. An actress could not but be touched by this off-stage applause heaped upon her; apparently the pair had followed her about from city to city in Austria and Germany; they knew all her roles, and the fine points of her technique. Really, it was extraordinary! "Why have we never met before?" she asked, and it did seem surprising, for they had so many friends in common. Kurt Meissner for example; Lili knew him well, and after they had exchanged reminiscences, Beauty let it be delicately understood that she had played in Kurt's life the same intimate role which Lili played in Graf Herzenberg's. And then the Fürstin Bismarck, and the Fürstin Donnerstein, and Emily Sonnemann —why, they lived practically in the same world! Certainly they must be friends, they must see more of each other.

Lanny didn't take anything for granted. He let the stage star know that they were the Budds of Budd Gunmakers and Budd-Erling Aircraft, and that his mother was the widow of Marcel Detaze. On chance that Lili hadn't heard of him, Lanny told about the Munich exhibition, and the painting of his mother, *Sister of Mercy*, which he had taken to the Führer at the Braune Haus. It would have been cheap to pull out the clipping and display it here; more *comme il faut* to prove it by the intimacy of his revelations concerning the great master of German destiny.

An American art expert made it plain that he had followed the career of Adi with the same fidelity he had given to Lili Moldau. He had been to Berchtesgaden, an honor which had never been vouchsafed to an actress maliciously reputed to have Jewish blood. He had been a guest at Karinhall, and at Göring's palace in Berlin, doors which Lili's shadow had never darkened. He had visited the Goebbels family. "Poor Magda!" he remarked. "The last time I saw her, at The Berghof, she looked very sad."

Lili replied: "You men know what you are!" Tactful, and as far as one should go in referring to the scandals of the *Regierung*.

Also, the Budds had connections in Paris; they were intimate friends of Mrs. Chattersworth, and of the de Bruynes, and the former Baroness de la Tourette; they had once leased the palace of the Duc de Belleaumont—in short, they represented for the *amie* of Graf Herzenberg a "find" of the highest value. "I would like you to meet *Seine Hochgeboren*," she remarked; "you will find him charming." Beauty replied, with exactly the right degree of *empressement:* "I know I should be proud to meet any friend of Lili Moldau's."

V

So mother and son came home well pleased with themselves. The promised invitation came by telephone next day; to meet Herzenberg at Lili's town apartment, and not at the château. That was no less satisfactory to Beauty, and Lanny had to pretend that it was the same to him. One step at a time—and such long delays in between! Lanny reported progress to Hofman and Monck, and they spent hours figuring over what they would do in the event that Lanny's social ambitions failed. Monck's time was running out, and he insisted that he could not ask for an extension. But how could they venture into the grounds of the château at night unless something could be done to those dogs—to say nothing of the nightwatchman who was almost certain to be on duty? Wait a day or two longer, and we'll see what Herzenberg is like, and whether or not he ever serves tea or gives dinner-parties at his concentration camp! Meantime, let's have another séance with Madame, and see if we can get Ludi to tell us any more news!

Beauty Budd and her preoccupied son dressed themselves again and drove to a fashionable apartment house near the Parc Monceau. There was *die schöne Lili*, playing the ingénue as she had done for twenty years or more, but now ad-libbing, as the American stage folk call it. She, too, must have consulted some "index," for she had learned about Lanny Budd's infatuation with the spirits and was primed for conversation on the subject. Did he know that the Führer and a group of his friends were deeply interested in all such mystical subjects? Lanny said he had heard it. Did he know that in the early days the Führer had always consulted an astrologer named Hanussen before he took any decisive political step? Lanny had been informed of that also. Then the actress inquired, did he believe in astrology? He said he had not had opportunity to investigate this abstruse subject.

Lili had recently consulted a fortune-teller in Paris who charged five hundred francs a sitting, which certainly indicated that she must have something. She had told the actress of incidents in her past too painful to talk about, and then had told her that she was going back to the stage and make a greater success than ever. "Of course every person who has ever had a stage career cherishes that dream, and I am wondering if I should try to make it come true. Would that count a proof of foreknowledge?" Lanny replied that it would be a proof of psychology, at any rate.

Seine Hochgeboren arrived: a shaven-headed Prussian with a dueling scar on his cheek and a monocle through which he surveyed you with what appeared to be a condescending air, though he may not have meant it that way. Certainly he had every reason to be cordial to a mother and son who possessed a knowledge of France and of the French fashionable world which might make them of the greatest use to him. His manners were suave, and your feelings were smoothed, your self-esteem flattered; the conversation was guided so that you were asked few direct questions but were led to reveal your habits and desires. It was as if a master of many servants was investigating a candidate for some especially important and confidential position.

This might be the case, of course, for Herzenberg had dealt with servants from childhood, and now had a large payroll at his disposal. Just what were these Budds and why had they sought an acquaintance with his *amie?* Were they as rich as they appeared? A great many smart people are like movie sets—all façade and nothing behind them. These Americans had a family fortune in the background, but did they command it, or might they be black sheep of some sort, devotees of the gambling tables, for example? If so, what were they prepared to offer, and what pay did they expect?

A Nazi overseer could count upon the certainty that such wordlings knew who he was and what he was doing in France; also, that they were not motivated by pure love of Germany, or of National-Socialist ideals. Lanny, in his turn, could assume that Lili had told her lord and master all that she had been able to learn about the pair. Also, one could be reasonably sure that two young officers of the Death's Head brigade had reported to their superior their clever feat in getting an American playboy drunk and hearing him blurt out the story of the Hooded Men and their plot. Even though Seine Hochgeboren might have known this already, it was confirmation, and held out the hope of future leakages.

So Lanny didn't have to recite that "spiel" with which he was accustomed to hypnotize Nazis, about how many times he had visited the Führer, and being an intimate of the Görings and the Goebbelses and the rest. He could be dignified and aloof, mentioning such mutual friends as Graf Stubendorf, at whose Schloss he had spent half a dozen Christmases since boyhood, and Emil Meissner, Kurt's oldest brother, now a General in the Reichswehr and a Junker of the inner circle. It was as if Lanny had been saying: "These are my credentials; and my way of presenting them lets you know that they are genuine."

VI

This was a busy, hard-driving man, and Lanny wouldn't make the mistake of assuming that he was interested in a tea-party chat. Said the visitor: "I have something on my mind that might be of use to you. My business does not permit me to take an active part in politics, but sometimes I come upon an item of information which seems important, and then it is a pleasure to pass it on. This may be something you know about, and if so, don't feel it necessary to comment. I am not fishing for information, but offering some."

"I appreciate your kindness, Herr Budd."

"I assume that you know Baron Schneider; but it may be that you haven't had contact with him lately. It happens that he is in a frame of mind to be of use to you and your cause. I won't need to say more, for you know what influence he has. Remember, he is not merely Schneider-Creusot, but also Skoda."

"Quite so, Herr Budd."

"I took a message from him to Kurt Meissner several weeks ago, and it may be that Kurt has acted upon it—he hasn't told me. Kurt is one of my dearest friends, my boyhood hero and exemplar; but I have an idea that his unhappy experiences have disturbed his judgment, so that he finds it hard to trust any person of the French race. You doubt-less know that he was a confidential agent of the Reichswehr here dur-ing the Peace Conference."

"I have heard something about it, Herr Budd, and we Germans are in your debt."

"Forgive me if I explain myself, for I want you really to understand me. I am a man of peace, both by profession and practice. My parents are American, I was born in Switzerland, lived most of my life in France, and had my holidays in England and Germany. In the last war my stepfather was killed fighting for the French and my best friend was nearly killed fighting for the Germans. I don't want to live through such sorrows again, and I believe there can and should be a genuine reconciliation between France and Germany. Kurt taught me that ideal as a boy, and he still accepts it in theory—but when it comes to a con-crete case, I have the idea that his reason does not dominate his attitude; instinctively, he simply cannot help disliking Frenchmen. I am men-tioning the matter to you with the thought that this may be less true of you."

"It isn't true of me at all, Herr Budd. I respect the French as a great people with a great tradition, and I am deeply obliged for your confi-dence. I would be glad indeed if I might have a chat with you about these and other matters."

"Certainly," replied the art expert; "whenever you desire."

"I have an apartment in town where my friends come occasionally. I will give you my telephone number, if you like."

"With pleasure," said Lanny—and inside himself he was saying: "*Damn!*" He got out his notebook and put down the number, acced-ing to Seine Hochgeboren's request that he consider it confidential.

Then he remarked: "I had the pleasure of visiting your château not long ago and looking at the paintings."

"I heard about it. I hope you found them worth while."

"I had the thought that you could hardly enjoy the daily confrontation with French military glory."

"Oh, well, one can't afford to forget history entirely, even while dreaming of a happier future."

So they played with each other, as two urbane men of the world; and on the drive home Beauty said to her son: "Did you really mean what you told him about your attitude to Germany?"

"Sometimes I think I do," replied the son. "I would almost be willing to turn into a Nazi if it would prevent another war between France and Germany."

"You are a strange fellow," said the fellow's mother. She was not very clear on the subject of the new ideologies, but had read somewhere that the Red dictatorship and the Brown were not far apart in theory and practice. All she could say now was: "If you were going to change your mind, why on earth didn't you do it before you broke up with Irma?"

VII

Lanny was one step nearer to his goal; but the steps were so many, and the time between them irksome! He could call up his new Nazi friend and ask for another view of those paintings, and by imparting information about French affairs and promising to get more, he could gain a position of intimacy with the whole Embassy staff. But would he ever get invited to spend a night at the château? Must he not rather assume that this was something out of the question; against policy, possibly even against orders?

He talked it over with his fellow conspirators. Should he drive to Belcour and there put his car out of commission and claim that it wouldn't run? But they undoubtedly had a well-equipped garage, with a mechanic who would quickly find the trouble—and possibly be suspicious as to its origin. Could he go as a visitor and fall seriously ill? Well, they would call a good German physician, and have a nurse to attend him, or perhaps an ambulance to rush him to Paris. Hardly would they leave him free to be sick by himself, and to wander about the grounds at night as a measure of convalescence!

Monck, alias Branting, had got himself an SS uniform. He was a Hauptmann, the rank he was used to in Spain, and the one befitting his age and solidity of frame. He had got the outfit from a tailor in one of the faubourgs, near to a motion-picture studio; he had said he was aspiring to a role, and the tailor, generously rewarded, had entered into the spirit of the undertaking and turned him out complete with all accouterments, according to a magazine illustration which Lanny had obtained. Now he strutted up and down his hotel room, halted, clicked his heels, threw up his right arm and heiled Hitler. Both his two associates had had opportunities to watch the Nazis in action, and they criticized his behavior, and finally pronounced him able to paralyze the will of any German nightwatchman. But what about the dogs? Rörich had told Lanny that they knew the German smell; but could Monck count upon that? Perhaps he had lost his in exile—and even acquired a Spanish smell!

They had their rendezvous, their car, their maps and blueprints, everything ready; they had figured out the last details of time and place. Their plans were at the stage of an army general staff which receives the order to invade a certain country and has only to reach into a pigeonhole and take out Plan 147B. But alas, all their plans, of whatever number, were timed for 0130, the military way of saying one-thirty in the morning. All depended upon Lanny's being inside the château at that hour, and being there as a guest, not as a burglar. Night after night passed, and he still spent them all in Paris.

VIII

The solution of their problem, when it came, was arranged by a kindly fate without any prodding; it was due to a development in French politics which none of them could have foreseen. A Corsican of Fascist sympathies, Duc Pozzo di Borgo, had fallen out with Colonel de la Rocque, tough leader of the Croix de Feu, and was waging ideological war upon him because of his "legalistic" tendencies, so offensive to the Cagoulards. The once-fiery Colonel had got nine million francs from Pierre Laval and had purchased *Le Petit Journal*, a newspaper of Paris with several hundred thousand readers; this had caused him to make peace with the government and promise to obey the laws. In short, he had become just another politician. The Duc had published the charge that the Colonel had received money from the French Foreign Office to build up his organization; the Colonel had replied with a suit for libel, and now the issue was being fought out in the courts— to the profit of the French public, which read newspapers of all political hues and agreed on only one thing—a delight in scandalous revelations concerning its statesmen, whom it called *cochons*, in English the short and ugly word "pigs."

And now to the witness stand came André Tardieu, recently Foreign Minister of the French republic, and testified that he had indeed paid public funds to Colonel de la Rocque for the upbuilding of the Croix de Feu, and that Pierre Laval, recently Foreign Minister and then Premier, had done the same. An immense sensation and, of course, fury among the "legalistic" sons of the Cross of Fire. Shortly thereafter the French Socialist Marx Dormoy received a visit from a mysterious black-clad gentleman who placed in his hands a heavy portfolio and departed without explanation. Dormoy, Minister of the Interior, was charged with the duty of protecting the republic from its enemies at home; and upon opening the portfolio he found that it contained full details of the doings of the Hooded Men and their plot to overthrow the government; the sources of their funds, and what amounts they had spent for guns in Germany and explosives in Italy; where these supplies were stored in several hundred secret places throughout France, and exactly when and how they were to be used.

Dormoy put all this before the Cabinet, and there resulted one of those seismic disturbances which go on day after day, shock after shock, until people in the neighborhood begin to wonder whether it may not be the end of the world, so often predicted by the prophets of the Christian religion. The Socialists, of course, clamored for exposure of the conspiracy and arrest of all the conspirators; but the conservatives pointed out that the plot involved some five hundred officers of the French army, many of them among the highest—and after such a housecleaning, how much army would France have left?

The Socialists, who had been on the point of overthrowing the Chautemps government, decided to stay on and fight within the Cabinet. Dormoy, blackbearded friend of the people, destined to be murdered by the Nazis in a few years, may have foreseen his fate and resolved to make the most of his time, warning the workers and peasants of the peril in which their Third Republic stood. Rumors began to appear in the papers, and little groups of men to meet and argue on street corners and in wineshops, as they do in democratic countries, to the distress of those who desire the world to stay as it is, and believe that the less the excitable masses know about public affairs, the fewer chances there are of tumults and increases in the income tax.

IX

It was Lanny's birthday, which came in the middle of November. He wasn't having any celebration, or even mentioning the event, out of consideration for his mother who couldn't bear the sight or sound or even the thought of the figure 38. Lanny got up as usual, ordered his orange juice and toast, and looked over his mail and his half-dozen Paris newspapers. Those of the left were full of dark hints of treason and sedition; knowing what it was all about, Lanny thought: "It may break at any moment; and what will it do to my plans?" He knew that Jesse Blackless had his ammunition ready and his guns primed; his speech would attribute the conspiracy to the Nazis, and would frighten those master-intriguers and make them cautious. The nephew had said: "Give me two or three days more."

He was going to send Monck out to the mill that morning. Jean had been told to find out where the Germans got the meat that was fed to their dogs. It would be necessary to poison them; an unpleasant thing to think of, but a human life was at stake. This happening would alarm the Nazis even more, and probably cause them to double their guard; therefore the burglary would have to be committed before the poisoning was discovered, and that meant a difficult job of timing.

A knock upon Lanny's door: a cablegram, which proved to be from Robbie. "Sailing Normandie tomorrow arrive Paris proceeding Berlin hope for your company." There had been a time, long ago, when such a message would have been the happiest event in Lanny's life. Now it was a nuisance, and one reason more for rushing things.

He shaved and dressed, and was about to leave for Monck's hotel, when the telephone rang. A woman's voice, which at first he failed to recognize; a woman in great agitation, breathless, as if she had been running and was barely able to gasp out a word or two; a woman speaking English with a French accent: "No names—terrible—police arresting—friend—best friend—mustn't say names—place in country— pillbox—you understand?"

The word "pillbox" told him; he knew of only one such. The speaker was Annette, wife of the younger Denis de Bruyne. "I ran to neighbors—for God's sake—help us!" She began whispering—as if that would protect the dread secret over the telephone.

"What do you want me to do?"

"Find the others! Warn them—keep out of way. You also! They are taking private papers—reading everything."

"I understand. Is that all?"

"Be quick! Others must not come home—you understand?"

"Perfectly. I will do what I can."

"Good-by."

So, the government had made up its mind to strike! They must indeed mean business, when they were raiding a home of such prominence as the Château de Bruyne. They would see the pillbox in the garden, and would soon find the cache of munitions; they would read whatever papers they could find in the home. They had caught Denis *fils*, but the father and younger son must be elsewhere, and it was up to Lanny to warn them. He called the elder Denis's office; the secretary had just come in, the employer had not. Lanny guessed that when a man is doing such work as overthrowing a government, his private secretary must have some idea of it. He said: "Ask no questions. M. de Bruyne is in very grave danger. It is necessary that you find him at once and warn him to disappear." The secretary replied promptly that he understood and would do his best.

Lanny repeated the procedure for Charlot. He too had not arrived, but the secretary, a woman, promised to find him. There was a club where the young man sometimes kept appointments, and Lanny called there, but without success. There was nothing more he could do; he couldn't be expected to go out and search the streets of Paris for those two. Knowing French politics as he did, he didn't think they were in serious danger, except of publicity and inconvenience—and possibly of blackmail.

Was Lanny himself taking any risks? When he gave his name over the telephone and helped seditious conspirators to escape arrest, he was making himself an accessory after the fact, and making it appear probable that he was an accessory before it. When the police went through those papers at the château, would they find the name of Lanny Budd as one who was carrying messages for the Cagoulards? If they searched the papers of Baron Schneider, they would be very apt to find memoranda concerning a message carried to an agent of the Reichswehr. Annette had said: "You also!"—and no doubt she had something like this in her mind. Lanny had caused her to believe that he was one of the Hooded Men at least in spirit, and the servants must have got the same impression. One of the first acts of the police would be to get the names of visitors from the servants. "M. Budd comes often, and he had dinner here with Baron Schneider!"

A blaze of lightning flashed in Lanny's mind. "By heck, I've got it! I'm a fugitive from justice!" He delayed just long enough to step into the adjoining suite and tell Hofman to get ready, they were going at once to see Branting, the problem had solved itself. He darted back to his own suite and threw a few articles of necessity into a small bag, including a book which he might try to read during a time of great stress. He wrote a note for his mother: "Gone a couple of days. Picture business." Then he and the locksmith bolted to the car.

X

Monck was awaiting them, and the son of Budd-Erling announced: "God has tempered the wind to the shorn Lanny!" He was in a lively mood, tempted to slap the two men on the back and invite them to dance the farandole. "No poison, no trouble at all! I walk right in and stay as long as I please! I have the right of asylum!"

He told them of the telephone warning, which had made him into a fugitive from justice. He had been working in the Nazi cause, and the Nazis knew it, and now, when he was in peril of his life, could they refuse him shelter? "Let them try it! I'll telephone the Führer, if necessary!"

The other two agreed that this did the trick, and they opened the cabinet of the general staff and took out Plan 147B. They had been over every detail a number of times, and now all Lanny had to say was: "Tomorrow morning, if you see the signal, and if not, then the next morning. Good luck, and thank you both with all my heart." They shook hands, making it a rather solemn moment, and Lanny took his departure. Monck was to drive out to the mill and see if Jean had picked up any additional information. Hofman had nothing to do all day, except perhaps to have another séance and see if Ludi or Tecumseh or Claribel had any suggestions to offer.

On the way Lanny stopped to purchase a couple of small bottles of cognac, which he put away in his bag. Then he drove to the Château de Belcour. To the gatekeeper, who knew him by now, he said: "Tell Leutnant Rörich I must see him at once. It is very urgent. *Ohne Aufschub!*" There was a telephone in the lodge, of course, and in a minute or so the gates swung open. Leaving his keys in the car but carrying his bag, Lanny went up the steps of the building two at a time, holding out his arm and saying his "Heil Hitler!" Then he grasped the hand of his Nazi friend. "Come inside," he said. "Something terrible has happened. Take me where we can talk privately."

"Everything is private here, Herr Budd," replied the other.

"I know; but this may be a matter of life and death."

He was escorted into what had once been the steward's office and the door was closed. In low tones the secret agent of the Hooded Men broke the news that his conspiracy had been discovered by the French police and that he and all the other conspirators were on the run. Lanny didn't have to depart from the truth very much. The charming Annette de Bruyne, whose hospitality Rörich had accepted, had telephoned the news that their home was in process of being raided and their papers searched and read. Lanny, at gravest risk, had got word to the other members of the family, and likewise to those persons who constituted his immediate contacts with the organization. It appeared that the whole conspiracy was being blown open; if the government had learned what was going on at the de Bruynes', it was to be assumed that they would know about hundreds of other places where arms were concealed, and would be making such raids all over France. "Being a foreigner," Lanny said, "I am in an especially dangerous position, and I could think of no place to seek shelter but here."

"*Aber!*" exclaimed the SS man, greatly embarrassed. "This is really most unfortunate, Herr Budd. We are in no position to offer shelter to anyone, because Seine Hochgeboren is an official of the Embassy, and his home is under diplomatic status."

"So much the better, *lieber Freund;* I assure you, the French police have no possible way of guessing that I am here. I haven't told a soul—not even my mother."

"*Leider, leider, Herr Budd*—how can I make it plain to you? We simply do not do such things. It is a question of the diplomatic proprieties."

"*Na, na, Rörich*, I am speaking as one *Weltmann* to another. This is for the cause, and we do not stand so strictly upon proprieties when Nazism is at stake. You know only a small part of what I have been doing; and I assure you that I value my life and my ability to work for the Führer more than I do the feelings of any Jewish-Bolshevik democratic republic." Those were the strings you pulled when you wanted to ring the bell in a National-Socialist soul.

"Believe me, *lieber Herr Budd*, I sympathize deeply. But you know I do not have the say in such a matter. I am only a junior officer."

"That I can understand. *Ist Seine Hochgeboren zu Hause?*"

"I believe so. I will put it up to him if you wish."

Lanny wished it; and while the Leutnant was gone, he strolled into the library adjoining the smaller room, and took a good look at the catches which held the French windows. When the head of the establishment appeared, the visitor was examining rows of French classics bound in very fine leather stamped with the crest of the Duc de Belcour. They went back into the smaller room and closed the door— just the Graf and his "refugee." Rörich had doubtless been told to keep out, and wasn't sorry.

XI

It was a funny scene; at least it would seem so in after years when Lanny could look back upon it: an exemplification of the classic formula, an irresistible force meeting an immovable body, and what happens? Underneath the velvet glove of the trained diplomat was the iron hand of the master of men, one of the *Herrenvolk* destined to rule the world. Seine Hochgeboren was absolutely determined that this American stranger or near-stranger should not find refuge in his home, which had been in the past and might be now a small-scale Oranienburg or Dachau. Lanny, for his part, had adopted the ancient French motto: *"J'y suis, j'y reste."* He was here, and he was going to settle right down and make himself at home, and nothing less than physical force would get him past the door—or one of those French windows of the library, the one Lanny had agreed to leave open that night; the third from the northwest corner of the building, with two catches at the top, two at the bottom, and an extra solid one in the center, holding the two sections together.

All with the most elegant manner—*suaviter in modo, fortiter in re!*— Lanny explained what work he had been doing for the cause of the Hooded Men, identical with that of the National Socialist German Workingmen's Party. He knew all the secrets and named the key names. Quite recently he had had lunch with Baron Schneider at his home, La Verrerie, in Le Creusot, and had been commissioned to offer financial aid to the Nazis through Kurt Meissner. He had been told how the arms were coming from Skoda, not Le Creusot, for better purposes of concealment. (He hadn't been told any such thing, but he knew it was sure to be so.) He had dealt with the key men, and for that reason the French authorities would be seeking him more than any other person.

Patiently Graf Herzenberg replied. The services of Herr Budd were appreciated to the full, and of course he could count upon all sympathy and assistance from the Nazi organization. But it would have to be at some other place than the home of an Embassy official. "We simply dare not offer such provocation to the French government. We do not permit any of our own secret agents to set foot upon these premises."

No less patiently, Lanny made his counter-reply. "I appreciate your position, Graf. I have never before forced myself upon any person, and it pains me deeply to do it now. But this is not a private matter and neither of us is a private person. I came to your estate because I thought of it, not as a home, but as part of the German Reich. I could not go to Kurt's, because it is an apartment house, and I am well known there. If I made a mistake, I am sorry; but I came in good faith, and surely it is your duty to protect me from our enemies."

"I grant all your points, Herr Budd, and, as I have told you, I will see that you are taken to a place of security."

"When you propose that, you are subjecting me to a risk which I feel is entirely impermissible. I do not think I am a coward——"

"I have never intimated such a thing, *mein Freund*——"

"My life has value to your cause, far more than I am at liberty to tell you. It is my duty to protect it, and yours to help me."

"I will see that you are taken in a closed car, and since it is an Embassy car, it will be covered by diplomatic immunity."

"If I am discovered in such a car, it will be exactly as awkward for the Embassy as if I were discovered here. Behind your high fence and inside these spacious grounds I am safe from all observers, and I protest most earnestly against the idea of taking me out upon a public highway during this crisis."

"After dark, Herr Budd?"

"Darkness makes no difference to the French police, for they have fast cars and flashlights. They will consider it far more likely that fugitives will attempt to travel at night, and they are accustomed to block the highways and stop and search all cars. Nor is there any safety in distance from Paris, for we have hidden our arms in all parts of France, and the search for our friends will be nationwide."

XII

So they argued back and forth; and when they had said everything there was, they went back and said it over again. Neither would give an inch; finally Seine Hochgeboren declared, firmly: "I deplore this misunderstanding, Herr Budd; but this is my home and I am charged with the responsibility for the care of it. The decision must be mine, and I can only repeat what I have said before: I cannot permit you to stay."

Said the son of Budd-Erling, with exactly the same amount of firmness: "I appreciate your position, Graf Herzenberg, and it puts me in a most excruciating dilemma. If you knew the facts concerning my duties and responsibilities, you would not dream of turning me from your door. But I am under oath not to reveal these; so what am I to do?"

"I can only act upon the knowledge which I possess, Herr Budd. If you have valid credentials, you must permit me to see them."

"Surely you know, my friend, that the last thing in the world a confidential agent would do is to carry credentials in a foreign country."

"No agent of Germany is working in this country without having some superior who knows him and will vouch for him. Tell me who that person is."

"What I tell you, Graf, is that you are mistaken. I have no superior in this country, I report to no one here and am known to no one here —at least not in my full capacity."

"Surely, Herr Budd, you know enough about our affairs to realize that I cannot accept such a statement without any sort of confirmation."

"All I can tell you is that if you force me to go farther, you will be making a mistake which you will greatly regret. I am a personally appointed and confidential agent of a person whose authority you will recognize."

"You will have to name that person to me."

"Despite the fact that I am under pledge upon my honor as a gentleman to do it under no circumstances?"

"I am fully capable of keeping a secret, Herr Budd; and anyone in Germany who knows me will trust me for that."

"I am sorry, I have to keep my promise. What I ask is that you permit me to telephone to Reichsminister General Göring."

"You mean to telephone from this place?"

"You make it necessary."

"You will give him your name?"

"By no means. I can speak a few words which will identify me to him; and I presume that you will recognize his authority."

"As it happens, Herr Budd, General Göring has no authority over me. I am an official of the Embassy, and my superior is Foreign Minister von Ribbentrop."

"I am sorry that my acquaintance with Herr von Ribbentrop is slight. Therefore, since you make it necessary, I have to ask to telephone to the Führer."

"*Wirklich, Herr Budd?* You enjoy a telephone intimacy with the Führer?" This was really too much!

"I am sorry that you put me into the position of seeming a braggart, Graf. The last time I visited the Führer at Berchtesgaden he was kind enough to give me the telephone number of Haus Wachenfels—pardon me if I am accustomed to speak of it by its old name, whereas you may know it as Der Berghof. Some time ago the Führer asked me to bring him a painting by my stepfather and I have neglected to do him that courtesy. If you will call him wherever he happens to be and say that the stepson of Marcel Detaze wishes to speak with him, he will understand it as code, and I am sure he will tell you that I am a person socially and politically acceptable."

For the first time the immovable body showed signs of being shaken. Said the Graf: "Even granting the truth of your claims, Herr Budd, it seems to me it would be most injudicious to attempt to call the Führer from a foreign country about a matter of so delicate a nature."

"Let me suggest an alternative. Would it be within reason for you to call Kurt Meissner and ask him to come out here at once on a matter of extreme importance?"

"That I could do, but it would be quite futile. Kurt has already assured me of his warm friendship for you, and nothing that he could add would modify the decision I announced."

"Kurt has told you of our friendship, Graf, but has he told you what he knows about the Führer's attitude to me? Unfortunately, Kurt was not present at my last visit to Berchtesgaden, when Herr Hitler was gracious enough to unbosom his soul and tell me of his true feelings concerning the French people. On that occasion he urged me to do everything in my power to avert misunderstanding between France and Germany, and I took that as a commission to do what I have been doing for the past year."

"Is that the confidential mission of which you spoke previously?"

"By no means. That was a public mission. I was charged to tell everyone that I had it directly from the Führer's own lips, and I have told it to hundreds of persons in the highest social and political and financial positions in France. Kurt has heard me say it more than once."

"Is that what you wish Kurt to assure me?"

"What I would like more than anything else, Graf, is to have Kurt tell you what I did for him under circumstances almost identical with those which have driven me to your home. I do not know how much you know about his work for the Reichswehr after the war; I have never asked him about it, and am not hinting for you to tell me. Suffice it to say that he was in Paris in civilian clothes and under a false passport at the time of the Peace Conference of 1919; he was a spy, liable to a military trial and to be shot at sunrise. He asked me for help and I gave it to him, instantly and without question. At that time I was secretary-translator to a member of the American staff at the conference; I was only nineteen, but I had proved my ability, and earned a career if I chose to follow it. I, too, enjoyed diplomatic status, and might easily have pleaded to Kurt the risk I would be running and the higher duties I owed to my country. But I raised no such objections. I took him to my mother, who hid him in her apartment for a week, and then I bought a car and she took him into Spain as her chauffeur. Kurt knows that we saved his life, and has many times said so."

"I do not doubt it, Herr Budd, and all this puts me in an extremely painful position. As it happens, Kurt knows nothing about the special circumstances which determine my position, and nothing that he could say would possibly affect my decision."

XIII

There followed a long and stubborn pause. Lanny was here, and didn't need to talk; he waited to hear what else his host had to say. At last came a new proposal: "Would it come nearer to meeting your wishes, Herr Budd, if I offered to send you into Germany?"

Lanny laughed. "Let me show you something." He took from his pocket the cablegram he had received that morning and handed it over. "You see, I should be very well taken care of in Germany. My father has important business relations with General Göring; he shares in the use of all the new devices and processes which the German Air Force possesses, and you can believe that there are not many persons who enjoy that privilege. The General personally escorted him to Kladow and showed him that wonderful military base. He not only invited me to Karinhall and introduced me to his wife, but he offered to present me with a hunting estate near by. I have never accepted any favor from him, but I have done him many, and when I travel to Germany with my father we shall have the pleasure of enjoying a great man's famous hospitality, and I shall tell him of intimate conversations about political affairs in Washington and New York as well as in Paris and London. Among other things I am sure *der dicke Hermann* will roar with laughter over the story of how I fled for shelter to Graf Herzenberg and what a devil of a time I had persuading him not to kick me out."

"I don't want to kick you out, Herr Budd," interposed the diplomatic official, obviously disturbed. "I, too, have orders which I am not at liberty to disobey, and which General Göring, as a military man, would be the first to understand."

"*Es kommt darauf an,*" said Lanny; the German way of saying that circumstances alter cases. "Now and then emergencies arise, and subordinates have to exercise discretion. I assure you that I don't expect to impose upon you very long—for France, which I know well, is a mercurial country; not for nothing is it called Marianne, a woman's name. Her tempests arise quickly and blow over even faster. I am not in danger of a French firing-squad as Kurt was, or even of a French jail; I am only afraid of their newspapers, which would break that shield with which I have protected myself—my profession of art connoisseur. If you knew what I have been able to do with it during the past few years you would understand that it must be protected against all mischances. That is why I thought I was safe in appealing to a man of culture and taste like yourself."

Lanny by now perceived the signs of weakening of his opponent in this long duel. He chose his most persuasive, *vox humana* tone, and pleaded: "I beg you to be reasonable, *lieber Freund.* I am here, I am safe, and it would be most distressing to have to depart. I assure you, I am a gentleman, and know how to behave myself. I will not meddle in your affairs, nor bore you with my company. I will, if you prefer, stay quietly in a room and read a book which I have brought. You may send me a little food, whatever is convenient, and I will keep your servants content with the proper *Trinkgeld.* When I feel the need of fresh air and exercise I will walk to the rear, completely out of sight of the road. If I may see the newspapers, I will be able to judge concerning this political thunderstorm, and when I perceive that it has blown over, I will take myself out of your way, skirting the dangerous city of Paris and heading for the fine old bridge which crosses the Rhine at Strasbourg. If on the other hand the danger seems likely to last, I will accept your kind suggestion and let you send me into Germany by whatever route you are accustomed to use."

The immovable body was moving—a bad prognosis for the future of the Third Reich! "I am forced to accept that compromise, Herr Budd, and to hope that your assurance of safety within these grounds will be justified by the event."

"*Meinen aufrichtigsten Dank, Graf.* You may be sure I will do everything in my power to repay your kindness." He held out his hand, and they exchanged a clasp. Then, smiling his best, the American added: "Let me assure you that my title of *Kunstsachverständiger* is not just camouflage; I really do know about art, and sometime during the day, if you find that you have leisure, I should be happy to take you about these fine rooms and tell you what I know about the painters represented here, and the historical significance of these different works. Since you have to live with them, it might amuse you to know about them."

"Thank you, Herr Budd. It happens to be a busy day for me, for somewhat the same reasons as for you. I am obliged to go into Paris, but if I am able to return before you leave, I will avail myself of your offer. Now if you like, I will have you shown to a guest room."

12

Observe the Opportunity

I

VICTORY in one battle meant the beginning of another. Lanny lay upon the bed in the pleasant second-story room assigned to him, and talked to himself without words. "Don't take it too hard. You have a lot of time to pass and you don't want your hair turning gray." He had brought with him Hans Driesch's book on psychic phenomena, and now set himself resolutely to reading. It was a subject in which the Führer was interested and that made it respectable; it was in the German language, and Lanny was going to speak, think, and be exclusively German until this battle was won.

There came a tap on the door. It was Rörich, friendly and smiling; might they have the pleasure of his company at lunch? Lanny assented; if they were going to treat him as a guest, that was to the good. As they went downstairs, the lieutenant grinned and whispered: *"Sie sind klug!"* Lanny had performed a feat in getting his own way, and Rörich was amused by it. He was glad to have company. Perhaps it becomes monotonous, running a concentration camp.

The meal was served *en famille*, as it were, in a small room which apparently had been intended for the upper servants. Present were the Third Secretary of the Embassy, the very haughty Herr vom Rath; Rörich and Fiedler, a stoutish Hauptmann Bohlen, a young Doktor Flügelmann with pince-nez and little black mustache; also a humble and quiet male secretary. They had a very unpretentious luncheon, consisting of *Wienerschnitzel* and a salad with a reasonably good *vin ordinaire*, followed by a *compote*. A man-servant waited upon them; Lanny had never seen a woman on the place, and didn't expect to— unless it was Trudi.

The thought of Trudi would come unexpectedly like that, and each time his heart jumped up and hit him under the throat. This was Trudi's place of captivity, and these were her captors, her torturers. Was the sharp-eyed Herr Doktor there to say when she had been whipped enough, and to make sure that she was kept alive? Was the round and rosy Hauptmann there to see that the two lieutenants didn't yield to feelings of a sentimental nature? Did the cold and reserved Rath prepare the reports to Berlin? Thinking such thoughts, Lanny had to smile and smile and let others be the villains. A strange thing, to be sitting in a chair putting stewed fruit into his mouth, and think- ing that Trudi might be right under his feet at the moment. One floor down, or possibly two? And what would she be doing and thinking? Should he wangle his way to the piano again, and play the *Ça ira*, to tell her he was here? He must do nothing unusual, nothing to attract attention to himself. Be polite and completely non-invasive, and give no excuse for anybody to wish him elsewhere!

The Hauptmann had telephoned to Paris and learned what the afternoon papers had in their early editions. Tremendous excitement, with headlines several centimeters high. The police had discovered a nationwide conspiracy and were seizing great stores of arms: machine guns and mortars, bombs and grenades, hundreds of thousands of rounds of ammunition. Since it was in the papers, the company felt free to question Lanny, and he told what he knew and more that he had guessed. He wasn't sure if he was a hero in their eyes or a coward; anyhow, he was a personality, and surely nobody would find him a bore.

II

Apparently Rörich had been put in charge of the guest. That suited Lanny perfectly, and after the coffee he said: "Shall we have a stroll?" They went out to the terrace, and he added: "We must go toward the back. I must not be seen from the road." They walked in a grove of plane-trees, which in America are called sycamores; the guest re- marked: "You must be happy, living in such a grand place. I don't suppose you have had it that way always."

"No, indeed," replied the young officer, and revealed that his father had been a shopkeeper, ruined by the postwar inflation; they had

had it very hard indeed. Lanny replied that things were far easier in Germany now, and there was reason to hope they would get better still. He didn't say how, for just then a dog barked, and he remarked: "Those friends of mine! Let us pay them a visit."

Their stroll turned toward the kennels. There were two shepherds and two dobermans, each pair in a separate pen of heavy wire mesh. They were glad to see visitors, and stood with their paws on the wire and their tails wagging briskly. "Oh, the lovely creatures!" exclaimed the American, and talked the language of those who have property to guard and the leisure to play with life. "You know, Rörich, you cannot really understand men until you have had an opportunity to study dogs. I am not joking; it is an amazing thing, how you see all human qualities, both weaknesses and virtues, in these mirrors of our personality. I suppose it is because they have lived by serving man for thousands of years, and have had to accommodate themselves to our dispositions. Whatever the reason, it is the fact that you will rarely in this life find a man who will be as utterly devoted to you and as single-minded in loyalty as a dog. You will find no child more eager for attention, or more ready for a romp, or more quickly aware of any trace of displeasure. As for jealousy, that is really comical. Have you made a special friend of any of these dogs?"

"*Leider*, I haven't had the time."

"Then they will not object to your manifesting interest in me. But I have one of these shepherds at my mother's home who can hardly bear to see my mother kiss me; and as for allowing me to pet another dog, that is out of the question—Pluto simply shoves his nose in and takes the other dog's place. If I order otherwise, he becomes so miserable that I cannot bear the spectacle."

The keeper came, an elderly man whose business it was to know dogs, and what the *Herrschaft* said about them. He and Lanny talked technicalities; Lanny said: "What are they fed?" and "What exercise do they get?" The man replied that they were turned loose at night and ran all over the place. The visitor made a move to open one of the doors, and he warned: "*Achtung, mein Herr.*" Lanny said: "We are old friends by now!" They discussed the instincts of watchdogs and what they could be taught. Lanny declared: "They know exactly what is in your mind. If you are afraid of them, they will give you cause for fear, but if you trust them they will deserve it."

He walked into the pen with the two shepherds; the man went with him, speaking words of command. It was a formal introduction, and the dogs came humbly. Lanny said: "*Schön Prinz!*" and "*Brave Lizzi!*"

He let them smell him to their noses' content; he patted them on the heads, and said: "I shall never have any trouble with anything so beautiful." The bitch was expecting pups, and he asked: "What do you do with them?" The man said: "We shall have to give some of them away," and Rörich added: "Would you like one?" Lanny replied that he would like nothing more, and would take it in his car the next time he went to the Riviera.

There were the dobermans, the old-style German police dogs, smooth-coated, black and tan, lithe and eager. The visitor said he didn't know them so well, and asked about their qualities. They were less excitable than the shepherds; more stolid, but hard fighters. He wished to make their acquaintance, and the keeper asked to go in first. The same introduction was made, and this pair also had full opportunity to learn Lanny's smell, his hands, and his English tweed suit and his shoes from New York. "My dogs remember my friends after years of absence," he said. He would have liked to add: "I suppose you don't need any nightwatchman"—but he was afraid this remark might be remembered if anything went wrong.

III

"Don't let me keep you from your work," he said to his friend. "I have a book, and am used to entertaining myself." He took a seat in one of the great leather armchairs of the library, and started the reading of a learned work by a professor of philosophy at the University of Leipzig. It had been comforting to Lanny that a scholar of this standing had taken the trouble to examine a layman's notes of experiences, and certify to their value as a contribution to knowledge.•

In his book Professor Driesch began, as all Germans do, at the beginning of the beginning; he discussed the problem: "How is *knowing* possible," and he pointed out the importance of remembering that the knower is a part of Reality, as well as the known. We are forced to assume that there exists between the knower and the thing known "a primordial relation, which we shall call *knowing potentia.*" Somehow the thing known affects the mind, and this affection takes the form of matter, and some matter which comprises what we call a flower affects some other matter which we call our body and our sense organs and our brain. Said the learned Professor Hans Driesch:

"This is a great miracle, and is by no means understood. Think of this: The ultimate result of the affection is a certain rearrangement of the electrons and protons in my brain—and then I 'see' the flower 'outside in space.' This in fact is a real enigma and will be an enigma forever. Things would be much easier for us to understand if the electrons and protons of the brain would 'see' *themselves*, but this, as you know, is not the case."

When Lanny read words such as these he knew that a man who had thought deeply was trying to explain to him in the simplest possible words ideas which were extremely complex. He did not read such words quickly, but stopped and pondered each sentence to make sure he understood its full meaning. He looked up from the page of the book at the very stately library which the Duc de Belcour had inherited from his forefathers, and found it strange to reflect that it was all "an arrangement of electrons and protons."

Lanny's eyes ran quickly over the outsides of hundreds of books, and these outsides affected the electrons and protons which composed his brain in a certain special way, for the reason that in the course of his life he had opened a great many volumes of the French classics, and so had acquired a special kind of "knowing potentia" for the language and history and philosophy and drama and fiction of the French. When he saw the name Racine on the leather binding of a volume, the electrons and protons of his brain began to dance in a certain special way, and when he saw the name Rochefoucauld, they danced in a way entirely different; it might be said with probability that there existed in the whole universe no other assemblage of electrons and protons which would have danced in exactly the same way as those of Lanny Budd. All this, surely, was to be recognized as "a great miracle!"

Some force which was "a real enigma" drew the objects which Lanny Budd called his "eyes" away from the leather-bound and gold-stamped volumes to the floor of the room, and along the floor to the third pair of French windows from the northwest corner. In front of those windows, on the soft carpet of dark green velvet, he saw a small coin lying, a franc, which had formerly been made of silver but was now made of base metal, and has on one side a figure of Marianne, or liberty, or the republic, whatever you choose to call her, sowing seed. Lanny couldn't see this with his physical eye, but he knew that this figure on the coin was turned up. He knew it because there wasn't really any coin there; he was seeing with what Hamlet called his "mind's eye" a coin which was going to be there sometime after one-thirty next morning, as a signal from Monck and Hofman that they were in the château. Ever since this signal had been agreed upon, Lanny had been seeing imaginary coins on carpets in front of windows, and each time the electrons and protons of his brain had been set to cavorting with a special and peculiar sort of violence.

Here was a problem which might have been found worthy of investigation by a professor of philosophy at Leipzig University. If the manner of the vibrations had been exactly the same as if the coins were "really" there, we should have said that Lanny Budd was suffering an hallucination. If such vibrations had continued in the same way for an indefinite period, we should have had to say that Lanny was mildly insane. But because the vibrations were such that Lanny knew they were different, we said merely that he was "imagining" the coin; he knew it wasn't "really" there, but expected it to be there soon, and felt now the things he was going to feel when he saw it "really" there. Yet the emotions he was going to feel were so violent that he couldn't bear them even in imagination, and took his eyes off the carpet and his mind off the coin that wasn't there, and forced himself to go back and read some more sentences from the learned professor's book.

IV

What did this authority have to say about the special kind of problem which had been puzzling Lanny's mind for so many years? Under the heading "Telepathy," he read:

"All our normal knowledge about another mind's contents is reached in an indirect way; we see and hear that the other being moves and speaks, and then infer that his mind is in a certain state. In the realm of psychic phenomena the indirect way is turned into a direct one. Sense organs and brain are excluded. The knowing goes from subject to subject immediately; the relation *knowing potentia,* therefore, must have existed also between them."

A strange thing, whatever way you looked at it. Lanny wondered which would seem the stranger—that we possessors of minds should be compelled to know other minds by the roundabout and complicated method of "inferring," or that we should now be coming to a stage of evolution where we were discovering another, a "direct" method. For hundreds of thousands, perhaps millions of years, men had been using the indirect method, and their minds were so set in it that they were unwilling, perhaps unable, to contemplate the possibility of the direct method. Yet, what a saving of time it would be! What a convenience—or possibly a nuisance! Like any power whatever, it would depend upon who was using it, we or the other person. What a different world it would make if ever it came into general use! A world so different that we couldn't imagine it, and wouldn't know how to live in it; some might prefer to commit suicide and take themselves out of it!

Here was Lanny Budd, for example; seated in a soft leather arm-chair, comfortably reading a book, or trying to. His wife whom he loved, the dearest being in the world to him, might be only ten or twenty feet away from him, lying on a bench in a stone cell in torment. He had been imagining her, or trying to avoid imagining her, for a couple of months; and here he was, this close, yet powerless to find out a single thing about her. Heavy stone walls lay between them, and the poet had been lying when he said that stone walls did not a prison make nor iron bars a cage. They made a prison for Trudi Schultz, and had obligated Lanny to carry on an elaborate set of investigations and intrigues in order to get this near; it would require a man in a Schutzstaffel Hauptmann's uniform and another with an elaborate set of steel tools to find out if she was there, and what was going on in her mind.

But here came this strange and mysterious possibility of mind reading, or telepathy. If it was a reality, the mind of Trudi would be able to flash a message into Lanny's mind, instantly and directly. Had she done something of the sort, that time when she appeared at the foot of his bed? He himself had tried it many, many times, in all ways and under all conditions: in the stillness of the night, when she might be asleep; when he himself was falling asleep, or just awakening; whenever his thoughts of her became vivid, and she might be thinking of him. Nothing had ever come in reply, but he kept on hoping.

He had read about the experiments of Coué, who claimed that it is not will but imagination which affects the subconsciousness. Since it was easier to imagine Trudi when he had reason to believe that she was so near to him, he sat now deliberately holding her in his mind, employing his art-lover's memory to visualize her. He saw her perfectly chiseled features, expressive of intelligence and of moral conscientiousness, of concern about truth telling and justice doing. He recalled her as he had known her ten years ago, young, eager, full of hope for her cause and for personal achievement in the work she loved; he recalled her as he had known her of late, when hope had been replaced by grim determination, when love of truth and justice had become stern anger against wholesale liars and killers. Fanatical, if you chose to use an unkind word, and by no means easy to live with, but commanding a husband's admiration and immovable loyalty.

He put his arms about her in love; he did not command her to come to him, but told himself happily that she was coming, that she was welcoming him and responding to his embraces. He permitted his senses to be warmed and his thoughts to be dissolved in memories of the oneness they had enjoyed for a couple of years. *Belle nuit, O nuit d'amour, souris à nos ivresses!* And in that sort of semi-trance his conscious mind waited, hiding in a corner as it were, trying to fool itself and pretend that it wasn't there, keeping watch for something that might possibly be a communication, a message from a beloved one who might be buried just beneath him in a dungeon of heavy masonry.

The trouble with all such experiments was, how were you going to know a message if you got it? How were you to distinguish between a thing from outside and the swarm of things you already had inside? Lanny had had a thousand imaginings concerning Trudi in that dungeon; he had had many others of her being elsewhere, including under the sod of France or Germany. How would he know which was the real "hunch" and which was self-deception. Even if he saw her, or heard her voice—how would he know that wasn't an hallucination, the product of his overstrained fancy? Tecumseh had called him a "highbrow," and had bade him become as a little child; but how did one perform that feat? Backward, turn backward, O time, in thy flight!

V

Dinner was a more formal meal, served in the great paneled dining room. The same men attended, but they now had two servants to wait upon them and there were several courses. The Nazis were no ascetics; they did themselves well, as you could see by looking at them. The afternoon papers had been brought out from the village, and everybody had had a glance at them; they all knew French, otherwise they wouldn't have had this assignment. Lanny learned that his efforts in Paris had been unsuccessful; all three of the de Bruynes were in prison, and likewise several of the other leaders whose names he had been hearing and using. All the papers were violent, raging in favor of their special point of view.

So the diners had plenty to talk about, and all expressed their opinions, mainly to the effect that the French were poor organizers and worse keepers of secrets. "It can't be done in a democracy," declared Fiedler; the well-informed Secretary vom Rath supported him: "That is why they are doomed." The consensus was that the chances of reconciliation between Germany and France were greatly reduced.

They wouldn't say in the presence of an American that this meant war, but such were the implications of their talk.

After the meal they repaired to the music room. Rörich had told them that Lanny was a musician, and of course his talents were at their service. "What shall I play?" he asked, and the Leutnant, who had known him first and had taken him up as a protégé, remarked: "Didn't you say you had played for the Führer?" It was up to Eduard vom Rath, the ranking officer, to suggest: "You might play for us what you played for him."

Lanny seated himself at the fine rosewood piano, and began the first movement of the *Moonlight Sonata*. It is a composition laden with grief; and here were five German males, full of good food and wine and ready to sink into a mood of exquisite melancholy. They were separated from the homeland, and from the women they loved; they didn't know when they would go back, and they turned all slow music into a *Liebestraum*. Beethoven had been born in Germany, and the fact that he had chosen to spend most of his life in Vienna was overlooked; that he had been a democrat and in rebellion against authority was quite unknown to these Nazis. They had been taught that he was one of the glories of the *Herrenvolk* and a proof of their superiority over all others. To enjoy him was honorable, and for a foreigner to play him was an act of homage.

When that movement came to an end, they asked for something else. Lanny's fingers began to fly, and there came rippling out upon the air a stream of lovely notes, a beautifully woven pattern of sound, gentle murmurs in the bass and little bird-songs in the treble—the *Waldweben* from *Siegfried*. The Führer loved Wagner above all other composers, and the Nazis had taken him over, drums and trumpets, slide trombones, bass tubas, and all. Wotan the Thunderer was their god, Freya was their sex dream, and Loki, the tricky one, was the head of their propaganda department. Siegfried was Germany incarnate, and when the spear was driven into his back every German thought of 1918. The Nazis were in the process of rewriting the legend, bringing the young hero back to life and making sure that this time he would be properly armed and guarded.

Lanny said: "Herr Kannenberg brought his accordion and sang for the Führer." He gave them a sample: "*Tiroler sind lustig, so lustig und froh.*" They gathered round and joined in, and that was a pleasant way to pass an evening that otherwise would have been one of nervous strain for Lanny. "There Was a King in Thule," "When the Spring

Comes and Looks from the Mountains," "Ah, How Is It Possible for
Me to Leave You?"—and so on and on—Lanny had sung these old
songs when he had visited the Meissners as a boy, and if he didn't
know the accompaniments he could make something up as he went
along. When his repertoire was exhausted, they suggested others, and
after he had heard the first verse he could play the rest. No matter
how many verses there may be, no German is ever known to tire;
nor will you find any one of them in the plight of most Americans,
who know the first two or three lines of their national anthem, and
then have to sing "La-lá-la-la-lá."

There came a pause, and Lanny said: "I will play you something
that these old walls have heard before." He pounded out the tune
that he had played on his first visit: "*Ah, ça ira, ça ira, ça ira—les aristocrats à la lanterne!*" Only Rörich would know what it was, and Lanny
looked at him and grinned. In his soul the husband was crying: "Trudi!
Trudi! This is for you! I am coming!" Was she there, and could she
hear it? He asked his subconscious mind but got no answer; instead,
he played and the rest of the company joined in singing: "*Mein
Heimatland, du schönes, du he-errliches Land.*"

The Germans have a poem to the effect that when you hear singing
you may lie down in peace, for evil men have no songs. The Nazis
were using this as one more camouflage, but for Lanny tonight it
held good.

VI

The company broke up shortly after eleven and the refugee retired
to his room. This was the worst period he had to spend, for he was
alone, and could not sleep. He sat in a chair and tried to read; then
he got up and paced the floor, back and forth, like a tiger in a cage.
He had had weeks to think of every possible thing that might go
wrong, but now he thought of more. The Graf had not come home;
perhaps he was spending the night with his lady, but, on the other
hand, he might come in late, or very early in the morning. Just what
would Lanny say if his host should find him in the act of opening a
pair of French windows in the library? "I am very restless, *Ihre
Hochgeboren.* I couldn't sleep. The news is bad. I want to walk outside." That would be all right; Lanny didn't care if they thought him
a coward. But what would he say if the Graf caught him in the act
of penning up the dogs? "They were barking, *Ihre Hochgeboren.*
They kept me awake." Not so good!

So many, many things might go wrong! They had picked a moonless night, and that wasn't subject to change; but there was a wind blowing, and the opening of a door or window might create a draft ·and cause some other door to bang. It was apparently blowing up a rain, something to be expected in this part of France in November; if the ground was wet, he would leave tracks in the house and so would his fellow conspirators. In the general excitement, would they remember to clean their shoes? And then that unanswered question of a night-watchman! What would he be, an old servant or a young SS man?

Resolutely Lanny picked up the book of the Leipzig professor, and forced himself to read a paragraph. Then he realized that he didn't know what he had read, so he went back and read it again. This learned scholar, after decades of investigation, had convinced himself that the phenomena of psychic research were genuine. "All minds are One in some last resort,"—such was the conclusion he drew. But all this meant to Lanny at the moment was: "Why doesn't Trudi send me a psychic message?" Then he would wonder: "Did she get any of my psychic messages to her?"

His thoughts moved on to the musical signal, his Blondel song. If she had heard it tonight, she had probably heard it the previous time, and what had she made of it? A long wait between signals, and she must have become discouraged; perhaps she had decided that it was merely a coincidence. After all, there were plenty of people in France who knew the tune of the *Ça ira;* it was in the books, and some German might have been curious about it, or perhaps have thought of making up Nazi words for it!

Lanny was trying to retrace Trudi's thoughts, using psychology where telepathy had failed. He had promised her that he wouldn't endeavor to find her; but perhaps she would understand that this promise was beyond his power to keep. Would that worry her, or would they have broken her spirit to the extent that she would want to be rescued? Perhaps she wouldn't have mind enough left to want anything, to know anything; they might have driven her entirely insane.

Oh, devils, that were committing such horrors upon human beings! Lanny recalled the seven men with whom he had just dined. All were "gentlemen," in the sense that they had good manners, they ate their food properly, they listened to Beethoven and Wagner, they smiled and discussed world events. Then they went down into the cellars of this building and applied physical and mental tortures to a woman, to break her will and reduce her to a cringing wreck, an imbecile or a gibbering idiot! They did it, not because they were savages at heart, but because they had been taught it as a duty; they had been drilled in a creed of diabolism, the vilest perversion of faith and morals since the Spanish Inquisition.

Lanny had taken up a feud against it, and was leading a raid upon it. But he was not at one with himself, because he doubted the wisdom of his course. He had got himself into a position of danger, and was getting two other men into a position even worse. If they should get caught, he would have three persons to worry about instead of one, and he would have a long and costly campaign on his hands. Trudi might forgive him, but could he ever forgive himself if he destroyed his position of advantage in the struggle against the Nazi terror? Cold reason told him that at this moment he ought to be in Berlin, finding out what he could regarding Hitler's intentions as to Austria. He ought to be dancing with some diplomat's wife or mistress, picking up gossip, instead of being shut up in a room by himself, holding a book in two hands which trembled, looking at his watch every minute or two, then listening to make sure it hadn't stopped running. Verily, "Time travels in divers paces with divers persons," and right now Lanny Budd was the one for whom it "stands still withal."

VII

When the lagging hands at last arrived at one-thirty, all these doubts and debates came to an end. All Lanny's faculties were needed now for the job of outwitting his enemies. He put on his overcoat and hat, also his kid gloves; he must wear gloves through all these operations, to avoid leaving fingerprints. Into the coat's capacious pockets he put the two bottles of cognac, also a tiny flashlight not much bigger than a fountain pen; you pressed a button at one end and a thin beam came from the other. Also, he had a handkerchief with a piece of twine securely tied to one corner; also a tape measure, and a well-drilled brain—such were the accessories required for Plan 147B.

He put out the light in his room and went to the door. Holding the knob firmly, he turned it and opened the door. Outside, a dim light burned in the hall; there was a row of doors, all closed, and behind them slept some of the Nazis, Lanny hadn't made sure which. Softly he closed the door and stole down the carpeted hall. If anyone met him, he had his formula ready; he was jittery and couldn't sleep.

Down the stairs, one at a time, stopping to listen. A night light in the entrance hall, but no sound. There might be a watchman inside the building, but he was not to be seen. Lanny had learned the arrangement of the rooms thoroughly and he slipped silently into the almost dark library. Everything quiet here, except for the thumping of the intruder's heart. He couldn't be sure whether that was loud enough to be heard upstairs.

The third window from the northwest corner of the building. Lanny had studied it from the outside and made sure there could be no mistake. French windows are like two narrow doors, and one of them is enough for a man to pass through. The one on the right opens first, and that was the one on which Lanny worked. He hadn't dared try the bolts in advance, and had wondered if they might be rusted in place. He tried the one at the top, holding his thumb under it to keep it from snapping suddenly. It was free, and he drew it carefully down. Then the one at the bottom, and last the one in the center, which held the two parts together. He opened it, and a blast of air struck him in the face. He reached his hand outside; there was a handle whereby the door could be opened from the outside when the bolt on the inside was pushed back; having tested this and made sure he would not be locking himself out, he slipped outside and closed the door behind him.

High up overhead, on the wall of the building, was a shaded flood-light of moderate intensity, shining directly down on Lanny's head; illuminating the loggia, the terrace, and the shade trees in the background. Lanny had been prepared for this, having seen it more than once from the road at night. He started a stroll which he hoped would appear casual. He could be sure at least that the noise of the wind would keep anybody from hearing the pounding of his heart!

Around a corner of the building was a second light; no doubt he would find one on each side. Visibility was good, as the airmen say. The sky was black and mysterious, and so were the trees in the distance; but all around the house was a belt of light and anyone approaching would stand out as if in bright moonlight. Lanny strolled around another corner, watching carefully, prepared for anything. This side had a porte-cochere; under it was shadow, and from this shadow came a challenging voice: "*Wer geht da?*"

VIII

Lanny had been prepared for this, and he met it with his best society manner. "Herr Budd," he answered, and came toward the porte-cochere. He was careful to keep his hands hanging, the palms open and the fingers extended; a harmless position, but not ostentatiously so. "*Sie sind der Nachtwächter?*" he inquired.

"*Ja, mein Herr.*"

"*Heil Hitler!*"

"*Heil Hitler!*"

"I am a guest in the château. You know me?"

"*Ja, Herr Budd.*" The servants had talked, of course.

"I couldn't sleep. I had to come for a walk."

"*Eine böse Nacht, mein Herr.*"

"You have heard perhaps what has been happening in Paris—the arrest of our friends?"

"*Ja, Herr Budd; sehr unangenehm.*"

"I am very much upset about it. I may be in danger, too. I had papers they may have found."

"*Leider, Herr Budd.*"

"You walk at night?"

"*Die ganze Nacht.*"

"May I walk with you?"

"*Gewiss, Herr Budd.*" Never one sentence without the "Herr," so Lanny knew it was an old-fashioned German. A man in his fifties, too old to be a perfect Nazi; perhaps a family servant of the Graf. He would have heard that Americans were free and easy in their ways, and would not be surprised if this one chatted as they strolled. Without doubt he had heard the visitor thoroughly discussed in the servants' hall; his riches, his clothes, his manners, his love of dogs, his playing and singing, his having visited the Führer.

"It is a terrible thing to know that your friends are being arrested and perhaps mistreated. I couldn't sleep and I couldn't read. I didn't want to disturb anybody, and I thought maybe if I got myself tired, I could get to sleep."

"*Ja, ja, mein Herr.*"

"I tried taking a drink, but I'm afraid of taking too much. I need to have my wits about me in the morning." He laughed, and took out one of the bottles of cognac, opened it, and took a pull, a small one. He put it back into his pocket. "It is easy to take too much when you are nervous."

"*Ja, mein Herr, das weiss ich gut.*"

IX

They strolled, and Lanny chatted freely, as he had learned to do with all sorts and conditions of men. "I don't suppose you can read French newspapers"—the guest set out to make himself a substitute therefor.

He told about the Cagoulard conspiracy, and how important it would have been for Germany to get a new government in France, one that would break off the alliance with the wicked Reds, which of course was aimed at Germany and could have no other meaning. "They want to do what they did in the last war, compel Germany to fight on two fronts at once, and of course the Führer will never permit that."

So the genial American explained French politics and the world situation to a humble *Diener*, and the *Diener* was impressed by his kindness, and every now and then would say: "*Ja, ja, mein Herr*," or perhaps "*Herrschaft*," which is equivalent to the English quality, or gentry, and is the same whether you are many or one. "*Was wünschen der Herr?*"—what does the quality desire?

Lanny desired another pull at the flask, and when he had taken it, he held it out to the man, saying: "*Wollen Sie trinken?*" This, of course, was unthinkable in Germany, and the man was taken aback and tried to refuse; but the genial American insisted that it was no fun to drink alone; he stopped while the man took a nip, and then, laughing, said that wasn't enough and made him take a real one, *einen richtigen.* "I have had too much; you take the rest."

He made the watchman drink until he coughed and sputtered; and after that they were real friends, and, as they strolled, Lanny told how the wicked Reds were working in Paris, with traitorous Germans to help them undermine the Fatherland, and how Lanny had tried to help in getting a new French government that would put down these evil Reds; but now, *leider*, the effort seemed to have collapsed, and Lanny didn't know what would happen; he might have to flee into Germany and give up his labors in Paris, at least for a time. It was extremely sad and he became a bit melancholy, and stopped and took another nip, and saw to it that Max—the nightwatchman's name—took a good one to brace him against the chilly damp wind of a November night. "Finish the bottle," Lanny said, and added, with a slightly tipsy chuckle: "I have another." Max obeyed.

It is well known that men who are in trouble are tempted to drown their sorrows in drink; but a serious and well-trained *Nachtwächter*, charged with a heavy responsibility, cannot afford to do such things, and *der arme Max* pleaded his duty. Lanny let up on him, and they took another circle of the château. The American *Herr* giggled and said he had had too much, but Hans would watch out for him; surely that was one of the duties of a proper *Wächter.* Max admitted that he had had to perform it upon occasions. He made a truly valiant effort to keep sober according to his honor. He was broken down only by

Lanny's assurance that this wasn't real cognac, only an imitation; what tasted like alcohol was only a flavoring, and it wouldn't make any able-bodied man really drunk. Have one more, in the name of *Gemütlich-keit!*

After a while the guest said that he was tired, and they might try sitting for a while; so they sat under the shelter of the porte-cochere, and Lanny took out the other bottle, loosened the cork, took a very small swig, and with laughter and mischief persuaded his companion to take a large one. *Ja, gewiss*, it couldn't possibly do any harm! He kept this up until he was sure the man had got as much on board as even a German could carry; then he said: "I feel warm and sleepy; let's rest." He deposited the bottle between them, and rested his head against the wall and began to breathe heavily. Presently he heard Max taking the bottle and heard a gurgling sound, so he felt sure his game was won. In a very few minutes the man was snoring loudly; then Lanny took the bottle and slipped it into his pocket and stole away.

X

One more duty, a dangerous one. Somewhere in these extensive grounds the dogs were roaming, and the visitor had to find them. Until they were penned up there was no possibility of entrance for any stranger, even in a Nazi uniform. When Lanny was a sufficient distance from the château, it was safe to call, and he did so. "*Ho, Prinz! Komm, Lizzi!*" He heard barking, and moved in that direction, calling now and then. It was so dark, and the wind in the trees so noisy, that the animals were almost upon him before he knew it. A moment of real fear when he heard them; but he mustn't permit that, for he had read that fear has an odor which betrays it to dogs.

Really, the visitor had no cause for worry; he had made sure of these friends, and now he spoke their names and they came in a tumult of greeting. They were perfectly trained and did not leap up on him and put mud on his clothes; they whimpered their delight and no doubt tried to shake their tails off, though he could not see it in the dark. He greeted all four by name, and patted them, and they crowded against him and had a lovely time with all the smells they had learned to know and which told them that this was a friendly god, coming to keep them company in the dark.

Of course they would follow him, along the familiar path back to the familiar kennels. It wasn't their usual time for entering, but if the friendly god opened the gate and took them in, it was not for them to question why. Both pairs knew their pens and their snug little houses, with fresh straw and old home odors. When the friendly god so commanded, they would crawl in out of the cold wind and sleep. The god would take all the responsibility upon his divine shoulders. He did so, and went out, fastening the gate behind him.

There was a corner of the château grounds bordering the highway which Lanny and his fellow conspirators had chosen because it was far from the gatekeeper's lodge and sheltered by shrubbery. Lanny would come to this spot and then count seven posts, which brought him to the one on which he would tie the handkerchief for a signal. Getting there in pitch darkness wasn't easy, but now and then he ventured a moment's flash from his light. The fence was of steel, and he counted the posts by hand, pushing his way past the bushes. Number seven had been chosen because it was plainly visible to anyone passing on the highway, and Lanny took out his tape measure and measured up six feet from the ground, and precisely there he tied the handkerchief, leaving a slipknot so that it could be untied. Six feet from the ground meant: "Everything is clear." Five feet meant: "Come again half an hour later." Four feet meant: "An hour later." Three feet meant: "The plan is off until tomorrow." Two feet meant: "Off for good."

Lanny's part was done, and it was his job to get back to Max and make sure the man's slumbers were not disturbed. If by ill chance he should awaken, Lanny would be ready with more brilliant conversation and the rest of the second bottle. The library had been chosen as the place of entrance because it was on the opposite side of the building from the porte-cochere, and it had been agreed that if there was a watchman Lanny would lure him to the latter spot and keep him busy there. If in any extreme emergency it became necessary for Monck or Hofman to call Lanny, they would give a faint imitation of a hoot-owl.

XI

The watchman was slumped over and still snoring. Lanny felt pretty sure that he could be counted out for several hours. The conspirator himself had nothing to do but keep still, and try not to let his teeth chatter, whether from cold or the excitement of a desperate adventure. Nothing to do but sit and imagine his friends coming up in their car, their lights dimmed to avoid attracting attention; they were supposed to make a round of the place every fifteen minutes, beginning at a quarter to two o'clock. When they saw the handkerchief, they would park their car a safe distance away.

They had in the car a light rope ladder, with hooks at the top, and Hofman, the smaller man, would stand on Monck's back and set the hooks and climb to the top, then pull the ladder over to the other side. Monck would hand up the box of tools and Hofman would take it down to the ground. Then he would climb up again, and keeping his perch on top of the spikes as best he could, let the ladder down on the outside for Monck. Hofman would slide down on the inside, and Monck would come up, drop the ladder inside, and slide down. All this would be done in darkness and silence, and if a car came in sight at the wrong moment, they would both have to hide in the bushes. Everything had been carefully rehearsed, and Lanny didn't need any telepathy to see it happening. But things might go wrong, and he saw those, too, and telepathy didn't tell him which was "reality."

The amateur burglars would have no trouble in finding their way to the château, for its gray walls stood up well lighted in the darkness. They would have to come into that floodlight and cross the terrace and loggia to the windows of the library. They would walk with dignity and assurance, having a story carefully prepared; Hauptmann Branting —that was to be his name—had come from Berlin with a confidential communication for Seine Hochgeboren. Hofman was his secretary, and they had had a breakdown of their car, and not wishing to disturb anyone so late they were prepared to wait under the porte-cochere. If they were caught inside the building, they would say they had found a window open; if it was a servant who caught them, the Hauptmann would overwhelm him with his authority: *Gestapo, Geheimdienst, zu Befehl, Herr Hauptmann, undsoweiter!* Only an officer would be able to meet such a charge of *Autorität.*

But suppose one of the officers happened to be restless, and to come downstairs as Lanny had done? Suppose the Graf himself happened to arrive inopportunely? These were chances the conspirators had to take, and now they were fears that Lanny had to confront. He had read of people's hair turning gray under this sort of strain, and he wondered if it was happening to him. He would have liked to have another nip of the cognac, but was afraid he might need it for the *Nachtwächter.*

The snoring continued, so loudly that if it had been a still night it might have awakened some of the sleepers in the rooms above. But the wind continued to roar and the trees to sway and creak. Lanny kept saying to himself: "It's all right now. Stop worrying!" He said: "Trudi! Trudi! We are coming!"

He didn't permit himself to stir until he was sure that half an hour must have passed since he had hung up the signal. That was time enough for the two men to have climbed the fence and got inside the château, and Lanny stole away from the stupefied watchman and around the building to the library windows. Softly and carefully he opened number three, and stepped inside; he closed it quickly to stop the draft, and then flashed his tiny beam of light upon the carpet. There on the green velvet carpet lay the coin that he had been seeing in his imagination for weeks. A French franc, with the figure turned up, meaning that his friends were inside the building! Oh God, oh God!

Lanny slipped out again, shut the window, and stole back to keep watch over the watchman. He sat on the steps of the porte-cochere, resting his chin in his hands to stop both the chattering of his teeth and the shaking of his hands. For the first time in his life he began to pray. "Oh, God, help them! Oh, God, help Trudi! Let them find her! Help me to bear it till they find her! Oh, God, have mercy!"

And then, after the fashion of modern man, he added: "Oh, God—if there be a God!"

13

My Life on Any Chance

I

THE hardest of all things to do in a time of danger is to do nothing. If Lanny had been under the necessity of talking to the nightwatchman and keeping that functionary's mind busy, that would have kept Lanny's mind busy, too. But just to sit there and listen to the man snore and watch for indications that he might be waking up—that indeed was a strain upon the nerves. Who might be awake inside this château at half past two in the morning? Somebody tending a furnace? Somebody keeping watch over prisoners? And what would they make of a strange Hauptmann Branting and his commission to investigate the contents of the dungeons and interview the prisoners therein? Would they obey orders and help him, or would they turn and run and alarm the household? Such problems offered endless scope to the imagination, and Lanny's mind hardly waited to complete one alarming episode before it started another.

Every now and then he would take out his watch and flash the tiny light upon its face for a moment. Never since the invention of clocks had a pair of hands moved so slowly. He had set himself a half hour as the proper time to allow, but he couldn't stand it; at the end of twenty minutes he got up and stole around to the library windows and slipped inside to look at the coin on the floor. If it had been turned over, it meant that the burglars had completed their errand and gone; it would then be Lanny's duty to put the coin in his pocket, go out and release the dogs, then re-enter the building, fasten the windows securely, and get back to his room as quickly as possible. But, alas, there was Marianne, or liberty, or the republic, or whoever it might be—still sowing the seeds of revolt, or enlightenment, or prosperity, or whatever that might be. The burglars were still at their work, and Lanny had to go back to his vigil at the porte-cochere and resume the imagining of difficulties.

He had heard Horace Hofman talking for hours about locks ancient and modern, and the kind one might expect to encounter here. Old ones might have been taken out, of course, and new ones put on. Vaults might have been built, with steel walls and modern safe locks, time locks, anything. These would present difficulties and take time, perhaps more time than could be counted on. The Meister-Schlosser had told many stories of human lives depending upon the speed of fingers which were insured for a hundred thousand dollars; so far, he had never lost out, but this might be where the record was broken. They had set four o'clock as the hour beyond which it would be unsafe to stay. Darkness lingered long at this time of the year, but the estate was a small farm, and farm workers go by the clock and not by the sun—at least they would do so in a well-ordered German establishment.

So Lanny went back to his post, crouching out of the wind and drawing his English tweed overcoat tightly about him; his hands were trembling but the palms were moist, so it wasn't the cold. The snoring began to be broken and replaced by mutterings, and Lanny's heart began to pound with a new fear. The watchman turned over, he made an effort to lift himself on one elbow. "*Ach, wer ist's?*" he groaned.

Lanny took out the bottle and uncorked it. "*Hier! Wollen Sie trinken?*"

"*Nein, nein!*" The man tried to protest, but Lanny bent over him, held his head, put the bottle to his lips. "*Trinken Sie! Er ist gut!*" When the man opened his mouth to protest, Lanny pushed the bottle in and lifted it. There was a gurgling sound, and presumably the liquor was going down his throat and not his windpipe. "*Gut, gut!*" Lanny kept saying, which is soothing to a German; at last the man sank back with a heavy sigh. That would do him for a while.

II

There had been a play called *Alias Jimmy Valentine*, about a safe-cracker who betrayed his identity by opening a safe in which a little girl had been accidentally locked. This man was supposed to have sand-papered the skin of his finger tips until they were raw; but Hofman said that was nonsense, for pain would destroy those delicate sensitivities by which you became aware of the dropping of a tiny tumbler. Ordinary locks you could open, as a rule, without too great delay, because you understood the principles on which they were constructed, and the weak points; by delicate probing you could determine exactly the location of the locking bolt and of the tumblers. But it always took a certain amount of time, and you had to refuse to let yourself be hurried or worried. Put your mind on it to the exclusion of everything else, just as if it were a problem in chess. Monck, alias Branting, would mount guard, and Hofman would forget there were such dangerous creatures as Nazis in the world.

Such, at any rate, was the program. How many locked doors would there be, and how could the invaders be sure which ones to open? Would the Nazis lock the door or doors which led into the cellars? Quite possibly; but again, it might be they would lock the doors of the different rooms in which they stored food, wine, trunks, and other property. If they had a number of dungeon cells, these would probably be in a separate part, and that part would be walled off and have a steel door, or perhaps more than one, to keep the sounds from being heard. Would they have a keeper inside this place at night, or would they just lock their captives up and forget them till morning? The French word *oubliette* means a place forgotten, or for persons forgotten, and the Nazis presumably would not let their slumber be disturbed by worries over their captives. If one died, it would be no great loss; but there might be one like Trudi Schultz who had vital secrets locked in her mind, and they might take special care of her and keep her guarded day and night.

Such had been the subjects of Lanny's thought for several months, and of long discussions among the three conspirators. Now two of them were finding out what they needed to know, while Lanny still could only speculate. No news was good news to this extent, that no alarm had so far been given. If that had happened there would have been lights coming on in the rooms above, and surely someone would have called to the *Nachtwächter*, or come to look for him. If the two burglars had found a guard in the cellar, they would use their arts to persuade him that they were Gestapo agents and must be obeyed; only as a last resort would they overpower him and tie him up while they worked. Lanny's busy imagination pictured such a series of events—he pictured many different series, and some of them caused his teeth to chatter so that he held his jaw tightly cupped in his hands.

This was certain: if any violence was used, Lanny's position with the Nazis would be pretty certainly destroyed, for he could never persuade them that he had not admitted the intruders to the place. The same might be true if the occupants of the château discovered in the morning that their woman prisoner had disappeared without a trace. Lanny might protest ever so earnestly that he had been asleep in his room and knew nothing about it, but they would be sure to trail him for the rest of his days, or until they solved the mystery. He could certainly not live with Trudi again, whether in Paris or London or New York. He could hear Trudi saying: "Oh, Lanny, you shouldn't have done it!" and his only plea could be that he had loved her more than duty. What would be her attitude to this form of constancy?—or would she call it inconstancy?

Lanny would listen for a few moments to the snoring of the watchman, and then he would go off on another train of speculations, few of them happy, many of them melodramatic. If there were untoward events of any sort, the Nazis would be sure to question the watchman, and it was hardly conceivable that poor Max could withhold the fact that he had been drunk, or refuse to reveal that it was the American guest who had got him drunk. The guest saw himself being summoned before a board of inquiry consisting of Seine Hochgeboren and his staff. Just how had he spent the night, and how had it happened that he had got the watchman drunk while keeping himself sober—especially since he had given Rörich and Fiedler to understand that he got drunk with extraordinary ease? Was he accustomed to carry bottles of cognac around in his overcoat pockets? And just where had he been on the estate, and would he be so kind as to let them examine his shoes? Just when Lanny had got through assuring them that he had not been anywhere but on the loggia and the drive, he would find himself confronted with the fact that his footprints had been discovered at a corner of the estate close to the highway!

III

From scenes such as this Lanny's overstimulated imagination would return to the immediate present. He saw a vision of Hofman on his knees before a dungeon door, fiddling with the lock, putting in one skeleton key after another, shaking his head and muttering: "It is too much for me." Was that a case of telepathy, or just his fears taking form? Did he really see Monck standing with his lips to an opening in a cell door, whispering: "Is that you, Trudi?" Perhaps that was Lanny's own painfully acquired knowledge of how dungeons are constructed.

They have to have airholes, unless it is intended to suffocate the prisoner. There is always an opening at the level of the keeper's eyes, so that he can look in, and a larger one at the bottom, through which he can shove food and water. These are closed by sliding covers which cannot be opened from the inside, but only from the outside; they would have to be left open at night, and even if they were closed, they couldn't be locked. Monck would open them, and if Trudi was there, and was conscious, the would-be rescuers would tell her what they were doing. They wouldn't speak the name of Lanny Budd, but they might say: "*Ça ira*"; also the Latin phrase, "*Bella gerant alii*," which was the password Lanny had used in his effort to get Alfred Pomeroy-Neilson out of the Franco dungeon. He had told Trudi this story and explained the meaning of the phrase; also he had told Monck.

Another half hour had passed. Max was still in his stupor, and Lanny made another trip to the library windows. He held his breath as he turned his flashlight on the carpet inside, and something seemed to give way in the pit of his stomach when he saw that the coin had not been turned over. It was nearly half past three, and they were still down in those cellars—doing what? Lanny was free to go back to the porte-cochere, crouch out of the wind, and do all the guessing he pleased.

"Give me time, and don't worry"—so Hofman had said; but now Trudi's husband discovered that this was beyond the possibilities of his mind. He was so worried that it seemed to him he just couldn't stand it. Had the two men been overpowered? Or had somebody locked them in? A curious fate that would be for a locksmith! Or had they got lost! That was a new idea which hit the waiting conspirator with painful violence. The plans of the building which they had obtained did not show what was underground. Certainly the passages must be extensive, and there might even be difficulties deliberately constructed; there might be trapdoors, or trick doors which closed when you passed through them. What more likely than that the Nazis had protected themselves by some modern device of the photoelectric cell, to keep their prisoners secure and to trap any unauthorized person who ventured into forbidden premises?

A nasty idea, and the longer Lanny held it, the more havoc it made in his mind. He thought: "When they pass a certain spot or touch a certain door, it may ring an alarm bell in Hauptmann Bohlen's room!" Lanny hadn't heard any bell, but he wouldn't have heard it in the midst of this windstorm. Even at that moment the Nazis might have pistols at the heads of the two would-be burglars and be saying: "*Hände hoch!*"

<h1 style="text-align:center">IV</h1>

The time came when Lanny couldn't stand it any more. If the men were lost, he had to find them; if they were trapped he had to free them. He had to put an end to the suspense which had been tormenting him for the past three months, and know if Trudi was there, and if she was herself, able to speak and to know what was happening. He had become obsessed by the vision of her behind a steel door, whispering through the aperture, and Hofman on the other side, unable to solve the secret of the lock. If that was the case, Lanny would get her out if he died for it; he would get Jean to hire half a dozen of the leftists among the village men, arm them with Budd automatics, and have them raid the château the following night, sever the telephone wires, hold up the inmates, and cut out the lock of the dungeon door with an electric torch!

Max was still in his stupor; and once more Lanny walked through the floodlights, turned the handle of the French window, and saw the curtains billow out in the wind. Quickly he closed the door and flashed his little torch. The coin was still heads up; and Lanny moved silently across the library and into the dining hall. Beyond that a pair of swinging doors led to a passageway; he had seen the waiters coming through these doors at mealtimes, and according to the plans of the building there was a large butler's pantry and beyond it the kitchen. From one side of the pantry a door opened to the cellar stairs, and that was as far as the plans showed. From there on Lanny would be groping his way.

The stair door was not locked. Lanny opened it with care, making no click, and stood listening. The silence was that supposed to be appropriate to the tomb. He flashed his torch for one moment and saw that the stairs were made of heavy blocks of stone, well worn by nearly two hundred years of use. One glance was enough and he shut off the light, which might alarm either his enemies or his friends. He went down the steps, one at a time, stopping to listen for the faintest sound, and using his utmost efforts not to make any. At the bottom was another door, and he tried it softly and found it was unlocked. Had Hofman unlocked it? He had said that they would close every door they found closed, so as to avoid attracting the attention of anyone who might happen to be passing.

The intruder flashed his light again. A long corridor, about six feet wide, running in both directions; walls of stone, and a number of doors of heavy wood, all having locks. Storerooms, no doubt; the locks were large and old, something that was to be expected. The conspirators had agreed that there would hardly be prisoners behind wooden doors without openings; also, a door which shut off the dungeon part of the cellars from the storeroom portions would almost certainly be of steel, or at least of heavy iron.

Which way had Monck and Hofman gone? Lanny might have told them to drop a scrap of paper for an indication; but the idea that he might follow them had never been contemplated. He had to make a guess, as they had doubtless done; he chose the direction in which he knew the main part of the building lay. Before he started he took a franc from his purse and laid it in front of the door. If his friends saw it, they might guess what it meant; in any case, it would serve to tell Lanny himself how to find the stairs again. He would count his steps, and make careful note of every turn he made.

One—two—three—four—five—six—seven. Lanny taking tiptoe steps, in black darkness, guiding himself by the walls; stopping every few steps to listen, and thinking that the crazy pounding of his heart must be echoing up and down the corridor like any other sort of pumping plant. He knew he was in the midst of dangers, and didn't try to deny to himself that he was scared. He wanted very much to be out of there, and all that held him was the desire to take Trudi with him. Try as he would, he failed to think of any plausible reason he could give Seine Hochgeboren for tiptoeing about in the cellars of that nobleman's country home at half past three in the morning. He could say that he craved a drink of liquor; but what about the half bottle of cognac he had in his pocket? Could he say he had found that in the cellar? They would surely ask him: "Where?"

V

Presently he came to a cross corridor, and there he stopped and listened long. Not a sound in this tomb. He felt about him with his hands and made certain of the layout; he had three directions to choose among, and no time to be wasted; he flashed on his light, down one corridor and then the next. He saw a shadow darting swiftly down one of them, and his heart leaped so that it hurt. A sound of scurrying feet—a rat. He and his friends had discussed this as one of the phenomena to be expected. "Rats go wherever men go," Monck had said; "they have better brains and will outlast us." The three had debated this idea; an ex-sailor, who had lived among rats and observed them closely, pointed out that men chose to think about a great variety of matters, but rats thought about nothing but taking care of rats. Their method was outwitting men and stealing their food. Also, they didn't fight one another, at least not persistently, and in armies, as men did. "And doesn't that prove they have better brains?"

Here they were, taking this old château for their own, and having nothing to do but burrow themselves into safe hiding places and get access to stores of food. Doubtless they compelled Seine Hochgeboren, and before him M. le Duc, to pay tens of thousands of francs every year for food for them. They had gnawed holes at the bottom of most of these wooden doors. Perhaps—oh, God!—they had got into the cell where Trudi had been confined, and eaten the ends of her fingers and toes on occasions when she lay unconscious. Doubtless there were cats also in these cellars; they do not concern themselves about strangers, and would make no trouble for Lanny—but one little terrier dog might bring all their plans to ruin.

Lanny went down one of the side corridors and found himself confronting a row of coal bins, filled to overflowing. This building had not been modernized, and all its rooms were heated by grate fires; the coal was shoveled into scuttles—here was a row of them. A large dumb-waiter, the invention of the American Thomas Jefferson, went up through the floor above. This was the rear of the building, and Lanny had stupidly guessed that it might be where the dungeons were situated—overlooking such commonplace necessities as coal chutes, and the delivery and storage of huge quantities of food and wine.

He retraced his steps, counting them carefully, seventy-four tiptoe steps, which are not so long. He found the coin on the floor and left it there; he went in the other direction, and it wasn't long before he came to another cross corridor. Again he felt about him, and listened, holding his breath. What sounds would his friends be making? Hofman would probably be crouched down, working on a lock, and the sounds he made would be so faint that he himself could hardly hear them. He might or might not be using a flashlight. Monck might be standing guard, or perhaps prowling in different directions to listen. Both men were wearing rubber overshoes. Both would be as nervous as Lanny, though their pride might forbid them to admit it. Certainly neither would thank him for sneaking up on them and causing their hearts to stop beating.

The explorer turned his tiny light down one of the cross corridors. It vanished into nothingness, and he tiptoed in that direction and found a large space piled solid with split logs: a store of wood for the great fireplaces above. Doubtless there was a dumbwaiter leading to a service room above. There was a great scurrying of rats here, and Lanny guessed that hundreds of generations of them had come to being in the interstices of those logs. Perhaps they never went out into the daylight, and had lost the power to see except in the dark. The thought came: "At what hour in the morning do the servants start to get coal and wood up to the floors above?"

VI

Lanny hastened his steps, exploring the anatomy of the ancient establishment of the Belcour family, favorites of King Louis the Sixteenth of France. Surely they had had enemies and the need to keep these enemies where they could do no harm. Even if it hadn't been so, even if they had relied upon the King to protect them, the architects would have put in dungeons, because dungeons were a proper feature of châteaux.

Lanny's gloved hands came to a door which seemed different from the others and he flashed the torch. Iron, black-painted, with rust in spots. He tried the knob softly, and it turned; the door came open, with the faintest trace of creaking. The intruder listened again; not a sound, not even a rat. He flashed his torch, and saw stone steps going down. Here was the place! He and his friends had agreed that if they could find a way to a second level in the cellars, that was where the dungeons would be. A place where the cries of the unhappy could never reach the guests in the banquet hall and on the dancing floor! A place where nobody could signal the unfortunates by playing Blondel songs on a grand piano!

Lanny took one step down, and then silently, oh, so carefully, closed the door, cursing its faint creaks. He didn't want to alarm his friends, and he could count upon it that they were here. Almost certainly the reason this door was unlocked was that the Meister-Schlosser had solved its mysteries.

As soon as the door was tightly closed, Lanny gave the signal agreed upon, an owl's hoot: "Hoo, *hoo!*" with the accent on the second syllable, long drawn. They had planned it for outdoors, where it would be more appropriate. Or was it conceivable that there were openings into these cellars through which owls might find their way? Would they be nesting in crannies up above the piles of logs, and pouncing on the rats that scurried on the floor? Just as rats have nothing to think about but rats, so owls would have nothing to think about but owls; and they, too, might outlast men, having brains enough not to fight their fellow-owls.

No answer to the call. With his gloved hands on the walls at each side of the narrow passage, Lanny went down, step by step—sixteen of them, and sixteen times he put his weight on the stones with painful slowness, for he had no rubber shoes to dull the sound. At the bottom the corridor went straight ahead, and he didn't dare to flash the light, but stood again and called, a bit louder: "Hoo, *hoo!*" This time he heard an answer, faint but prompt. Some other owl was in this subterranean tunnel!

Lanny wasted no fraction of a second, but went toward the sound, as quickly as he could on tiptoe. There was a turn in the passage, and when he came there, the beam of a flashlight appeared suddenly full upon him. He stopped, and flashed his own tiny light, and there was the spectacle he had been imagining for the past two hours; Hofman on his knees before a door, with his metal box of tools beside him, and Monck on guard behind him with a torchlight in his hand. One glimpse was enough for all three, and they shut off their lights at the same moment. Lanny came to the locksmith and whispered, barely audibly: "What have you found?"

"There is somebody in here."

"Is it Trudi?"

"We can't be sure. We hear groans; nothing else."

"Man or woman?"

"We can't tell that."

"Can you get the door open?"

"I think so. I am working." Not a word more; he went to work. Monck drew Lanny a short way into the corridor, so that they would not disturb Hofman. The German whispered: "Why did you come?"

"I thought you must be in trouble."

"The dogs are penned up?"

"Yes."

"Is there a watchman?"

"I have him blind drunk. I don't think he will move."

"Everything else O.K.?"

"So far as I know. Have you opened any of these other doors?"

"We haven't had time. We had to open three doors on the way here. I've listened at all the cell doors and heard nothing. All the slots are closed but this one, and that seems to indicate the others are empty."

VII

Hofman whispered: "Hush!" and they fell silent. He was working in darkness, guided by his senses of touch and hearing. He had some kind of instrument in the keyhole and was moving it ever so gently. Only he could hear the sounds, and know what they meant; that was his business, at which he had worked and played most of his life. Lanny would have liked to listen at those other doors, but he was afraid to move a muscle; Monck had listened, and that had to be enough. Time, which had stood still for Lanny, was now racing for all three of them.

Suddenly there came a clicking sound, and a whisper: "I have it!" The lock turned, and the door creaked on its hinges. In the second which that took, Lanny and Monck had moved to the locksmith's side, and when he flashed his torch into the cell, all three pairs of eyes were as one.

The place was about ten feet long and eight wide. It had no window; only the two openings, one at the top and one at the bottom of the door. The air was fetid, and had the smell of dried blood which Lanny had learned to know in Nazi dungeons. In the far corner, to the right as you entered, was an iron cot, and on it lay a figure covered with a dirty gray blanket. Hofman stepped in and they followed, all three with their torches turned on. In that bright light they saw that the prisoner was a man, stoutish, gray-haired, and with a straggly gray beard which might have taken a week to grow.

In the light the prisoner stirred and groaned, but did not open his eyes; he was alive, but perhaps not much more than that. There were wounds on his head, unbandaged, and the blood had run over his face.

Apparently he had been left here to die, if he chose to do so. Beside the cot was a plate with dry bread, a tin cup, and a pitcher with water. Whether he was able to help himself to these was apparently no concern of the men who had left him here.

"He looks to be a German," whispered Monck; but of course one couldn't be sure, since there are so many types of Germans, and they have been so thoroughly mixed with bordering and invading peoples through the centuries.

Lanny suggested: "Your uniform may frighten him. Better wait outside for a bit."

Monck went out, and Lanny poured some water into the tin cup, and sprinkled it into the man's face. He stirred and moaned, but did not open his eyes. Lanny whispered: "Lift up his head," and Hofman set his torch on the stand and did as requested. "The whole back of his head is bloody," he declared.

Lanny put the water to the man's lips and tried to get him to drink. Lanny had to take one gloved hand and press his jaw down to get his mouth open; then he poured in a little water and the man swallowed it. He began to moan: "*Ach! Oh weh!*"—which confirmed the guess as to his nationality. He laid his head down, but still he did not speak, and Lanny said: "I'll try a little cognac."

He took the bottle from his pocket and uncorked it. Hofman raised the poor fellow again, and Lanny poured in a few drops of the liquor; this started the man to coughing, and Lanny waited, then tried a little more. At the same time he murmured: "*Wir sind Freunde*"—we are friends; and then: "You have nothing to fear."

The man opened his eyes, which were pale blue; one had been badly bruised and may have been useless. Lanny went on whispering reassurances, but perhaps his words were not understood. There was terror in the prisoner's face, and he cried faintly: "*Nicht peitschen!*" Do not whip me!

Lanny repeated, over and over: "We are friends. Do not be afraid." But the prisoner began to whimper in a faint voice. Evidently nobody had come into this cell for any purpose but to torture him, and whatever else they told him would be a trick.

Hofman whispered into Lanny's ear: "We cannot stay. Our time is up." But Lanny had no idea of leaving without some further effort.

"I have an idea," he said. He pulled off the blanket, revealing a sickening spectacle; the man had apparently been whipped on both his front and back; the former was a mass of bloody stripes. But Lanny was hardened to Nazi methods and didn't stop for comment; he hastily folded the blanket, and said to Hofman: "Lift him up." He placed the folded blanket so as to prop the man's head up, facing forward; then he sat beside the victim, leaning over him, and flashed the tiny torchlight into his eyes. Lanny began to murmur softly: "*Wir sind Freunde*," and "*Keine Angst!*"—don't be afraid. Then in a sort of singsong, slowly: "*Sie wollen schlafen*"—you want to sleep. "*Sie wollen schlafen, Sie wollen schlafen!*"—over and over. Lanny had read somewhere that you cannot hypnotize a man without his own consent; but perhaps a man in a daze like this wouldn't know how to refuse. Anyhow, why not try? He went on and on trying, in spite of Hofman's whispered protests.

The prisoner was staring into the light, and perhaps he was getting the words; his whimpering ceased, and apparently he was being calmed. Lanny began passing his free hand before his face, just below the beam, not interrupting it entirely. He changed his formula: "*Sie schlafen—Sie schlafen. Schlafen—schlafen.*" It is a good singing word, with a broad "a" as the Germans say it; and after seemingly endless repetitions of it, the eyes closed. The man might be in a trance, or he might be asleep, or he might be dead. It wouldn't take long to find out.

VIII

Lanny shut off the torch and bent close to the man's face, whispering: "We are friends. *Freunde, Freunde.* We won't harm you. Tell me who you are. *Was ist ihr Name?*" He kept repeating these words, until at last there came a reply, so faintly that Lanny couldn't be sure whether he heard, or whether his own imagination was supplying it. He wanted Hofman to hear it too, so he said: "*Lauter. Noch einmal. Ihr Name.*"

This time Hofman could hear, and what a jolt it gave him! First Paul, and then Teicher, the first name pronounced "Powl," in German fashion. The name that both Lanny and Hofman had heard in the séance room from the lips of the old Polish woman, supposed to be speaking for Ludi Schultz! The old man who was kind, and who had tried to help Trudi, and who was being tortured by the Nazis! This was he!

"*Sagen Sie, Paul,* there was a woman prisoner here?"

"*Ja—eine junge Frau.*"

"What was her name?"

"*Nein, nein!* She wouldn't tell! She didn't tell me! *Ich weiss nichts!*" Evidently this question terrified the victim.

"Don't be afraid, Paul. We are friends. Your friends and her friends also. Was her name Trudi?"

"They said that was her name."

"The Nazis said that?"

"But she wouldn't say. She wouldn't tell me." Still the terror.

"What did they do with her?"

"They beat her, but she never talked."

"Is she here now?"

"No, they took her away."

"Where did they take her?"

"To Germany."

"Why did they do that?"

"Because she wouldn't tell them anything."

"They didn't kill her?"

"I don't think so."

"Why did they beat you?"

"I tried to help her."

"What did you do?"

"She wrote a letter and I tried to take it out. They were watching me and they got it."

"Who was the letter to?"

"A French name, I forget. Long—something."

"Longuet?"

"That is it."

Lanny needed to ask no more. Manifestly, Trudi couldn't have written to him, or to any of her comrades of the underground. She had thought of Jean Longuet, editor of the Socialist newspaper in Paris; she had heard Lanny talk about him, and knew that Lanny had been sending him secret news from Spain. He was well known, and to name him would be revealing no secret to the Nazis.

Monck came in from his vigil in the passage. "It is a quarter past four and we are taking a grave risk."

"One moment," Lanny answered. Turning to the prisoner, he said, in a firm voice: "Paul, you will not tell anyone that we have been here."

"*Nein, mein Herr.*"

"You will not remember that we have been here. You will forget. *Vergessen—vergessen. Verstehen Sie?*"

"*Ja, mein Herr.*"

"You will sleep and get well. *Schlafen und gesund werden.*"

"*Ja, mein Herr.*"

With Hofman's help Lanny laid the victim flat again and put the blanket over him. With quick strokes of his handkerchief Hofman wiped the pitcher and cup, so that not even the marks of gloved hands might be left on them. Bending over the prisoner's face, Lanny whispered: "You will wake up." He snapped his fingers. "You are awake."

They couldn't delay to make sure. Monck took the American by the arm, guessing rightly that it was hard for him to tear himself from this scene, and that he might be a little weak in the knees. "Come," he commanded, firmly, and led him to the door. All torches went off, and they came into the corridor, and waited while Hofman fiddled with the lock. They heard it faintly click. "O.K.," he whispered, and Monck picked up the heavy box of tools, he being the sturdier man. They went down the corridor, softly but swiftly.

IX

No reason for delay now; they had only one thing to do, to get out. They went up the stairs, and closed the door at the top. Apparently Hofman had made a passkey, for he needed but a moment to lock it. In single file they went down the long corridor in the upper cellar, feeling their way by the walls. Had they counted the number of steps? Lanny didn't ask; it was enough that he had counted, and now counted again. He knew the turns, but didn't have to prompt the others, for Hofman, in the lead, took them straight to the proper door. Lanny flashed his tiny light for the fraction of a second, just long enough to pick up the coin which he had laid on the floor. Hofman opened the door softly, and when the others had gone through, he closed it behind him, but did not stop to lock it; he was willing to let it be supposed that some careless person had forgotten to lock it.

They went up the flight of stairs on tiptoe, and waited while Hofman slowly and carefully opened the door which led into the butler's pantry; he held it open a fraction of an inch, listening. This was a moment of danger, for there was a good chance that some servant might be getting early to work. But there was no sound, and Hofman opened the door all the way. When the others had passed through, he closed it, and again did not stop to lock it. Lanny didn't ask if it had been found locked; he was sure that Hofman knew his business, and time was galloping for them.

Into the dining room, and past the long table of French walnut at which Lanny had eaten a meal and might eat more; past the historical paintings upon which Lanny had discoursed to Rörich. A dim light pervaded these rooms, and the three intruders looked in every direction, all their senses alert. Across a wide hall, and then into the library, and over the soft velvet carpet to the third window from the northwest corner. Hofman stooped and picked up the coin, and then opened the half-window, really a narrow door. A blast of wind, a long blast, while three men slipped through; then he closed the barrier behind them.

Had the watchman awakened? Had the dogs been turned loose? These were chances they had to take, and there was nothing to be said about them. "*Au revoir*," whispered the locksmith, and Lanny replied: "See you in Paris this morning." The two started across the floodlighted loggia, a paved and uncovered space in front of the château. They did not run, but moved with the dignity appropriate to an SS Hauptmann charged with secret duties by the Gestapo. Hofman was now carrying the tool kit—for of course it was unthinkable that an officer would perform such menial service. Lanny did not wait to watch them, but walked with his practiced casualness around the building to the porte-cochere.

The watchman was still breathing heavily, and that was to the good, though Lanny's peril was still far from over. He had to wait for a period of ten minutes, that being their estimate of the time required for the men to get to the steel fence and climb it. Once they were out of the light, they could carry the box of tools between them and make good time. The ladder was hidden in the bushes, and it wouldn't take them long to get it up and climb over. But there was the possibility that some car might be passing; a peasant cart might delay them quite a while. It wouldn't do for them to be seen climbing the fence with a heavy box, and still less would it do for the dogs to be turned loose until they were safely over.

X

So Lanny had to sit there and think about Trudi, and realize that he had proved all the worst that he had imagined. In that cell, or in one of the others adjoining, she had spent something like three months, being whipped and tortured by those half-dozen cultivated monsters with whom Lanny had eaten meals and might have to eat more. A feeling of nausea came over him, and he had to clench his hands and set his teeth tightly together. He wished that he had brought along his Budd automatic in his bag; he saw himself carrying it in his pocket when he went down to breakfast, and suddenly producing it and shooting down those men in a row. But no, it wouldn't do the least good; he was fighting not men but a government and a system of thought, a set of ideas. The day might come when guns would be used, but it wouldn't be one gun; it would be millions and perhaps tens of millions.

He had got here too late. The delay was something he would never be able to forgive himself. But what could he have done? Everything had depended upon his becoming a guest in the château, and how could he have managed that a day earlier? Should he have tipped off the Socialists in the French government as to the Cagoulard conspiracy and thus caused the raid earlier? Possibly he might have done so; but the idea had not occurred to him until the telephone call had come from Annette de Bruyne. He couldn't have given his name in an accusation which involved the de Bruyne family; and would the French cabinet have acted upon the basis of anonymous charges? No, that was just a crazy idea, one of many with which Lanny would torment himself, because he had to blame somebody for this tragic *dénouement*.

He had failed completely, and forever, so he told himself, with sickness of heart and soul. The Nazis now had Trudi inside the vast dungeon which was Germany. They had taken her there to kill her, because they couldn't break her will, and killing was what they did with the bravest and best. Lanny had no way to find her, and would never even know what had happened to her—unless some day she would appear at the foot of his bed in the night, or unless she would speak to him with the voice of Tecumseh. All Lanny's elaborate efforts had been for nothing; all the time and expense, bringing Hofman from New York and Monck from Spain; all Lanny's own time and labor, when he might have been really doing his job as presidential agent.

It was good to crouch there in the darkness and shiver with cold and grief and rage all combined; it helped to pass the time, which was again standing still. All Lanny could hope to save out of this misadventure was the ability to go on deceiving the Nazi-Fascists. He still might fail at that, for Paul might not obey the hypnotic suggestion, or Max might stay drunk and tell who had got him drunk. The dogs might make a disturbance, the two burglars might be delayed in getting over the fence, somebody might see Lanny coming in at the library windows—oh, yes, there were plenty of mishaps to be imagined, and to keep Lanny looking at his watch. It might even be that some of the Nazis would be using hypnotism or telepathy, clairvoyance or trance mediumship. Two could play at that game, and Hitler had men who knew all about it. You fought the devil with fire, and then discovered that he had discovered a new and hotter kind!

Oh, God, oh, God, poor Trudi! Lanny would have to give her up; yet, no sooner did the idea cross his mind than he knew that he couldn't do it. Already he began thinking about ways to find her in Germany. Who would have her in charge—Hitler himself, or Göring or Goebbels or Ribbentrop or Himmler? Could Lanny find that out if he stayed with the Graf and cultivated his friendship? Poor fool—so the son of Budd-Erling called himself—sitting here dreaming about such achievements, before he had even made sure that he could escape detection and the complete ruination of his career!

XI

The little imps or hobs or whatever they were that were sitting on the hands of Lanny's watch and keeping them immovable at last had to let go; the ten minutes' period was up, and Lanny arose and walked quietly to the rear of the building and back to the kennels. Nobody was there, at least not in sight. The dogs heard him coming and were on the alert; they weren't used to being turned out at this hour, but whatever the friendly god did was all right. He opened the gates and they followed him; he closed the gates behind them and told them to run, and away they went into the darkness. They might find the scent of the men and might lead their keepers to discover the tracks, but if the invaders had got away in their car there would be no solving of that mystery.

Lanny returned to the porte-cochere. He grabbed the watchman by the shoulders and shook him, saying: "*Aufstehen! Aufstehen!*" The man began to groan and protest; no doubt he had a headache that he wouldn't forget for a long while. He must be roused sufficiently to get on his feet, and be made to realize his own danger, that of losing his job, a terrible thing to an elderly citizen of Germany, where everybody is regimented and his life-time record is on file. Lanny kept on shaking him, more and more vigorously, and commanding sternly but not loudly: "Wake up! *Aufwachen, Sie Esel!*"

Lanny ventured a flash of his torch. By one of the pillars of the porte-cochere was a hydrant, used for sprinkling the flowers and washing the drive. Lanny turned it on slightly and got a little water in his handsome Homburg hat and went and threw it into the watchman's face. He did it a second time, and by dint of more shaking and pulling he got the poor fellow onto his feet. "Now, walk!" he commanded. "*Sie sind betrunken, Sie armer Narr!* If they find you this way, you will be sent back to Germany. *Verstehen Sie?*"

"*Ja, ja, mein Herr.*"

"All right then, keep walking. Don't let anybody know you have been drinking. Don't say anything about me, or they will get it out of you. You understand?"

Poor Max began to stagger along, with the American half holding him up. *Ja, ja,* he understood everything, and was terrified; *ach leider,* and *Herrgott,* and *bitte um Verzeihung, Herr!* And then *Oh weh, oh weh,* which is the equivalent of the English woe, and *bitte sehr,* which is please very much—everything a poor terrified elderly *Diener* could think of. "We have left undone those things which we ought to have done; and we have done those things which we ought not to have done; and there is no health in us,"—so runs the English formula, and this abject Pomeranian made it all up in his own language. Lanny would shove him along and catch him when he stumbled, and keep saying: "*Vorwärts, marsch, machen Sie sich auf die Socken!*— Keep moving and don't sit down or you will fall asleep again and they will find you drunk."

"*Ja, ja, mein Herr! Danke schön, mein Herr!*"—and so on. Lanny knew there were still a couple of hours before dawn in the middle of November, and if the man could be sufficiently frightened and would keep on his feet, he would get over his spree and get to his bed without attracting attention. Lanny walked him all the way around the château, and then dared not stay with him any longer. He gave a final set of injunctions and obtained a final set of promises, and then went up to the loggia, scraped his feet thoroughly, and went in by the library window. Inside, he closed the window carefully, and fastened all the bolts; he took one glimpse around to make sure that the coast was clear, and then went quietly to the stairway. Still there was nobody about, so far as he could see. He went softly up the stairs and walked down the corridor to his room. He hadn't failed to note which was his own door; he turned the knob and slipped silently in; he closed the door and locked it, and then went to the bed and dropped upon it and began to weep softly to himself—partly for Trudi, and partly in reaction from the frightful strain under which he had been laboring, not for three hours, not for three days, but for the three longest months of his life.

XII

Lanny did not sleep at all. He lay on the bed and rehearsed his night's or rather his morning's work, and tried to see if there was any flaw in the perfect crime. He searched his overcoat for smears of blood which might be difficult to explain; he found several on the sleeves, but they were small, and he rubbed them with a damp handkerchief. Fortunately tweeds do not show stains conspicuously. He washed his hands thoroughly, not forgetting his fingernails; he scraped and polished the soles of his shoes, and saw to it that the scrapings went down the drain. He hung his hat over his reading lamp, with the light turned on to dry it quickly. He shaved and put on a clean shirt, and when he went down to breakfast he looked reasonably fit and self-possessed.

Did any of the Nazis have anything on their minds? If so, they were as good actors as Lanny. The morning papers from Paris were there, and everybody looked into them eagerly, and then talked about what he saw. Arrests were continuing, and *l'affaire Cagoulard* was occupying the attention of all France. *L'Action française*, which espoused the cause of these bold brave heroes, charged in flaring headlines that the exposure was the result of base betrayal, a jealousy vendetta by the partisans of the Croix de Feu. It was a feud between Léon Daudet and Duc Pozzo di Borgo on the one side and Colonel de la Rocque on the other, and the Nazis at breakfast agreed that it was conclusive proof of the impossibility of dealing with the French, so feminine and unstable, so poisoned through with the virus of individualism and democracy.

Lanny agreed with everything; and after he had had coffee and toast, and felt better, he borrowed one of the papers and sat in the library to read it. Incidentally he had a good look at the third window from the northwest corner and made certain that the carpet was not too dirty and that the long velvet curtains hung properly. When his reading was finished he sought out Eduard vom Rath in the office, and said: "Herr vom Rath, I have been reading the news and thinking things over, and I have made up my mind that this is one of those tempests in a teapot, of which I have seen so many in this unstable nation. I no longer feel that I am in serious danger, so long as I go about my art business and keep away from those who are having trouble with the police."

"*Ich verstehe, Herr Budd.* It has been a real pleasure to have you with us."

"I know that Seine Hochgeboren is disturbed at having me here, and his reasons are obvious and proper. Will you be so kind as to present him my compliments and let him know of my decision?"

"*Selbstverständlich, Herr Budd.*"

"I know that courtesy requires me to thank him personally for his hospitality, but under the peculiar circumstances it would not be wise for me to call on him, or even to telephone or write him."

"*Ja, ja, das wird er einsehen.*"

"If he calls up, you can tell him that the guest has departed, without using my name; and when you see him, convey to him my deep and sincere gratitude for his courtesy."

"With pleasure, Herr Budd."

"Do not mention to anyone that I have been here, and be sure that I shall be no less careful."

"Your discretion is appreciated, Herr Budd, and we all enjoyed your company."

"Be so kind as to say my *Lebewohl* to the rest of your staff, since I do not wish to interrupt them at their work. *Heil Hitler!*"

"*Heil Hitler.*"

XIII

Speed the parting guest! Lanny went up to his room and put his few belongings into the bag. His car was brought under the porte-cochere, scene of never-to-be-forgotten experiences. He drove away, never to return, or so he hoped; at least, not until this château had again become French, and he might undertake the marketing of some reasonably good paintings.

The conspirator had made so real to himself the possibility of being involved with the Cagoulards that he took the precaution of phoning Hofman at his hotel, to ask if everything was all right. The locksmith met him on the street, and after making sure they were not being trailed, they took a taxi to Monck's hotel. There, what a bull session they had! Three veterans of a war—and all the world knows how old soldiers like to fight their battles over again. They wanted every detail of Lanny's story: how he had managed to force himself upon Graf Herzenberg, and the various persons he had met in the château, and how the dogs had behaved, and the nightwatchman. All these matters had been the subject of anxious speculation, and now to hear the true story was like being taken behind the scenes of history.

They had failed in their purpose, but they had done their best, and Lanny hastened to assure them that he realized this. The task he had undertaken had lain beyond his power; both Hofman and Monck had been convinced of that from the beginning, and had told him so. They saw no hope for the woman artist, and as sensible men they could not pretend otherwise. A locksmith could break into a French château, but not into the citadel of Nazism; as for Monck, alias Capitán Herzog, alias Hauptmann Branting, he said that he had a company of hard-fighting men waiting for him up in the red hills of Aragon, and that was the place where Trudi Schultz could be saved if anywhere.

The trio enjoyed a sleep, and then a bath and a meal. In the evening Lanny had a talk with each of them separately. Monck insisted that he had failed, and that the sum paid to him should be reduced accordingly; but Lanny said that the Capitán had done everything he had agreed to do, and the failure was not his but Lanny's. Monck had got into touch with his wife through the underground, and she and the children were expected in Paris in a couple of days; they settled on the arrangement that Lanny was to get a hundred thousand francs from his bank, about four thousand dollars, and during the next few days Monck would occupy himself in changing these for notes with different serial numbers. With one half he would purchase American Express Company checks for the use of his family, and the other half he would turn over to the underground for the continuing of Trudi's work.

Professor Adler, he reported, had somehow got wind of Trudi's kidnaping and had fled from Paris, but now he had returned. He had raised a gray beard, and was no longer a clarinetist, a conspicuous occupation; he was living in a different workingclass district and planned to support himself by doing translating. Only three persons were to know about him, Lanny, Monck, and that injured man about whom Monck had told Lanny in Spain. Lanny was to write Adler a code letter and they were to meet on the street, as in the old days. This was like having Trudi back again—the most important part, so Trudi would have told him, and so the Trudi-ghost would continue to assert. At least it would give him a reason for selling more pictures and making more money.

XIV

Hofman had not been told that Trudi Schultz was Lanny's wife, and so it was necessary for Lanny to conceal his grief when the locksmith was present. The locksmith had become convinced that Trudi was dead, and he said so flatly. As for Monck, he considered it the part of kindness to convince Lanny of the fact, in order that he might not go on wasting his efforts. When they were alone together, he said this, and Lanny thanked him, saying: "You may be right, and I fear you are; but surely I have to make certain before my mind can feel at peace!"

"How do you expect to make certain?"

"I have an idea that I am going to get Hitler to tell me." Then, seeing his friend's surprise, he added: "Don't think I'm crazy. So far it's just an idea, but it might work out. Hitler is a believer in occult phenomena, I've been told; and if I can get him interested in spirit communications, he might take the trouble to verify them."

"*Por dios!*" exclaimed the Capitán. "If you pull off that one, will you promise to let me know about it?"

"We'll have a dinner somewhere, and I'll tell you the story. But meantime, don't forget, all this is as close a secret as anything on this earth."

Later on Lanny had a private talk with Hofman, who still insisted that he didn't want any payment for his part of this job; he had had a delightful trip to Paris, had seen the sights and heard the news, living *en prince* in the meantime; what more could a man want?—especially when he had failed in the job.

Lanny replied: "You opened every lock."

"I got a free education," countered the Meister-Schlosser—"in two different subjects, psychic research and the insides of Nazism. Both are worth while to me, and I wouldn't take a lot of money for them."

"Do this," suggested the host. "Follow your hobby for a few days here in Paris. I have to wait for my father, and meanwhile you may find some old locks that you would like to add to your collection; if so, let me buy them for you and feel better in my conscience. I might need you again some day, you know."

XV

Lanny had to go and see his Red uncle and wind up matters there. The nephew was teaching himself discretion, and didn't tell Jesse the story of what had happened at the Château de Belcour; he just said: "That enterprise failed to come off, so you can pay Jean and tell him to forget it and move out of the mill." He didn't ask for an accounting and Jesse didn't offer one.

They talked about the Cagoulard exposé, as everybody in Paris was doing at the moment. Lanny was afraid the delay had spoiled his uncle's story, but Jesse declared: "If I had sprung the news in the Chambre everybody would have said it was a *canard;* but when the government springs it, some of those scoundrels get at least a few days of jail—damn their dirty souls!"

The *député de la république française* went on to reveal an amusing aspect of the affair. A very discreet representative of the Croix de Feu had come to him and explained how they were planning to expose their traducers; they had heard rumors that M. Block-léss had been collecting information along these lines and they wanted it to add to their own and turn it all over to the government. At first Jesse had been unwilling to trust the man, but the latter had managed to convince the deputy of his good faith; he wanted the data so badly that he offered to pay, and Jesse actually sold a copy of his notes for ten thousand francs, a most unexpected contribution to a Communist campaign fund. "Every little helps," he said; and Lanny replied with an even more pointed adage: "Extremes meet!"

Hofman knew where to look for locks, and he found a collection of ancient Egyptian contrivances which a dealer was holding in the certainty of some day interesting a rich American. Hofman told Lanny, and that rich American was interested. It appeared that the pyramid makers had designed such a good lock that no one had ever been able to think of a better idea. The only difference was that modern lockmakers had steel and precision instruments, whereas the Egyptians had had only wood. Hofman explained:

"They fastened their doors with a long hollow bolt and staple made of teak, the hardest wood they could find. Into the upper part of the staple, or housing, they fitted several loose pins that dropped into matching holes in the bolt and held it in place. The key was a flat stick of wood, generally thirteen or fourteen inches long for a street door, with pegs on the end to correspond to the pins in the bolt. To unlock the door, the Egyptians stuck the key through a round hole in the wall, lifted the pins until they cleared the bolt, then drew back the bolt by pulling the key which held it by pegs sticking in the pin holes. Egyptian locksmiths carried their finished keys about on their shoulders like a bunch of fagots."

"What does this dealer want for his collection?" asked Lanny.

"He wants sixty thousand francs, but that's much more than I would let you spend."

"I would pay it cheerfully," said the son of Budd-Erling, in whose pockets money always burned a hole. "But you can be sure your dealer doesn't expect to get his asking price—not even from an American. Offer him thirty thousand."

"I offered thirty-five and he laughed at me."

"Did you give him your name and address?"

"I did; and I told him I was leaving for New York in a couple of days."

"Bide your time. He hopes to get fifty thousand, and will take forty; but don't say more than thirty-five until you report to me. Remember, I've been buying and selling art works in this city for some fifteen years."

Hofman took the advice, and bought the collection for thirty-eight thousand francs of Lanny's money. He brought the locks home and spread them out on the bed and explained them to his friend. They had been used, no doubt, to secure the granaries or other treasure houses of some wealthy Egyptian, perhaps a pharaoh, nearly three thousand years ago. They had been carefully cleaned, and still worked, and the Meister-Schlosser was as delighted with them as a child with a big doll which shuts its eyes when you lay it down. When these two parted, it was indeed "*Au revoir*" and not "Good-by." Hofman said: "If ever you have anything as novel and entertaining as your last assignment, don't fail to let me know." He grinned, and added: "When I was a boy we used to say things like that, and finish with: 'I don't think!' "

BOOK FOUR

In the Midst of Wolves

14

The Jingling of the Guinea

I

ROBBIE BUDD arrived in Paris. He had got news of the arrest of the de Bruynes on board the steamer, and on the boat-train had got the newspapers and brought himself up to date. The French police had arrested a hundred or more conspirators, and at least a score of them were persons of wealth. Robbie's sympathy was with such persons, anywhere in the world and regardless of what they had done, provided that it was for the benefit and protection of their class. The government of France had Socialists in the cabinet, and that was enough to prove it incompetent and dangerous. Men who had tried to get rid of it might have been indiscreet, but you couldn't really blame them.

Robbie was in an especially embittered mood just now, because the near-Socialist government of his own country had broken his proud will. He had announced that he would go out of business before he would have anything to do with labor union organizers, but when it came to a showdown, he had felt himself obliged to consider the interests of his stockholders. There had been sitdown strikes all over the country, and the New Dealers were trying their best to prevent any more of them. Robbie had been plainly told that he wouldn't be allowed to have one; there was that most outrageous "Wagner Act," having to do with labor relations, and there were dark hints that delays in the placing of government orders might be experienced by employers who refused to meet union representatives and work out agreements.

Robbie was having a hard time, and he simply couldn't have gone on without government orders. It was humiliating, outrageous, an insult to his dignity as a man and his right as a citizen; but he had been forced to bow to the will of these new tsars, the bureaucrats, and their allies and political supporters, the walking delegates, the labor union racketeers. It was a political conspiracy; these fellows had put up half a million dollars to elect Roosevelt, and now they came to collect their price. It meant the death and burial of what Robbie had learned to call the "free enterprise system." It didn't occur to him to mention what amounts he and his associates had put up in the effort to defeat Roosevelt, or the use they had made of the government in the good old days when nobody had disputed their control.

Lanny had had many a wrangle with his father over such questions, and was resolved never to have another. He listened to the story of how Robbie, unwilling to meet the usurpers himself, had delegated the unsavory job to one of his vice-presidents and a couple of superintendents; how then, greatly to Robbie's discomfiture, the usurpers had succeeded in persuading this trio that their men earnestly desired to increase and improve the Budd-Erling product, provided they could have some reasonable say about the conditions of their labor and a fair share in the profits thus earned. Poor Robbie had found himself backed up against the wall. "Big Steel" had surrendered to this hold-up, and so had General Motors. What could a poor "little fellow" do?

And so, Budd-Erling had become a union shop; the racketeers had the right to tell Robbie whom he could employ—or rather they had the right to say that the new employee couldn't go to work until he had got a union card, and had agreed to let the company deduct a percentage of his pay and turn it over to the union. The "check-off system," it was called, and the money would be used to extend the power of the union to other plants—or perhaps to enable the gangsters to have free trips to Florida, who could say? The hypocritical Lanny remarked that the world was changing, and nobody seemed to know how to stop it.

I I

Denis de Bruyne and his sons had tried to make some changes in their French world, and apparently had got themselves into serious trouble. Robbie wanted to hear all that Lanny knew about it; he was deeply distressed, and perhaps it was his duty to go and visit the prisoners; would Lanny come along? The son replied that he had thought the matter over and decided against going. This was a factional quarrel of the French, the most bitter that could be imagined, and they wouldn't want foreigners mixing in it; Lanny's business as an art expert would be knocked into a cocked hat if he were suspected of doing so.

What was really troubling Lanny was the possibility that the de Bruynes might say something to his father, indicating how deeply

Lanny had committed himself to them. Robbie wouldn't understand that, and Lanny couldn't very well explain it. "If I were you," he said, "I'd think twice before calling at the prison; it surely wouldn't do you any good with the government. You must realize that the Cagoulards had a hanging list, and many members of the government know that their names were on it. Their fury is easy to understand."

"What do you think they'll do to the prisoners?"

"Keep them in jail a few weeks to frighten them; but I doubt very much if they'll ever be brought to trial. There are too many important figures involved, people who will be moving heaven and earth to suppress the story."

"After all, I don't suppose there's anything I can do for Denis or the boys."

"Not a thing in the world. What is done will have to be done by Frenchmen."

So the cautious businessman remarked: "Perhaps it might be the part of wisdom for me to wait until I have seen Schneider, and found out what he wants."

"I should advise that strongly. The de Bruynes know the situation, and their feelings won't be hurt. They understand that we can't help them, and they don't need anybody to cry over them."

"Frankly, Lanny, I'm having a hard time. The recession is getting worse every day. I've taken a huge gamble in the belief that aviation is going to increase. It would be a great load off my mind if I could get a real order from the French right now."

"Well then, you had better keep away from the Cagoule. Many of the army officers sympathize with it, but dare not show their feelings at present, and Pierre Cot, the air minister, is a leftist, and one of those who are fighting in the Cabinet for the full exposure of the conspiracy. You are up against much the same sort of thing as at home: *le New Deal*, the French call it."

III

Robbie had telegraphed Baron Schneider from the steamer, notifying him of his impending arrival; and now at the hotel was an engraved card requesting the honor of the company of M. Robert Budd at the town house of the Baron that same evening. Lanny had received a similar invitation at his hotel. Beauty's heart would have been broken if she had been left out of such an affair, so Lanny telephoned the Baron's secretary, saying that his mother was in town and asking if it would be agreeable for him to bring her. The result was another card arriving by messenger within the hour.

Robbie got out his "tails" and had them pressed, and with one of his waggish grins asked his son: "Shall we wear hoods?" Lanny replied that the Baron would slip money to secret conspirators, but would not invite any of them to his home in this crisis. There one would meet the most fashionable crowd, plus the politicians of the center and right, and any sort of famous persons who might enjoy the favor of one of the most powerful men in France. The same sort of evening affair that Robbie had seen in the days when Lanny had been "Mr. Irma Barnes," and they had leased the palace of the Duc de Belleaumont, so that Irma might learn the duties of a *salonnière* under the guidance of Emily Chattersworth.

They engaged a uniformed chauffeur from Denis's taxicab company to drive Lanny's car and deliver them in proper state before the doors of the mansion. There between nine and ten o'clock was *tout Paris* arriving, with the traditional red carpet under its feet and striped canvas canopy overhead. Black-clad gentlemen with the correct white ties, and others in uniform with chests covered by decorations; the ladies in the much greater splendor permitted to them: gorgeous furs from every part of the earth and jewels from its depths; evening gowns of every hue, and snow-white or pink bosoms and arms and backs; coiffures so elaborate that the ladies exhausted themselves sitting up to have them prepared and then dared not lie down for a moment's rest. A splendid scene, as Lanny had foretold, comparing it to a dead fish such as he and his father could see on the beach at Juan on a dark night, shining with gold, silver, green, purple, shimmering and pulsating, fascinating to the eye—so long as you kept to windward of it.

The Baron received them cordially and said that he had been looking forward to the meeting with Robbie; would he and his son come to lunch on the morrow? "I don't suppose I have to introduce you to anybody," added the host, "since you know so many in my country. Consider yourselves at home,"—the utmost a Frenchman could say to foreigners.

Robbie Budd, who had been doing business as a munitions salesman in Europe since the beginning of the century, had met most of these military gentlemen and knew what their insignia and decorations meant. He had been a steel man, so he could talk shop with François de Wendel; he had been an oil man, so he could exchange greetings with Sir Henri Deterding, and chat with him about what had happened since their meeting at The Hague. He had attended several of the great international conferences in the interest of Budd Gunmakers, then of New England-Arabian Oil, and more recently of Budd-Erling; so he could chat with the diplomats and politicians, also with the great ladies, the duchesses and marchionesses and countesses who favored them. Beauty knew them, too, and had paid many a one to bring to luncheon or dinner some general or cabinet minister or great capitalist whom it was important for a salesman or promoter to meet privately.

IV

The great world of Paris was fluid, almost as much as that of New York. Persons of prominence lost their influence and new ones took their places. Writers and other intellectuals, musicians and other artists lost their vogue, and one met them in the cafés but no longer at fashionable soirées. Speculators lost their money and disappeared; others made sensational gains, and they and their chosen ladies made their appearance, having been properly coached and equipped by couturiers and modistes, and by ladies of fashion who had fallen into need and lived by giving help to the newly arrived. All this was especially true of politicians; they began, as a rule, by making violent speeches of a leftist character, and when they had got the votes, they accepted "campaign funds" from the big businessmen; each one acquired a rich *amie*, and after he had been taught how to handle a knife and fork, he made his entrée in the salons, where people were curious to meet him because his name had been in the newspapers.

Of late it had become the fashion for successful statesmen to go to the Comédie Française for their favorites. This state-owned institution had been since its founding two and a half centuries ago a lure which drew the most beautiful and charming ingénues from all over France. On the stage they enacted roles of luxurious passion, and off-stage they enacted the same roles with even greater ardor—this being even more essential to their careers. Their eyes were turned in the direction of the prominent politicians, and especially the Cabinet ministers, who had the appointing of director and assistants, and whose word could determine the assignment of roles, of publicity in the press, and all the other desirabilities of *la vie parisienne*. Intrigues went on incessantly, shifts took place, and a great part of French public life was occupied with speculation concerning who was who and with whom.

Lanny was behind the times with that sort of news; but when Beauty came to Paris she hurried off to lunch with one of her smart friends and to tea with another; she would come back loaded up with information

—and don't call it "idle gossip," for a deal in airplanes might depend upon the good disposition of one of these young creatures, and the first job of a businessman might be to go to the theater and see her in the embraces of some lover, and note the fine points of her technique. Nowhere in the world was acting more conscientiously rehearsed or traditions of the stage more religiously preserved, and if you understood these matters you were a person of culture, and knew how to flatter a popular actress and cause her to speak well of you to her patron. You might be ever so staid a family man from the land of the pilgrims' pride, but you had sowed your one wild oat when you were young, and here was your shrewd and well-trained ex-mistress, knowing the great world of Paris and London and Berlin, and ready to take your arm and be escorted about a drawing-room, whispering information into your ear, and introducing you to exactly the right ones. It wouldn't hurt you in the least to have this *grand monde* know that the mother of your son was still your friend; this *monde* would believe what in Newcastle, Connecticut, would be called "the worst," but here it would be considered a touching instance of fidelity, which ladies of maturing years, trying to hold onto their lovers, would observe with envious sorrow.

Beauty would say: "That is Yvonne Roux; she is seen everywhere with Herriot. The one next to her, in cerise crêpe-de-chine, is Hélène Manet —she is always invited with Tardieu." Later, on the ballroom floor: "You know Georges Mandel, I believe; that is Angelique Beaulieu he is dancing with—she also is a *pensionnaire* of the Comédie." After they had taken a turn or two: "There is Mlle. Poussin with Yvon Delbos, the new Foreign Minister." Robbie would observe a youngish man, tall and thin, pale and timid-looking. "He was a professor before he became a politician," the well-informed Beauty would add. "He is believed to be very conscientious, and intends to marry her. Right now she is playing in one of the Molière comedies."

There were wives present, also, and now and then Beauty could point out one in the same room with the *amie*. The contrast would be pathetic, not to say tragic, for the wives were what the politicians had been able to get when they were young and poor and had not the same range of choice. Now the wives had grown old along with their partners, and some of them were stout and some were gawky, and no art of dressmaker or cosmetician could conceal their defects. What heartaches they must suffer to see their life partners publicly disporting themselves with young hussies, and leaving the wives to such tenth-rate chances as they could find! There is an old song which tells about after the ball is over, after the dancers gone; many a heart is weary, many a heart is sad—and it might also have been recorded that many a husband is getting the very dickens from his wife.

V

In the library Lanny came upon a group of gentlemen and two or three ladies who preferred serious conversation. The center of the group was a shortish heavy-set man with dark overhanging eyebrows, dark straight hair beginning to thin, a long nose and a wide drooping mouth which gave him a somber, not to say melancholy appearance. Lanny knew him, because he had been a professor of philosophy in Nice, and one of the ornaments of Emily's Riviera salon. In that drawing-room a tactful hostess had guided the conversation, calling upon this person and that and making sure that each had a chance to display his intellectual wares. But here was no such circumstance; here two or three persons had asked the writer, Jules Romains, what he thought about the situation of the country, and others had joined the group and stayed so long as they were interested. There was nothing unusual about this; Lanny had seen the same thing at one of Emily's lawn parties at Les Forêts, where a troop of lovely ladies had listened spellbound while Anatole France poured out a flood of ironic wit; again in London, where Bernard Shaw had kept a roomful of people entertained for a full hour without one of them interrupting; again at the Genoa conference, where Frank Harris had produced a monologue about Shakespeare, like a stream of molten gold with rubies and emeralds and diamonds shining in it.

Here it was different, for this was a deadly serious man, delivering a message to a nation in serious trouble. M. Romains, now in his early fifties, was a voluminous writer, and among his output were volumes of plays and poems which were called "Rabelaisian," a French way of permitting what in English would be called "off color." But now he was at work upon a series of novels portraying the manners of his time; and in between these labors he was carrying on a crusade of a dignified and exclusive character to save his country, according to the best lights of one of her eminent philosophers and littérateurs. Here he was telling the story of his efforts to a dignified and exclusive audience; the sort of people who knew the inside workings of the machinery of statecraft, and set the switches and pulled the levers which determined the destiny of France.

M. Romains had taken many journeys in his country's interest and at his own expense. He had talked with the statesmen of fourteen European lands. Three years ago he had traveled to Berlin and delivered a lecture under government auspices. Brownshirted leaders had been summoned from all over the land to hear him, and one of the top-flight Nazis had said to him: "You know, no private individual has ever been received like this in Berlin." The philosopher-novelist had also been welcomed by the King of the Belgians, who had discussed frankly that country's attitude to the gravely threatened war. As M. Romains told about these matters, you couldn't doubt that he was patriotically in earnest, but also you couldn't help feeling that he was intensely impressed by his own importance.

His plan was the one known as *le couple France-Allemagne,* and it meant reconciliation with Germany, by the simple method of giving the Nazis whatever they demanded. For example, he had had the idea that the Allies should have got out of the Saar without the formality of a plebiscite. Lanny happened to know that Briand had been trying to work out some compromise on this question as far back as ten years ago; but apparently M. Romains didn't know that, and certainly it wasn't up to Lanny to correct him on his facts. The philosopher-novelist seemed to have the idea that the Saar settlement had been a matter between France and Germany, and that the plebiscite had taken place under French military control, whereas the fact was it had been a League matter, and French troops had been withdrawn nine years before the plebiscite was held.

Among the members of that attentive audience was Kurt Meissner, who had met the Frenchman many years ago in Emily's drawing-room. Evidently he had put his opportunity to good use, for it was just as if M. Romains had sat in a seminar conducted by the Wehrmacht's agent, had absorbed the entire doctrine, and was now giving an oral dissertation to demonstrate what he had learned and get his degree. His discourse embraced the complete Nazi program for the undermining of the French republic: warm protestations of friendship; unlimited promises of peace; the sowing of distrust of all politicians and of the entire democratic procedure; and, above all else, fear of the Red specter. The Reds kept faith with nobody, their country was a colossus with feet of clay, their army a broken reed upon which France persisted in trying to lean. The republic had to choose between Stalin and Hitler; between an illusory military alliance and a secure and enduring peace.

The words burned Lanny's tongue: "M. Romains, have you ever read *Mein Kampf?*" Of course, Lanny couldn't say them; but he wondered, how would this somewhat self-conscious idol of the bourgeois world have replied? Lanny recalled the Max Beerbohm cartoon in which a drawing-room fop is asked if he has read a certain book, and replies: "I do not read books; I write them."

V I

The next day Lanny drove his father to that same mansion, and they had a lunch in which a whole pheasant was put before each of them. Afterwards came a quiet chat in which two men of large affairs had a chance to develop their acquaintance. The munitions king of Europe spoke with frankness; he was gravely concerned about the state of his country, and the developments in military aviation which seemed about to put all other kinds of military equipment on the shelf. He didn't speak to Robbie as a big man to a little man, but rather as one who might become little to another who was certain to become big. This was immensely flattering to the visitor, but Robbie wasn't the one to swell up and burst; he knew what he had, and had worked many years ,to get it; also, he understood how business is conducted, and that when a big man invites you to his palace and offers you his finest old vintage wines, he wants something and wants it badly.

Robbie Budd was an associate of General Göring, and had been taken into the inside of the new German Air Force, and no injunction of secrecy had been laid upon him. Quite the contrary, it was Göring's policy to frighten his opponents and get what he wanted without having to fight; therefore, technically equipped visitors were encouraged to come and look and then go out and talk. This was Robbie's game, too, and had been ever since he had listened to his father's instructions as a boy; the way to sell munitions was to go from one country to the next, and tell each how far ahead the others were. So Robbie laid the paint on thick, and Charles Prosper Eugène Schneider looked at the picture and shivered deep within his soul. Yes, even though he knew the game as well as the son of Budd Gunmakers, having been taught it by *his* father and grandfather—and he was older than Robbie.

France's deadly rival had outdistanced her, and was leaving her hopelessly behind. Germany had become that which every gunmaker in the world had dreamed all his life, a country putting everything it had into armaments; reducing the wages and lengthening the hours of all its workers and bidding its munitions men to build all the plants they could, in the certainty that they would receive all the orders they could fill, and keep their machines going at full speed twenty-four hours every day, Sundays and holidays included. Most favored of all was the

Air Force commander who, while he looked like a comic stage character and dressed like one, was at the same time one of the most competent executives in the modern world, driving his subordinates with a whiplash and getting the orders of his Führer carried out with utter loyalty and no scruples.

That was a nightmare, a nightmare, exclaimed Baron Schneider; it kept him awake night after night, seeing the calamity that hung over France. His miserable, incompetent government, hopelessly corrupt—who knew that better than the Baron, who had been buying it for half a century? But of course he didn't say that to his visitors. What he said was denunciation of the wretched system of prototypes to which the French air ministry was committed; the economical illusion, the pinchpenny insanity of having models of the very best planes, and the means of making them quickly, and imagining that that was national security!

"You can't fight battles with mating-jigs," said Robbie, dryly.

"Of course not! And now these politicians have taken over my plants, having no idea how to pay for them and at the same time asking me how to run them! We have all this confusion and miserable wrangling—and right in the midst of the gravest peril our country has faced since Sedan."

VII

What was it this badly worried monarch of munitions desired? Well, first of all he wanted Robbie to tell him the truth about the performance of the Budd-Erling P11, about which he had heard fabulous reports. When Robbie told him, he shook his head sorrowfully, saying that the best of the French prototypes, the *Morane*, couldn't equal that. Then he wanted to make sure if Göring had these secrets, and what use he was making of them; Robbie could answer the first part of this question, but said he could only guess about the second; *der dicke Hermann* was wide awake and not missing any tricks. Robbie said he had given first chance to his own country, and then to the French and the British; he named the men he had approached and who had turned him down. "That left me no recourse but the Germans, if I wanted to keep in business."

"Of course, of course," said the Baron. "It is too bad you did not come to me. I had some power in my own country at that time. Now I am not allowed to do anything, or to own anything except bonds. I am supposed to be laid away upon a shelf. But being a man of action, I am not happy there, especially when I learn what Thyssen and Krupp von Bohlen and the rest of them are doing."

The munitions king of Europe went on to explain that he could not persuade the French air ministry to buy enough planes of French manufacture, and it was even less possible to persuade them to buy foreign planes, for then to the reluctance of a semi-pacifist government to spend money would be added the opposition of great French private interests. It had been the idea of the Baron to buy personally a hundred or two of the very newest Budd-Erlings, and train men to fly them privately; then in case of an emergency he could present them to the army. But now had come this wretched exposé of the Cagoule, which the Baron took as an infringement of his personal privacy, just about as Robbie took the C.I.O. invasion. There was no helping it, of course; a sensational press was playing up every item it could unearth, and would rush to proclaim that the master of Le Creusot was setting up a private air force and training it, for the purpose of threatening Paris and forcing the government to obey his will.

"I have to think of myself as an outcast from my own country," declared the great man, sadly. "I have to go abroad in order to save France from itself." He explained that he still owned Skoda, which was in the town of Pilsen, and the Czechs still granted him the right to make goods and to buy and sell as he pleased. Would Robbie be willing to manufacture a hundred fighter planes for immediate delivery in Czechoslovakia, and would he go in on some sort of arrangement to send his experts to that country and assist in establishing a factory for the manufacture of Budd-Erlings?

Robbie of course was delighted to get a large order, and said that because of his sympathy with the Baron's cause he would give it priority over everything else. He would be proud to be associated with so distinguished a concern as Skoda in the fabricating of planes, and would make the Budd-Erling patents available. But the Baron must understand that certain features of the Budd-Erling were protected by General Göring's patents, which were not under Robbie's control.

The Baron sighed and said it was too bad that the Germans had got ahead on everything; it looked as if the French would have to make friends with them, willynilly. "I have been talking on the subject with this well-informed son of yours. It is a question whether their Führer is a man whom we can trust. What do you think, M. Budd?"

"My son has had the advantage of knowing Herr Hitler personally," replied Robbie, cautiously. "I have not."

"*Eh, bien, M. Lanny?*"

Said Lanny: "Anyone would be assuming a grave responsibility who gave advice on that subject, M. le Baron. All that I can say is that you have to make up your mind to be either an ally or an enemy. It is not possible to be half-way between."

"It is extraordinary what discretion this young man possesses, M. Budd, and what an insight into our French situation."

Robbie was surprised, for he had never given his son credit for such valuable possessions. He remarked, deprecatingly: "Lanny has lived all over Europe, and has had unusual opportunities to hear opinions."

"One can hear all sorts of opinions in my drawing-room, M. Budd; the problem is to sort them out and select those which are sound. I should be glad if your son would come to see me now and then and tell me what he has learned; and this applies to you also, for I perceive that you are a man who has foreseen how the world is moving and has placed himself in a strategic position."

That was high-class flattery, and not to be rejected. Robbie perceived that Baron Schneider, ten years older than himself, was looking for someone to carry burdens for him. He had intimated in a delicate way that he would expect to pay generously. Robbie said he would think over the proposals and be ready with definite offers in a couple of days; the Baron replied that he had no doubt they would be fair, and he would have his technical men work over the details and his lawyers assist in drawing up the papers. He sent his visitors away happy; Robbie remarking to his son: "This may prove the biggest thing that has ever come my way."

VIII

Beauty Budd was still in Paris, and she wouldn't have been herself if she hadn't been thinking her own thoughts and scheming her schemes. The incomparable Lanny was involved with some woman, and was keeping her hidden, even from his adoring mother who had never failed to excuse everything he did. Manifestly, the reason could only be political; this woman, a German, was doing some of that dangerous underground work which had so frightened Irma and had caused the break-up of Lanny's marriage. At present Lanny was heavyhearted and preoccupied, and what could it mean except that the woman was in trouble, and perhaps Lanny also? Could it be that she had gone back into Germany? Most probably so, for Lanny stayed in his apartment a lot, read endless newspapers, and played the piano in a restless and distracted way. Beauty knew him so well that she could tell his moods by what he played and how he played it. She was right in the same hotel, watching him like a hawk; she knew that he had been away only one night, and that certainly would not have been the case if the woman he loved had been available. He was much more assiduous than that, and accustomed to having what he wanted.

Perhaps right now was a chance for Beauty to have what she wanted. Sophie Timmons, Baroness de la Tourette, had come up from the Riviera for a lark, and now Beauty phoned to Emily Chattersworth, who came to town, and those three old stagers put their heads together. They had done so on previous occasions, trying to decide the destinies of this eligible but provoking man. Here he was thirty-eight—the dark secret was shared among the three who had known him from baby-hood—and still drifting around at loose ends, a prey to any designing female who came along, instead of having a wife and settling down to raise a family in some place where these three conspirators could have the fun of watching. It was they who had made the Irma Barnes match—so promising, they still couldn't understand how it had failed.

The new wife had to be an American, they decided. There was a large American colony in Paris, and many visitors, and after due can-vassing they pitched upon a damsel named Mary Ann Everly, a nice old-fashioned name for a debutante, just out of Bryn Mawr and doing her grand tour with her mother. She had soft brown eyes and a gentle manner, a quiet young thing; they all knew that Lanny disliked the noisy ones who would chatter while he wanted to read the speeches in the previous day's Chambre. No less important, the family had scads of money; old Philadelphia people, the father a banker, Episcopalian and everything proper. The girl was modern—they all learn the facts of life nowadays, and talk about whatever comes into their heads.

The way it was arranged, Emily was to invite the mother and daugh-ter to lunch, and Beauty and Sophie were to keep out of the way, since it would look too pointed if the whole crew were there to gang up on Lanny. Not that they could fool him anyhow, but they must do their best. Emily would keep the mother busy, and Lanny and the girl would go for a stroll in a great beech forest, haunted by the ghosts of thou-sands of German soldiers—but the girl wouldn't know that, and Lanny wouldn't mind, knowing how all France was haunted by the ghosts of soldiers of every nation and tribe. Or he could take her paddling in a canoe on a little artificial lake. The match with Irma had been made at Sept Chênes, Emily's place above Cannes; the locale now would be different but the strategy the same.

IX

Lanny had mailed a set of notes to Gus Gennerich, calling attention to the fact that his previous account of the Cagoulard conspiracy had been sustained in every detail; also predicting that there would be no prosecutions, and that the share of the army and air force in the conspiracy would be hushed up. Later he sent a memorandum confirming his statement that the Nazi embassy had a château near Paris where they held and tortured anti-Nazi Germans, and suggesting that it might be well for the F.B.I. to look into the rumors that such Germans in New York had been kidnaped and spirited on board the *Bremen* and other steamers.

Now he prepared a summary of the state of the French air force as compared with the German; adding that he had got this direct from Mr. Tailor and it could be accepted as authoritative. Going over all this in his mind, Lanny decided that it constituted a good week's work for a presidential agent. If all hundred and three of them turned in as much copy, F.D. would have his hands full indeed.

As usual Robbie had invited his son to accompany him to Germany, and this time the son accepted. Since he hoped to make use of Kurt on this trip, he stopped in at a music store and purchased a new four-hand piano arrangement of an orchestral work by Hindemith; then he phoned Kurt, asking if he should drop in and practice it with him. Kurt couldn't resist this temptation—despite the fact that the composer was a modernist; this poison had so infected Europe that not even a fountainhead of Nazi propaganda could entirely escape its effects. They sat side by side and pounded away for an hour or two, Lanny making some mistakes and Kurt correcting them; that was their old relationship, so they finished in a glow of satisfaction.

Lanny told of his plans, and said: "You know Robbie has an important deal with Hermann Göring."

"I have heard so," replied Kurt, whose business it was to know everything. "It's been useful to us, and still more so to Robbie, I imagine." A typical Nazi assumption, which Lanny accepted with due humility.

"Are you going home for Christmas?" he inquired, and when Kurt answered in the affirmative, Lanny added: "I expect to stay a while, because I've been neglecting Hermann's picture business and he may want me. We'll get Heinrich Jung, and have a regular old home week. Perhaps we can call on the Führer."

"I'll see if it can be arranged," said Kurt. "He's likely to have his hands full very soon. Schuschnigg has been making a lot of trouble and may have to be taught a lesson."

It was an indiscretion, of course. Kurt was human, in spite of being an exemplar of the master race, and he couldn't resist the temptation to show an adoring friend and pupil how much he knew about his great leader's purposes. Lanny would get off another rush note to Gus, saying that there was reason to expect an invasion of Austria in the new year.

X

Coming back from this visit, Lanny found a message to call Emily Chattersworth. He did so, and was invited to lunch at Les Forêts the following day; some friends she especially wanted him to meet. Lanny, suspicious as a much-hunted stag, guessed right away that the does were after him again; however, he couldn't say No to an elderly doe who had been a second mother to him, and was now growing feeble and didn't get about very much. All right, he would come; after all, yearling does are pleasant to look at, and it couldn't do any harm to browse for a while in company with a carefully selected one. Lanny went up to see his mother, and found her looking as innocent as any tame doe in a paddock. She asked how Kurt was, and was politely surprised by the news that Lanny had had a call from the châtelaine of Les Forêts.

Mary Ann of the Philadelphia Everlys proved to be about the nicest Everly ever. She was twenty but looked even younger; rather small, with the sweetest little round face, a tip-tilted nose, and wide brown eyes taking in every feature of this fascinating new old world. Of course she couldn't really be as innocent as she looked; one glance at her competent mother, and Lanny could be sure that Mary Ann had been told what she was here for, but perhaps with a warning that this was a dubious man, who had been divorced by a monstrously rich wife because of "incompatibility of temperament." But that wouldn't keep him from being an object of curiosity. Emily, old darling, wouldn't have failed to mention that he was an art expert of high repute, having some of the wealthiest collectors at home as his patrons.

Lanny knew that he was there to entertain these visiting ladies, and he pulled out his best bag of tricks. He talked about this very splendid home and the many interesting sights he had seen here: Anatole France discoursing on the lawn, and Isadora Duncan dancing in the drawing-room, with Lanny playing, scared stiff for fear she would notice how many notes he was missing. And the famous people who had frequented Emily's salons—a roster of the great names, not merely of France and England, but of far-off places such as India and China. Part of the time Lanny had been too young to understand all they were saying, but he remembered their faces, and what people had said about them, which was enough to constitute culture in the smart world.

He described Hansi Robin playing the violin here, and Lanny's half-sister Bess falling head over heels in love with him. He made a funny story of his proud New England stepmother, shocked by the idea of her daughter marrying a Jewish fiddler, and the surprise she had got when Hansi visited her home town, and everybody treated him as if he were the grandson of the Jewish Jehovah. Hansi and Bess were now in London, and next week Hansi was scheduled to play with one of the Paris symphonies; he was going to give his rendition of the Bruch concerto, which Lanny said was something not to be missed. Courtesy suggested that he should invite his hostess and her guests to hear it, and when the older ladies accepted, Mary Ann was so happy as to seem almost but not quite indiscreet.

She had come abroad to see the places and things she had been reading about since childhood, and was prepared to renew all the thrills she had ever experienced. Her eagerness was genuine and quite touching. After lunch Lanny took her for a stroll in the beech forest, and told her how a whole division of the German army had been trapped here; he described the scene of wreckage after the battle, and showed the stumps of trees which had been shot into splinters. He told about the elderly librarian, M. Priedieu, who had been so shocked at the sight of the boches dumping the Louis Quatorze furniture out of the windows that he had dropped dead.

When they came back to the drawing-room, Emily asked Lanny to play for them, and he obliged. Doubtless Chopin is well known in the Quaker city of brotherly love, but its topmost social set might have difficulty in fitting him into its code of etiquette and ethics. He was an impulsive and unhappy lover, and the invasive and dominating George Sand carried him off and broke his heart and then made a novel and autobiography out of it. He died miserably of tuberculosis, and the only joy he had was putting his melancholy and anguish into music, along with the glory of his proud race. He made for himself a style which in course of the years became synonymous with piano technique; the sweeping phrases fitting the instrument as a well-worn glove fits the hand.

Lanny played the F-sharp minor polonaise, which Liszt admired so extravagantly, and about which he imagined strange things. It is tempestuous music, full of martial clashes, and not easy to play; but if Lanny made slips, the ladies wouldn't know it. When he got through, there were tears in Mary Ann's eyes; she tried furtively to wipe them away, because a public display of emotion was so contrary to her mother's code.

XI

Beauty of course wanted to know everything that had happened; she always did, and complained because Lanny left out the most interesting details. She wanted to pretend that she didn't know whom he had met; he said: "Old goose! She's a very nice girl, and I invited them to the concert tomorrow. But I'm not going to marry anybody, and I've told you often enough. Some day I'll tell you the reason, but at present I'm not free to, so you'll just have to trust me and forget it."

He had a row of seats for the concert; he was taking Beauty and her husband, and Sophie and hers, and Zoltan, as well as the other three. Robbie didn't care for highbrow music, and anyhow he was to have a final conference with Baron Schneider before leaving for Berlin the following day. Lanny went to Hansi's hotel to meet the couple and swap news with them. They were among the few who knew that he was helping the underground, though he had never told them how. He told about Kurt and what he was doing, and about the de Bruynes, and what he had found out about the Cagoulard plot. On this account he mustn't be seen in public with either Hansi or Bess, but it would do no harm for him to attend the concert, or to come to this hotel after making reasonably sure he wasn't being followed. He had brought the Hindemith score, and he and Bess played it; Hansi listened but didn't care much for it. The ultraradical in politics was a conservative in music.

It seemed to Lanny that his brother-in-law had never been better than in his rendering of the melodious and charming Bruch concerto that evening. He always made a good appearance on the platform, tall, dignified, and wholly concerned with his art. His pale ascetic features and large dark eyes gave an appearance of melancholy appropriate to a Jew in these tragic times. He had had two rehearsals with the orchestra and his performance was impassioned yet without flaw. Concert audiences in Paris are fastidious, but when they get what they want they do not stint their applause. They called Hansi out half a dozen times, and he played as an encore one of his favorites, a movement

from a Bach solo sonata, very austere, and difficult to make effective
after the sonorities of a large orchestra. The audience gave him another
ovation, and his appearance was a triumph.

What would be the effect of all this glory of art upon a young lady
of susceptible age and romantic disposition? She sat next to Lanny, but
he had forgotten about her, being concerned with the technical side
of what his brother-in-law and friend was doing. So might a relative
of the daring young man on the flying trapeze have watched his gyra-
tions and held his breath at the perilous moments. But when it was
safely over, Lanny noticed that Mary Ann wasn't applauding, but sat
rigid with her hands clasped together tightly in her lap and the knuck-
les white. He knew that she was having an emotional experience, and
thought: "Maybe she's fallen in love with Hansi—and if so, that let's
me out!"

But no, it wasn't that way; Hansi was wonderful, but he was a god
that had come down out of the skies and would return there—along
with his wife. Lanny was the host who had selected this entertainment
and provided the tickets; and the three elderly Norns who had taken
charge of Mary Ann's fate had no idea of letting him retire to his soli-
tude again. When the concert was over, Mr. and Mrs. Parsifal Dingle
and the Baroness and her husband just disappeared without a word.
The majestic Emily, accustomed all her life to preside over social
arrangements, remarked to Lanny: "I'll take care of Zoltan and Mrs.
Everly; you drive Mary Ann." It might seem a wee bit pointed, but
the *salonnière* knew that Lanny was leaving for a long stay, and it was
now or never.

XII

Had Mary Ann been told what was going to be done? Probably not.
But the mother must have been told; she had looked this prospective
son-in-law over, and had doubtless made inquiry concerning Budd-
Erling Aircraft. So there was Lanny, driving on the brilliantly lighted
boulevards of Paris, with this small-sized package of quick-burning
powder on the seat beside him. Chopin and Max Bruch and a magnificent orchestra and *la ville lumière* and a thousand years of French history were all mixed up in her soul, along with a handsome man who
still looked young and who spoke with a soft voice and seemed to have
all the languages of Europe and all the culture of the ages on the tip
of his agile tongue.

He wasn't supposed to take her home right away, of course; he could propose a drive, perhaps in the Bois, and if they stopped a while in a sheltered spot, that would be according to the etiquette of this automobile age. But without any such preliminaries he said: "Mary Ann, may I talk to you frankly for a minute or two?"

"Certainly," she replied, and shivered inwardly.

"You are a lovely girl, and if I were free I should fall in love with you, I am sure. But, unfortunately, my heart is pledged."

"*Oh!*" she said, and all the life seemed to go suddenly out of her voice.

"My mother doesn't know it; or rather, she doesn't want to know it, and keeps fighting against it. It is a very sad story and I'm not free to tell it; but I owe it to you to be frank, so that you won't think I am indifferent to the lovely qualities that I see in you."

"Thank you," she said; "I appreciate it." She didn't say: "You are presuming a great deal as to my state of mind," or any artificial thing like that. She didn't mind his knowing that she liked him.

"I am taking a great liberty, I know; but I have lived most of my life on this old continent, and I really know what I am talking about—far more than I am able to tell. Take my advice, see all you can while you are here, and try to understand what you see, but then go home and don't come again. And above all, don't ever think of marrying any European man."

"You really think they are that bad?"

"There are noble exceptions, but your chances of finding one of these, or of recognizing him if you found him, would be slim. In general, European men do not feel about women as you would expect, nor about love or marriage. But that is not the main thing I have in mind; I mean what is coming to Europe and its people. Don't tie your fate to it, and don't give your heart to anyone whose fate is already tied to it, as mine is."

"You mean another war?"

"I mean a series of wars and revolutions that may not be over during your lifetime. You may live to see this great city laid in ashes, or bombed to dust and rubble. You may see the same thing happen to many other cities, and half their populations killed, if not by war, then by plague and famine."

"Oh, how horrible, Mr. Budd!"

"I'm not free to tell you what I know; you just have to take my word that I have special information that has caused me to say to my best friends: 'Get out of Europe and stay out.'"

"How soon do you think this will begin?"

"Within a couple of years at the outside. It may be next spring; it depends upon circumstances which are beyond anyone's control or guessing. When it comes it will be like a series of strokes of lightning, and I'm not sure that three thousand miles of ocean will be enough to protect anyone from them. But go back to Philadelphia, and marry some man of your own set that you have a chance really to know."

She might have made a saucy answer, but she was frightened, and shocked out of all pretending. She said: "Mr. Budd, you are being really kind and I am grateful." He knew that she would be bound to assume that he was in love with some married woman, and that suited him. But evidently it didn't suit her entirely, for she added: "If ever you find yourself near Philadelphia, let us be friends."

15

To Have a Giant's Strength

I

ROBBIE and his son went by plane, because Robbie was in a hurry and the season was not favorable for motoring; they could just as well rent a car in Berlin. They put up at the Adlon as usual, and since they had telegraphed for reservations, the reporters were soon on hand. The Nazis proclaimed themselves revolutionists, bringing in an entirely new order, but the fact was they slavishly followed the customs of the bourgeois world in all things that had to do with power and prestige. When an American airplane manufacturer came to consult Reichsminister General Göring, it was an acknowledgment of Germany's newly won importance. When his son, an art expert internationally known, came with him, that was an event of lesser importance but not to be overlooked. Each newspaper had in its *Archiv* the items already published about the Budd family, and dug them out and wove them into the new story. Always Lanny writhed, thinking of his old-time comrades, now underground, reading these items and despising him as one of the renegades, the band-wagon climbers, the worshipers of the bitch goddess Success.

Robbie had telegraphed the fat General, and soon after their arrival came Hauptmann Furtwaengler of his staff to invite them to lunch at the Air Ministry. It was an enormous granite building, the ugliest in the city, which was saying a lot; the newspapers said it had three thousand rooms, but you could never count entirely upon Nazi newspapers. *Der dicke Hermann* had a palatial suite here, and welcomed them in a military costume of cream and gold suggestive either of interior decoration or a musical comedy chorus. He made himself such agreeable company that Lanny, who liked nearly everybody, had to keep saying to himself: "This is the man who burned the Reichstag; who ordered the blood purge in Berlin; who is going to turn Europe into a slaughter pit." Hitler, of course, was the driving will, the prime mover, but his function was mostly making speeches and devising slogans, while this great lump of lard was the executive and the preparer of all future executions.

Lanny had been raised in the midst of killing instruments and his privileged life had been based upon their sale at a profit; but he personally had never killed anybody, and it had always required a psychological effort for him to understand a killer, to imagine what must be going on in his mind. This fat Hermann had been trained for killing since early youth, and probably through his childhood had been taught worship of the old German heroes who had made killing their sole business on earth and had then been carried off to Valhalla to have their reward in the form of unlimited barrels of beer and barrel-shaped maidens. He had been a brave and skillful killer in the great war, but had been licked at it. Now he was going to have another chance, and this time he was going to win. That coming revenge was the sauce that flavored all the food he ate and the beer he drank; the expectation of it was the motive of all the prodigious labors he performed.

One other impulse drove him—personal vanity. He was the master executive, the great one to whom the others came for orders. All Germany knew this, and the rest of the world, both friends and enemies, would acknowledge it in the future. In this vanity lay the root of the great man's hospitality; he had to have people to admire him, to serve as mirrors in which he might contemplate himself. He personally designed and ordered his bright-colored uniforms, literally scores of them; they externalized his glory, and first he surveyed himself, so as to see what his visitors would be seeing, and when they saw it he read the admiration in their eyes.

Secretly, of course, they might be amused, but that did not trouble

Der Dicke too much. After all, it was a game they were all playing,
and it was the mob they had to fool and impress: the great German
masses which lined the sidewalks twenty deep when their old-style
robber baron drove by in his huge six-wheeled automobile, baby-blue
in color. These masses went into the factories and toiled twelve hours
a day to make the equipment for the coming war; they gave their
sons to be drilled and got ready to spread the fame of the fat General,
soon to be Marshal, all over Europe; to enable him to ride in triumph
into one capital after another in the baby-blue limousine—equipped, of
course, with bullet-proof glass.

II

That was what these Budds meant to Hermann the Great. They
came overseas to him—not he to them. The father knew a lot about
planes, and had given some first-rate ideas, in exchange for second-
rate ideas and enough cash to keep him going. The son went about in
drawing-rooms of the enemy, and from his chatter much useful information could be gleaned. Both of them admired Hermann, gazed
with open-eyed wonder at his marvelous works, and bowed before ·
the future which he was preparing.

Did they really mean all the admiration and friendship they expressed? Probably not; for most men are motivated by greed and fear,
so Hermann believed, and he took them as they were; at present he
fed their greed, and in due course would teach them fear. Meantime,
they were good actors, and we all enjoy attending a show now and
then; so, press the button, and lackeys will come, wheeling tables
loaded with broiled venison, also *Rebhuhn*, with asparagus grown
under glass, peaches frozen in California, and other delicacies from
those seven seas which *Der Dicke* intends to master with his new air
force. While planning and arranging these matters he does himself
well, telling his exploits past and future and laughing uproariously,
boasting to Robbie of the wonders his scientists have invented, making
jokes with Lanny which cause that ivory-tower dweller to blush
slightly, accustomed as he has been to the sophistications of the old
world and the crudeness of the new.

This old-style German robber baron is devoted to his Führer. He
recognizes that it is Adolf Hitler who has shaped the Nazi doctrines
and built the Nazi Party; who has bewitched and captivated the German peasants and middle classes, something which Hermann could
never have done. Hermann began as a humble *Leutnant* in the trenches,

and has risen to be General and is promised a marshalship, the highest of all military ranks. That is enough; Hermann will build the Wehrmacht, and especially the Air Force which is designed to be its crown and apex, the breaker of stalemates, the crusher of Maginot Lines and whatever else the foe may have.

Incidentally, it means that the marshal-to-be will make himself the richest man in the world; he has set up the Hermann Göring Steelworks, the biggest of all time, and will add to them everything his army may take. Privately owned, of course, with no nonsense about nationalization—for has not the Führer said that Bolshevism is the Public Enemy Number One? Isn't it fear of Bolshevism that is enabling Germany to undermine and destroy the governments of every country in Europe? So, why shouldn't Hermann get rich—and boast of his riches to poor Americans, who make thousands of dollars while he is making millions of marks?

"You must come and see my new airports," says the world's future owner; and then: "You must come to Karinhall. Emmy said not to fail to bring you." Emmy Sonnemann, former stage queen, has settled down and got started on the way to presenting her husband with an heir. Her picture is in the illustrated papers almost every week; an example for every German woman below the age of forty-five; what they are all urged and even commanded to do. Block-wardens in all the humble districts go the rounds inquiring of the women whether they are pregnant, and if not why not, and they had better produce good reasons or the government will take action in the matter. Birth control advocates are shut up in concentration camps and abortionists are executed without ceremony, for the Führer must have soldiers for his future task of ruling the world. Hermann adores Emmy, and as a reward for setting a proper example to the German *Volk* she can have anything in the world she asks for; she is the first lady of the Fatherland—the Führer being a bachelor, and, in the eyes of the German *Volk*, a saint.

III

They had a very good time at the luncheon, and it was prolonged while they sipped *Rheinwein* and Hermann and Robbie smoked long black cigars and talked about their business affairs. When they were through with the preliminary stages, they discussed the state of Europe, and when they came to France with its tricky and futile politicians, Lanny told a story which *Der Dicke* pronounced *kolossal*.

As Lanny told it, his old friends the de Bruynes had got themselves head over heels into the Cagoulard conspiracy, and at the moment when Denis *fils* had been arrested and the father was fearing arrest, he had entrusted certain especially compromising papers to Lanny's keeping, thinking they would surely be safe in the hands of an American. But Lanny had been tipped off that the French police were watching him, and he had tried in a great hurry to think of some place where he could hide and be safe. It happened that a few days previously he had met Graf Herzenberg at the home of Lili Moldau, the actress, and he had the impulse, perhaps foolish, to seek shelter at the Château de Belcour. Lanny repeated the long argument which had taken place between himself and Seine Hochgeboren; really amusing, for of course the Graf had been badly scared at the idea of the French police finding Cagoulard documents in his home. Lanny told how he had sought to assure the Graf that he was a friend of Hermann's, and the Graf had refused to believe him, and how alarmed he had been by Lanny's proposal to telephone to Hermann from the château.

Lanny narrated all this in a way to bring out its humorous aspects. He didn't know, but thought it a safe guess that Hermann didn't like Seine Hochgeboren, and wouldn't mind his having been embarrassed in this sort of opera-bouffe adventure. Lanny said he realized that he hadn't been able to do very much to help Hermann in his work, but he had done his best, and had certainly done a great deal to help Kurt Meissner in meeting the right people in Paris. *Der Dicke* was gracious enough to say that Lanny had helped him considerably and certainly had the right to be protected in Paris. That was good to hear, for Herzenberg would be bound to meet the General sooner or later and to ask about Lanny; indeed he might already have asked—which was Lanny's reason for telling the story. Hermann wanted to know what had become of those papers, and doubtless would have been willing to pay a fancy price for them; Lanny answered casually that he had turned them over to a trusted friend of the de Bruynes, and was glad indeed to have got himself clear of the mess.

He talked freely about the Frenchmen who were most active in the plot, and Hermann asked if Lanny would object to his making notes of the names. Lanny said: "Certainly not; but I believe they are all well known to your agents in Paris." To this the fat General replied: "That may be, but I like to know things myself, and have a check on my agents." He had until recently been head of the Gestapo, but a former schoolteacher named Himmler had taken over these all-important functions.

Somewhat to Lanny's surprise, Robbie referred to Baron Schneider as one of the backers of the Cagoule; that was a weighty secret, and one which the Baron would hardly have wanted revealed at present. But Robbie had come here hoping to place a good cash order with Hermann, and he knew that the way to make sure of it was to let it be known that he had already placed a good cash order with Eugène; no confidences counted for anything in comparison with that, and so the name of the Baron went down on the list, along with those of Michelin the tire man and Deloncle and General Duseigneur and Comte Hubert Pastré and the rest; not forgetting Pétain, marshal of the army, and Darlan, admiral of the navy.

. Lanny could see the Reichswehr marching into Paris as a result of those pencil marks which the Kommandant of the German Air Force was scribbling on a pad of paper. Robbie could see it, too, though probably not so clearly. He had made up his mind that he didn't care, provided he could keep America out of it, and have Budd-Erling put to work on a big scale for America's protection. That was Robbie's philosophy in a nutshell; take care of your own house, and to hell with Europe!

IV

Hitherto when Lanny had come to Berlin with his father he had had affairs of his own; but now he seemed to have nothing to do but accompany Robbie everywhere, listen to Robbie's conversation, and ask questions about what he saw. This was a most gratifying development to the father, and brought back to life a dream which had died long ago—that his first-born might decide to follow in his footsteps and take over part of his burdens. Robbie's two sons by Esther were active in the plant, and he had no fault to find with them, but they didn't have Lanny's imagination or his knowledge of world affairs. Robbie had to be careful not to show these feelings at home, but Lanny knew what was in his heart, and was touched by the older man's willingness to explain everything, his pleasure in his eldest son's company and in the fact that the dangerous Pink tinge seemed to have faded out of the son's mind.

Robbie had been told, or had read somewhere, that this was something entirely normal. The young had their fine enthusiasms, and then in course of the years they learned what was possible and what wasn't. With Lanny this process had taken so long that Robbie had come to despair about it, but now it seemed to have come about all at once, a quite magical transformation. Lanny no longer met any Reds or Pinks and no longer had their papers on his table; more important yet, he no longer made the "smart cracks," the cynical remarks by which you could recognize the type. The father had been deeply hurt because his favorite son had repudiated all his ideas; and now to have him reverse his attitude was heartwarming indeed.

So Robbie had talked freely about Big Steel and Little Steel, about Alcoa, the great aluminum trust, and the various power combines allied with it; about Standard Oil of New Jersey and its arrangements with Germany concerning patents on the making of artificial rubber; about the du Ponts and their sale to Germany of the discoveries of their vast research laboratories. All these matters concerned Robbie, because they had to do with airplanes in one way or another. Planes had to fly faster and higher, they had to be stronger and at the same time lighter—the safety of the country, the mastery of the world, might depend upon ten-miles-an-hour difference in speed, or a .50- instead of a .30-caliber machine gun.

At the moment the Germans had the fastest fighter, but Robbie had a new one in the "mock-up" stage that was going to knock them all cold. Robbie's only problem was to get the money to complete this new model, without having to run into debt and risk losing his company to some Wall Street syndicate, as had happened in the sad case of Budd Gunmakers. A distressing thing to come here to Germany and see the research men with all the resources of a great government behind them, and to know that at home people were asleep, and leaving the burden to be carried by a few farsighted individuals, nearly all of them "little fellows" like Robbie Budd!

V

The General sent Furtwaengler to escort his guests and show them the wonders of the newly completed D.V.L., the institute for aeronautical research. To Robbie it was one of the great experiences of his life; he got from it thrills such as Lanny would have got if in the National Bibliothek he had stumbled upon the hitherto unknown manuscript of a tenth symphony by Beethoven. Great Jehoshaphat, these people had built a wind-tunnel in which they could test their models for speeds up to four hundred miles an hour. (Three hundred and twenty was the best that Robbie's new model was expected to produce.) They were training their men in air-reduction chambers, accustoming them to electrically heated suits and oxygen pumped into their lungs, so that fighter planes could get on top of bombing planes, even those equipped with sealed cabins and superchargers. Air war was going to take to the stratosphere, and the nations that didn't get there first would never get there; they would be licked in the first day, or night, of combat.

Most of these improvements were foreseen, but they were supposed to belong to the future; the Germans, however, were going to turn the future into the present. They could do it because their men at the top had the vision; because Göring had been a flyer, and had gathered his old buddies about him and put them in charge. These men knew what air war was, and what it might be; they had been licked once, and knew why, and how to get ready for the next time. All German science, all German discipline, all German wealth, were being directed to this end, so that when *Der Tag* came along, the German army should have an air cover to protect it, first to drive its enemy out of the skies and then to crush his defenses and enable the Wehrmacht to march where it would.

Meantime, in the other countries, what? Robbie Budd didn't wring his hands, for he wasn't of that type, but verbally he did just that. Muddle, muddle, muddle! The Royal Air Force was good, what there was of it, but its control was in the hands of men who still thought in terms of the last war; men who had never flown, and who looked upon airplanes as a convenient but uncertain device to enable army commanders to find out what the enemy ground forces were doing. Brass hats on the land, and on the sea admirals loaded with gold lace, pacing the bridges of great battlewagons with magnificent dignity and resenting airplanes as lawless, impertinent, and bad form.

In France it was even worse; their air force was a pitiful farce, and their program of nationalization in the face of the German threat was lunacy. As for America, that was a story which Robbie had told his son a hundred times. We had an air force of the right size for a Central American republic, and after a manufacturer had met a hundred different kinds of tests, most of them three times over, and had filled out forty-seven blanks in quintuplicate, and had been insulted half a dozen times by men who knew one-tenth as much about planes as he did—then he might get an order for ten units and the promise that Congress would be asked to budget twenty more, but a subcommittee would cut it out.

VI

Aviation was something new in the world, and at every stage of its development it had broken the rules and defied authority. When Lanny

had been a tiny toddler on the beach at Juan, two bicycle manufacturers in Ohio had built themselves a frail contraption out of spruce-
wood and canvas, and on the sand dunes of the North Carolina coast
had learned to keep it in the air for several minutes. Nobody had paid
any attention to them, because everybody knew that it couldn't be
done. Even when they went back to their home town and in its
suburbs were flying circles around a field, the newspapers refused to
pay attention to the doings, because they had been hoaxed so often
and the public was tired of "flying-machine men."

Such was the attitude manifested at every stage of air development.
A decade or so ago the army had court-martialed and discharged its
most capable flying general, because he not merely told what bombing
planes could do to battleships, but proved it. The men who conducted
those proceedings were in command of the army today, so declared
Robbie Budd, and they would have court-martialed *him* if they had
had any way to get hold of him.

But Budd-Erling had a few supporters in the air corps, and one of
them, a colonel in the reserve army, happened to be in Berlin at this
time. Charles Lindbergh was his name, and when he was a youth he had
performed an unorthodox and presumptuous action, stepping into
a little flivver-plane on Long Island and heading out across the Atlantic. When he landed at Le Bourget airport near Paris some thirty-
four hours later, he was the first man to make a solo flight across the
ocean, and had become one of the most famous men in the world. He
was a shy and retiring person, and didn't enjoy it; when he found he
couldn't walk on a street anywhere in his native land without being
surrounded and mobbed, he grew irritated, and took to being gruff
to newspaper reporters, an offense unprecedented in the vast over-
grown village called America.

Then came the tragedy of the kidnaping and murder of his little
child. The uproar of the trial was a crucifixion for the young airman,
and after it he moved to England to live. He had made a lot of money,
and had married a banker's daughter and become conservative in his
political views; perhaps he was that anyway, because his father had
been a "radical" congressman and his family life had been unhappy as
a result. Anyhow, Herr von Ribbentrop, the Nazi champagne salesman who had been made ambassador to England, saw an opportunity
to make use of a naïve middle-western American for his propaganda.
The Nazis were getting ready to fight, but of course didn't want to
fight if they could frighten the world into giving them what they
wanted. It suited them to have the world believe that Germany pos-

sessed overwhelming might in the air, and a tall, dignified, and honest young Swedish-American was picked out as the trumpet to blow this news to the world.

"Lindy" was invited to be General Göring's guest, and apparently he found it possible to enjoy living in the General's country. He came a number of times, and was received with every honor, and even given a decoration. All doors were open to him and all secrets revealed—or so he was made to believe. He flew his lovely young wife in their small plane over Germany, and saw that all along the Swiss and French borders the Germans had built an airport every twenty miles. He was escorted through giant factories, and estimated that Germany was building twenty thousand planes a year, and could double the number at will. He examined the planes and decided they were better on the whole than those of any other nation. He had not been forbidden to tell these things, and since they seemed important he told them freely, and persons in other countries who didn't want to face the facts were greatly annoyed.

VII

Colonel Lindbergh was a man after Robbie Budd's own heart, and one whom he would have chosen to have as a son. They agreed in practically all their ideas; they were interested in mechanical constructions and bored by what they called "sentimentality" of all sorts. They accepted the Nazis at their own valuation, as "conservatives" whose function was to put down Communism. In spite of the fact that one had flown the Atlantic and the other was talking about planes to fly it every day, both belonged to the group which was coming to be called "isolationists." They desired to see their country settle down within its own borders and arm itself to such an extent that no country or combination would ever dare to attack it.

So now these two sat in the Budd suite and discussed what they had seen and learned in the four great nations of the Western world, the only nations that really counted, in their way of looking at things. They knew each other's minds, and didn't have to waste time in preliminaries; they spoke a technical language, and neither had to explain his terms to the other. This applied not merely to the different makes of planes, their performances, and the hundreds of complex gadgets they contained; it applied to the techniques of flying them and the places to which they were flown, the companies which owned them, the stocks and bonds and other financial affairs of these concerns, and the personalities of those who financed and administered them. The only thing the air Colonel had to explain was the term "perfusion pump," a device which he was trying to perfect for the surgeon Alexis Carrel, a kind of "artificial heart" which would be used in certain emergencies.

Lanny listened to all this, and tried to remember as much as he could of the things which seemed to him most significant. He wondered if he, too, was becoming "conservative" in his middle years; anyhow, he found that he agreed with his father more than he had ever thought possible. Since the last war he had believed himself a pacifist, and had been embarrassed to bear the name of one of the "merchants of death"; but now he was convinced that France, England, and his own country ought to have military planes, as many as they could get in a hurry—yes, even if it allowed Robbie Budd to make a fortune, and to say to his son: "You see, I was right!" Later, when occasion permitted, Lanny would shut himself up in his bedroom and make careful notes of what he had heard, and pin them in his inside coat pocket right over his own "perfusion pump."

VIII

The great six-wheeled limousine called at the hotel for the Budds— establishing for them, so far as concerned the employees and many of the guests, a status equal to royalty. They were covered with a bearskin robe and driven to the ministerial residence, across the way from the Reichstag building, whose burned-out dome had been left unrepaired as a reminder to the German people never to forget to hate the Reds. Lanny thought of the tunnel which connected the two buildings underground, and through which Göring's men had come to set the fire. This was a story so melodramatic that nobody but Reds would believe it, and if you had told it to anybody else in Germany you would have been turned over to the Gestapo.

The deviser of this clever political stroke emerged from the palace he had won. He looked more immense than ever in a voluminous blue military cloak, with a black fur collar and hat; the coat reaching to the ankles of the shiny black leather boots. The great man occupied a full half of the wide rear seat, and his two guests the other half. A staff car followed for their protection, and *Der Dicke* started asking Lanny about the attitude of the British toward Germany's newly declared resolve to protect her minorities in the lands to the east of her. Lanny told of discussions he had heard.

The British, like the French, had to make the difficult choice between Nazis and Reds, and the fat General grinned as he listened to Lanny's account of their perplexity. Their Foreign Minister, Lord Halifax, former Viceroy of India, had visited Berlin in the previous month, ostensibly to attend a sportsman's exhibition which the General and his staff had got up. Göring was Master of the Hunt and Game Warden of Germany, while Halifax was Joint Master of the Middleton Hunt, so they had been two buddies. They had wandered around in a vast hall looking at the stuffed heads of slaughtered game from all parts of the earth, and his Lordship had received on behalf of his government the first prize for a display of overseas trophies.

Two men more incongruous it would have been hard for any cartoonist to imagine: the English nobleman, tall and drooping, with a pale, cadaverous face; stiff and solemn, deeply pious and praying both publicly and privately over everything he did; Göring, on the other hand, a throwback to the ancient Teutons, a tub of guts and a pair of bloody hands, a bellowing laugh and a restless will unchecked by the smallest scruple. He permitted himself the pleasure of telling his American guests about this visit. The noble Lord had done his best to pin Germany down to an agreement to be content with practically nothing. That was the "appeasement" idea of the new Prime Minister, Chamberlain, who kept offering it, and wondering why it was not welcomed. There had been a time in the world's history when the British had wanted things and had taken them; but now they had persuaded themselves that nobody was ever again going to take anything.

Said Robbie: "I believe they will let you have a few things, provided you can convince them that nothing British is involved."

"We have given them that assurance many times," replied the host. "There are Belgian and Dutch and Portuguese colonies of which we might reasonably claim a share. As for the people of German speech and blood who have been cut off from us by the Versailles treaty—we simply do not understand why the British are so determined to keep them in exile. If the British cannot endure to see Germany grow strong again, they will have to enforce their idea with some something more powerful than Anglican High Church prayers."

IX

The horn of the car moaned its long blasts while they sped over the low flat land of Brandenburg and came to the Schorfheide with its forests and the well-fenced game preserve. It belonged to the German government, but the old-style robber baron had calmly taken over the use of it—and who was there to say him Nay? A hunting lodge had been good enough for the Kaiser, but not for Göring, who had turned it into a palace and named it Karinhall. A long graveled driveway brought the baby-blue limousine in front of a wide-spreading two-story building of stucco or concrete, having a doorway like an ancient castle narrowing to a sort of stone tunnel as if for defense—one of those vestigial architectural features which Lanny had explained to Leutnant Rörich at the Château de Belcour. There were elk's antlers over this entrance, and many sorts of hunting trophies on the walls of the great hall inside; for of course a military man has to keep in practice, and when he can't have men he uses animals, which are cheaper, but not too cheap to be good form, in Germany as in England.

Lanny had visited this place with Irma, but that had been three or four years ago, and many trophies had been added and many gifts received since then. The Führer had had printed a special edition of *Mein Kampf*, as big as an atlas and with the most elegant binding imaginable. This had been set up on a table of corresponding magnificence, with a candle on each side always burning, just as in a church. Behind it, on the wall, was a Madonna and Child, and this seemed to Lanny the oddest combination an interior decorator had ever thought up. Had the General and his associates overlooked the fact that the subject of this work of art had been a Jewess?

Also there was a ceremonial Japanese sword which Robbie and his son were invited to inspect and wield—at a proper distance. There was an album containing photographs of the Air Force Commander's "first seventy airfields," and Robbie, of course, didn't have to pretend his interest in this. There was the shrine to Karin, the Swedish baroness who had been Hermann's first wife, and for whom the place was named; candles burned before it, and outside was a marble mausoleum holding her remains, brought from Sweden with ceremonies at which Hermann and Adolf had marched reverently side by side.

Also there was the lion cub—always a new one wandering about the house, despite the fact that one of its predecessors in favor had mistaken the General's white trouser leg for a birch tree. Upstairs the visitors inspected the most elaborate playroom they had ever seen, a floor made into a toy village with trees and all accessories, and running around it and through it a triple railroad track with toy trains. The great man sat at a desk and pressed buttons, and the trains shot here and there, through tunnels and over bridges. "My child will play with these some day," he said; the pregnancy of Emmy was soon to be made known to the German nation.

They dined in the long hall, at a table seating twenty-four guests. Only half the seats were occupied, mostly by officers of the General's staff, including Lanny's old friend Furtwaengler. After the meal the great man excused himself for a while, saying that he had reports to read. Robbie sat down to study the album of the first seventy air-fields, and Lanny wandered about looking at art treasures and wondering from whom they had been expropriated. They included immensely valuable Flemish tapestries, portraying naked ladies of the Rubens style of architecture. As the great man's *Kunstsachverständiger*, Lanny knew that his patron's taste fluctuated between the two extremes of the most magnificent costumes and none at all. At the foot of the table in the dining hall, facing the General and his wife as they sat, was a marble Aphrodite Anadyomene, and elsewhere in painting and statuary you observed naked Greeks and helmeted and bemedaled Germans, about fifty-fifty.

X

In the library before a fireplace the lovely Emmy Sonnemann had seated herself upon a sofa, and not in the middle. She said: "Come and talk to me, Herr Budd." Did she intend that he should occupy the other half of the sofa? He thought it the part of wisdom to take a chair three or four feet away.

He could look at her better from that vantage point; and she was meant for looking at. Maternity in its preliminary stages seemed to become her. She was a large woman, but well proportioned; she had played Brunnhilde at the Berlin Staats-Theater, and could have played the Venus de Milo if anybody had written a drama on that theme. She had regular and lovely features, expressive of gentleness and kindness; bright blue eyes, and blond hair which had not required chemical treatment. Of all the Nazis, she was the one who came nearest to their professed Nordic ideal.

She was the first lady of the Fatherland, and one of the best known of its public figures, owing to her long premarital career. All Germans had seen her on stage or screen, and felt that they knew her. Mostly they knew only good; for though she had taken up the duties of a queen, she played it as a stage role, and everybody had the comfortable feeling that she was that kind of queen. In private life she was easygoing, comfortable, a bit naïve. Theatrical folk are supposed to be bohemian, but when they become successful, they are glad to turn bourgeois, and that was Emmy Sonnemann. Millions of people in Germany would have paid half their worldly goods for a ticket of admission to Karinhall and the privilege of sitting on the other half of that sofa; Emmy wouldn't have minded, but would have chatted amiably with each, and given the money to the *Winterhilfe*.

She said: "You don't come to see us very often, Mr. Lanny Budd."

"I have had to stay at home and help my father," he apologized. This wasn't true, but he couldn't say what he had really been doing.

"Lanny is a very nice name," she remarked. "May I call you that?"

"All my friends do," he replied. Doubtless she would have liked to add: "Call me Emmy"; but her husband, *Der Dicke*, might not have approved.

"You had a wife when you were here before. Then I heard you were divorced. Tell me about it."

Was that royalty speaking, or the stage world? In one case it would be a command, in the other just normal curiosity. Lanny took it for the latter and said: "It's a complicated story. Our tastes were too different. Irma had been raised in a huge palace on Long Island, and I in a little villa on the French Riviera. I just couldn't get used to being so very formal and magnificent."

"Oh, how well I understand!" exclaimed the first lady. "Sometimes I am so bored, I think I can't stand it. But then I remind myself how it used to be at rehearsals—doing the same thing over and over, and never getting it quite right."

"The public seems to have thought you got it pretty right," remarked Lanny, gallantly.

"*Na, na!*" exclaimed the one-time star. "Everybody flatters me, but you don't have to."

"I assure you quite sincerely that I saw you in several of your roles, and you were always lovely."

"*Ja, vielleicht;* I was good to look at, when they fixed me up and got the lighting exactly right. At the end I was beginning to show my age, in spite of anything they could do."

Lanny exclaimed with all sincerity: "This is an experience unique in my life: an actress admits her age when she doesn't have to!"

"But you know all about me, Lanny. I was a successful ingénue when you were a little boy."

"You must have been a very young ingénue; and anyhow, I didn't know about you then."

"To tell the honest truth, I was never a very good actress. I tried desperately hard, but I lacked the temperament. The directors wouldn't give me emotional roles, and my feelings were terribly hurt; but now I have thought it over and realized that they were being kind to me."

Lanny didn't know quite how to take such a confession. She was being frank—but would it be safe for him to be? He remarked: "May it not have been that you were too good for some of the roles, Frau Göring?"

"*Ach, mun,* you are being beautiful. That is the very explanation with which I comfort myself. I have never hated anybody very much that I can recall, and certainly I have never wanted to kill anybody. I like to see people happy, and I do what I can to help them. But nobody seems to want to see people like that on the stage."

"It is not the fashion of the time," admitted the art expert, consolingly. "But you have got what you want out of it, and so you can look back philosophically." He wasn't sure if that was true, but certainly it was up to him to assume it.

XI

The first lady of Naziland had commanded him to be seated, and had taken charge of the conversation. Presumably she had some purpose, and etiquette required Lanny to give her a chance to reveal it in her own way. There was a lull, and he waited; then suddenly she remarked: "I am still playing a role, Lanny. I have to be a great lady, and the stage and screen directors taught me everything about it. But one thing they never did teach me, and that is to be entirely happy."

"Ah!" exclaimed Lanny. "Whoever could teach that role would become the greatest director in the world."

"I don't like cruelty," the woman went on. "I don't like to see people suffer, and I can't help suffering with them. I am not supposed to say this to anybody in the world; but I have the impression that you have the same sort of feelings. *Nicht wahr?*"

"Yes, that is true," admitted Lanny. "I surely don't like cruelty." He couldn't say less about himself.

"Tell me this: How do you feel about the Jews?"

"Some of my best friends are Jews," he replied. After he had said it, he remembered that in New York the Jews had taken that up as a sort of shibboleth, by which you could recognize the anti-Semite who didn't wish to admit his prejudices. But after all, what else could anybody say? And what more?"

"You know how it is in the stage and screen worlds. The Jews seem to love art; at any rate they know how to run it, and how to make money out of it. So I made friends among them; some of them I became really fond of, and now they get into trouble, terrible trouble, and they write or send somebody to me, begging for help; and what can I do? I try to help one, and before I succeed there are several more. They think I am all-powerful, but I am not, I assure you."

"I can believe you, Frau Göring."

"Tell me honestly, what do you think of our policy toward the Jews?"

This indeed was a poser for the son of Budd-Erling, here on Budd-Erling business, or supposed to be! Was he going to forget that this lady's husband was the founder and still the nominal head of the Gestapo? He believed that she meant what she said, and was not just trying to probe his mind and get something out of him that might be of use to her husband. But he surely mustn't go too far on that belief!

"*Meine liebe Frau Göring,*" he said, "I have suffered over this problem just as you have. I have conceived the most intense admiration for your Führer, and confidence in his program as the salvation of German culture and a means of preserving order all over Europe. But I don't regard the Jews as anything like the menace that many people do, and I think the Nazis have harmed their cause with the rest of the world by what they have done."

"Hermann feels the same way," replied Hermann's wife. "If he had the power, he would put extremists like Streicher out of office. He tells me that you have Jewish relatives, and made some effort to help them get abroad several years ago."

"That is true," Lanny admitted. "Hermann was very kind to me indeed." Long practice had taught this presidential agent to keep a straight face while listening to statements which tempted him to irony. *Hermann der Dicke,* like many another man in a high position or a low, was telling his wife the truth but not the whole truth; he surely wouldn't want her to know that this magnificent Karinhall was full of art treasures which he had wrung out of Johannes Robin by torture in the cells of the old red brick police prison on the Alexanderplatz.

Said the first lady of the Fatherland. "I go to my husband and ask him for exit permits for this Jewish artist and that, and he gets them for me. But he has so many problems and works so hard, and I hate to burden him with more cares. A man has a right to be happy when he comes to his wife, don't you think?"

Yes, Lanny thought so; also, he thought the former star was being extraordinarily indiscreet, and that he was on a spot and must be extraordinarily cautious. He replied: "I am hoping that now, when the Party is so securely in power, these unfortunate incidents will diminish."

"I fear it will be exactly the opposite, Lanny. The Party is in power, but our problems are by no means solved. The lower elements take pogroms as a sort of sport; and some of them make money out of it, too, I have been told."

XII

This conversation was interrupted by Robbie, who came strolling into the room. He was invited to take the place next to Emmy, and he started asking about motion-picture salaries in Berlin as compared with those in Hollywood, a subject of which no one in the profession ever wearies. Lanny sat quietly, supposed to be listening, but his thoughts were far away; he was having one of his internal discussions with Trudi.

Some part of his mind was always on her, and especially so in Berlin, the city of her birth and of his meetings with her over a period of years. He could never approach the Adlon without seeing his car parked on a certain spot in front of the hotel, on that night when the Gestapo had been hunting her, and he had parked her there while he went inside to fix matters up with Irma. He and Robbie now had a different suite, but all rooms in a great hotel look more or less alike, and the Trudi-ghost—as well as that of his love for Irma—haunted the bed in which he slept. It is not a good thing to have two wives in the same bed—so any Turk could have told this grandson of the Puritans.

Lanny was thinking: "Emmy is sorry for the Jews and helps them to get passports. Mightn't she become sorry for Trudi, a blond Aryan like herself? A woman artist of extraordinary talent, who has fallen under the suspicion of the police because of the activities of her late husband!"

Lanny went through an imaginary scene in which he told the first lady of Naziland this plausible and most touching story. He had every right to have been on friendly terms with art circles in Berlin prior to the coming of the Nazis; just as much as Emmy had to have known the stage and screen personalities. And to have met some Socialists, just as Emmy had met some Jews! And to have taken up a young woman artist of talent, and made her work known in Paris, and helped her to earn small sums! Later he had heard a rumor that Ludi, her husband, had been arrested and interned. Trudi, he was sure, had never been politically active, her one preoccupation being to sketch correctly the lineaments of every unusual-looking person she met. "Would you not be willing to make inquiries about her, Frau Göring, and perhaps go and see her, and help her to get away to America, where she could not possibly do any harm to the Nazi regime?"

Thus Lanny's imagination, lively as usual. No doubt he could persuade Emmy to cause the ordering of a report on the case of Trudi Schultz. A dossier would be laid on the desk of the Reichsminister General, who, among his manifold duties, had charge of the government of Berlin. That dossier would be labeled: "Trudi Schultz, alias Mueller, alias Kornmahler, alias Corning, alias Weill—and perhaps other names that she had never told to her second husband. Not exactly consistent with the ivory-tower attitude! The dossier would reveal that she had been one of the most active workers of the Social-Democratic Party's underground; that she had distributed literature from a secret press, whose operators had been caught; that she had procured the purloining of confidential documents from the General's own office and had smuggled them out of Germany by some method unknown; that after her flight to Paris she had been the source of large funds for the underground, and the best efforts of the police had failed to discover where she had obtained these funds.

That last was the fact which would stick out like a sore thumb from any report the General might get: really tremendous sums of money, tens, possibly hundreds of thousands of marks, from an unknown source; and would the stupidest General in the Nazi army fail to exclaim: "*Ach, so!* She is friend and probably mistress of this glib-tongued and plausible American playboy!"

That was where all Lanny's flights of imagination ended. He had given Trudi his pledge that he would go on giving money to the underground, and risk nothing that might direct the attention of the Nazis to himself. He had certainly broken that pledge in Paris; and how many more times would his pitcher go to the well before it got broken?

XIII

Upstairs in their adjoining bedrooms, Robbie Budd and his son might have talked over the events of the day, as guests all over the world are accustomed to do when they retire for the night. But Lanny had warned his father: "Remember, there is nothing more likely than that rooms in Karinhall are wired for dictaphones." It sounded like melodrama, but Robbie well knew that such things were done, and not only by Nazis. There were sound-detecting devices which could be hidden under a bed or behind a dressing table, and would magnify and record in another room the faintest whispers. Father and son had agreed that their conversation must be of a neutral character, and that if ever they said a word about anyone in Naziland it would be complimentary.

Now Robbie went to his suitcase and got a sheet of writing paper. Using the back of his suitcase and not the desk which was provided in the room, he wrote a few words, and then beckoned to Lanny, who came and read: "Don't talk so much to the woman."

"*Gosh!*" whispered the younger man. He wanted to say, or to write: "She pinned me down," or something like that; but obviously, this was no time for argument.

The father wrote: "Remember Donnerstein's story?"

Lanny nodded. He wasn't ever going to forget that very lively woman friend of Irma, who lived all over Germany, picked up delightful gossip, and retailed it with eagerness which would have landed her in a concentration camp if she had not belonged to the highest social circles.

Robbie wrote again: "The Heilbronn dentist," and showed the words.

"O.K.," said Lanny—this being something it was safe to say out loud.

He had passed on to his father one of the Fürstin Donnerstein's choice tidbits, having to do with a dentist who had known Emmy Sonnemann in the small town of Heilbronn where she had been born, and had written her a letter congratulating her upon her splendid marriage. In the course of the letter he had named a total of eighteen different persons in the town, telling the news about them. All these persons, plus the loquacious dentist, had been arrested by the Gestapo and brought to Berlin, where they had been held and cross-examined for weeks. Not one of them had any idea what it was all about; and when the ordeal was over, they each received a hundred marks and carfare to their homes, with the injunction to say nothing about what had happened to them.

"Jealousy is madness," wrote the father; and the son nodded several times more, saying: "O.K., O.K." No matter what advances the lovely Emmy might make, she wouldn't get another tête-à-tête with the son of Budd-Erling. Not only is jealousy madness, but Hermann might become a madman on slight provocation. He had been a dope fiend after the death of his first wife and had been confined in an asylum in Sweden. Under the strain of the gamble for world power which he was taking, he might well have fallen victim to the habit again. In any case it certainly wouldn't help Robbie Budd in getting airplane contracts to have this world gambler pick up the notion that Lanny was making himself too agreeable to the first lady of Naziland.

The son took the paper and wrote: "You are right. Sorry." Then Robbie carried the paper into the bathroom, set fire to it with a match, and held it carefully until it had burned down to the last square inch. He pulled the lever and sent the ashes down to a region where it might reasonably be assumed the Secret State Police would not follow; and along with the ashes went the last trace of Lanny's notion that he might get Emmy Sonnemann to help him get Trudi Schultz out of a Nazi prison!

16

Fuming Vanities

I

BACK in Berlin, Lanny found messages awaiting him. One was from Heinrich Jung, and Lanny had several reasons for wanting to see this ardent young Party official. He called him up, saying: "Come to lunch," and Heinrich replied, in English: "Delighted." He was proud of his English, proud of his rich American friend, and proud of an invitation which took him among international smart society.

Sixteen years had passed since Lanny had first met a humble student of forestry, son of the Oberförster of the Schloss Stubendorf estate. Heinrich was rounder now, and even rosier in the cheeks, but otherwise not greatly changed; blue eyes, close-cut blond hair, a brisk manner. He lived on hope and enthusiasm, and kept a bland smile as a permanent feature of his landscape. He had just been promoted to a post of greater responsibility in the Hitlerjugend, and had a new uniform with new insignia. He was happy in it, but at the same time modest, attributing his rise not to his own merits but to the discernment of the great organization of which he was a part. He had hitched his wagon to a star. and that star had turned into a nova, brightest of shining suns.

Heinrich didn't have any important secrets that Lanny could extract from him, but he was interesting as the perfect type of the Nazi zealot, the finished product of the Hitler educational machine. Lanny watched him with the attention he would have devoted to an ant under a magnifying glass: a bundle of energy and zeal, laboring with blind fury all day and most of the night, responding precisely and automatically to various stimuli, and never stopping for an instant to question the ends he was serving. Heinrich had that peculiar Jekyll-and-Hyde quality of the Germans, which made it possible for him to be a warmhearted and amiable friend, and at the same time capable of most shocking cruelty. Heinrich himself had never committed any murders, but he justified them all as serving the great German purpose, and Lanny could never doubt that if the Führer should give the order, Heinrich would draw a gun in the Hotel Adlon dining room and shoot off the top of Lanny's head. He wouldn't enjoy doing such a deed, but he would know that it was necessary; otherwise the greatest man in the world wouldn't have commanded it to be done.

The *Herrenvolk* were fulfilling their destiny, and Lanny was one of the comparatively few Americans who understood and honored what they were doing. Heinrich Jung was completely naïve about this; the idea never crossed his mind that a member of the American privileged classes might believe that it was *his* race rather than the German which was destined to come out on top in the great world dog-fight. No, because the Americans had their own job to do, and a full-sized one; the greater part of their continent was still in the hands of others, and the Nazis granted them full rights to it. There were some who were even willing to concede South America, also; Heinrich avoided that question, because the Germans were strong there, and what the Germans had got they had to keep. The greater part of American culture, all that was best in it, had been contributed by the Germans, and that was one reason why Heinrich could feel so cordial to Lanny Budd; Lanny was part German, and the *Herrenvolk* could take him in, and his countrymen could become equal members of the future ruling group—that is, of course, after the Jews and the poisonous Jewish influences had been eliminated from their country.

Heinrich talked, as he always did, about the wonderful organization he was helping to build all over the world, and its achievements in making over the youth of Germany, and those of German race outside. There had never been anything like it in history; it was modern science applied to mass psychology, under the guidance of a supreme genius in that field. Heinrich had attended the *Parteitag* at Nuremberg in September, a five-day jamboree which was for every Nazi what the pilgrimage to Mecca is to the devout Moslem. Heinrich described all the ceremonies, and repeated the gist of the speeches. Everything in the world was going to be made over, and the Nazis had begun with history. Heinrich had learned at Nuremberg an entirely new history of Germany, and of the rest of the world in relation to Germany; he didn't know any other history, and he never read any book, magazine, or newspaper except Party publications. Lanny had to exercise the utmost care never to say anything that would clash with this friend's firmly rooted ideas.

II

There was a peculiar way in which Heinrich Jung was connected in Lanny's mind with Trudi Schultz. Once on the official's desk Lanny had observed a copy of one of the underground pamphlets which Trudi had written and caused to be printed in Paris and shipped into Germany. Some loyal member of the Hitlerjugend had turned this wicked thing over to his superior, and Heinrich had communicated with the Gestapo about it. Now Lanny said: "Do you ever see any more of that anti-Nazi stuff of which you showed me a sample?"

"No," replied the other; "not for some time. I think that sort of criminal activity has come entirely to an end."

"You have a marvelously efficient police force, I know."

"It's not only that, Lanny; it's the *Zeitgeist*, it's something that you will feel if you stay for a while. The very soul of the people is changed; they have been made over in the Führer's image, and it is impossible for any German to stand out against this influence. They all see that he has solved their problems for them; everybody has work, everybody has security, everybody has a sense of pride in belonging to the Führer's great organization and sharing his wonderful dream."

"I feel it, believe me, Heinrich. I make it my business to talk with the plain people wherever I go."

"You should come to Stubendorf this Christmas and meet the people there. It would give you an insight into what is coming soon in European affairs."

"You know I have never wavered for a moment, Heinrich, in my attitude to the question of the return of Stubendorf to Germany. I resigned my humble post on the staff of the Peace Commission because

I didn't approve the decisions on that and other border districts. And don't think it was easy to do; I made a lot of enemies, and put an end to what might have been a chance for a diplomatic career."

"I have never forgotten it, Lanny, and never shall. The issue is coming rapidly to a head now, and not because of our propaganda in the border states, as you will read in the lying foreign press. It is simply because our Germans in exile also see the Führer's success, and want to be a part of this new order he is building. Stubendorf is like a boiler under which you build the fire hotter and tie down the safety-valve. Our people simply will not endure to be governed any longer by incompetent and corrupt Polish officials. You will not find a single person who will say anything but this."

In the old days, Lanny would have got off some wisecracks; for example: "It might be different if I could understand Polish." But now he was playing a game, and he asked: "Is it the same all along the border?"

"*Absolut!* From Gdynia and the Corridor, all the way to the south of Austria, and even into parts of Hungary and Yugoslavia."

"I suppose the first move will come in Austria. At least, that is what people seem to expect in England and France."

"What is coming is in the Führer's mind alone," replied the loyal servant. "He does not tell me state secrets."

"Have you seen him recently?"

"I don't trouble him unless there is some important reason. Many people who had the good fortune to know him in the old days presume upon that circumstance, but I have always been careful not to."

"Not many can say that they came to see him in prison, Heinrich."

"That is true, and he doesn't forget. But I do my job, and he knows that I am doing it, and that is enough."

"Would you like to take me to see him again?"

The official's face lighted up, but then quickly became shadowed again. "Do you think it would be wise, Lanny? He is in the midst of heavy labors and has to make difficult decisions."

"Well, I don't want to intrude, but it happens that I have met a number of important persons in England and have listened to a lot of talk. Also, I have been on the inside of efforts in France to set up a government that would break off the Russian alliance. General Göring found my story interesting, and the Führer might do the same."

Lanny told of his dealings with the Cagoulards, and of his flight to the country home of Graf Herzenberg. It pleased Heinrich greatly, because it showed Lanny definitely on their side, something which

Heinrich had been trying to bring about for sixteen years. He said that, and added: "You see why we Germans can never trust a nation like France, whose governments are so unstable that we never know what to expect."

"I suppose you are right. It is a real tragedy that our coup d'état failed."

"You couldn't help it, Lanny. Nobody could do in France what we have done in Germany. Our revolution stems from the people; it is a general movement, with a Führer who is of the people and understands their soul. The French are incapable of producing such a leader, or of recognizing and following him if he appeared. All you could get there was a subsidized conspiracy, a pitiful sort of *Putsch;* it was fundamentally reactionary, and if it had succeeded, you would soon have made that discovery."

"I am afraid you are right," replied Lanny, meekly. He was interested to observe that what Heinrich said about the Cagoule was almost identical with what Leutnant Rörich had said in the château. Had Dr. Josef Goebbels discussed this pitiful French *Putsch* over the radio, and had they both been listening? Or had they been taught out of the same Nazi textbook?

Anyhow, Lanny got what he wanted out of this meeting. Heinrich said: "I'm sure the Führer would be interested in that story. I'll call up and see if an appointment can be made."

III

Another of the messages at Lanny's hotel was from the Fürstin Donnerstein; she was having an *Abend,* and would be happy if Lanny and his father would come. Lanny said: "You will meet important people." So Robbie put aside some calculations which he had promised to General Göring, and they were driven to the white marble palace on the swanky Königin Augustastrasse, belonging to a Prussian landowner and diplomat of the *Kaiserzeit.* The princess was some thirty years younger than her husband, a nervous, high-strung woman who smoked a great many cigarettes and was bored by her life without knowing why. She had met Irma on the Riviera years ago and they had become pals; now she hadn't heard from the heiress for a long time, and wanted Lanny to tell her why. Lanny knew that she was a tireless tattletale, and what she really wanted was to probe the mystery of a divorce which had intrigued smart society in half a dozen capitals.

But now, with many guests to welcome and entertain, was not the time to approach this subject. The tall blond Hilde said: "Oh, Lanny, you must come to see me—and soon! Do promise." Then, in a whisper: "I have the most delightful lot of gossip—*wirklich prima!*" Lanny said promptly that he would call up without fail.

He and Irma had been about in Berlin society, and a lifetime in Europe had trained him to remember faces, names, and titles. Also Robbie had met many of the leading businessmen, and had the same sort of training; his German was shaky, but he rarely had to use it, for practically all these people knew English. Presently father and son were engaged in conversation with a dark somber-appearing man who knew the steel industry of Germany to the last ingot, and who was greatly concerned to know the meaning of the present business slump in America; what was the government going to do about it, and was there any chance of the steel men in America cutting their prices on the world market? This was Fritz Thyssen, pronounced Tissen, one of Germany's great industrial masters, and, by his appearance, one of the saddest and most badly worried men in Naziland.

Presently he remarked: "I don't sell much steel abroad these days, but they have to let me sell a little, in order that I may have the money to buy postage stamps and other things that require cash." What a world of meaning was in that sentence, for anybody who understood the code! Here was the man who, more than any other, was responsible for putting Adolf Hitler in power; who had brought Adi to the Rhineland and got the steel men together at a secret meeting, so that an ex-painter of picture postcards could explain to them that he didn't really mean his terrifying program of "abolition of interest slavery" and "nationalization of department stores." Thyssen personally had put more than five million marks into the Nazi treasury at times when the Party had been on the verge of financial collapse.

And now for a matter of five years he had been making the discovery that Adi was a man who kept no promises and had no conception of loyalty to anything but his own "intuition." Now this Catholic steelmaster was in the position of a man who has got a mad bull by the tail; he cannot let go, but has to hold on with all his might and be dragged in a bone-breaking career. He had dreamed of making tractors and promoting German agriculture, but instead he was commanded to make cannon and tanks, and for these products he had to take treasury notes, which were promises to pay on the part of the Nazi government, and were good inside Germany for the reason that all other German big businessmen were in the same plight as Fritz. That was the reason he looked as if he wanted to cry, and why he risked his freedom and indeed his life by making snide remarks to an American manufacturer who was still free to produce what he wanted to produce—even though he wasn't always sure that he could sell it after it was finished!

IV

The Donnersteins had engaged a *Sängerin* from the opera to entertain their guests, and Lanny listened with pleasure to the rendition of a song cycle by Hugo Wolf. It appeared that music was the only thing he still had in common with the Germans. So long as you left out the large section of music which bore the names of Jews, you were free to sing and to listen freely, and to express pleasure or lack of it without fear of the Gestapo. Therefore, ye soft pipes, play on; pipe to the spirit ditties of any tune provided its Aryan!

Robbie hadn't much time in Berlin, and preferred to put that little to business uses. When Lanny came out of the concert-room, he found his father seated in an alcove in conference with another Nazi notable: a large powerful man of about Robbie's age and looking oddly like a cartoonist's idea of a Prussian Junker; a square, knobby head close shaven and a square bulbous face very red; a small gray mustache and large spectacles, watery blue eyes and a sausage neck with a prominent Adam's apple, enclosed by a tall and tight old-fashioned stiff collar. Every now and then this gentleman would give a violent swallow, and then a nervous adjustment to his collar, as if he thought his Adam's apple might have knocked it out of position. His gestures were of violence, even when his voice was a whisper.

It was the great Herr Doktor Horace Greeley Hjalmar Schacht, a financier with a craving for publicity, who had been on both sides of pretty nearly every political movement which had appeared in the Fatherland since the days of the Kaiser—and what a number of them had cursed that unhappy realm! At present the Herr Doktor was Finance Minister to the Nazi regime, which meant that he was the issuer of those treasury notes which the fear-filled Fritz had to take whether he wanted to or not. The minister was apparently engaged in a confidential talk with Robbie, for when Lanny approached, he fell silent in a rather obvious way, as if to ask: "Who is this *Eindringling?*"

Robbie said: "This is my son, Lanny," and the Herr Doktor rose to his feet, clicked his heels and bowed from the waist. Robbie added: "Bring up a chair, Lanny," and then, to the other: "My son is to be trusted as I am."

So the Finance Minister resumed his monologue. It appeared that he was in the same mental state as the steel king; extremely unhappy, and overwhelmed by an impulse to pour out his soul to an influential American. Dr. Schacht's country was heading straight for bankruptcy, and the highest financial authority in the government was as helpless to prevent it as the humblest German laborer who received paper marks in his pay envelope and hastened to spend them at the nearest *Kolonialwarenladen*. The Nazis were undertaking a program of military preparation, and at the same time another of public works; making cannon and tanks, and at the same time building swimming pools and monuments! "What do they mean to do?" queried the Herr Doktor, and Lanny couldn't be sure whether it was tears or just rheum in his eyes. "We go on blindly issuing paper of a dozen different sorts, and even now our short-term paper is at a discount on the market. When the long-term obligations fall due, how can we meet them? How can anybody imagine it will be done? I have figures showing that seventy per cent of our total national income is going into government work of one sort or another at the present time, and what is that going to leave for sound business as you enjoy it in America?"

This lamentation went on for quite a while. The great financier placed his hand over his heart, covering the gold swastika which dangled there; he swore that the flood of printing-press money was the work of the radical element in the National Socialist German Workingmen's Party, and that he, a man who had been backing sound finance all his life, assumed no responsibility for the measures to which he was driven and for the orders his pen was signing. "*Leider!*" and "*Unglücklicherweise!*" and "*Zu meinem grössten Bedauern!*" began or finished nearly every sentence the Nazis' financial wizard spoke. Robbie Budd wondered: Could he be thinking of forsaking his native land and asking an influential American to help him get a job in one of the great Wall Street banks?

V

When the *Abend* was over, the Americans walked back to their hotel, along Unter den Linden, with its seeming-endless double row of great tall pillars, each with a double eagle on the top. They went on foot, because they wanted to get some fresh air into their lungs and also because they wanted to talk over the evening's events. Robbie said: "What an amazing thing, that two of this country's biggest men should blow off steam like that! I thought you told me there was no free speech here!"

Lanny explained as best he could. "These are two very exceptional men. The first"—he wouldn't use names, even in a low tone on a nearly deserted boulevard—"I believe was sincere; he is about at the end of his rope, and my guess is he's due for a fall. As for the second, he is one of the world's greatest rascals, and all I can say is, if he wasn't engaged in fooling you, then he certainly managed to fool me."

"What could his purpose be?"

"I'll wager he has made that same speech to several hundred foreign businessmen in the course of the present year. He wants you to believe that Germany is on the verge of bankruptcy, so that you'll go home and spread that good news. The Herr Doktor is concerned to have Americans carry on in the good old way, and not imitate the shrewd devices which he has thought up which enable Germany to put seventy per cent of her income into purposes that would scare you to death if you understood them."

"You're giving them credit for a devilish lot of subtlety, Lanny."

"For just as much as I would credit the devil himself. They have as good brains as there are in the world, and have put them to the task of blinding your eyes while they get ready to cut your throat."

"And yet you say the fat fellow"—Robbie wouldn't name General Göring—"tells me all about his war preparations in order that I'll go out and frighten Englishmen and Frenchmen!"

"The fat fellow is thinking about the immediate situation—the moves which are planned against the border states during the next year. He wants to bluff England and France just as Mr. Big in Italy bluffed them over Abyssinia, and as they are both doing over Spain right now. But our financial Doktor is a long-term man, and his idea is to persuade you that the whole thing is a house of cards and is bound to collapse of its own weight. That being so, the democracies can go on taking things easy, and won't have to arm, or fight for their lives—until it's too late."

"Well, it's certainly a new line of talk from a banker," commented Robbie. "He'd have a hard time getting money in Wall Street with it."

"He knows that's all past and over; he's got all he ever can. What these people want now is to be let alone for two or three years more, and then they'll be ready for anything that can happen."

"You still hate them like poison, don't you, Lanny!"

"I understand that my father is here to get contracts, and I'm helping him. But it's no good letting you fool yourself, and when you ask me questions, I tell you how I see it. That's strictly between you and me, now and in future, of course."

"Oh, sure," replied the father; "and I'm grateful for what you are doing. At the same time, of course, I hope you're mistaken."

"Nobody could hope it more than I," replied the son.

VI

All this time, while Lanny was playing about with smart Berlin society, a voice was crying in his soul: "Trudi! Trudi!" He was in the same position as to her that she had been in as to her former husband; she had endured some four years of grief and frustration, with nothing to do but wait and fear the worst. In the end Lanny had been able to persuade her that if Ludi had been alive he would surely have found a way to get word to her. In this case Lanny could be sure that Trudi would make no such attempt; she would never whisper his name, to say nothing of putting it on paper. He must count her among the dead; one of many thousands of casualties in the secret war on Nazism, a part of that age-old war for freedom which has been going on ever since the soul of man awakened and discovered itself in slavery.

A hundred times Trudi had said to him: "It is bound to happen; and when it does, forget me, and go on and do your work." So here he was, trying to find out what Hitler was going to do about Stubendorf and the Corridor, about Austria and Czechoslovakia; which would come first, and how soon, and would they resist, and what action would England and France take? In the course of this work Lanny had to go about and meet the leading Nazis, eat their rich foods, drink their choice wines, and never fail to wear an agreeable smile; whenever he found this possible, his conscience would begin to gnaw, and he would say: "I am being corrupted!" When he found himself enjoying the goodfellowship of *Der Dicke* or the rapier wit of Reichsminister Doktor Goebbels, he would have a sick feeling inside, and would punish himself by driving home past the prison on the Alexanderplatz where he had gone to see Johannes Robin, or the Columbus Haus where he himself had once been held under suspicion.

Would they be keeping Trudi in one of these places? Or would they have brought her to Germany only to kill her? Monck had insisted that the latter must be the case, and had warned Lanny not to waste his energies. Of course, if Lanny seriously believed in spirits, he could go on with those experiments; but no more burglaries! So now, when the husband came home from an *Abend,* he would prepare himself for sleep, put out the light, and lie for a while in darkness and silence. He would compose his mind and say: "Now, Trudi." He would wait and watch, concentrating his thoughts upon her, saying without words: "All I want is to know where you are." But no voice ever spoke and no figure appeared at the foot of his bed. Darkness and silence in his soul as well as in his room.

VII

Robbie Budd left for home; he would spend his Christmas on the steamer. Kurt arrived in Berlin on his way to Stubendorf, and called Lanny at the hotel, inviting him to come along. But Lanny said No. He had already met Graf Stubendorf in Berlin, and no longer had any sentimental feelings about the Schloss or the Meissner family either; they were all German, and getting ready for war, and full of Nazi rage and Nazi propaganda shams.

Heinrich had telephoned, saying: "Our great friend will see you shortly; but today is not a good day, because something bad has happened and he is annoyed." Lanny knew better than to ask questions about such matters over the phone; instead he kept his promise and telephoned Hilde, Fürstin von Donnerstein, who exclaimed: "*Grossartig!* I am simply bursting with news! Will you come and have tea?"

He drove to the white marble palace, and found that his hostess had invited no one else. She was the mother of three children, but still young; her colors were fading and she made up for them with more cosmetics than Lanny found attractive. She was tall and thin for a German woman, with a nervous, distracted manner; she would rattle on for a while, and then suddenly stop and start off on a new topic. Her speech was ninety per cent English and ten per cent German, or vice versa, whichever you preferred. Lanny knew that in spite of her high social position she wasn't happy; he suspected that her marriage to a man a whole generation older than herself had not proved a success. However, she was proud, and talked only about other people's troubles; that was satisfactory to Lanny, who had met numbers of unhappily married ladies and had learned many stratagems for keeping himself a sufficient distance away.

Like Rosemary, Hilde had to know about her friend Irma, and why she and Lanny had broken up. He had to give her something in return for what he wanted, so he explained the differences between his temperament and Irma's, giving the latter the benefit of all doubts. Nothing about politics, of course; it was just that he was bohemian in his tastes, while Irma enjoyed only the most proper people. Hilde would be certain that there must have been another man or another woman, and would be alert for the slightest hint as to which it was. But Lanny insisted that with Americans a divorce could happen without any sexual trespass. Irma had since found the perfect husband, but really and truly, she hadn't had her eyes on Lord Wickthorpe when she had divorced Lanny. Hilde heard this with lifted eyebrows, and exclaimed: "*Ach, mein lieber!* If I had ever in my life met a man as trusting as that, I should have fallen in love with him *sofort.*"

This might be what in café society in New York was known as "making a pass at him." He was supposed to say: "Is it too late?" or something like that. But this proper grandson of the Puritans remarked: "Irma and I always trusted each other, but I knew she wasn't happy, and was sorry about it. We agreed to remain friends, and never let our little daughter know there had been any trouble between us."

"What cold-blooded people, you Americans!" exclaimed the Prussian princess. "It seems to us *ganz unglaublich* that a nation should have set to work deliberately—*kaltblütig*—to provide a place where you can go and hide for a few weeks and come back with a new partner! *Schrecklich!*"

"It isn't quite like that," smiled the grown-up playboy. "We seldom create anything deliberately; we discover what we call a 'good thing,' and then a lot of people rush in to make use of it. Nevada is a large state which consists mainly of deserts and mountains. It has a small population who haven't many ways to get rich, and one of its frontier towns discovered that quick divorces and wide-open gambling would bring tourists with checkbooks in their pockets. It's about the same thing as Salzburg discovering that a music festival could be made to pay, and that tourists like to dress up in short brown leather pants and hats with a *Gemsbart* on them."

"*Salontiroler,* we call them!" laughed the Fürstin, who had a summer home in those mountains, and had been expecting a visit from Irma and Lanny on the very day when their marriage had gone *kaput.*

VIII

A maidservant wheeled the tea service into the drawing-room, and then departed, closing the door. Hilde poured the tea, and then, as part of the ritual, took the "cozy," a sort of padded tent which was put over the teapot to keep the heat in, and set this object carefully over the telephone. There existed in Berlin the widespread belief that the Nazis had some sort of device whereby they could listen in on conversations, even when the phone was disconnected. Lanny doubted very much if it was so, but his knowledge of electrical matters was not sufficiently great for him to risk his own life or that of his friends upon it. He had seen this tea-cozy procedure in more than one home, and was never surprised if any host or hostess rose suddenly and stepped silently to a door and opened it to glance outside. Sometimes the person would apologize, and sometimes go on as if nothing had happened.

Hilde took a peek out of two doors, and then drew her chair a foot or so closer and turned on the gossip spigot. "*Also*, Lanny, have you heard the news about *unser kleine Doktor?*"

There might possibly have been many little doctors in Naziland, but for Hilde and her guest only one. He was short and frail-looking and dragged a club foot; to make up for these defects he had a pair of keen observant eyes, a lightning-swift mind, and a mouth so wide that when he opened it and shouted, the whole world heard him. He was one of the two most dreaded men in Naziland, the other being Himmler, head of the Gestapo. Now Hilde was radiant with delight, and though she spoke in a half whisper her voice carried a thrill. "Jupp" at last had got what was coming to him—from a screen comedian who had objected to nothing more serious than Jupp's having forced the actor's young wife to submit to his advances.

The popular Gustav Frölich had lain in wait for Jupp and given him a sound drubbing; whereupon Jupp had appealed to Himmler, who had had the actor thrown into jail; whereupon the actor's friends had rallied and given Jupp an even more complete working over, so that now he was laid up, giving out that he had been hurt in an auto accident. *Herrlich!* The Moscow radio had got the story and broadcast it last night—had Lanny happened to be listening? *Die ganze Welt* listened to Moscow these days—it was the only way you could get the truth about Berlin. Magda Goebbels, the little doctor's wife, had got the facts that way, and now she was giving Jupp a third licking, the worst of all. *Unschätzbar!*

IX

Lanny had had the honor of meeting the Goebbels couple early in his Nazi career. In his efforts to aid Johannes Robin he had appealed to Heinrich Jung, who had taken him to Magda. Lanny never knew just what had happened after that. Apparently it had been Dr. Robert Ley, head of the Nazi Labor Department, who at first had the bright idea of grabbing a Jewish millionaire and his yacht; then Dr. Goebbels, who called Dr. Ley a drunken rowdy, got the bright idea of taking him away from Dr. Ley; then Reichsminister Göring, who called Dr. Goebbels a deformed monkey, had the bright idea of grabbing him away from Dr. Goebbels. Of course Lanny wouldn't say a word about this to Hilde; he just said that he had been in the Goebbels home, and had found the little doctor a witty and delightful companion.

"He is a double personality," commented the woman; "when he takes his public role he is so bitter, so *grausam*, it makes you shudder."

"I suppose he takes a professional attitude toward his work. He began as a journalist, and newspapermen all have to do what in America is called 'taking policy.' When such a man goes into politics, he carries over the same attitude."

"*Ach, ja*, but does he have to be such a *Raubtier* toward young women?" Hilde got up and went to the door of her drawing-room, opened it, and then came back. "This wretched deformity has the whole stage and cinema world at his mercy; it is part of his propaganda department, and every young and attractive actress must come to his bachelor apartment in the Rankestrasse and submit to whatever indignities he cares to inflict. And poor Magda has to hear about it over the Moscow radio—not to mention all the anonymous letters."

"The last time I saw her was at the Berghof," said Lanny. "I thought I had never seen an unhappier-looking woman."

"She greatly admires *Die Nummer Eins*," replied Hilde, who even in the privacy of her own home was afraid to say the word Führer. "Some say she goes there to pay the little doctor off; *aber*—it would be better not to say, even if one knew." A pause, while a struggle between loquacity and security went on in the soul of the Princess. Apparently the latter won, for she dropped the sex-life of the Number One Nazi.

"Do you know Magda's story? She was an orphan, brought up by a wealthy Jewish family—and what a strange reward they have received! She married an elderly millionaire, Herr Quandt, who took her to New York, hoping to distract her restless mind. She rewarded him by demanding a divorce with a handsome alimony. Then she became a convert to our new racial religion, and her income was found useful at Party headquarters. She became *Die Nummer Eins'* dear friend, and there have been many times when he was in fear of poison and she alone was trusted to prepare the vegetable plates with one poached egg which he adores. She was, as you know, *eine Schönheit*, and many men fell in love with her. I suppose she thought our Juppchen offered the surest road to wealth and fame. At that time, you know, Göring was not married, so she expected to become our first lady. When the cabinet was formed, and Hermann was in it but Jupp was not, she entered upon a period of mourning; but finally Jupp became a Reichs-minister, and Magda began to bloom. You should see the estate they have acquired on the Wannsee; and the entertainment they gave there last July—*fabelhaft*—it was like *A Midsummer Night's Dream*, only much more of everything. An island called the Pfaueninsel, and you go to it by a bridge of boats, held in place by men in livery; and on the other shore you find the SS men all in white uniforms, and lovely maidens in white—what do you say? *Maillots?*"

"Tights."

"You see a thousand huge artificial butterflies lighted from within; a dancing stage for a thousand guests, and forty men mixing drinks, and such foods as you would expect only at a royal banquet; after supper a ballet and then fireworks—such a racket that all the diplomats wonder, does the Propaganda Minister tell them that all art and hospitality and *deutsche Gemütlichkeit* are to end in war?" The Fürstin interrupted herself. "What do you think, Lanny? Is it so?"

"*Liebe Hilde!*—you will have to ask the Reichsminister."

"*Jawohl!* It is so anyhow with *die arme Magda*—her happiness has ended in domestic war. Her mail full of unsigned letters, and broadcasts from Moscow concerning her husband's black eye! *Preis und Ehre sei Gott!*"

X

Lanny had to be careful while drinking tea with this free-spoken member of the Prussian aristocracy. In the old days he had been free-spoken himself, and Hilde was proceeding on that basis. She was talking *to* him, but he had to remember that before long she would be talking *about* him. He took occasion tactfully to remind her that he was General Göring's art expert, and that his father was the General's business associate. "I have had to learn to keep my thoughts to myself in many different parts of the world," he said. "Don't expect me to express opinions on Nazi personalities." That must have disturbed her, for she said no more about Nazi personalities for a while.

Irma had told her about Lanny's psychic experiments, and now he mentioned the cross-correspondence they had got in Berlin, and how he had just revisited one of these mediums and got additional messages from his grandfather. Hilde wanted to know how such things could happen, and he told her his theories or guesses. She said the Nazis were trying to repress astrology and fortune-telling, on the ground that it was nonproductive activity; but several of their prominent leaders dabbled in all sorts of mystical and occult ideas.

"I have heard that stated concerning *Die Nummer Eins*," remarked Lanny, leading the conversation to where he wanted it.

"*Ja, wirklich!*" exclaimed Hilde—and again the gossip-spigot was turned on. "Do you know the story of Hanussen?"

"I have heard that he was killed because he made some unacceptable prophecy concerning a high eminence."

"*Nein, nein, glauben Sie's nicht!* That is the sort of story that people make up because it pleases them. My husband met Hanussen, and attended one of the séances he used to give for the Berlin élite. He was a Jew, you know, but that was in the days before *die neue Ordnung* was installed. Hanussen was an astrologer, and some sort of *Genie*, people said; when he went into a trance he foamed at the mouth, and the things he told were often quite terrifying. It is true that he predicted the death of *Die Nummer Eins*—but after all, we have to die some time, *nicht wahr?*"

"Why was he killed?"

"It is one of our dreadful stories. He became wealthy, and loaned large sums to Graf Helldorf, who was one of the first of our Prussian nobility to take up with the Nazis, and became president of our Berlin police. He is a gentleman of more extravagant tastes than his estates warrant; also he is one of those whose *Liebesleben* is somewhat different—I was going to say from the usual, but perhaps I had better say from the non-Nazi. Anyhow, Hanussen made the mistake of letting Helldorf give him notes; and when the sums had grown very large and the first of the notes was due, Göring had the Jew-astrologer killed, and the notes have never since been presented at any bank."

"You know, Hilde," remarked the visitor, "your *Nummer Eins* has said that he is building a regime to last for a thousand years. I should say——"

"*Ja, Lanny?*" said the woman, expectantly. She had heard him say clever things, and was eager for his comment.

But it was one of the times when Lanny bit his tongue. He had been on the verge of saying that what Adi had done was to provide Hollywood with plots for a thousand years; but the Princess might consider that a *mot* and pass it on. He remarked, tamely: "I wonder if some fortune-teller made that thousand-year prophecy."

"I have never heard it said."

"Do you know if Adi consults such people at present?"

"I've heard no mention of the subject."

"I'd be much interested to know. I take these psychic matters seriously, and I am wondering to what extent his powers are derived from subconscious forces. He might use hypnotism without even realizing it; and it may be that his extraordinary self-confidence is due to his conviction that he has some kind of supernormal support."

"I haven't the least doubt he believes that, Lanny. He calls it his intuition."

"It is the same thing, whatever name you give it. Socrates talked about his *daimon*, and Jeanne d'Arc about her St. Michael. I'd be tremendously interested to know if this dynamism is supported by some medium, or by some psychic procedure, a ritual, or prayers, or act of worship. What does he do when he has a spell of discouragement?"

"They say he falls into a fit and chews the rug."

"Yes, but there is nothing medicinal in a rug. Sooner or later he gets up and goes to work to overcome his obstacles. I'm interested to know if there is somebody who goes into a trance, or who sits over a magic spring and breathes gases like the Delphic oracle, and tells him that he is a man of destiny and that all the world is going to belong to him before his end."

"I'll see if I can find out for you," replied the Princess. "One has to be careful asking questions about these matters, of course."

XI

Hauptmann Furtwaengler telephoned to say that Seine Exzellenz was having a shooting party at Rominten over the week-end, and would Herr Budd like to accompany him. Lanny said: "*Mit Vergnügen!*" He knew that Robbie had made an excellent deal with *Der Dicke*, and would wish the intimacy to be cultivated—but not with Emmy! This time would be safe, because Rominten lay away to the east from Karinhall, and in Germany ladies as a rule do not go on shooting parties; especially not ladies who are on the way to presenting their nation with an heir apparent.

The baby-blue limousine called again, and now Lanny and the General had the rear seat to themselves, except for a bearskin robe. It was a cold afternoon, and a light snow was falling; the mournful horn sounded incessantly while the great man went on pumping Lanny dry on the subject of French and British statesmen of all parties. Hermann's body might be lazy, but his mind was surely not; he was better educated than any other of the Nazi leaders whom Lanny had met, and whatever he heard he retained.

Rominten was what the British call a "shooting box," and had a thatched roof like a peasant's hut; but inside it was roomy and comfortable. Besides Furtwaengler and the other adjutants and aides-de-camp there was one of Göring's Swedish brothers-in-law, Count Rosen. Maidservants waited upon them and brought a supper consisting of half a dozen choices of game. Afterwards, Lanny played the piano and they sang, as at the Château de Belcour. Never again would he sing German songs without remembering the mental strain of that earlier occasion; he could play with one part of his mind, and with the other be thinking: "Trudi, where are you?"

Trudi had been taken away from Belcour, and this fat man with the bellowing voice was her keeper. When he retired to his bedroom to read "reports," was there one about Trudi Schultz among them? Or had he already ordered her killed, her body burned, and her soul forgotten? "Dead men tell no tales" has been the creed of tyrants and criminals since the beginning of human time, and the formula includes female as well as male saints and reformers. Lanny's face wore a smile and his fingers tripped lightly over the notes of a sentimental love song, while the mind which controlled them was thinking about pressing the trigger of a machine gun.

In the morning the company was called before dawn, and Lanny was put into a sleigh, along with the Hauptmann and an Oberstjäger-meister, also a keeper who had charge of the particular beat they were to visit. Outside was complete darkness, except for the stars shining like jewels; the two-horse sleigh sped silently along a wood-road through a deep fir forest, and meanwhile the keeper told them where they were going and what they were expected to do. Their goal an open glade, the haunt of a great "sixteen-pointer," a stag which was expected to come out with his hinds to feed upon what grass could be got by pawing in the snow. Herr Budd, as guest, would have the first shot, and the Hauptmann would be second; the "Colonelhunter-master," being attached to the estate, had to be content with shooting the partridges, hares and other small game which appeared upon the table three times a day.

XII

They came to the *Hochstand*, a platform some twenty-five feet high with a ladder at the side. They climbed up silently and mounted guard, not speaking even in a whisper, flexing their muscles to keep warm, and peering by the gray light of dawn to make out the forest and meadow. It was bitterly cold, and the first thing they saw clearly was the white streamers of their own breath. But soon the scene grew clearer, the fir forest, carefully kept, so that only the great trees and the proper number of smaller were left. Presently the animals put in their appearance, and they, too, were carefully kept, fed from hayracks when grass could no longer be found; the hinds were never killed, and the stags only when they had attained their full growth. It was a great honor to be invited to have a shot, and a great fall in prestige if you missed.

Lanny had to wait a considerable time for a clear shot; for of course it would not do for him to hit the wrong animal. The leader of this herd could have no idea of his danger, but it really appeared as if he were purposely keeping one of his ladies between himself and his foe. The men were tense with excitement, standing rigid as if they were parts of the *Hochstand*. Lanny was excited, too, but always there was that other part of him, saying: "What would Trudi think of this waste of time and money?" He recalled how she had urged him to cultivate the fat General; some other of her comrades had been doing the same, and had stolen precious documents from *Der Dicke's* files. While Lanny's eyes watched the stag, the underground part of his mind was saying: "I wonder would Monck know who that person was? And could he put me in touch with him?"

"*Achtung, die Herrschaften,*" whispered the keeper. The great antlered beast had taken a couple of steps forward, exposing his front half, and Lanny raised the rifle which had been put into his hands that morning, and which he had never fired. He knew all about guns, and had been taught to shoot in his boyhood; he had visited other shooting-boxes, and had studied a book which gave diagrams of the bodies of stags and showed the location of the heart from several angles. "X marks the spot," and Lanny raised his rifle and aimed at it with care. He pulled the trigger, there was a report, and the great creature dropped in his tracks. That was all there was to it, except that the two officers wrung his hands and patted him on the back. The rest of the herd had vanished into the forest, so the hunters descended from the stand and drove back to the "box" to learn what had happened to the other parties.

They went out again before sundown, and waited at another stand. This time there were two stags in sight, and Lanny offered the first shot to the Hauptmann, who had done him many favors. They argued in whispers, but the officer insisted that it would be displeasing to Seine Exzellenz; so Lanny shot first and got his, and then, as the herd did not run, Furtwaengler got his, and all were happy.

Sledges came and brought in the carcasses, and laid them on the lawn in front of the house. A bonfire of pine branches was built, and the Jäger wearing dark green uniforms and carrying horns in their hands, stood lined up behind the trophies, while the Hauptjäger read off the list of the kills and the names of the killers. The keepers of the herd had a name for each stag, and Lanny learned that he had killed first Heinie and then Stax. The General made a brief speech of thanks to his guests for the service rendered, and then the Jäger raised their horns and sounded the *Hallali*, or death of the stag. The notes were echoed back by the tall trees of the forest, and in the starlit night the scene was so beautiful that all parts of Lanny's mind forgot his wife for a few minutes.

But not so a little later, when Göring asked if his guest would like to have the head mounted and take it to his home. Lanny said: "*Danke schön, lieber Hermann.*" He remembered the time when he had smuggled Trudi's stolen documents out of Germany in the back of one of Hermann's paintings for which Lanny had found a customer in America. A stuffed and mounted stag's head would offer an ideal hiding place for papers or jewels or whatever it might be. Lanny would ask the hotel to store the trophy for the present, against some emergency which might arise in the career of a "P.A."

17

Dangerous Majesty

I

"IT IS a great honor the Führer is doing you," said Heinrich, in that formal manner which he assumed when speaking of the greatest man in the world. "He hardly ever sees foreigners nowadays, except diplomats in his line of duty."

"*Gerade drum!* It'll be good for him to have a change of scenery now and then." Thus Lanny, with that free and easy American manner which half-frightened and half-fascinated a Party bureaucrat.

The appointment was for four, at the Chancellery. The weather had turned mild, the sun was shining, and they walked from Heinrich's office, past many cold white marble monuments to German glory. New buildings were going up, mostly of gray Swedish granite; they were part of the public works which the Herr Doktor Schacht had lamented. Lanny was committing no breach of confidence when he told of the Finance Minister's anxieties. Heinrich commented: "These mighty structures will be here long after the Herr Doktor's name is forgotten, and everyone will recognize them as one more proof of the Führer's manifold genius."

There was the "Old Chancellery," which had been built for the Hohenzollerns, but had not been good enough for a one-time painter of picture postcards. He had added to it the so-called "New Chancellery"; three-storied, massive, and rectangular, looking like a military barracks transplanted to the Wilhelmstrasse. In its upper stories were halls devoted to his greatest works, the models of the new city hall, the administration buildings, and of stadia and baths, layouts of whole cities, *Prachtbauten* which he was going to cause to arise. Heinrich had brought his friend early, at the great man's own suggestion, in order that these marvels might be shown to him.

The stern-looking SS guards gazed suspiciously at all visitors, even one in Heinrich's uniform. However, this pair had the proper cards of admission, and Lanny displayed the proper fervor as they wandered through the vast corridors with red marble floors and Gobelin-tapestried walls. Precisely on the stroke of four they presented themselves to the double guards in front of Der Adolf's private study. Over the double doors was a sort of coat-of-arms with "AH" inside the design. The visitors were passed in to the secretary, and by him ceremoniously into the inner sanctum.

In the Berghof and the Braune Haus the Führer had chosen modernism and simplicity; but here he had apparently been overcome by the spirit of Berlin, which is that of barbaric magnificence. He had set himself to outdo Mussolini in the colossal size of his office. It was paneled in dark wood, and had high broad doors leading out to the park of the Chancellery. There was a capacious fireplace, with a lifesize Bismarck over the mantel and a statue of Frederick the Great near by. The Führer's desk was at the left, an awesome distance away; it was flat-topped and large, and on it Lanny observed books of military strategy, a magnifying glass, a row of colored pencils, and, unexpectedly, a pair of spectacles, never worn in public for reasons of prestige.

Enormously high ceilings and glittering chandeliers, heavy draperies and thick rugs rather dwarfed the ex-painter, who was nothing much to look at. He was clad in a blue civilian suit with white shirt and black tie, and if you had passed him on the street and hadn't seen him in the newsreels you would have taken him for a reasonably successful grocer or a *Beamter* of the lower ranks, say a customs official like his father. He had grown stouter since Lanny had seen him last; his cheeks were rounder and also his nose; the little dark Charlie Chaplin mustache must have been growing also, but that could be reduced with less trouble than *embonpoint*.

He was in his amiable mood; indulging himself in the luxury of meeting one of his adoring followers, and a visitor from the land of wild Indians and cowboys. In his youth Adi's favorite reading had been a German romancer by the name of Karl May, whose endless volumes dealt with the noble redskin and his conquest by German emigrants on the plains. Since then the subcorporal of the World War had learned that America had heavy industry and could produce cannons and shells, but his thinking about the continent was still colored by his early imaginings. He would have been glad to have Karl May's America for his friend, and the son of Budd-Erling meant to him a glimmer of that hope. So this was not just a social call but a diplomatic *démarche*.

He shook hands with both his guests, and when he had them seated, he opened up on Lanny at once: "I thought you were going to send me a Detaze."

"I assumed you would have forgotten all about it, Herr Reichs-kanzler," said the art expert.

"Why should you wish me to do that?"

"I thought you were just being polite."

"I can be polite in less expensive ways. I wanted the painting be-cause it will give me pleasure, and because I am doing what I can to promote friendship between the two countries, and to bring our two cultures together."

"I owe you an apology for my negligence. I will gladly make you a present of one of our best Detazes."

"You made that offer before and I told you I could not permit it. You said the pictures were for sale and I asked to buy one. I am not a rich man—you perhaps know that I do not take any salary for this office I hold—but the German people read my book, and I derive royalties from the sales, and can afford to indulge my taste in art to a modest extent. Tell me, what do Detaze landscapes bring on the market?"

"The prices have varied considerably, Herr Reichskanzler." Lanny did some quick mental arithmetic. "Some of the smaller works have sold for as low as eight thousand marks; on the other hand, at our show in New York, before the great panic, we sold several for as high as forty thousand marks."

"Let us compromise," said the Reichskanzler. "Would you consider thirty thousand marks a fair price to pick me out one of the best land and seascapes?"

"In view of the advertising it would bring, Herr Hitler, I should consider I was taking an unfair advantage of you."

"Not many people get an opportunity to do that, so you had better make use of it. Send me the painting with a bill in regular form and it will be paid."

II

The Führer talked about art for a while, and the efforts he was making to promote sound taste in the Fatherland. He didn't defend his tastes, he just stated them with quiet finality; in the course of five years nobody had ventured to dispute his authority on the subject, so it was perhaps only natural that he should consider the matter closed. Art existed for the purpose of inspiring the people with sound Nazi ideals; it was a branch of Dr. Juppchen's Department of Education and Propaganda, and the fact that Juppchen was just now laid up with a black eye didn't invalidate his principles nor stop the work of their inculcation. The Führer had that very morning received a visit from his old and dear friend Magda and had laid down the law to her in the plainest terms; there was to be no divorce and no more scandal in the *Parteileitung;* as soon as Jockl—so the Führer called the little doctor in the doctor's Rheinland language—was out of bed again he would be summoned to the presence and have the law laid down to him: he would live on terms of outward amity with his wife and he would assign parts to young actresses on their merits and without any other price: otherwise the Führer would apply to Jockl the Nazi laws requiring sterilization of all persons who possessed hereditary physical defects, which included clubfoot.

Of course Hitler didn't say any of that to his visitors. It was Hilde who would tell it to Lanny at their next meeting; it might be that the detail concerning sterilization had been added by Hilde herself, or by the person who had passed the delicious tidbit on to her. It is not only in Naziland that the great and famous are the subject of gossip, and that it has a tendency to grow like the fish that gets away from the angler.

Adolf Hitler forgot very little that was of importance to his cause, and he remembered that at their last meeting he had charged the son of Budd-Erling to inform the French people of his friendly intentions toward them. Now he listened with pleasure while the visitor told how he and his friend Emily Chattersworth had helped Kurt Meissner to meet persons who were socially and financially prominent in Paris, and how all three had helped to spread the message of peace on earth and good will toward Germany. It was of course important for Hitler to understand the Cagoulard movement, how strong it was and what reliance he could place upon it; and here was a man who had, apparently, lived in the very center of that movement.

Lanny talked freely, and Adi listened attentively. He trusted few persons altogether, but he had to trust many part way, and to determine how far in each case was the first duty of a man of affairs, a seeker of power. The last time this plausible American had come visiting, his rich wife had been enthusiastic for National Socialism, while the husband had been reserved and noncommittal. Now he had changed, and said it was because he had seen the wonderful work the Führer was doing. And that was all right; many persons were being convinced by that method, and not all of them were climbers and self-seekers. Some were idealists, a type to which Adi considered himself as belonging. Because of his social position this middle-aged playboy from overseas could accomplish a great deal without any special effort. In these days of complex organization an engineer who understands a great machine can do more work by pushing a button than a thousand laborers can do by all their toil and sweat. The Führer of the Nazis was looking for such social engineers, and as he listened to Lanny Budd he was thinking, first: "Is this the real thing?" and second: "How can I harness him and put him to work?"

III

Lanny talked about the French statesmen, their incomes, their connections, their financial and journalistic backing, their lady loves and other weaknesses. He talked about the men at the top in the money world of Paris, the inner circles of the two hundred families. He told of Baron Schneider, and that uncertainty which tormented the soul of a munitions king, who knew that he had either to co-operate with Hitler or else get ready to fight him, and couldn't make up his mind which. This amused the Führer, and he rubbed his hands together and slapped his thighs, as was his way when pleasurably excited.

Then Lanny got launched on his story of the de Bruynes, and how he had got the news of their arrest, and had sought refuge in the home of Graf Herzenberg. That was a priceless tale, and Adi bubbled with delight, and abandoned some of that caution which he was trying to teach himself, never with entire success. Seine Hochgeboren was one of those haughty Junkers whom a humble army sub-corporal was now having to battle and subdue to his will; one couldn't expect a man who in his youth had been reduced to sleeping among the bums not to distrust, and in the depths of his soul to hate, one of those great estate owners who kept their land and their privileges through all wars and revolutions, and now were tolerating a mob-leader, a rabble-rouser who could be made to serve their purposes for the moment.

Adi had known this rich American for a matter of ten years, and he knew that Kurt and Heinrich had known him since boyhood. There could be no question that he really moved in the circles of which he told. Let him go on and talk, as he seemed to enjoy doing, and reveal his tastes and his ambitions. That was the way to win men, and to keep them in one's service. If right now, for example, this man could be tactfully caused to pay a visit to Vienna, he might meet on intimate terms the associates of a statesman whom Adi called "*dieser verdammte*

Schuschnigg," and ascertain what promises of support he has received from Mussolini, and how far the Italian windbag could be trusted—if at all!

IV

Just as the Führer was trying to make up his mind to approach this delicate subject, his visitor suddenly shifted the conversation. "*Eure Exzellenz,* I have been having some unusual experiences along the line of psychic research, and it occurred to me you might like to know about them. I have heard that some years ago you carried on experiments along this line."

"I am still a believer in many occult ideas, Herr Budd; but I have had to discourage these activities in Germany, because I have found such a mass of fraud connected with them, and credulous people are swindled unmercifully."

"No doubt that is generally true, though I myself have been fortunate in escaping it. Eight years ago my stepfather discovered a medium in New York, an old Polish woman, and we brought her back to the Riviera with us. She has lived in our home ever since, and we have had every opportunity to check on her activities. I have kept notes of my sittings with her, and my stepfather has done the same. Many days we drew blanks, but on others events took place which took my breath away."

"That interests me of course, Herr Budd. Tell me more about it."

"One of our friends who sat with this medium was Sir Basil Zaharoff. They met in a hotel room in Dieppe, where he had come as a stranger, and I am sure that Madame had no idea who he was. As soon as she went into her trance she began crying out about guns going off, and people shouting curses at the sitter. Then she introduced relatives of Zaharoff, and it was embarrassing, for they accused the old munitions king of actions which he denied. Finally the spirits made it so uncomfortable for him that he jumped up and left the room. Subsequently I verified one of the charges in the files of the London *Times* some fifty years back; it seems that he had pleaded guilty in the Old Bailey police court to the charge of having converted to his own use one hundred and sixty-nine sacks of gall belonging to a merchant in Greece. The medium had given the number of sacks, though I doubt if she had ever heard of gall as an article of commerce. I know I hadn't."

"That is certainly an extraordinary story, Herr Budd."

"Zaharoff was so impressed that after a long interval he came back, and for years he used this medium to communicate with his dead wife, the Duquesa de Marqueni. Early this year I happened to be having a séance with Madame at my hotel in Paris, and I was told that the spirit of Sir Basil had just arrived. Afterwards I went out and got a paper with the news of his death."

"I have never had any experience so convincing as those. Where is this medium now?"

"She was in Paris when I left. My mother was intending to take her back to our home."

"Would it be possible for me to see her sometime?"

"Surely, if you are really interested. Would you like me to bring her to Berchtesgaden?"

"I should be most grateful. If you would let me pay the cost of the trip——"

"Do not trouble about that. We have taken her to visit friends in London and other places, and have never failed to be rewarded by some interesting development. I must give you fair warning—the spirits are no respecters of persons, and Sir Basil is not the only one of our friends who have been embarrassed by what has come out in a séance."

"I am one who has nothing to hide, Herr Budd—unless it be matters of state, of course."

"In those the spirits manifest little interest. But I think you would like to hear of one incident which occurred to me some three and a half years ago. I was having a séance with Madame in my studio at home—the building which was used by Marcel Detaze. I take her there because it is quiet and the influences seem to be soothing. The paintings are Marcel's, and a fine library on the walls was willed to me by my great-uncle who was a Unitarian minister in Connecticut. This was on an afternoon, and the mistral was blowing outside, rather noisy in the pine trees and cypresses of the Cap d'Antibes. Madame gave a violent start, as she does when anything painful comes up. Her control, an Indian chieftain called Tecumseh, doesn't usually let himself be upset, but now his voice trembled as he said: 'A spirit has just come over; a little man in civilian clothes. He has just been shot. I see him lying on a couch covered with yellow silk; blood is pouring from a wound in his neck, and from other wounds. It is a great room with high ceilings; he is an important man. Others are running in excitement, some trying to help him, others crying out. I hear the word Doll—is that a name? He is not a doll, but a small man. He calls for a priest, but none comes. He fingers a rosary, and so I think the man is a Catholic.' Such was the scene, Herr Reichskanzler, and I made my notes of it; the date was July 25, 1934, and as soon as the séance was over I called up the newspaper office in

Cannes and got word that Dollfuss had been killed in Vienna about three hours previously."

"An amazing story, Herr Budd; truly, it deserves to rank with Swedenborg's clairvoyant vision of the great fire which destroyed so much of the city of Stockholm. You know that case, I suppose?"

"I have read it somewhere. I do not tell this particular experience very often, because it rests on my word alone, and people find it too hard to believe."

V

The fact was that Lanny had never told this story before, and didn't expect to tell it again. The reason was, no such séance had taken place; he had made the story up because he wanted Hitler to talk about Austria, and this was the bait. There was no risk involved in the telling, for Madame never knew what went on at her séances, and by Lanny's own account no one else had been present. Now he waited, in the mood of a fisherman who looks over the side of his boat and sees a large black bass approach the bait, and taste it or smell it, whatever a bass does. Finally, he takes it into his mouth. Glory hallelujah!

Said the Führer of all the Nazis: "You doubtless know, Herr Budd, there are people who say I had something to do with the killing of poor Dollfuss. I assure you, he had plenty of enemies of his own, and they needed no hint from me."

"I can readily believe that, Herr Reichskanzler; the situation in Austria is a miserable confusion."

"Basically it is quite simple. The Austrians are German people, and belong to the *neue Ordnung* which I am establishing. Some of them have been misled by false propaganda, originating in Moscow or other poison centers; but as soon as the Austrians understand what I am doing and planning, they will see where their true interest lies, and nothing will be able to keep them out of my Reich."

Lanny had laid a train of powder and set fire to it, and now all he had to do was to sit and watch it burn. He knew from previous experience that whenever the Führer got started, he became spellbound by his own eloquence, by his clear and logical train of thought and the vision of the wonderful things he was going to do with Europe when he had got it. His plans were so rational, so perfect, that no man could reject them when he understood them, and no man could fail to understand them when they had been explained as the Führer was explaining them now. That some men preferred what they called "liberty" to what the Führer called *"Ordnung"* was a sign that they were men of abnormal minds, and such minds could not be tolerated; if they refused to be convinced, there was nothing to be done but to exterminate them. That was a messy business, and the Führer was strongly disinclined to it; what he wanted was for people to submit peaceably, and he wanted this especially in Austria because German blood was sacred in his eyes. He wanted this clever American to confirm his own conviction that the mass of the Austrian people would be pleased to come in with their German brothers, and would repudiate the little group of self-seeking aristocrats, headed by Schuschnigg, the Jesuit-educated Chancellor who was in alliance with the Mediterranean and therefore racially inferior Mussolini.

VI

"Are you familiar with Vienna, Herr Budd?" inquired the Führer, suddenly.

"I have paid a few visits there in the course of my professional work. I have seen a number of fine paintings in those old palaces in the quiet secluded third and fourth Bezirk."

"That reminds me of something I have long had in mind. I should like to have several good Defreggers, and I have been told that there are some to be found in Vienna."

"I have seen several there. Vienna is surely the place to buy paintings now."

"His genre pictures of peasants give me great delight. You know I was born in that country, and look over a good part of it from my windows."

"Be assured I have not forgotten that magnificent view. As to Defregger, I have several of his works listed in my cardfile, but unfortunately I did not bring it with me to Berlin."

"If at any time you should happen upon a representative work, you might let me know. Don't mention my name, of course, for that would raise the price."

"I never name my clients under any circumstances, Herr Reichskanzler."

"Vienna is an interesting place just now," continued Adi, with seeming casualness. "Unless I am misinformed, important events are impending there."

"I doubt if you are misinformed," replied the American, with a quiet smile. "Other people await events, but you make them."

It was not easy to resist such tactful flattery. The Führer realized more and more clearly that he was dealing with a personality, and he ventured a further advance. "It is true that I have sources of information; perhaps I have too many, and am too familiar with their weaknesses, their desire to impress me with their omniscience. When I put their reports side by side, it is as if I employed a score of astrologers to tell me what is going to happen, and their readings increase my uncertainty."

"We have a way of saying it in America, which I might translate: *Alle verschieden und keine zwei ähnlich.*"

"That is it exactly. If at any time you should find yourself in Vienna, and be in position to meet some of the key people, I should be interested to know your reaction to them. In making the suggestion, I assume that men in your position, and that of your father, have an immediate interest in the effort I am making to keep Bolshevism from spreading into Western Europe."

"You do not have to explain that to either of us, Herr Reichskanzler." Lanny said it hastily, for he knew that mention of this subject was like pulling the trigger of an automatic gun—and one so heavily loaded that it might go on shooting for the rest of the afternoon. "Give me an idea what information you would like to have, and I'll do my best. I gather that the situation in Vienna changes rapidly, and persons whose opinions and intentions are important one day may be of no consequence the next."

"I see you know the city well," remarked the Führer.

Lanny smiled inside himself. He had learned a lot, and was learning more every moment that he listened to this discourse. There was no way Hitler could say what he wanted to know about Austrian affairs without revealing what he didn't know, and what he feared. He wouldn't say why he wanted his information, but that wasn't necessary, for Lanny could be sure that his purpose in life was not the collecting of Austrian painters. The fact that he was so direct and so urgent meant that the crisis was coming to a head. The fact that he didn't trust Mussolini, with whom he had made a deal only a few weeks ago, meant that he was thinking of exploding the Italian windbag and wondered whether the explosion would kick back in his own face. The list of those Austrians whom the Nazi Führer didn't trust proved to be a complete roster of those now active in the country's public life, and the things he wanted to know about them were like a row of big letters on an illuminated signboard, spelling one single word: "ANSCHLUSS." To give its full meaning in English would require a dozen words: "Invasion, and incorporation of the Austrian republic into the Nazi Third Reich."

VII

When Lanny had got everything he wanted, he rose to leave, saying politely that he hoped he hadn't taken too much of a busy man's time. The busy man replied, even more politely: "Not at all, Herr Budd. I have talked for an hour without a break, and hope I haven't worn you out. It is my weakness, due to the intensity of my convictions."

"I have rarely been more interested in my life, Herr Reichskanzler," —and the secret agent wasn't lying in that.

"When may I hope to see you again?"

"I have to go to Switzerland on a picture deal, but that shouldn't take more than a few days. Then I will go on to Vienna, and see if I can find you a good Defregger, and anything else of interest. I'll come and report, and if you are still interested I'll have my mother put the Polish medium on a train and send her to Berchtesgaden or wherever you say."

"*Herrlich, Herr Kunstsachverständiger!*"

The great man turned to his adoring official, who had sat in a chair for two solid hours without once opening his mouth. "*Nun, Heinrich, wie geht's bei Dir zuhause?*" When Heinrich replied that nothing could be better with him, the Führer patted him on the back, exclaiming: "*Mit tausend Männern wie Du könnte ich die Welt erobern.* How do you say it in America—'lick'?"

"I could lick the world," supplied Lanny, and so the two visitors went out laughing.

"*Herrgott, Lanny!*" exclaimed the Oberförster's son. He was walking on air, so thrilled by the interview he had witnessed, and the secrets he would carry in his bosom from that hour on. He wanted his friend to come home with him and celebrate, and offered to open his best bottle of wine; but Lanny said No, he had several matters to attend to before leaving for Geneva, and the Führer's business was urgent, as Heinrich knew.

As a matter of fact Lanny had only one thing to do, which was to sit in his hotel room and go over in his mind all the information he had gathered. The reason he was going to Switzerland was to write it out and mail it in a free country; he would never put anything on paper in Naziland. He had tried to think of some way to send a letter out by his father, but he knew that the papers of travelers were examined, and anyhow he didn't want Robbie to become familiar with the name and address of Gus Gennerich. The thing to do was to step into a night express, and in the morning be in Switzerland or Holland where mail was safe and nobody searched your hotel room in your absence.

Also, Christmas was only two days off, and Lanny was lonely. He didn't know a human soul in Naziland to whom he could voice his feelings, and the Trudi-ghost was poor company at this season. The Germans still celebrated Christmas, but the Nazis did their best to turn it into a pagan festival; anyhow, after Lanny had been among them for a while the food they served him began to turn sour on his stomach. Hansi and Bess were giving a concert in Geneva, and after that in Zurich, and they were among the eight or ten persons who knew Lanny's true convictions, and to whom he could talk out his heart.

VIII

So, up into those high valleys, full of clear blue lakes which feed the Rhine and the Rhône and the Danube and the other mighty rivers of Mid-Europe. *Auf die Berge will ich steigen, wo die dunkeln Tannen ragen!* In the morning Lanny looked out upon a dazzling white landscape which quickly became painful to the eyes. Tier upon tier of towering snow-clad peaks, glittering like Christmas-tree tinsel; they had been here hundreds of thousands of years before he had been here to look at them, and they would remain for hundreds of thousands after he was gone. The thought made him feel lonelier than ever, a stranger in a world that was strange in many different senses. Nature, so beautiful in some of its aspects, was harsh and frightful in others, and Lanny was one of those softhearted men who desire that the human insects which have taken possession of the planet and call it their own should help one another to meet and overcome the menaces of nature, instead of 'creating others even worse, the new scientific ferocities called *Machtpolitik* and *Blitzkrieg*.

The train followed its course around the shore of the ice-clad Lac Léman, and came to the old city of watchmakers and moneylenders which Lanny Budd had visited so many times over a period of years. His first action was to ensconce himself in a hotel room, set up his little portable, and put upon paper a dangerous and exciting sequence of words. Everything he had learned in Germany, including details as to the strength of the Luftwaffe, and the fact that Adolf Hitler, by his own statements, was going to be in possession of Austria within the next couple of months; by some trick if he could devise it, or otherwise by invasion. He was quite sure that Mussolini was too heavily involved in Spain to interfere, and that the British and French governments were in the hands of men who wouldn't like it but would have to lump it. Presidential Agent 103 agreed with these expectations, and cited evidence of a first-hand character to support them.

The "P.A." made only one copy, and he didn't leave it in the machine or his bureau drawer. He sealed it tightly in a double envelope, addressed it to Gus Gennerich, marked it by way of a French steamer, and mailed it at the post office. Then he went for a walk on the windswept avenue which fronts the lake and struggled against a fit of profound depression. He had done a long and difficult job, far indeed from what he would have preferred to do. He had done it under the command of the Trudi-ghost, and also of his own conscience; but could he persuade himself that he had accomplished very much? Granting that F.D.R. received these reports and read them, how long would he remember what he had read, under the pressure of ten thousand other duties? And what would he do about it? Lanny had been getting the New York papers both in Paris and Berlin, and it seemed to him that Roosevelt was following the program which some French wit had attributed to Léon Blum: "One speech forward and two steps backward." Under pressure of bitter attacks from the isolationists, the President had taken back a good part of his "quarantine speech," and since then he had kept quiet. That was all the dictators wanted, of course: for their opponents to do nothing, and leave it for them to do everything.

IX

The old city of Geneva had been a center of world discussion and sometimes of world action for the past seventeen years; and now the League of Nations had just completed and was putting to use its fifteen-million-dollar peace temple. It was spread wide, with magnificent terraces and flights of marble steps; a long white structure of four stories, built on three sides of a rectangle and having heavy columns which suggested the Greek, even though they were square. Lanny, who had visited Greece, and studied its history as well as its art, knew that the Greeks had had Amphyctionic councils which had sought to reconcile the jealousies of a score of tiny states, but without success. Proud Athens and stern Sparta had fought a deadly war, and then, after an interval of preparation, a second and deadlier. It seemed to Lanny that there were many parallels to the Peloponnesian Wars in the present rivalry of Britain and Germany; he knew they were preparing to smash each other's cities into rubble and dust, and here in this shining new temple of peace men were laboring with such brains and conscience as they possessed to avert that horror.

Lanny ate his Christmas dinner in the home of Sidney Armstrong, who had been a permanent official of the League since its start. Lanny had first met him on the staff at the Peace Conference; a young liberal, but one who had chosen not to protest when the time for protest came. So he had got a job, and was holding on to it, still not protesting when the time for protest had come—and gone, so it seemed to the son of Budd-Erling. At the same time, Lanny reminded himself that he enjoyed independent means, whereas Sidney had only his salary, and had acquired a wife, three children, and an expanded waistline.

Janet Sloane was the wife's name, and she had been the official's secretary; an efficient and at the same time very lovely young woman, with fluffy brown hair and lively brown eyes not easily to be forgotten by Lanny Budd. He wondered, had Janet ever told her husband about that little passage of love which had taken place between her and Lanny shortly before her marriage. He had taken her to dinner, and found her so interesting that he had driven her all the way around Lac Léman, a matter of some ninety miles. When they were parting she had asked him to kiss her just once. It was while his heart was pledged to Marie de Bruyne, otherwise he would very probably have married her; and what a difference that would have made in his life! No Irma Barnes, with all the contacts with the smart world that she had brought; no Trudi, with all the dangers she had brought! Indeed, it was hard for Lanny to think of anything in his present life that would have been the same; in all probability he would have settled down in Bienvenu, and extended his own waistline, and had three lovely children—though of course they wouldn't have been the same as these three.

The Armstrongs were a comfortably settled couple, and to all appearances happy. Janet considered her husband a well-informed and useful publicist, and she was helping him by entertaining and cultivating the stream of important personalities who came to the various Assemblies and Councils of the League, and often stayed to serve on this committee or that. She was bound to be thinking how different her life might have been if she had married this brilliant and fascinating grandson of Budd Gunmakers; but Lanny was most discreet, and did as little as he could to disturb her imagination. He ate his share of Christmas goose, and of plum pudding which had been sent by Janet's family in America; he played the piano for the children, and afterwards sat for hours listening to the conversation of a practicing exponent of international order and security, a bureaucrat who was fighting not merely for his job but for his faith.

The bureaucrat was, as Lanny found, not too greatly discouraged by a succession of failures. The League still stood, and its new palace, which provided its permanent officials with sumptuous offices, was a symbol and a permanent promise. True, many small states, mostly Central and South American, had withdrawn, but that was because they were poor and had fallen behind with their dues, politely called "quotas." Germany had withdrawn a few months after Hitler took power, and Japan after she had been censured for her raid on Manchuria. Italy had withdrawn just a couple of weeks ago, after using the League as a platform for the denouncing of all who opposed her invasions of Abyssinia and Spain. But Sidney, on the whole, was glad to have them go, for they had behaved as rowdies and bullies and not as reasonable men. The permanent official admitted that Europe's affairs were at a crisis, but it would be weathered, as others had been. A way would be found to teach the dictator states that they could not get along without their neighbors.

Lanny would have liked to ask: "What way is there but war?"—but of course that wouldn't have done. This serious-minded, middle-aged chair-warmer with the round, rosy face and horn-rimmed spectacles blamed most of the world's present woes upon America's failure to join the League and put its immense influence upon the side of law and order. He deplored the bloody conflict in Spain, but insisted that the Communists were in full control in Valencia, and thought that when Franco had won, as he was bound to, he would settle down and become a conservative statesman. He had hoped the same from Hitler and Mussolini, and was waiting to see the decent elements in those countries arouse themselves and take control.

To Lanny he was a mine of information about the various personalities prominent in international affairs. Occasionally he would say: "Don't you think so?" and Lanny would reply, discreetly: "I haven't your sources of knowledge, Sidney," or: "You are the one to tell *me*," —and found that this satisfied the permanent official. After an afternoon and evening, Lanny was in position to return to his hotel and prepare another report for Gus Gennerich—important and interesting, but without a single ray of sunshine in it.

X

Hansi and Bess arrived; they didn't put up at the same hotel with

Lanny, nor appear in public with him, but he would go to their rooms and stay, and listen while they rehearsed their recital. For Lanny it was like coming home; he kept little from this couple, only his dealings with Roosevelt and Trudi. He had told them that he was collecting information for an important purpose, and they took it for granted that this meant Rick—as in part it did. Bess still wondered why he didn't get a wife, and was prepared to co-operate with Beauty to this end; but she didn't bother Lanny about it, and both musicians listened gladly to what he told them about Europe's affairs.

When it came to Communism, Lanny would say: "Well, maybe so; I'm not taking any sides." They knew it was a polite evasion, and had learned to accept it and avoid arguments. They had their formulas, simple and satisfying. Nazi-Fascism represented the last stage of capitalism on its way to collapse; the Nazi-Fascists were gangsters whom the capitalists hired to protect them, just as Henry Ford and other great capitalists of America had done in the effort to keep labor unions out of their plants. If these gangsters now and then took to blackmailing their employers, that, too, was according to precedent. When finally the gangsters were overthrown, capitalism would fall with them, and there would be nobody but the Communists organized and able to take control.

Lanny would smile and say: "Well, I have a sister who will become a commissar, and a brother-in-law who has been made a Distinguished Artist of Soviet Europe; so I'll probably get by." Meantime, he would go on sending data to Eric Vivian Pomeroy-Nielson, who wrote under the pen-name of "Cato," and was quite sure that when the British people had been sufficiently informed, they would turn out the semi-Fascists and appeasers of Fascism and install a democratic regime; also to Franklin D. Roosevelt, President of the U.S.A., who pleaded that he couldn't go any faster than his people would let him, and asked his friends to trust him while he gave the dictators rope enough so that they could hang themselves.

Lanny sat quietly and inconspicuously in a large audience and listened while Hansi and Bess played a Mozart sonata, and then the very fine César Franck, which was one of Hansi's favorites, and which he had chosen to play on a notable occasion of his life. Two sensitive Jewish lads had come to Bienvenu to meet the wonderful Lanny Budd, about whom their father had been telling for years; two dark-eyed shepherd boys out of ancient Judea, transplanted magically to the French Riviera, playing fiddle and clarinet instead of harp and shawm. Hansi had been so nervous that he had hardly been able to hold his instrument; but as soon as he had got going and the lovely first theme came floating to Lanny's ears, Lanny realized that here was a musician who combined tenderness with dignity, and whom no demonstrations of technique would distract from the great purposes of art.

Now here he was, a recognized master; and again the lovely theme came to Lanny's ears, full of memories of which a French organist, its composer, had known nothing. Lanny saw little Freddi Robin, sitting near and watching his older brother, his hands locked tightly together, his whole body turned to stone with fear that one finger might be misplaced by the hundredth part of an inch; dear gentle, sensitive Freddi, who had grown up to be a steel-nerved hero and had been tortured by the Nazis to the edge of his dreadful death.

Strange are the whims of fate, and stranger still the alchemies of the spirit which turn suffering into beautiful art! "For deeper their heart grows and nobler their bearing, whose youth in the fires of anguish hath died." The soul of Freddi Robin had passed into his brother and sister-in-law, and when they played the music he had loved, something magical came forth from strings of gut and wire, and even casual strangers such as this audience in Geneva felt that they had been taken into some temple and were witnessing some valid rite. That is what art is, a process of creation, which makes itself a part of life, and builds new life in its own image, immortal and eternally operating within the soul of man. One accent of the Holy Ghost the heedless world hath never lost!

XI

The concert team moved on to Zurich, and Lanny traveled on the same train, for it was on his way to Vienna, and he needed the sustenance of great music to give him the courage to face another bout with the Nazis. He knew, of course, that when he entered that hell of intrigue and greed, when he put himself on exhibition as a court favorite, a privileged guest not merely of *Die Nazi Nummer Eins* but also of *Die Nummer Zwei*, he was bound to stir into life a million little demons of jealousy and suspicion. Who was this handsome and elegant stranger, and by what right did he intrude into the Holy of Holies, violating all the canons of national exclusiveness and racial domination? What did he want?—for manifestly nobody comes to visit a sovereign who does not want great prizes, either for himself or for others. His father was an airplane manufacturer—but couldn't the

Fatherland make its own planes? And what secrets could a Yankee sell that were half so precious as those he would wangle or steal? Watch him closely, for he is a menace—so a score of court favorites would decide, persons who would have given their eye teeth to be invited to Karinhall or Rominten, to say nothing of spending two hours with the Führer in his splendid study in the New Chancellery.

So Lanny did not visit two Red musicians on the train, but sat quietly reading a safe book on the psychic researches of the sound and racially respectable Baron Schrenck-Notzing. In Zurich he went to a separate hotel, and then phoned for Hansi's room number, and went to it without giving his name at the desk. They had their meals in the Hansibess's rooms, and Lanny went into the adjoining room while the waiters brought the trays. None of these precautions seemed excessive to the musicians, for they knew the Nazi spy system, and that only their international reputation kept them safe from harm. Anybody might be a spy or worse, and when this Red pair were driven to the concert hall, their agent accompanied them and had two able-bodied male friends along with him. Such was life in a city which lay only a dozen miles or so from the Nazi border.

Lanny was sitting in the lobby of his hotel, reading the news from Vienna in the local German-language newspaper. He chanced to look up as there passed him a slender, blond-haired woman; her blue eyes met his brown, and both gave a start of recognition; then she passed on swiftly, and went to the desk and got her key and disappeared into the elevator—called also the lift, *l'ascenseur, der Fahrstuhl*—for Zurich is a city where you are never sure what language you are speaking. If you go south, you will have Italian thrown in; if you go east you will hear a Tirolean dialect which will puzzle you unless you know German very well; in remote valleys you will hear varieties of Romansh, a language which has come down from ancient Latin.

Lanny sat thinking about Magda Goebbels. She it was, without question; and what was she doing in Switzerland? The last time he had seen her was at Hitler's retreat, Der Berghof; he had thought then that she was the unhappiest-looking woman he had ever seen, and he thought the same now. He could not say that she was pale, for the ladies do not leave themselves that way; but she was as thin as ever, and haggard and *harcelée*. She was out of Germany—and did it mean for good?

Lanny wasn't much surprised when a bellboy brought him a tightly sealed note, and he read, in English: "Dear Mr. Budd: Could I have the honor of a brief talk with you? Room 517."—and no signature. He said to the boy: "No answer," and sat for a while in further thought. She wasn't likely to be a spy; she had troubles enough of her own, and would be wanting advice, help, money—or possibly just to pour out her heart. To listen to high-placed, unhappy ladies was surely part of a presidential agent's job; and Lanny was free to do it, for this was international Switzerland, and not America, where high-class hotels catering to the family trade maintain a guardian angel on every floor to make sure that no gentleman enters a lady's room unless he is registered as the lady's husband or father or son. Here no one would pay any heed if Lanny entered the elevator and stepped off *au cinquième* or *Nummer Fünf*, and went to a certain door and tapped gently.

XII

"*Wie schön dass Sie kommen, Herr Budd!*" exclaimed Magda, with intense feeling; but there wasn't any gush about it, and she didn't stop for social formalities, to offer a drink or to ring for *Kaffee*. No, she was in grave trouble, and said: "*Bitte, nehmen Sie Platz,*" and then: "*Ich muss mich entschuldigen.* You remember when you came to my home in Berlin, and asked me for help, I did what I could—it turned out not to be very much, but that was not my fault, it was out of my power."

"So I understood, Frau Goebbels."

"I have never forgotten how you told me the story of poor Johannes Robin and his terrible trouble. You may not know it, I was brought up by a Jewish family and have a host of Jewish friends; you cannot imagine what I have suffered to see their plight and to be helpless to do anything about it. Now my own turn has come—I am in the most awful distress, Herr Budd."

"I am sorry to hear that, Frau Goebbels."

"I have the keenest recollection of your kindness—that was four and a half years ago, if I remember—but I have not forgotten what I thought: here is a really kind and generous man, trying to get something for somebody else, not for himself. I have not met so many since then, Herr Budd."

"They are not so easy to find in our so-called *grosse Welt*."

"*Ja, leider!* If only I could have known it when I was younger! I have nobody to blame but myself for the wreck of my life. I have been a vain and silly woman. I had a kind husband, and a most elegant estate in Mecklenburg; my every whim was indulged, but I did not have sense enough to know that I was well off. I was taken in by formulas, by high-sounding phrases. I had dreams of glory, I thought I was going to make my mark on history—in short, I was ambitious."

"It is a common failing," said Lanny, consolingly.

"It should be left to men! Women should ask nothing but to be safe from the evils that men inflict! Nothing but a home, and a place to hide from horror and shame! I suppose you know what sort of man I am now married to. All the world has heard it over the radio."

"I didn't happen to listen; but I have heard talk."

"I cannot stand it any more. I am prepared to die rather than stand it. I have brought my dear children out of Germany, never to return. I have nobody to help me but my two maids, and I desperately need advice. Where are we to find safety?"

"That is a difficult problem, Frau Goebbels." Lanny had decided in advance that he would take time to think that problem over!

"*Um Gottes Willen,* you must help me! At least give me the benefit of your knowledge of the outside world. Not for my sake, but that of these pitiful children, who must not be made to pay for their mother's vanity and folly. If only you could know what I have suffered! What has been told over the radio is not the hundredth part of it, Herr Budd." The woman got up suddenly and stepped to the door of her room, opened it swiftly, and peered out. She closed and locked it, then took her costly fur coat, which had been flung upon the bed, and spread it over the table on which the telephone stood. All this was the familiar ritual in Naziland, the preliminary to confidential conversation.

XIII

Magda Goebbels drew her chair close to Lanny's, and lowered her voice. "*Mein Freund,* will you permit me to tell you just a little of the realities of National Socialism? And will you promise never to hint at me as the source?"

"Most surely, *gnädige Frau!* And will you, in return, never mention that you have talked to me?"

"That is only fair. I am throwing myself upon your mercy; what is it you say?—throwing discretion to the winds. I am desperate, and do not care what becomes of me—only for my poor little ones." She caught her breath and then rushed on: "I do not know what is in your heart concerning our *neue Ordnung,* and be sure I shall not ask you for the smallest hint, not even watching the expression on your

face. All I will do is to tell you what I have experienced. My first
husband was one of those who joined with Thyssen and other mag-
nates in putting up money to aid a certain great man—I won't use
names——"

"The Big Shot, we say in America." Lanny could still smile.

"*Richtig!* I listened to him shoot, and the thunder deafened my ears.
I thought: This is the greatest man in the world. This is the man
who is going to make over Germany and bring order to all Europe.
I became completely converted, completely demented—what is it—the
devotee of some cinema idol?"

"A fan."

"*Das ist's!* I make no excuses for myself; I was a vain and silly fool,
but at the same time there was genuine admiration, a desire to help
and serve. The human heart is not simple, you know."

"Indeed I know, Frau Goebbels, and I am prepared to make allowances. Nobody can question that the Big Shot is an orator, and a
dynamo of energy."

"I came to Party headquarters to work, in order to be near him.
I gave my money to the cause. I aspired to be known as the perfect
Parteigenossin. I demanded a divorce from my husband, and broke
with my old life entirely. I dreamed of the day when the Party would
come to power and my hero would be able to accomplish in Germany all those wonderful promises. I gazed upon him with adoring
eyes, and he saw it, of course, but he did not respond, and I thought
it was because he was a man of saintly life, a consecrated man, thinking
only of the German people and the National-Socialist cause; so I
adored him all the more. I began to hear rumors that there had been
women in his life, and still were, but they were such dreadful stories
that I refused to believe them—I even denounced to the police one
person who had repeated them. You have heard those stories?"

"I have heard many."

"They are all true, the very worst; but I didn't find it out until
later, too late. Jockl fell in love with me—I was beautiful in those days,
and he was an ardent wooer. He has a brilliant mind and can be most
charming when he wishes. It was all for the cause; I would help him,
I would become his first assistant, I would be put in charge of women's
fashions in Germany—all sorts of things like that. I thought I could
do great things, and wanted to be admired and to have titles and
honors. *Die Nummer Eins*—the Big Shot—came to me and asked me
to marry Jockl, and become some day the first lady of the Fatherland. This was before the Party took power, and long before Göring's

marriage. So I became Frau Josef Goebbels and bore my darling Helga; and almost at once I made the cruel discovery that my husband cheats in love as he does in everything else in the world. He is one of those lewd men who want every young woman they see; he wants a new one every night—he must have the thrill of conquest, the excitement of unveiling, the novelty of solving a new problem, discovering a new set of reactions. I stood it because I had to; I was a woman among the Nazis, and there must not be any scandal in the *Parteileitung*. Am I boring you, Herr Budd?"

"Not in the least. You are not surprising me, either."

"You saw me at the Big Shot's home in the mountains, the evening you came there with your wife. Did that surprise you?"

"Not especially; but I thought you looked very unhappy."

"I was in such a state of terror that I could hardly keep my teeth from chattering. I came very near asking to be allowed to go away with you and your wife. It is the most horrible thing—I can hardly bear to speak about it." She got up and went to the door again, opened it and looked out, then returned, and lowered her voice almost to a whisper: "You know, perhaps, a little concerning sexual pathology?"

"Surely, Frau Goebbels."

"The great man is impotent; he, the most powerful in the world, cannot accomplish what his commonest soldier, his humblest *Diener*, can do. He is frightfully humiliated, he struggles against his frailty; he becomes excited, hysterical; he raves, he foams at the mouth; he blames the woman. He makes her do unspeakable things; and she obeys because he is the master, because his will is the only law in the land, because there is no one who would dare to help her, because, if she defied him, he would have her whipped until the skin had been stripped from her naked back. If she should escape to a foreign country, he would have her relatives seized and tortured—because you see, he demands loyalty, and does not permit scandals in the *Parteileitung*. Such is our *neue Ordnung*."

XIV

So at last Lanny had the truth about matters which had puzzled him greatly. A presidential agent had information which he wouldn't put on paper, even in Switzerland, but would deliver *viva voce* in that room in the White House. Said he: "It is a tragic story, Frau

Goebbels. You must know that it is a very old story, and is in the medical books."

"I am not going back to it. I have made up my mind—I will end my life first. What I want is to go to America, where women are safe. What I am asking from you, Herr Budd, is advice about getting to America."

"It is not especially difficult. You can go into France and take a steamer from a French port."

"But I must have passports, and that troubles me; the delay, and the danger in the meantime. I shall be in terror every moment; I dare not let my children out of my sight. Can you not help me to get passports quickly?"

"I am terribly sorry, *gnädige Frau;* I have no influence with the State Department, and would have no idea what to do except to follow the regular routine. Also, I must point out to you that I am an unmarried man, and if I became active on your behalf, the gossip-mongers would have a story ready to their hands, and one that could surely not help your case."

The second lady of Naziland sat with her hands locked tightly in her lap, staring ahead of her as if turned to marble. Her lips barely moved, as she whispered: *"Gott in Himmel,* what am I to do?"

He answered: "I will make a suggestion. My former wife, Irma Barnes, is now Lady Wickthorpe, and a person of influence. It would be a simple matter for you to travel through France and enter England as a tourist. Then ask Irma to see you and help you."

"Will she remember me?"

"She remembers you well, and has spoken of you often. I would advise you not to say anything to her about the Big Shot, because she is one of his ardent admirers. But she has doubtless heard about your husband's misconduct and will be prepared to sympathize with a wronged wife. She has the same reason for gratitude to you that I have, with the difference that she is a woman and therefore not a cause of scandal. She undoubtedly knows the American ambassador in London, and would actively interest herself on your behalf."

"Thank you, Herr Budd. I was sure that you were a kind man."

"It is difficult to be kind nowadays, and often dangerous. Let me suggest that you do not mention our meeting to Irma, or to anybody else—ever."

"I have promised that, and you may count upon it."

"It is not wise for me to stay longer; so—*Auf Wiedersehen.*"

He went out into the corridor, and observed, standing near the elevator, a gimlet-eyed man of a type which all Europe was learning to recognize—the Nazi in civilian clothes. Lanny didn't go to the elevator, but turned into the stairway and went down fast to his own floor. In his room he packed his belongings, rang for his bill, paid it by the bellboy, and left the hotel by a rear entrance. He stepped into a taxi and was driven to the depot. From a telephone booth he called Hansi at Hansi's hotel and said: "Something has happened which makes it better for me to be elsewhere. Write me to my home. By-by and good luck."

Lightning Source UK Ltd.
Milton Keynes UK
29 May 2010
154850UK00001BA/137/A